GOOD FOR THE JEWS

ALSO BY DEBRA SPARK

Twenty Under Thirty, editor
Coconuts for the Saint
The Ghost of Bridgetown
Curious Attractions: Essays on Fiction Writing

GOOD FOR THE JEWS

Debra Spark

THE UNIVERSITY OF MICHIGAN PRESS · ANN ARBOR

Copyright © by the University of Michigan 2009
All rights reserved
Published in the United States of America by
The University of Michigan Press
Manufactured in the United States of America
⊛ Printed on acid-free paper

2012   2011   2010   2009   4   3   2

A CIP catalog record for this book is available from the British Library.

Library of Congress Cataloging-in-Publication Data

Spark, Debra, 1962–
    Good for the Jews / by Debra Spark.
        p.   cm. — (Michigan literary fiction awards)
    ISBN 978-0-472-11711-6 (cloth : acid-free paper)
    1. Jews—Wisconsin—Fiction.   2. Madison (Wis.)—Fiction.
3. Jewish fiction. I. Title.
PS3569.P358G66   2009
813'.54—dc22   2009020595

Warm thanks to Colby College, the Corporation of Yaddo, and
The MacDowell Colony for their generous support during the
writing of this book.

FOR GARRY

Smoke at the horizon. A lone tendril corkscrewing up. Probably a brush fire. That's what Alex Decker usually thought, when he saw smoke. He'd been in Chicago for work. Earlier, passing the Milwaukee exits, he'd told himself to stop, visit a museum, drop in on a friend. He could do that sort of thing now. But he drove on, impatient for home, for that specific moment when the undulations of corporately owned farmland gave way to the tremendous line graph of the city. Madison, Wisconsin, was miles off, though—and home forty miles beyond that—when Alex saw the smoke. At first, it was a thin, white spiral. Then three distinct puffs, as if a giant lay just beyond the horizon, trying to blow smoke rings. Alex noted all this, but absentmindedly, as he might have taken in the garish shafts of light penetrating a distant cloud—lifted, it seemed, from some storybook Bible—or later, the smiley face spray-painted into the "U" of the obscenity on the sign for his exit. After a wry tick of pleasure, his curiosity faded. He had one errand in Madison—the pharmacy (a prescription, razor blades)—before home.

In town, he parked. As he opened his car door, a faint siren began in protest. Or maybe the siren had been there all along, and Alex heard it only now that he had stopped. His son, Doug, as a child, had loved the siren sound. Nothing excited him as much as a rescue vehicle. Even now that Doug was a teenager—and in any case, not stepping out of the car with his father—Alex silently exclaimed, "Oh, honey. A fire truck!" As if fire trucks—or ambulances or police cruisers—were all about joy. Not crime or injury. Still Alex was sanguine. Or inured to apocalypse. Who wasn't? At a certain point you had to admit that what was coming at you was coming at you. Then go ahead and live your life.

Not that he had always felt this way. Five years earlier, a week after the World Trade Center tragedy, Alex had visited Jackson Reiser, a fishing buddy whose wife had just given birth. Alex held the infant, taking comfort in his small weight. In the wake of disaster, everything good had to be noted and valued. "Pretty day," he cooed at the baby. "Pretty day." He walked to the window, thinking to show the boy the light chop on the lake, the orange of the leaves, the heartbreaking sunshine of a Midwestern fall day. But the blue sky was no longer empty. From the far shore, giant cotton balls of smoke rolled over the lake. A bomb, Alex thought. *They've bombed Madison.*

"What's that?" he called to Jackson, who was in the kitchen, getting tea.

They've bombed Madison. His limbs felt cold, hollow, as if evacuated in preparation for the terror that would soon fill them. He snuggled the baby closer to his chest, considered the heroics that might be required of him in the next twenty-four hours. But then Jackson came in with some of the twiggy stuff he liked to drink and said, "That? Oscar Meyer, I'm guessing. We get the exhaust from the plant whenever the wind's blowing this way."

Alex sniffed, decided that the air smelled of frankfurters. First time a hot dog ever made him feel safe.

"God, I thought it was . . . like . . . a terrorist act or something."

"Hey, buddy," Jackson said, extending his arms for his child, "it *is* a terrorist act. Corporate terrorism."

"Right-o," Alex said, thinking of a handless man he'd seen around town. Alex had the idea that the guy was a processor at the wiener plant until the plant decided to process him.

"It's no joke," Jackson said. "The enemy is here. Right at hand."

"Did I say he wasn't?" Alex asked, but distractedly, not wanting to enter into this particular conversation. He'd only signed up for purchasing a stuffed toy and visiting a baby. As concessions went, the awful tea was as far as he would go.

Now, as Alex headed back out of Madison for his place in Ridgeway, the smoke—it came from somewhere near the stadium—darkened into greasy black plumes. Something inorganic was burning, a metallic stink in the air. So not a brush fire. Maybe a home, its toxic heart—all those computers and microwave ovens—revealed in incineration. The sirens grew louder, blared on. Perhaps several homes, or some shops along Park Street, had caught fire. It was Friday. Around six by the time Alex bumped up the drive to his home. He'd been at a conference: "Superintendents in the 21st Century: How Leaders Promote Student Learning." These days, when Alex traveled, it was invariably for such things. The real work of the conference was getting there and back.

A conflagration on his answering machine, too. The red light beeping and beeping. Twenty-two messages! The first—the first worrisome one—from Valerie: "Alex, are you there? I hope you're in town. Can you come home? *Now?* Doug really needs you."

It was the word "home" that frightened him, even more than the wobble in Valerie's voice or the subsequent message from the chief of police: "Afraid I've got some bad news about one of your students."

Valerie's home hadn't been Alex's for over a year.

Part One

THE YEAR OF THE DRESS

She appeared to every man as a member of his
own people.
—Talmud, *Megillah*, 7a

Fire is the ultra-living element. It is intimate
and it is universal. It lives in our heart.
—Gaston Bachelard, *Psychoanalysis of Fire*

Chapter One

APRIL–MAY 2005

❦

As far back as Ellen could remember, she'd been told there were two categories of things in the world: what was good for the Jews and what wasn't. The TV news was bad for the Jews. Mose—her cousin, though he was almost forty years her senior—and his volunteer efforts in the community . . . that was good for the Jews. The Messianic Jewish temple gaining ground in Madison . . . that was definitely bad for the Jews. "Bunch of crazies. *Meshugge*," Mose would say and tell a story about how the Lubavitch Jews in Brooklyn stoned his mother—his own mother!—because they saw her shopping for food on the Sabbath.

"Stoned her!" Ellen said, amazed, when first told this. She'd read Shirley Jackson's "The Lottery" in high school.

"Well," Mose admitted today, as Ellen began to clean his apartment, "they threw *a* stone at her." Ellen was twenty-five and had lived with Mose between the ages of six and eighteen, first in California and then in Wisconsin, but she was only now hearing the whole of the story.

Mose's job was good for the Jews. He taught American history at a progressive high school, had come all the way from San Francisco over a decade ago to take the job.

You'd think for all of this that Mose would be a regular attendee at synagogue, but he rarely went. His job was what occupied him. While she wiped down the stove, splattered with soup, he complained about two new classes—"Theater of Oppression," and "Who Am I?" She ran water for the mop. The cleaning was a weekly favor that she'd imposed on Mose. She didn't like to think about what his place would look like without her help. "These classes, I'm telling you," Mose said, as he pulled on his coat. "They teach students to value what they make, no matter what. 'Here, it's shit, Mommy. I made it. Isn't it good?'"

"Mose!" Though he was always direct—and had worked for years as a plumber, which might have made him cavalier about excrement—it wasn't like him to be gross.

Mose folded a supermarket-shopping list into his pocket. He didn't like to stay while she worked, said he hadn't raised her to labor for him. "Worse," Mose said, as he left on his weekly errand, "the classes make these kids think of themselves as victims. They identify with victims everywhere. They are all for Palestinian rights. They don't see the complications."

Which wasn't good for the Jews, of course.

But maybe he was a tad paranoid, Ellen thought, as she turned her attention to the kitchen floor.

Or too obsessed with his notion that America produced citizens wedded to the idea that they'd been wounded. When she was in college, Mose even leveled this criticism—of viewing oneself as a victim—at Ellen, as if the weight of her early loss was a backpack she stubbornly refused to take off.

"That's not true," Ellen had insisted. If anyone held on to the past, it was her sister, Barbara.

"Phhw. Can you even remember them?" He meant her parents. "No. You were too little."

But she wasn't. Ellen was six when her parents died in a car crash and had many memories of life before Mose: of her mother bringing her to school on the first day, of her parents driving off for dinner at a restaurant, of her father telling her to play outside with Barbara. Actually, most of her memories *were* of her parents' leaving, her strongest being of a creepy couple who came to babysit while her parents went to Carmel for the weekend. The couple's dog soiled the living room carpet, and the wife baked trays and trays of cinnamon rolls—not for the girls to eat; she sold them somewhere. There was a baby, too, with a diaper always sagging and full. Ellen was so frightened by the couple's disorderly ways, she took two showers a day, just to cry.

Ellen vaguely believed in her own premonitionary powers. Back then, the couple had heralded the future, the loss not just of her parents but also of her parents' patterns, their knowledge of how things were done. (No cookies before breakfast; the Batman placemat for Barbara; the Robin placement for Ellen. Lights out at eight.)

For the seven years that they lived with Mose in California, Barbara and Ellen shared a bedroom. Friends and mere acquaintances deluged them with presents—the poor things. After the car crash, someone gave Ellen a talking Barbie. She'd always wanted one. But now the doll terrified her. She had wished for something, and she got it. Only her parents had to die first.

"I remember it," Barbara said one night, when they were still small and tucked in, a gap between their beds, across which they extended their arms, so they could fall asleep holding hands.

Everyone said the girls had been asleep at the time of the crash.

"I wasn't asleep," Barbara said. "I . . ."

"Don't tell me." Ellen started to shriek. "I don't want to hear, I don't want to hear, I don't want to hear."

By the time Mose arrived in the room, both girls were in tears. "Ellen Myrtle. Barbara Ruth. What's the matter here? What's the matter here?" He ordered the two into his arms.

"Nothing," they sniffed. It was always a big deal when Mose used their middle names. And then Barbara said, in a small voice, "Can we have a cookie?"

"Chocolate chip OK?" Mose asked, and that was precisely the problem. They could ask for anything, anything but what they really wanted.

Now Ellen's wants were decidedly non-material. Three years out of college, she hoped to marry. Mostly she wanted children of her own, though that desire was a small bird's heart—no roaring engine—inside her. It would happen, she knew, when it would happen.

Or maybe she didn't want anything really, maybe wanting was just too terrible.

Ellen packed cleaning supplies back into Mose's front closet, then scribbled a note. "Gone home. Don't forget to walk." Outside, the day

9

was fair, if chilly. She unlocked her bike, then began to ride the fifteen or so blocks from Mose's small apartment in a rehabbed elementary school to her small apartment in a converted mansion, supposedly designed by a disciple of Frank Lloyd Wright, though that attribution made no sense; the single Wright house that Ellen had seen was supermodern, all horizontal lines. *Her* place had a grand gray stone terrace, a massive central staircase. Dark wood for the floors and molding. Off the narrow hallways, single people lived their hermetic lives. Ellen's own apartment consisted of two rooms—the bedroom and a living room with mullioned windows. The kitchen was built into a wall. Just a sink, small stove and half-refrigerator.

At home, her fingers still smelling of the various potions she'd used at Mose's, Ellen started the weekly cleaning of her own place. She liked to clean, liked anything designed to make life feel simpler and clearer. She started in the bathroom, scrubbing the peacock-and-cream tiles, the claw-foot tub, old-fashioned and perfect. The room put her in mind of her pre-adolescent self, holing up in the bathroom of Mose's San Francisco apartment. It was the only room that had a lock on the door. Ellen used to fantasize about how she might live in the small space—sleep in the bathtub, store cereal boxes on the shelves above the toilet. At synagogue, in those same years, during the annual showing of *Night and Fog*, she'd retreat to the cold, gray bathroom, the sill under the single translucent window strewn with dead flies. There were things in this world she didn't want to know about. She ran the hot water in the tub, encouraged the suds from her eco-friendly cleaner down the drain. She might not know what was good for the Jews, but she knew what was good for her—a single, relatively unobservant Jew—and that was a small spot, hers and safe, outside of which the world could do what the world needed to do.

Chapter Two

APRIL–MAY 2005

❦

*I*t started with the dress. Or ended with it, depending on your perspective. Not that it wasn't a beautiful dress. Sleeveless with a white bodice that laced tight in the front and under that a big flouncy skirt. When she first saw it, Valerie Decker pictured a sylph-like maid—"Milkmaid!" she actually thought "milkmaid"—lifting the voluminous skirt so she could run (barefoot, of course) through a green field spotted with delicate white flowers. Really! What had Alex been thinking, when he purchased the garment in New York? A new Midwest trend? Royal balls? Subarus out; liveried pumpkins in?

"You could wear it to that whatsit," Alex said, flapping his fingers toward the backyard window, as if at some glamorous spot, farther east on the continent.

"That what whatsit?"

"You know, that thing you put together. For the Oscars."

Valerie rolled her eyes. She directed Madison's Center for Artistic Exchange, down on State Street. Alex was talking about the Center's annual fundraiser, held in a turn-of-the-century casino. This was east of the city at a resort once favored by Chicago mobsters. People did glam up for the event, and a local antique shop hired models to slink around dinner tables, as if they weren't watching but attending the Oscars.

So, whatever. She left it alone. Leaving it alone being her métier when it came to Alex. But then he had one of *his* annual events, the yearly fishing party, which involved more alcohol than fish, and much running from sauna to frigid lake and back again. Alex's college roommate had found a place in Door County, and now six of them drove there every year. It *was* a pretty spot. Valerie had visited herself once, in warmer weather. Just after she and Alex married, they had gone there, taken a ferry from the uppermost point of Door County to Washington County island, and rode their bikes around, laughing even as they got caught in a ridiculous downpour. Then back to an inn on the mainland for towels, dinner and sex. (It helped to remember that sex part, now that she lay in bed, wishing for a partner as she had when she was eighteen; someday, perhaps, it—it being what? love? the love of a man? a roll in the hay?—would happen to her, too.)

At any rate, the dress. The night before the departure for Door County, the men always gathered for a big dinner at the Deckers. Chili, cornbread, beer. Too many potato chips. Stuff they never ate the rest of the year—being the kind of men who ran every morning and fretted about heart disease. But the men—or so Valerie told her friends—were preparing to be stupid. And the food helped. On this particular night, the night of the dress, they'd all had too much. Doug—thank goodness!—was out. In Chicago with his band, his first big-city gig. Not that the sight of men indulging would be anything new to him. Valerie lazed in bed, still dressed but propped on her pillow, reading *The Age of Innocence*. She was having her own little party with Edith Wharton, good friend.

The phone on the bedside table rang once, Clara Massengill calling to remind Alex and Valerie about a dinner party that she was having for Hyman Clark, the new principal at Sudbury High. It had started an hour ago. Had Alex forgotten? Not missing a beat, Valerie chirped, "How strange! I was just going to call *you*. Alex's had to go down to Iowa suddenly. Something wrong at his family's farm. He wanted me to send his regrets. I'm *so* sorry. I should have called earlier. Honestly, it slipped my mind, what with me worrying about his folks and all."

"Shoot," Clara said, and Valerie sensed she was less distressed about Alex's troubles than the symmetry of her dinner table. Clara had been having dinners for the new principal all week, atoning for her own abrupt, mid-year departure from Sudbury with this last obligation.

Tonight was the final dinner. By next week, Clara would be in Boston, and Hyman Clark would be at the helm of the school.

Back to Edith Wharton, Valerie thought, hanging up the phone and settling into her pillow. Her bedroom, its umbers and coppers, never failed to please her: the dark wood moldings, the bed piled high with pillows, the accumulation of Turkish rugs and kilims on the floor, over the back of the stuffed chair, even hung on the wall like a painting. She was the pasha of a mini-textile kingdom. Elsewhere, the house was more restrained.

"Hey, honey," Alex shouted up the stairs.

"What?" Valerie called back, not yet moving.

"Honey," Alex shouted again, and Valerie pulled herself from bed.

"What?" she barked, from the top of the stairs. Alex had come to the bottom. He grinned, the hall light glinting off his perpetually sunburned forehead, his eyes unfocused, clearly engaged with whatever conversation he'd just left. She said, more kindly, "Yes?"

In the background, she could hear the small TV in the kitchen going, laughter. And then one of the men saying, "Oh, shit." She didn't know why they hadn't moved into the living room.

"Put on that dress and come down here. I want to show the guys."

"What are you talking about?"

"The dress. The one I got for you in New York."

"Are you crazy?" she whispered, but loudly, as if she could make her voice simultaneously strong enough for him and too soft to reach his friends in the kitchen.

"I want the guys to see it." He called, "You guys want to see this dress, don't you?"

Alex's friends began to chant, "The dress, the dress, the dress." In the morning, they'd all feel like asses.

"No," Valerie said.

Alex climbed a few stairs, running his hand over the banister. Valerie flashed on Doug, years ago, home from summer camp, racing down the stairs, saying, "I missed this," meaning he missed the feel of his palm on the banister. What a sweet boy he was. And always had been. "Come *on*," Alex insisted. "I told the guys you would. It'll be embarrassing now if you don't."

"It will be embarrassing if I *do*." She had not been able to impress on Alex, back when he'd first presented the dress, that it was not appropriate for a middle-aged woman, cut as it was for the breasts to plump up over the bodice, á la a French whore. Not that Valerie knew anything about French whores, but that seemed to be the idea.

"Come on, honey," Alex began. "You look great in it. You've got a great figure." Admittedly Valerie complained on occasion (well, once a day) about her body, but that wasn't the issue here.

"No," she said, and that ended it.

*T*he marriage, that is. The dress ended the marriage. Alex returned from Door County, still nursing his grievance. "You humiliated me in front of my friends." Not, she gathered, because she hadn't modeled the dress, but because her refusal turned his request into something thoughtless and sexist—which it was—but that hadn't been his intention. His intention had been playful. He bought this extravagant dress on a lark; his friends should see it!

And then: "You always humiliate me in front of my friends."

"You can be sharp," a friend said, when Valerie recounted the conversation.

"Sharp? What are you talking about? Like when I say 'the sound of his voice makes me grit my teeth'? Well, I don't say that to *him.*"

"I don't think he really likes being called Stress Boy at dinner parties."

"Stress Boy! That's a term of affection."

Still dressed in fishing clothes, Alex stood over Valerie, who lay in bed trying to read. He said if she couldn't support him, he'd move out.

"Support you? What do you mean, support you? Agree with every dumb idea you have? You're right. I can't do that."

Alex stared at her, stricken, as if she'd finally outdone herself in cruelty. She wished she hadn't used the word "dumb," that she'd been able to modulate her voice. But even as she wished this, she declared, "If you want to leave, leave." Their fights always circled back to theatrical ultimatums.

"OK, then. I will."

Valerie didn't think he meant it, but while she was at work, he packed a bag and moved out to Ridgeway, where they had a second home, largely unfinished because Alex was doing the interior work himself. Alex's friends—he told her, over the phone—thought he'd made a good decision, and Valerie, unable to let anything go, and even though the idea of a final split terrified her, said, "Oh, of course. Wouldn't want to make a move without the advisors."

Later, Valerie told Doug—home from his first solo weekend in the city, buoyed by his taste of independence and perhaps other undiscloseable experiences–that Alex was taking a little break from home life.

"What's that supposed to mean?" Doug asked, instantly alarmed.

"Like a vacation. Only he's staying out at Ridgeway." She kept her voice even. She wasn't going to be one of those women who tried to ruin her child's relationship with his father.

Doug looked confused, then frightened. "No, *really*," he said.

"Hun, I'm not sure. I think you'll have to ask your father." *Oh, God,* she thought, her eyes tearing. *They were really going through with this.*

If it had been a bigger city, if Valerie had been able to avoid him, if Doug wasn't Alex's child, it would all have been easier, but there Alex was—at her doorstep to pick up Doug for the weekend; at her doorstep to ask for files from his old office; at her doorstep to say he hoped Valerie didn't mind, but he was beginning to date a little.

"Mind? Oh, of course not," Valerie said, breezy, a modern woman unfazed by such things. "Date away." She minded all right. They'd been apart for all of a month. Worse, she knew how the world had changed. Joel, one of her divorced friends from the university, had filled her in. "Dating" didn't mean you asked someone out. It meant you visited www.match.com, e-mailed, then met a stranger for coffee. Later, dinner. By date two, women asked men, "Where is this going?" so that even the marrying kind were scared off. As for date one: "The blow job is the new kiss goodnight," Joel confessed, appalled but clearly doing what was required in the new world order.

Leaving Alex on the steps for a moment, Valerie went to the kitchen and returned with a bag of dried, pitted dates. She poured them into her own hand, then shoved them into his. "Here," she said, "I've got dates, too. Have as many as you want. Stuff your big fat face full of them."

"Jesus," Alex said. "What's the matter with you?"

He was charming, that was what was the matter with her. She knew he'd appeal to women. It took time to realize he wasn't as smart as he seemed; it took marriage to see his pouchy belly pressed up against the bathroom sink, as he leaned toward the mirror to trim his nose hairs.

And Valerie. It didn't matter what she was like. The only single men around were of the dropout, I-tried-too-many-pharmaceuticals-in-the-sixties variety. Of course, people had affairs. Supposedly they did, but who wanted to be involved with a man who would cheat on his wife?

It was hard not to think of *her* own beginning with Alex, now that *he* was starting anew. One day in grad school—right before either of them had declared an interest in the other—Alex and she went for a walk in a residential neighborhood just west of campus. This was at the University of Iowa, where they were students, Alex working toward a Ph.D. in educational administration, Valerie going for her M.B.A. Dirty snow hugged the roads, but the ground was dry, the air warm— or warm for Iowa in April. "We're having a heat wave," Alex sang as they started off. "A tropical heat wave." It had felt like that. Fifty degrees and birds trilling, real birds, not the massive ravens—those plump undertakers—that stayed all winter.

Alex and Valerie meandered through a neighborhood choked with run-down rentals. All their friends lived here. The streets were tucked behind an anachronistic hospital, a brick structure with no apparent relation to the gleaming University Hospital down by the river, with its research center and medical students. Amid unkempt patches of lawn and porches sagging under the weight of living room sofas, a cramped grocery sold grad student necessities—no fresh vegetables, endless cans of soup and, now that the laws had been deregulated, bottles of wine. People used to drive to the state liquor store on the highway for even the most innocuous wine cooler. "These days," Valerie told her college friends, most still back in New England, "you can stop in the drugstore for whiskey and toothpaste. Land some tequila and gummy worms at the QuikTrip."

Grad students who weren't from the Midwest examined the quirks of the state with great anthropological interest. Pig roasts, corn detasseling and Laundromat bars . . . oh, the customs of this country! As Alex and Valerie neared the grocers, they considered Iowa City's Laundro-

mat bar. Overnight, it had morphed into a Laundromat bar/tanning salon. What else might an enterprising Iowan add to the list?

"Crime and death-scene cleaning?" Valerie suggested.

"That makes sense," Alex said, his voice so reasonable that it flipped
and became a mockery of reasonableness everywhere. "But then why
stop there? Why not do . . . oh, animal and bird abatement?"

"Abatement," Valerie snickered.

"All this thinking is giving me a headache." Alex stopped walking. "I
must have a chocolate bar!" He raised his arm importantly, finger
pointing toward heaven, as if he were the ruler of a vast kingdom, a
monarch pronouncing on his desire. Alex was athletic and handsome
then, not sunk into the snowsuit of fat that he later donned as readily as
he donned the mantle of school superintendent, as if they were both
cloaks he'd meant to wear all along. (Within weeks of their split, Alex
had exercised the fat off. This determination so like him. If he was going to do something, he was going to do it.)

Alex took the stairs to the grocers two at a time, then reemerged
from the store, bar paid for and already half-unwrapped. "My dear," he
said, "will you share this with me?" And then he'd kissed her—their
first kiss—on the nose.

It was best not to think of things like kisses on the nose just now
though. "Animal abatement," Valerie whispered in Alex's ear, the first
time they went to bed, "is *such* a turn-on." It was best not to think of
that, either, all their joking. It was best to remember that time, early in
their Madison years, when they had a fight, and Alex stormed out of the
apartment, and Valerie circled town, trying to find him. (Where was
Doug when this happened? He would have been a baby, but she could-
n't place him in the memory, and yet how could she have gone looking
for Alex, if Doug wasn't safely in someone's care?) Finally Valerie located Alex's car (a yellow VW, not hard to hide) outside what was then
called the Fess, a bar in a hotel of the same name. It was something else
now—the Big Poodle, the Great Dane, the Yucky Dog. Inside, at the
bar's long wooden counter, Alex sat flirting with a woman, her hair
gelled into dangerous spikes. At Valerie's approach, the woman
swiveled her head, her long branching earrings—could they be shel-
lacked bird *claws*?—whapping against her jaw, scratching in alarm.

"Hello," Alex sneered. He didn't invite Valerie to sit down. Still Valerie half-hoped Alex would stand and comfort her, for who did she go to when she needed comfort but him?

Alex and the woman waited for Valerie to speak, and because no words formed in her head, because she was genuinely stunned that he'd be rude to her in front of another woman, she reached for his bottle of beer. "I've always wanted to do this to you," she said and poured it over his head. Or started to. Alex grabbed her wrist and pushed her out of the bar, through the hotel foyer and onto the sidewalk, where they continued the argument from earlier. Who remembers anymore what these things were about? What could generate such passion? Valerie didn't come from a family, or world, where people behaved this way. She came from snobs. New Englanders without money but snobs nonetheless, her parents permanently encamped in the faculty housing at Bradbury Prep: Dad the much-beloved choir master, Mom appreciating the free housing, the good education for Valerie, and the many rich people coming and going. Not that she put it this way, but that was the idea, more or less. After graduating, Valerie attended nearby Amherst. *You'd never have gotten in if not for Bradbury,* her parents enthused, Valerie's academic achievements being, apparently, about her parents' wise choice of employment. So Valerie escaped as soon as possible for the Midwest, finding herself, in the months before Alex, smitten with construction workers and farm breakfasts—everything for which she hadn't been raised.

"Bitch," Alex whispered in her ear and grabbed Valerie's wrist again. She slugged his arm. Valerie's parents often argued but were as likely to strike each other as to spontaneously combust while spreading jam on their crumpets, an affectation they'd acquired from one of the Bradbury parents. "Disorderly household," Valerie once read in Iowa City, in the newspaper's quaint police reports. Someone had been arrested for a disorderly household; at the time, Valerie had looked at the mess in her kitchen sink and said, "Uh-oh."

Oh, it didn't matter what she told her Madison friends. Alex and the ludicrous dress didn't start it. Not really. The dress just ended what was there all along.

As for the woman at the bar, a week after the fight—apologies made, presents bought, exhaustion finally lifting; why, oh, why, did they let things get so far?—Valerie visited her gynecologist.

"I'll get Suzy for the internal," the doctor said. Valerie obediently scooted herself into position, remaining knock-kneed, as she supposed she must, till everyone was gathered for the occasion.

Suzy entered with all the efficient good cheer of someone used to offering comfort to the healthy. Jewelry cuffed her ear cartilage. She looked vaguely familiar. "You OK?" she asked gently, as the doctor inserted the speculum. A poster above the examining table featured a photograph of a white kitten, holding onto a branch. "Hang in there, baby," it said, though for those acquainted with sex, birth or super-sized tampons, how traumatic could an internal exam be? Now there was an idea for a game show. "Can You Top This?" Each of the female contestants would try to outdo the other with stories about ob/gyns and their idiotic ceiling posters.

"Oh, sure," Valerie turned to smile at Suzy, only realizing, mid–pap smear, who the spiky-haired nurse was.

*E*ach year, the Center for Artistic Exchange picked a theme, and then their various performances, educational programs and exhibits would relate, somehow, to that theme. "What's next year's theme?" people were always asking Valerie. Under her supervision, the center had done "Aging in America" and "Childhood and Its Discontents." This year's theme was "The Stranger Comes to Town," which had been semi-disastrous for the Center's daycare. "The Pied Piper" terrified the kids, and their parents—alive to news reports of abductions and molestation—weren't too happy either.

In the year of the dress, when people asked Valerie about next year's theme, she answered, "Hate." She said it simply, more wry amusement than anger in her voice, but no one ever cooed, "How interesting," or followed up the answer with another question.

𝓑ike paths criss-crossed Madison, but the road to Mara Maud—a cosmetology school located in a strip mall west of town—was busy and shoulderless. Still, Ellen regularly braved the ride down University Avenue for her friend Tamar, the school's receptionist. You'd think the school would have no trouble finding people to volunteer for free services, but there had been a few incidents. "You can't trace that gangrene to our cuticle scissors," Maud insisted in court, and the judge agreed. Even so, people started to call the place Sweeney Todd's.

"Now," said Tamar, "it's like flying an airline after a major crash. Things are more likely to be clean here than anywhere else in the city."

Tamar was supposed to find clients for the beauty students, and Ellen did what she could to help. She'd already offered up her body for a pedicure, haircut, two chair massages and a makeup application. Tamar wanted her to have a facial, but Ellen wouldn't; she was self-conscious about the tan mole on her face, a miniature mouse curled below her right cheekbone. Ellen routinely propped her face on her palm, hoping nobody would notice. She'd once even asked a plastic surgeon to remove the mole, but he refused, saying the scar from the surgery would be far worse than the mole, and why should a pretty girl like her worry about something no one could see anyway?

Ellen felt ashamed, as if she were the kind of person who'd want face-lifts and tummy tucks as she aged, but she wasn't vain, just concerned with basic maintenance. It was like tuning up her bike. A responsibility. And though she didn't wear makeup beyond lipstick, she liked to have her toenails painted, her fingernails shaped, her legs waxed. It made her feel as if she'd finished doing the laundry of herself, folded and ironed everything neatly, that she was in order.

The "technician" responsible for today's "treatment" was Kristen Howard, who'd just finished her first semester at the beauty school.

"She flunked client relations," Tamar confided as she guided Ellen to the massage table on which Ellen was to rest. Tamar had attended a different beauty school but been hired on the strength of her tattoos—elaborate vines and birds that she'd designed for her arms alone. "You have to tell me if she says anything outrageous."

Ellen raised her eyebrows. "Darling, I don't think so."

"Oh, come on," Tamar goaded. They'd been friends since junior high, conjoined (initially) by the poorly attended events their synagogue's rabbi planned for Madison's always-disintegrating Jewish youth group. "I guarantee you'll get some dirt."

"Well, I'll be too much of an upright citizen to share it."

"Ph-shht," Tamar said, a deflating beach ball sound. She knew she'd get her way in the end. "Like my hair?"

Tamar was wearing it in two small buns, little knobs behind her ears.

"Looks great."

"Anyway, you're going to like this. I told her to do the herbal body wrap. It'll be like she's making you into a human burrito. You'll sweat out your toxins."

This appealed. Ellen was working, half-consciously, on purity. Whole foods. Filtered water. Pajamas—not that she could afford it—of organic cotton.

"So clothes off," Tamar said, giving Ellen a quick kiss goodbye, "get between the sheets, and Her Awfulness will arrive."

Moments later, a dark-haired, statuesque woman pressed into the room. "Hey, I'm Kristen. I'll be your technician today." She wore a short, fitted black skirt and peachy-pink shirt. With her high heels and makeup, she might have been a person spritzing perfume at a department store. "So we're going to do a body wrap today?" She'd pulled her hair tightly back from her head and secured it in a bun. ("Looks like her eyeballs are going to pop out," Ellen's mother once said of a neighbor who wore her hair in a similarly severe fashion.)

"Oh, yeah, thanks," Ellen said, embarrassed, her eyes tearing slightly at the memory of her mother's words. She could recall her mother saying, "Did you go to the potty?" and get similarly choked up. Everything she could salvage from the first six years of her life was precious.

"So what do you do for a living?" Kristen pulled back one corner of the massage table's sheet and started to scrub the front of Ellen's leg with rough salt.

It was always nicer when the beauty students didn't want to talk, when you could just drift away. "I work at a daycare."

"Me?" Kristen said, not responding to Ellen's information. "I'm a witch, though I'm also getting my certificate here, of course. I need a day job."

"Oh." Ellen didn't know what to say to this. "What kind of witch?"

"You think I'm going to say a good witch, right? You think I'm going to say I'm one of those Wiccan people?"

"I guess," Ellen agreed cautiously, expecting Kristen to elaborate, but she didn't. New Age music, punctuated with bird chirps and babbling brook water, played softly in the background.

Kristen made a rolling motion with her forefinger, and Ellen understood she was to flip over onto her stomach. She did so, and Kristen continued her work, rubbing salt over Ellen's back. Once Ellen was completely covered, Kristen said, "This salt preserves your skin. No, really! It's just like you were a hunk of meat, and I cured you. I could hang you in a back closet for months, and you'd still be fresh as a daisy. But"—Kristen patted Ellen's shoulder—"instead I think you should rinse all this off." She held up a towel that Ellen was to step into.

"Um . . . OK."

"Oh, don't be embarrassed. I've seen it all and then some."

"Right," Ellen said. Still she felt weird, *unusually* naked, as she pushed herself up, rotated onto her bottom and angled one leg then the other off the table.

"You go shower in the bathroom on the left, just outside that door," Kristen said, pointing. When Ellen returned, Kristen gestured to a thick blanket on top of what looked like a large sheet of foil. Ellen was to lie down.

"So now I'm going to put some of this oil on you—it's scented with myrrh—then I'll wrap you up and go away for a stretch."

"Myrrh," Ellen chimed. She wasn't a gardener. It was a plant, as far as she knew, that only grew in the Bible.

"I'm actually an evil witch," Kristen announced, companionably, almost flirtatiously, as she started to rub oil over and behind Ellen's shoulders. "I'm as bad as they get."

When she didn't laugh at her own words, Ellen imagined that Kristen was going to lean over and kiss her, as if this patter were some secret lesbian mating ritual that everyone in Madison, save she, knew about.

Ellen was a virgin herself; the only twenty-five-year-old virgin in the world, she supposed, and anything that smacked of a come-on scared her. It wasn't as if she hadn't been the object of attention. People always told her how beautiful she was. "Wholesome." She heard that a lot. And: "You could be a model." She once even had headshots taken, on the sly, for Mose would never approve of such a thing. But then the idea of modeling seemed foolish to her, too. She wasn't particularly eager to be noticed. Still, it did occur to her once, while at a college party, a boy standing with his forearm leaning against the wall beside her, the back of his other hand lightly brushing her cheek, that a boyfriend, or even a lover, would ruin things for her; that beauty, once possessed, wasn't beauty. Or something like that. The thought wasn't fully formed in her head, and yet it had pulled her through college. Lately though it seemed dumb. She should just get the sex thing over with already.

"What are you waiting for?" Tamar had asked her recently. "It's not like the first time is earth-shattering for anyone."

"Yeah, I guess," Ellen said. "I'm sort of waiting not to feel judged."

"What are you talking about?" Tamar had cried. "People are always telling you how pretty you are."

Ellen twisted her lips into a frown. It wouldn't do to say *that* made her feel judged.

"Well, enough of that," Kristen said but continued to rub oil into Ellen. Perhaps she'd exhausted the subject of the dark side.

"Ever had your eyebrows waxed?" Kristen inquired in a clipped tone.

"No."

"You really should."

Ellen offered a noncommittal, "Hmm."

"And a bikini wax. God, you definitely need that."

Ellen flinched. Barbara had been her instructor in the vagaries of feminine hygiene, but this issue had never been broached. If there was a reason to stop helping Tamar, it was the salon's sense that a woman's body was an endlessly pruneable forest. Somehow *wrong* in its natural form, a suggestion that took Ellen back to her adolescent self: ever visiting the bathroom to check if her tampon had leaked, to tuck toilet paper under her armpits, to splash water on her sweaty face. Even then, people regularly told her she was pretty, but she'd never *felt* pretty; she'd felt gross.

Kristen wrapped a warm blanket around Ellen, securing its edges under her feet and torso. "Be back in thirty minutes," Kristen said. "You should just relax."

Ellen tried to keep her mind blank, not to use the time to figure out what she needed at the grocer's or to remind herself to call Barbara. But she felt odd. Not because of Kristen exactly. And it didn't have anything to do with work. What *was* it? She tried not to *be* distressed, but observe her distress. Something—a bit of last night's dream—winged through her brain, disappearing before she had a chance to catch it. She pictured, for no particular reason, a fold of fabric carved in stone and draped over a woman's marble calf. If it was a dream pulling at her, perhaps she should let it be. A few nights ago, she dreamed she'd taken a down elevator, hoping to go from Town—which seemed to be floor 5— to Home—which was on floor 2. But she'd accidentally stepped off on floor 3, which was the Third Reich. For days, she lived more in that dream than out, thinking only of how she might inform those in the real world of where she was stuck. But already it was too late. In the logic of the dream, she could get off the elevator but not back on.

There was a knock on the door, and Tamar stepped into the room. "Want some water?"

"How can I drink wrapped up like this?"

"I'll get you a straw."

"No, thanks."

"Did she tell you that she was a witch?"

24

"Yes! What's *that* about?"

"I think she's really pissed at her boyfriend."

"That's an interesting way of dealing with it."

"She has a way of making people feel lousy about themselves. I hope she didn't try that on you."

"Not exactly." Ellen didn't like to get others in trouble. Still, *that* was it. Kristen's comments judged Ellen, made it clear that the way she'd chosen to live—or the way she'd chosen to live in her body—was wrong.

"Tut, tut," Tamar clicked her tongue. "She's coming back. By the way, did I mention she's really a he?"

"What are you talking about?"

"She's a guy; she's going to get the operation. But he has to live as a she, before she does it. Sometimes I think her problem is that she's jealous. You know, of all the women here."

"Wow."

"Did you guess? I mean about her being a man?"

"God, no. It wouldn't have occurred to me. I mean, *really*."

Ellen, fair-haired and fair-skinned, felt rather masculine herself as she left the beauty school. Oily and warm, she had the unhappy idea of herself as a Chia Pet—a badger—exuding endless unwanted hair. She bent to fumble with the lock on her bike. Behind her, someone said, "Hey!"

Still squatting, Ellen shaded her eyes with one hand and looked up. She didn't register anything for a moment, and then a person—a looming silhouette—blocked the sun. Ellen stood and saw an athletic man, his nose a little pink, his hairline receding, though he had a full head of curls, comically unruly. He grinned, then gave a little wave of his hand, as if to a small child.

"Ellen, right?" His red lower lip glistened, and Ellen remembered a bisexual friend saying that kissing men with beards reminded her of being with women. Ellen had been a little shocked at this; she was retrograde that way—still surprised by the sex lives of others.

"So how have you been?" the man said.

Who *was* he? Ellen flipped the Rolodex of her recent encounters: someone from the Willy Street Food Co-op? Another volunteer theater usher?

"Maybe you don't remember. I sat down at your table. I didn't have my beard then."

"Oh, yes," she began. "Alex Decker, the superintendent. From the terrace."

One afternoon last spring, she'd been sitting behind the University of Wisconsin's union, and he'd asked to share her table. She'd pulled her legs from the green metal chair on which they were propped. The terrace chairs with their backs shaped like sunbursts were decidedly uncomfortable, but (some wise designer must have reasoned) virtually indestructible. Plus they were all chained to the tables. Students would steal anything.

"Thanks," Alex had said, as she lifted her face to the sky. It was the first warm day after months of cold, and everybody was out on the union's back patio, which descended in shallow steps to Lake Mendota. "Student?" he asked. Someone was grilling brats down by the water, and she could hear the metal clinking of buoys tending to the university's sailboats.

"No," she said, bringing her eyes down to meet his, unsure if she wanted to be drawn into conversation. "Not anymore."

"What are you now?"

"I work in a daycare." She'd kept her hands on her sunglasses, but this felt rude, so she ventured, "You?"

"I'm the superintendent for schools."

She laughed, probably with more suspicion than mirth. "Not really."

"I'm not the superintendent of schools?"

"Alex Decker doesn't have a beard," she said. "I've seen his picture in the paper."

"I grew one. I needed to make a change. Not shaving was the only thing I could think of." He waited a beat, then added, "I've also lost a bit of weight recently." He looked down at his torso, as if just remembering where the wayward pounds used to be.

"Well, that's a strange coincidence . . . " Ellen began slowly.

"It doesn't look like *you're* growing a beard . . ."

"I'm . . . I'm related to Mose Sheinbaum. He's sort of my adopted father."

"You're kidding! I hired Mose Sheinbaum . . ."

"I know. For Sudbury High School, for the at-risk kids."

"Oh, that's a misperception. It's not just at-risk kids at Sudbury. And also you shouldn't call them 'at-risk.' That makes their qualities seem like deficits."

"Which qualities?"

"Oh," Alex had wrapped his forefinger around his chin, as if considering. "Mainly their criminal records, their inability to read . . . that sort of thing."

"Mose is still there. At Sudbury, I mean."

Alex had nodded. "I knew that. I think I did. He always was one of our best teachers. Of course, I haven't been principal there for many years."

"Right," she had said, then run on, complimenting Alex about his work, because Mose *had* always admired him, and she *could* remember a few specifics—like that he'd arranged it so that the district's students could take sign language for their language requirement or get course credit for social action. It was funny that it had taken so long for her to place him.

"On the terrace, that's right," Alex said now. "We talked about Mose Sheinbaum, as I remember." He made a puppet-talking gesture with his hand, as if they'd gabbed endlessly.

She put her fingers to her brow and tapped, as if was all coming back to her now, though, in truth, she felt a little dizzy.

Usually Ellen didn't let small interactions slip by her. Since girlhood, she'd collected minor encounters, didn't dismiss their value. Back in San Francisco, there had been a cookie place where she guiltily stopped a few times after school. She invariably joked about how she shouldn't be eating sweets, even as the Ethiopian clerk handed her a cookie, damp and swollen with chocolate. Then one day on the evening news, she learned he'd been murdered. A hold-up. "Kids on drugs," Mose said. "I bet that's who did it." Ellen knew nothing of the cookie man beyond his sweet smile as he dispensed change; surely he'd not understood half of what she was saying during their quick transactions. And he, too, knew nothing of her. And yet she carried him with her, reminding him (wherever he was) that she valued him, that she mourned, even though she didn't know him. It made a difference that he had once been here. To his family, yes, but also to her, a stranger whose life

27

brushed his. In this way, Ellen believed, she honored her parents, who must have made a difference—though there was little evidence of it—to someone beyond Mose, Barbara and Ellen.

"Are you all right?" Alex asked, squinting, then reaching out to touch her protectively on the forearm, as if she might need to be steadied.

"Yes, I'm sorry. It just took me a second to remember." Ellen shook her head, as if it were her hair that prevented her from being present to the moment. "What's up? Skipping school?"

"Well, it's actually hard to skip school when it isn't in session."

"Oh, yeah. I forgot." Even if it hadn't been summer, the school day would be long over by now. The day felt bothersome, all jumbled up with too many non sequiturs. Witches. A male-female. Her own untended self.

"Not that I don't *want* to play hooky."

"Oh, hooky," Ellen said, almost dreamily. She'd always had a perfect attendance record.

"I'm going to go get my BB gun and shoot squirrels," he said, and gave what Ellen assumed was a Davy Crockett swagger.

"Is that what kids did when you were young?"

Alex cocked the side of his mouth. Perhaps this was too much of a reminder that Ellen's own generation of hooky players was more likely to dress in goth clothing and murder classmates.

"No. More sneaking of liquor, as I remember it, back in the Dark Ages."

Ellen remembered a bit of her dream: something about dancing and that stone drapery she'd flashed on earlier. The dream slipped away then returned in full, finally poking through the weave of the day. Last night, she'd dreamed about *Wisconsin*, the gold-gilded statue that graced the State Capitol Building's enormous granite dome. In Ellen's dream, the figure—with her badger-topped helmet—was dancing. But there was something grotesque about her movements, the lifted knees too emphatic, the pounding arms scary, *Wisconsin* on uppers. Ellen had been subconsciously in thrall to the dream all day.

"Actually," Alex checked his watch. It was almost six. "Now that I have what I need"—he lifted an Ace Hardware bag—"I *am* going to sneak some liquor." He paused, looked at his feet. "Could I convince you to join me?"

"Oh," she said, surprised. Out drinking with the superintendent of schools? It hardly seemed like something that anyone, let alone Ellen, would do. "Hmm," she added, slowly considering. This didn't seem wise. She felt fuzzy. Kristen said to drink a lot of water after the body wrap, otherwise she'd get dehydrated. Why had Ellen dreamed of a statue, of all things? And why did she feel like she, somehow, *was* the statue, with its edgy, frenetic movements, as if she were a cartoon drawn by a Parkinson's patient? Ellen had the idea that she was occupying two narratives—the one in her life; the one from last night's dream—and the vague suspicion that if she accepted Alex's offer, the two narratives would merge. "Yeah," she heard herself saying. "You could."

"Leave the bike here," Alex said. "I can drive."

She hesitated, then thought better of her hesitation. Were they going on a *date*? He *was* cute. She could see how somebody might be interested. A night with him wouldn't end at a bar with drunken athletes or in some club where music played so loud that you had to shriek to be heard. He was such a clear grown-up. "OK," she said. "That's be great." Then, "No, wait."

"Yes?"

"I work at a daycare. I told you that, right? When we talked on the terrace?"

"I think you did."

"I work at the daycare that . . . the one that the Center for Artistic Exchange runs."

"You work at Sugar Plums?" Alex asked, half-laughing. "Well, well."

Ellen rarely dealt with the Center's administrators. Still, everyone in the daycare knew that the Center's director, Valerie Crowley-Decker, was divorcing her husband, Alex, this Alex, the one before her with his vanishing beard and wet lips and unexpected invitation.

Chapter Four

APRIL–JUNE 2005

Mose Sheinbaum had a story he liked to tell about the day he met his wife, God bless her soul. They'd gone to the same party, an afternoon picnic in San Francisco's Golden Gate Park. After, he suggested they go for a walk, and they ambled for a long time, out of the park to the beach by Playland, then up the hill, past the Cliff House to Sutro Park. There, on the cliff, with the Pacific Ocean spread out before them like a personal gift, he asked if he could take her to dinner sometime. She smiled but said, "Maybe I'm too old for you." She *was* ten years his senior, and he'd heard friends at the picnic say there must be something wrong with her: in her thirties and not yet married. So he told her no, no, he was an old soul, older than his actual years, already worn out, in fact, by the afternoon's exercise.

Rachel looked confused, as he'd hoped she would.

"Yes," he said. "My feet . . . they're aching with all this walking."

"Not really," she said, slowly, aware she was being tricked, but not yet sure how.

"I can't take another step," he declared, then placed his palms to the ground and kicked his legs up, change raining from his pockets. He walked like this toward the sea, his legs (she said, later) waving wildly, tentacles above him.

The way Mose looked now—osteoporosis having bent his six-two torso into a question mark—who would believe this story? Mose barely believed it himself, and yet to this day, he could feel the press of the sandy path's pebbles in his hands, hear Rachel's sharp shriek of pleasure and surprise. Mose had heard she liked a man to be a little *meshugge*, and he'd aimed to comply.

A year or so into their marriage, Rachel confessed she'd been put off by his oceanside antics. A showoff for a husband? That was something she didn't need. She could tell him this, because he so clearly *wasn't* a showoff. Or silly, another thing she worried about after the stunt. If she were alive now, she might have added "agile" to the list. He wasn't that either. Not any longer.

"You don't always make," Rachel admitted, but kindly, "the best first impression."

If this wasn't true, her words made it true. Even now, decades after her death, Mose—given to reflection, but not undue self-reflection—hesitated before meeting new people, always wondering what mistake he'd make and eager, before he opened his mouth, for another chance to acquit himself.

"*My* goal in life," said Smitty, "is never to attend a dinner party."

"Laudable," Mose allowed. "You're what now?"

"I'm an art teacher. I work with you," Smitty said, his voice rising with this second piece of information, as if his answer might be wrong.

Mose pulled into the Massengills' short driveway. Clara Massengill was Sudbury High's departing principal, and this was her farewell dinner party. "I'm asking how old you are," Mose said. He had never been able to figure Smitty out; the man seemed to live apart from the conventional norms of society: without family, without transportation (thus Mose's assistance tonight) and largely without companionship.

"I'm forty-two."

"Well, forty-two is a good age to give up your dreams," Mose said. His own aspirations were more convivial. He liked a gathering, liked the easy talk about recent movies, political outrages or arthritic knees. Nothing comforted so much as the unoriginality of one's emotions. *Why, others felt the same way, too!* How nice. How very nice. And, as far as Mose was concerned, a free dinner was a free dinner. Even if it was for work. Still, he shared some of Smitty's concern. Someone new to

31

meet, after all. And not just any-old-someone, but Hyman Clark, the new principal.

Smitty gazed longingly at the baby-blue velour seats of Mose's Buick Regal—a rich man's car, though Mose was no rich man. "It's so nice in here," he said with no apparent sarcasm. "Really roomy."

"Glove compartment sleeps six," Mose observed.

But Smitty didn't smile. He squinted at the small brick home to his left. Mud lined the path that led to the front door.

Should Mose confess the car had a name? That Barbara and Ellen called it Stanley, which was short for Stanley-Make-Me-A-Malted? But then Smitty never really warmed to the clannish humor of Mose in the presence of his girls . . . or another Jew. It was part of the reason he wasn't a closer friend. That and his age. For Mose, younger people didn't qualify for grown-up status. Half the time, he wanted to tell Smitty to cut his shaggy hair and tuck his shirt into his pants. Or at least to stop wearing t-shirts with obscure slogans to work.

"I'm just not good at these social things," Smitty said.

"You're the art teacher. You're not supposed to be good at these things. Still, we've got to go in." Mose opened his car door and struggled to his feet. They were already twenty minutes late. When Smitty didn't move, he leaned back into the car and commanded, "Son, get your ass out of that car."

"Cripes," Smitty deadpanned, as he pushed open his door. "You can be scary."

Inside, guests were gathered in seats around a coffee table laden with cut vegetables, dips and cheeses. Clara Massengill appeared to have made no preparations for her upcoming move. The Tuscan platters that hung on her walls like paintings hadn't found their way into boxes. No one had bubble wrapped the lamps with their hand-painted shades or in any way disturbed the perfect order and cleanliness of her small home.

"Come sit," Clara called solicitously when she saw Mose. "Aren't you looking dapper tonight?" As he made his way awkwardly across the room, one of the English teachers rose from her chair and said, "Here. You have to sit here."

"Thank you," Mose said. It hurt him to stand still for any length of time, hurt him more to accept a seat from a young woman, but what could he do?

"So, Mose," Clara began once he was settled. Clara gestured to a tall man with a bowtie, the only stranger in the room. "*This* is Hyman Clark. Hyman, this is Mose Sheinbaum, our history teacher." Smitty didn't bear introduction, it seemed. He was routinely overlooked this way, which was part of the reason Mose liked him.

Mose rose (painfully, this being his plight since his spine had crooked itself) and leaned over the coffee table to shake Hyman's hand.

"Pleasure," Hyman said, standing himself. His face had the grainy texture of Cream of Wheat.

"No, no," Mose said, shaking his head. "The pleasure is all mine."

Sudbury High was an expeditionary learning school. ("School as field trip," Mose explained to the uninformed.) It was open to everyone in the district, but heavily recruited near-dropouts. Not exactly a charitable group. On Monday, they'd take in Hyman's bowtie, his blue blazer with the three gold buttons at the cuffs, his balding pate and the unaccountably squashed face—the human version of a pug—and they'd have him for lunch. Even small-boned Clara—who was so prim and formal, who always dressed in tailored suits—had two faded eagles tattooed on her forearms. She might be a grown-up now, but she'd been a badass in the past, and the students loved her for it. She was "mean," they said, to want to move to Boston.

"So sorry," Hyman smiled, "my wife couldn't be here to meet you. She came down with a little something."

Mose nodded, as if in sympathy. "My wife, too. She came down with a little something. What she came down with was Death."

"Oh." Hyman jerked his head back, as if he'd been slapped. "So sorry."

"No, *I'm* sorry." Mose flushed. Why had he said this? It was so obviously the wrong thing to say. "That was twenty years ago."

A muscle under Hyman's right eye began to twitch.

"Oh, don't worry. Really. I know lots of people who have come down with it." Mose wasn't making his joke any better. Good Lord, what if Hyman Clark's wife *was* seriously ill? At home, sleeping off the effects of her latest chemo treatment? Mose cleared his throat and said more seriously, "It's really good to have you here. I'm hoping for some shop talk."

"Oh, yes," Clara cried in a way clearly meant to return Hyman to the general audience of the living room. "We're *all* happy to have you here."

Mose sank back into his chair. He'd have liked to descend further, through the floor and into Clara's basement, which would be, he knew, well-kept, the floor swept clean and the hot water heater shining, a perfectly reasonable place to eat his dinner. Instead, he asked the English teacher what novel she was teaching this semester.

Beside him, Clara declared with giddy enthusiasm, "Now everybody. You have to try the *gimpfli*. We've cut it up for the cheese, so you can't quite tell, but it's the Swiss version of a croissant!"

In her eagerness to smooth over the moment, Clara might have been a dybbuk, suddenly possessed by the ghost of Mose's wife, clearly saying (if in a code only Mode could understand), "You *still* don't make the best first impression."

"*The Heart*," the English teacher said—and because no one had heard Mose's question, it sounded like a random, if all too true non sequitur—"*Is a Lonely Hunter.*"

In his classroom, a little over a week later, Mose looked down at his watch. The period had ended, but no bell had rung. Perhaps it was broken? "OK, everybody," he said, stopping himself mid-thought, his students confused but willing to forgo clarification if it meant their day was over. "Tapes in. Tapes out. That's class."

Mose always ended classes with this proclamation. Then with the tape exchange. Students dropped the tape they'd listened to on the previous night into one box, and Mose handed them the listening assignment for the next session. For today's class—final period American history—Brandi Carter manned the "tapes in" box, a task she undertook with considerable sexual brio.

"I hope you were kind," Mose heard her purr at a boy. "Did you, you know . . . rewind?" And then, in more of a dominatrix manner, to another classmate, "Where's your tape?"

"Forgot it."

"You know you can't get past me without a tape." Her tone was both strict and suggestive, her body constantly dancing between a breasts-forward, back-arched come-on and a child's slump, as if embarrassed by the stance she'd just tried. Today she wore a too-tight white blouse, over a lacy . . . what-did-they-call-those-things, the things that looked like Victorian stays? . . . giving the impression she was about to burst from her clothes. Just last week, Mose had overheard a boy in the men's room say, "Which would you like more? A blow job? Or to try and get past Brandi without a tape?"

Adolescence was hard enough in the fifties, when Mose was young. Now he didn't know how kids got through their days. So much suggestion. And yet repression was the order of the day. You spent your life learning how not to act on your desires. It didn't matter that all around you, adults weren't following suit. A girl in Mose's first period class was pregnant, thanks to her mother's boyfriend.

Luckily, Brandi—her short hair mussed, as if she'd just risen from bed—turned dutiful when the classroom emptied. "Excuse me," Brandi called. "Mr. Sheinbaum?" She sounded like the officious secretary she was surely destined to become. "We only got thirteen 'The Cold War's and one 'Korean War,' if you can believe it." There were eighteen students in Mose's class.

"Thanks, Brandi." Mose extended his arms for the box of tapes. "I'll take care of this now."

She shrugged, then said, "Mr. Sheinbaum. You know you have to watch us kids. We're not all on the up and up. If you know what I mean."

"Thanks, Brandi," Mose repeated as she shouldered her bag and left.

Tonight, the kids would be listening to "McCarthy and McCarthyism."

Outside, it was still raining. Inside, the lights hummed. Mose sniffed, taking in his classroom's smell of sweat and wet dog hair. On a sunny day earlier in the month, the building's heat had been abruptly and nonsensically turned off. No matter that it often snowed, right through May, in Wisconsin. Today, after lunch, the heat finally clanged noisily on, and students started to disrobe, one girl bounding up to the classroom's temperature gauge to note that it was now seventy-five degrees. But Mose never managed to warm up. Now he felt in need of a mitten for his nose, which was particularly chilly, as if he were the damp canine responsible for his room's odor.

A bell rang to indicate that school was over. The principal's secretary announced something that Mose couldn't understand, the particular distortion of his classroom's intercom rendering all messages unintelligible.

Not long after, Smitty poked his head into the classroom.

"Sir," Smitty said.

"Come in, come in," Mose said, propping himself on the edge of his desk.

Smitty entered, leading with his chest. On another man, this would have looked pompous, but not on Smitty. On Smitty it just looked, as so much about the man looked, wrong.

"*Fear no*—what?" Mose said, gesturing with his chin to the words on Smitty's black t-shirt. A pilly cardigan hid the end of the sentence. Smitty pressed his hand to his chest, almost coyly, though Smitty was the least flirtatious person Mose knew, so much so that even though he was single, the students never speculated on his personal life the way they did with other unattached teachers. Mose perhaps being the only other exception, since he was old enough to be, in the minds of the students at least, beyond romantic matters.

"Not telling," Smitty said, then quickly opened the doorway of his sweater to flash the word "art" at Mose.

"Of course!" Mose said victoriously. " 'Fear no art.' What else for the art teacher? I will try to follow your injunction."

"Might I have left my gloves in your car?" He scratched his head vigorously, as if trying to loose the answer from his scalp.

"You might have and you did," Mose said. "If you want to wait a minute, I'll go out and get them."

Smitty peered out the window. Mose followed his gaze; the rain seemed peevish. A day or two more of this weather, and it would just seem boring. "You headed home?" Smitty asked.

"I am. Want a lift?"

"I wouldn't mind." After a beat, Smitty moved his glasses to the bridge of his nose and peered over his square frames to say, "That was quite a performance at Clara's."

"Not my finest hour," Mose admitted.

"Well, maybe he won't remember." Smitty was quiet, then added, "Hyman Clark," as if Mose might not know to whom he was referring.

"We can only hope," Mose said. "Though *you* didn't forget."

"No, no, I'd never forget *that*."

Here, another adult might have dissembled, but Smitty's charm was all in his failure to charm.

"Maybe I should do something," Mose said.

"Like what?"

"Oh, I don't know. Apologize? Grovel?"

"Well," Smitty offered, "maybe he didn't really notice."

Mose hoped Smitty was right, but there was one thing Smitty didn't know. Sometime during the Massengills' dinner party—after the meal, but before dessert—Mose had glanced at his watch. Looking up, he'd caught Hyman's eye. Mose was about to smile when Hyman said, in the stern voice of a principal—and why was *that* a surprise?—"You have somewhere better to be?"

"Well, there's bed," Mose had said, again trying for a joke. "We moldering old folk"—Mose had at least ten years on everyone at the table—"we get very shaken up by all this festivity."

But his words hadn't entertained. He could already imagine Hyman, in some meeting with the powers-that-be, talking about how to get rid of the deadwood in the system. Fear tap-tap-tapped behind Mose's ears, and Mose brushed it away. Foolish to think, with all his years of good student reviews and his awards (more than one!) for teacher-of-the-year, that he'd be set aside for a handful of ill-chosen words. Clara had always encouraged him when he said his plan was to teach far past sixty-five. She knew the idea of retirement frightened him. Whatever would he *do*?

"OK," Mose said. He headed to the closet, pulled a dark coat over his crumpled jacket, loosened the knot at his neck. "Let's quit our place of employ, before I'm overcome with shame."

*O*nce home, Mose arranged his things. Papers for later, coat to dry out, mail (the usual bills and flyers). But before he attended to all this, he dialed school. He wouldn't sleep tonight, if he kept worrying about his behavior with the principal. When Hyman came on the line, Mose explained who he was (thinking/hoping that Hyman didn't remember him, what with all the new faces, Hyman new to town and new to his job, etc, etc.).

"Well," Mose cleared his throat, ready to get to the point of his call, "I was wondering if we could meet for coffee some time. Have a chance to talk."

"Oh, yes," Hyman agreed distractedly, "we'll have to do that." Mose prepared to suggest a possible time when Hyman added, "Thanks for your call," and hung up.

Once Mose realized he was listening to a dial tone, he hung his own phone up. It rang immediately. Mose supposed it would be Hyman, calling to explain: *phone trouble, so sorry*. And why not? So much at the school had been breaking down lately.

Instead, Ellen's voice came chirping through the receiver. "Mose? It's raining."

"Well, I can see that, darling." Outside, the sky looked like pilling gray felt. The plinking in the puddles on Mose's small terrace grew larger, and Mose encouraged the drops along.

"So you know what that means . . ."

"The forced march is cancelled?" Mose stood for the window, where he twisted his neck to get a better look at the dirty fabric of the sky.

Ellen fretted over Mose, and in recent months, their weekly lunches had become weekly walks. Osteoporosis had aged Mose. *Milshik* or *Felshik*, so went the meals of his youth, and what had he been thinking? He always went for the *Felshik*. Not so his vegetarian charge, a poster child for physical fitness. She biked everywhere, and the effort made her all the prettier. Glowing with health. That's what people said. A cliché, but true. She clearly thought exercise would do the same for Mose. No point in explaining that it wouldn't. When it came to his bones, what was done was done.

"No, sir. The forced march is forced indoors," Ellen announced. "So I'll see you at the Shell?" The Shell, the University of Wisconsin's giant sports center, gave Mose a headache. For five dollars, you strolled on a track that circled several basketball courts, while you suffered—amid the echoing bounce-bounce-bounce of basketballs—the buzzing white lights that hung from a catwalk, high above.

"You'll see me," Mose said hesitantly, imagining that he should stay in, wait for the principal's call, even though he already knew the call wouldn't come.

$\mathscr{M}$ose arrived at the Shell to find Ellen exuberant—her general response to the prospect of exercise. He was glad she was happy—bouncing in and out of a runner's stretch—but her delight deflated him. Ellen: a human gerbil. *Run, run, run. Oh, happy, happy. Now, water. That was good. Run, run, run.* Hadn't he raised her to aspire to more than mere motion?

"Let's go," Ellen said, hooking her elbow companionably through his, as if they were little old ladies out for a walk. Mose shook her off. He needed that arm for balance.

"Ellen!" a young man cried, abruptly stopping mid-run. They never got far without bumping into one of her chums. This boy was practically naked, shirtless and black-shorted, his slight but perfectly formed chest wet with exertion.

"Hey, Mike. You've met my father?"

"Don't think I have." Mike extended his hand for a shake, his grip clearly saying, "I'm a good man, full of respect for your generation, and well able to provide for your daughter," before continuing on.

In fact, Mose was not Ellen's father, though it often seemed easiest to introduce him as such. Barbara, Ellen's sister, usually just spelled things out. "Hi, this is my cousin Mose. He raised my sister and me." If strangers asked why, Barbara punished with information. Nosy bastards. She said: "My parents were killed by a dead man." Or: "My real parents were done in by a milk truck."

Either way, as Mose explained to his own friends, the facts were the same: a man, a massive coronary, a truck careening across a California highway meridian into the front of a paltry car. The girls in the back were unhurt, if you could call living through such a thing being unhurt. There had been something galling about having only corpses to blame: the heart attack victim unable to control his truck, once he was dead; Barbara and Ellen's parents who should have bought a sturdier car, which they surely would have, if they'd had the means.

The means. Who had the means? Not Mose, then working as a plumber in San Francisco, but he took the girls in: little Ellen and Barbara. Now not so little and living on their own, Barbara married to a librarian and settled in far-off Maine, and Ellen still here in Wisconsin, in her tiny apartment overlooking one of the city's four lakes. She worked for an hourly wage at the Center for Artistic Exchange. The outfit had an on-site daycare, and for over two years now, that's where Ellen had spent her days, thinking up ideas for circle time and doling out snacks of mini-carrots and pretzels in Dixie cups.

"So any plans for the summer?" Mose asked, as they settled into their pace around the track.

"Plans?" Ellen said, confused.

"Oh, you know. I was just wondering what was out there, job-wise."

"Well, I *have* a job."

Already Mose's back hurt. "Sometimes I think of myself at your age."

"I know," Ellen said pleasantly, though there was no invitation to continue in her voice. "I know. But twenty-five then was different than twenty-five now."

"Sure enough."

Their lives had been neatly split. Hers in childhood, his in middle age. Not long after his wife's stroke, the girls came into his life, and from the ashes of their collective misfortune—for by his mid-forties, Mose felt ruined: bored, grief-stricken, and lonely—Mose rose. He worked in the trades then, but he went back to school—San Francisco State for his B.A., then his master's. The girls should know the importance of education. He was fifty-two, Ellen almost thirteen, and Barbara seventeen when they left California for Wisconsin.

For a small city, Madison offered a lot, anchored as it was by the university and the State Capitol building. Still, it might have been another country: the doughy citizens at the farmer's market who hawked their wares, promising cheese curds so fresh they squeaked. And who, exactly, was it that appreciated food that protested its own consumption? And then there were the fish boils—a barroom treat, fish smothered in sticks of melted butter. Out in the suburbs, towns were dotted with ugly statues of "wee people." Little elves or trolls. Mose wasn't sure what they were supposed to be, or why he should be charmed by them. Even now, twelve years into life in the Midwest, he felt as if he were living abroad. One of the oldest synagogues in the country was here, though kept as a museum piece in the park. Hard to believe any Jews predated Mose in this city, though he saw them (with his own eyes) at Angel Towers, the high-rise nursing home where he served hot meals, once a week, and was often instructed to "Please stay away from the food cart." The rotating staff never quite remembered that Mose was a volunteer, not an inhabitant.

"Are we done?" Mose turned to Ellen.

"Done?" she said, squinting. "That's three laps. We only just started."

"Honey." He didn't want to disappoint her, though shouldn't she sense his limits? "This is all I *can* do."

"We'll sit and talk then," she said, gesturing toward the few wooden bleachers that hadn't been pressed flat against the length of the Shell's enormous wall.

"Hey, Ellen," another boy cried and waved, as he made his way around the track.

"So what's new in your life?" Mose began, once they were sitting.

"Oh," she sighed, but not unhappily. "Nothing, really. The kids." She meant the kids at the daycare. "And then just home and friends."

"And who was that fellow? The one who just went around."

"Oh, Steve. He's an environmental engineer. I know him from . . ." She thought a moment. "Oh, of course, Tamar had a thing for him. But I guess he didn't for her."

"That's too bad. And how is Tamar?"

"The usual, you know."

But Mose didn't see Tamar anymore, not now that the girls were grown, though he used to see her twice a week, back when he was driving Ellen to and from Hebrew School. He'd been glad for Ellen to have a Jewish friend—some connection to her tradition—though Tamar's flamboyance was always a bit much for him. Mose's years at Sudbury made him largely immune to shocking teenage behavior, but still he'd been shaken by Tamar's manner during her bat mitzvah—the long slinky dress she'd worn with platform shoes, the way she toddled over to the bimah, while holding the slit in her dress closed, then sat back in her chair, stopping the nervous chewing of her bottom lip only to glower at her parents. If you could flunk a bat mitzvah, she'd have flunked, but grade inflation was everywhere, even in the rabbinate, and the rabbi, who had to say something kind about the adult that Tamar was destined to become, said he'd always noticed the girl had a fine eye for fashion. It didn't surprise anyone when she chose beauty school over college.

"And that other boy who we met back there?" Mose pointed to where they'd been standing when they met Mike.

Ellen looked squarely at Mose and said, half a laugh in her voice, "The answer to the question that you are trying not to ask is 'No, I'm not seeing anyone.' And when I am, and when I'm ready to share that news, I will, so you don't need to ask."

"OK, OK. Point made, point taken."

"No offense meant," she said.

"None taken."

There was a time when the questions went the other way, when Barbara and Ellen made endless inquiries about Mose's female friends, as if surely he'd fall in love and provide them with a mother. But after his wife's death, Mose was in no condition to date. Who did he want but her? Just when he might have been ready to reconsider, there was that unusually high PSA test, and then the prostate cancer. This was when he was still in San Francisco. Mose had been afraid of scaring Barbara and Ellen—how much loss could they take? The day of the diagnosis, Mose sat in his kitchen considering how he would manage everything. There was a lot to weigh, but he could think only of Ellen's panicked crying, earlier in the week, when her helium balloon floated away. Ellen had wanted to let the balloon go, to see what would happen.

"But will it come back?"

"No, honey," Mose had said.

"Never?" Ellen's voice trembled, and Mose told her that it might lose its helium, then come down in front of some family's apartment. A long crying jag ensued. Finally, in a tiny voice, Ellen had said, "I hope it's a *really nice* family." A conversation that would have made some sense if Ellen was three at the time, but she was six, old enough not to grieve balloons.

So Mose never told Barbara and Ellen about the surgery. Instead, he sent them, young as they were, to sleep-away camp for two weeks. They were gone for the stretch of his hospitalization and initial recovery. A bad time for him. ("Will they come back?" he'd wanted to ask the surgeon about his erections. "Never?" Was there an age at which you didn't feel upset about this loss?)

But he had a romantic life, all right. Not that he was advertising it. Look at Philip Roth (or was it Nathan Zuckerman?), fellow prostate cancer survivor, devil with the women—or to the women—who couldn't (if you trusted the subtext of his books) function anymore. He'd channeled all his crazy brilliance into his work, and look what he'd achieved. *Portnoy, Goodbye, Columbus.* Good books, all right, if a little too much about his member. But *The Plot Against America. American Pastoral.* There you saw it! What that man could do when he took his mind off what was between his legs!

Mose wasn't making any claims for himself, of course. But he had a passion, too. And his passion was his work.

Chapter Five

JUNE 2005

✦

$\mathscr{A}$lex was in college before he started dating women or going to bars or doing all those things from which he'd felt excluded as a teenager. Now that he was forty-two, it seemed everyone else had grown up and out of it. No one really wanted to hang out in a bar wondering what the night might bring. No one arrived at a party hoping some new woman might be in attendance. Sure, Alex's marriage had fallen apart, so it made sense that he'd be thinking about women, but he'd been thinking about them all along. Not that he ever cheated on Valerie, but he always had a flirtation going, a crush. He couldn't quite accept that the mind-blowing sex you had in the first weeks of a relationship was all the mind-blowing sex you were going to get . . . ever. That all the excitement—the pure narrative excitement of a night out, as if a man weren't a life, but a really good novel—was going to disappear. Even when he'd been happiest with Valerie, marriage made him feel flat. There was no suspense to it. He no longer went to social gatherings with a sense of possibility. What might the night bring? When he was a young man, before the evening ended, he might land in some unknown woman's bed. When Alex added up the number of nights this had happened, when a night's possibility became an actuality, his sense of expectation made no sense. The likelihood that an evening would turn into a real encounter was right up there with the chance that a woman would knock on his door and come crawl into his lap. He was lonely in the stretch before he met Valerie, but still he longed for the sense that something might happen. Marriage gave him the feeling that his hand was dealt. Shuffle things as he liked, he was never going to get another queen in his particular deck.

Valerie and Alex were twenty-five when they married, twenty-seven when Douglas was born. There had only been half a dozen single years, and yet those years tugged at Alex. Not because he was happy then—all those crazy girlfriends!—and not because he wanted to succumb to adolescent daydreams about seducing this one or that, the patter that would get him into bed, the women he would pick up at a hotel bar while traveling. After all, there rarely *were* any women in bars, and when there were, they weren't looking for someone. They were reading books. And even if he met someone, he wouldn't do anything. The sexual world roiled beneath this, the real (and repressed) world, but there was no road from here to there.

Now that he had a woman in his car—and not just any woman but that knockout he'd met on the Union terrace last spring—Alex found his manner vacillating between paternal and wannabe flirtatious (and could there *be* a more repulsive combination?). Did she have her seat-belt on? (Paternal.) Did she need help? As she struggled to get the seat-belt, long ago jammed by a wayward piece of Douglas's bubblegum, across her chest? (Vaguely lascivious.)

"So where to?" he finally said.

"Huh," she sniffed. "What would be good?" She scanned the horizon, as if the answer might be out there. Her hair was wet in the back, as though drying from her morning shower. "I'm not much of a drinker," she admitted. He'd dared himself to talk to her on that day last spring, had asked himself, "If you hauled a panel of judges onto the terrace and asked them to select the beauty queen of the hour, who would they pick?" It was her, the blond, no question, and just for that reason, he'd forced himself over to her table, sloshing his beer on his wrist as he went. He'd probably looked like an old lech.

"Well," Alex glanced at his watch. It was just after six. "It doesn't need to be a drink. Is it too early for you for dinner?"

"Not at all. I always eat early. Better for your health, you know."

"Everyone I know likes to eat late," Alex said, not even sure if this was true. "Proves they've got an exciting life, I suppose."

"Well, I definitely don't have an exciting life."

"Huh. No boyfriends? No late nights partying?" Valerie always railed at the use of "party" as a verb.

"No, not at the moment. Boyfriend, I mean. As for late nights, I'm kind of a morning person."

"So what *do* you do, in the evening?"

"Oh, this and that. Visit with friends. Go for a run. Or . . . I've got a sewing circle. With all these old women. That's been pretty cool."

Alex had been heading to a restaurant that he frequented near the Capitol Building, but the place—with its extensive wine list, waiters in chefs whites, locally grown greens arranged into careful little salads—struck him as too formal for a girl who might find a sewing circle charming.

"I know where we should go. Ever been to Hazel's?"

"Oh, no, I keep hearing about it. It's out in the country, right? Past the Hop? I love that place."

"I thought you weren't a late-night person." The Hop was a country-western bar. Sort of a dive. Valerie and Alex had visited back when they first came to Madison, not long after that movie about Patsy Cline came out, and half their friends were swept up by the romance of hard-knocks and cowboy bars.

"Well, I like to dance," Ellen said, "and I've been taking country swing lessons."

"You're kidding? Well, let's go dancing."

"You know how to swing dance?"

"Yessir, if there's one thing I know, it's country swing. Ever since I was a kid."

"I don't really have any friends who are into swing."

"One time . . . years ago now . . . I went to the Hop with my wife, and I tried to flip her over my back. I used to do that with everyone, even my mother, when my family went to the roadhouse. This was back in Iowa where I'm from. The whole family always went dancing. Anyway, I flipped my wife over, but she didn't get what I was doing, so

46

she tried to unflip herself. She slid off my back onto the top of her head."

"My God!"

"You're not kidding. She ended up with a mild concussion." He glanced over to her, then back to the road. "That's the thing about dancing. You just have to let the man lead. You know, just give in to it."

"That's exactly what our teacher says!" Ellen enthused, as if charmed by the coincidence.

"The problem," Valerie had told Alex—long after her concussion was over and when they were talking not about dancing but her difficulty having orgasms, despite Alex's diligent attentions—"is that I've never been able to give into anything."

The malls on Madison's perimeter were disappearing in Alex's rearview mirror. They were finally out in the country. Alex switched the air conditioning off and rolled down his window. "Feels good out here."

"Well, maybe we *should* go dancing," Ellen said.

"Sure, let's do that," Alex said. He propped his elbow on the window. "And to think that I went to the hardware store for a stepstool."

"I'm sorry?"

"I didn't find one." When she didn't say anything, he added, "I moved a few months ago."

"Oh, I should have guessed that. I mean, I know that you and Valerie are . . ." She waved her hand to cover the words "breaking up." She was silent, then said, "I don't see her much at work, but . . . could we not tell her about this?"

Alex looked over at her.

"Maybe it would upset her?"

Oh, it would upset her all right, and though he didn't think of himself as mean and didn't plan to let her know about this evening, he realized that was part of the pleasure.

Hazel's occupied an old stone building, bordered by two cornfields, just where you'd expect absolutely nothing to be. To get there, you took the highway, then turned onto a road that crossed a stretch of land that looked more like Iowa than Wisconsin: fewer hills, vegetation largely razed. And then there it was, an old stone cottage, sitting in a knoll of trees with wispy leaves. The place had a fairy tale feel to it. "Because," Valerie used to say, "we can't figure out what those trees are. So the whole place feels unreal."

Now on the road that led to Hazel's, Ellen said, "Look."

"What?"

"A fire. Don't you smell it?"

As soon as she said this, wisps of dark smoke, like low-lying clouds, drifted toward them. Then, off to the left, flames appeared, beyond a stand of trees. The smoke was denser there, and from deep within the black-gray, a blossom of red-orange unfolded itself.

"A brush fire, I'm guessing," Alex said.

As they drove closer, the flames became more distinct: orange and brown, spluttering behind the trees.

"Kind of big for a brush fire," Ellen said.

"It's a field," Alex realized, as they crested a hill. A giant rectangle of flame appeared below them. "They've set it on fire."

"How are they ever going to put that out?" Ellen asked, a touch of panic in her voice. "Maybe we should call 9-1-1?"

Alex gave a snort of a laugh. "No, honey." He wondered instantly if this sounded patronizing. "They're burning it on purpose. To clear it. Sort of an odd time of year to do it, though."

The road brought them closer, then right by the fire. Alex slowed the car, so they could watch the blaze, a gauzy curtain of flame giving off waves of heat. As a boy, Alex had imagined walking through such sheets of fire, as if through a maze, knowing he'd emerge unharmed. Because he was magic. Because he was a super-hero. He'd been a bit of the nerdy outsider as a kid, so that's how he thought of himself: as in disguise.

"Wow," Ellen whispered, still staring, her face illuminated, as if the biggest candle in the world had chosen to shine right on her. "It's like some burning Rorschach test."

"What?" he said, though he registered her words a moment after he asked his question.

"Just, you know," she said and turned her eyes back to the road. She clearly didn't want to repeat her observation. "All the things inside it."

Hazel's was lit by candles and a fireplace, as if in allegiance to the drama outside, though Hazel's décor actually hadn't changed in decades. Nor, it seemed, had the matronly waitresses in their black skirts, white shirts and sensible white shoes.

When the waitress came to take their drink order, Ellen said, "I guess I need a second to decide."

"And how about your dad?" the waitress asked cheerily. "Do you know what you'd like, sir?"

"I'd like you to know that she is not my daughter . . . and whether you have . . . um . . . Macallan's."

"I'm so sorry," the waitress said, sounding genuinely embarrassed. "I'll have to go check with the bar." She scuttled quickly away.

Ellen smiled briefly, then purposefully crossed her eyes. "Now I'm afraid she'll card me."

How old *was* Ellen? Younger, of course. Young enough to be his daughter? Good God, Alex hoped not. They ordered—steak for him, salad for her—and the dishes arrived almost too quickly. "So . . . when I talked with you that day at the Union, you said Mose Sheinbaum was something like your father, your adopted father. What's that mean exactly?"

"Oh," Ellen sighed. "It's kind of a long story." She seemed both willing and reluctant to explain.

"Well," Alex smiled, hoping he didn't appear pushy. "I've got ears." He waved his hand, as if beckoning the story over to his side of the table. "So why don't you try me?"

"Oh, I'm going to sound like the poor Little Match Girl. But"—she settled her napkin on her lap—"my parents died in a car accident when I was six. Our cousin Mose took us in and raised my sister—Barbara, she's older—and me. There wasn't any other family who could really take us. Mose had a wife, but she was dead. Everyone was dead." She said this last as if it were a joke. "Everyone but Mose—who insists he's half in the Great Beyond as it stands—but that's what happened. He took us the year I started school. First grade. It was a week after my birthday. The accident was, I mean." She stopped talking, then smiled briefly. "And . . . I don't know . . . what else can I tell you?"

He started to say he was sorry, but then she said, "Oh, yes. I had an ice cream cake from Carvel's. Only the icing wasn't made of ice cream. It was red gel, and it looked like blood. But that was before."

"Before?"

"The cake. It was before they died."

Had Alex even known Mose had kids? Well, not kids, but dependents, people in his care? He wasn't sure. Years ago, Mose had told Alex about a plan by two members of Sudbury's advisory board to oust Alex from Sudbury—from his own school! the one *he'd* founded! At the time, Alex had convinced the men to resign. If not for their willingness to go, he couldn't say for sure where he would be now. To date, that was the principal fact that Alex remembered about Mose, but as Ellen spoke, he dredged up other things: how Mose had always opted out of after-school activities and the extra salary that came with a willingness to coach a sport or oversee a club; how Mose had never been available to chaperone dances or take students on overnight field trips.

Alex's meal was almost done, Ellen's just begun. He was always embarrassed by how quickly he ate, a bad habit left over from boyhood, but then he realized Ellen wasn't much focused on her meal. Maybe a career dieter, he thought exhaustedly. He'd like to meet a woman who wasn't endlessly preoccupied with her weight. "There's not much of a family resemblance between you and your . . . er . . . cousin."

"I know," Ellen said. "Everyone says that."

Alex didn't tell her that he found her beautiful; he had the idea she would be put off by such a compliment.

"And your sister. What's she like?"

"She's kind of . . . Well, she's really smart. Definitely the smart one."

"*You're* smart." Something flickered across Ellen's face, and Alex sensed he shouldn't have said this.

"Well, not really, I'm not a student or anything. I think that was a disappointment for Mose, but I'm practical. And my sister . . . see, she isn't. Being intelligent . . . mostly it's just made her unhappy."

"I'm sorry to hear that."

"And you? I've been telling you all this stuff, but . . . what about you? And I know you just . . ."

"Divorced. Yes," he said. By now he had the narrative down pat. You *needed* a story about a divorce just like you needed a story about how you met your wife. And people seemed to think the one was as easy as the other, though you met your wife on a single day and left her—or at least Alex had left Valerie—over the course of many years. Alex told people that he and Valerie were just at different places in their lives and that they were still friends, but he had no idea if this was true.

"Well, you know her, so I guess I should ask what *you* think of my ex."

"Oh, I couldn't say. I don't really work with her." Alex could remember when Valerie first rented out space to "Sugar Plums." The business referred to itself as a "Creative Arts Center"—not a daycare—which was how it came to be housed in the Center for Artistic Exchange's basement. "I just see her now and then. Mostly when I go to the gallery openings."

"And you don't have an impression?"

"No, I do." She laughed a little.

Alex raised his eyebrows. "And . . ."

Ellen hesitated, then said slowly, "I think she's . . . formidable."

Alex laughed. "What's that supposed to mean?"

"I don't know. I guess I'm scared of her. She's so . . . you know."

Ellen shrugged, and Alex thought of all the words she wasn't saying: judgmental, smart, funny, nervous, unforgiving, despondent. Those were the words *he'd* use, but they didn't have much to do with how Valerie appeared in public. She was generous to friends and co-workers. She was warm—he'd realized many years back—to almost everyone *but* him.

"Well, Valerie and I broke up, because she held me in . . ." His voice surprised him by cracking slightly. He cleared his throat. "Contempt. Not that she criticized me. I can handle criticism. It was the contempt I couldn't take."

"I can't imagine someone feeling that way about you. Not that I know you that well, just you seem . . ."

Alex waited. He very much wanted to know how he seemed, but she didn't finish her sentence, just brushed her fingers toward him and said, "Well, you know."

What would Ellen do if he tried to touch her? He didn't want to risk it, but then he reached across the table and put the pad of his thumb briefly to her bottom lip.

She smiled. In pleasure? Embarrassment?

"That was a relief," she said.

"What was?"

Ellen didn't say anything. Perhaps she was going to change her mind. Then she added, "That thing with your . . . your . . . what's it called . . . your thumb."

"Dessert?" the waitress came by to say.

"Oh, no," Ellen said, as if the woman had asked about something far more serious. The waitress left to get the check, and Ellen reached across the table to squeeze Alex's fingers. "Dad," she said. "Let's go dancing."

A band played from a lit platform in the otherwise dark, semi-cavernous expanse of the Hop. Tables clustered at the dance floor's edge, and waitresses zigzagged behind chairs, picking up beer bottles and good-humoredly suffering patrons' jokes.

"How many lessons?" Alex called over the too-loud music, as he and Ellen made their way to the dim dance floor. Most of the men wore jeans, but there were a few dancers in zoot suits, complete with partners in Mary Janes and flared skirts.

"Five. We've just done the Lindy Hop. Oh, and the jitterbug, of course."

"Well, then that's what we'll do."

A long-ago lesson: women didn't need to know how to dance, men did. They'd do fine, if Ellen could follow his lead, and she did, quite easily, as if the ability to sense where another person was going was no skill at all.

When Alex flipped her over his back, Ellen spun effortlessly over—no Valerie she—landing on her feet and squealing, "Oh, my God. Do that *again!*"

Into his pleasure crept some guilt: awkward Valerie stumbling over the breakwater at an East Coast beach. Her bad balance and general inability to trust her body. When it didn't irritate him, Valerie's faltering moved him. In the end, fear was the one passion to which she couldn't help but succumb.

They danced steadily, till the band took a break, then they sat, ordered more beers, while a k. d. lang CD played "I'm Down to My Last Cigarette." They drank silently, and Alex worried—as he always worried—over the quiet. Comfortable silence: unless you were alone, that seemed like a complete oxymoron. Finally, he leaned toward her ear and said, "Want to learn the St. Louis Shag?"

"Never heard of it," she said distractedly.

Maybe he'd brought his lips too close to her ear? He pulled himself up in his chair. "Some people call it the Imperial Swing. My dad was from St. Louis, so it's sort of a family favorite."

"It's kind of cool you went dancing with your family. I can't imagine doing something like that."

"Well, another time, another place." Alex rested his chin on his palm and squinted into the dark. Was he the oldest person here? "I can't quite imagine dancing with my son, so it's something that ended with my generation, I guess." And just as well. The dancing had been a bright spot in Alex's determinedly dull childhood. His parents hadn't wanted him to go to college, and when Alex insisted, they laughed at his choice of the University of Iowa over Iowa State. Did Alex think Shakespeare was going to teach him how to run a farm?

"Well, so come on," Ellen said, slapping his forearm, as if he'd been resisting. She stood, took his hands and pulled him to his feet. "Teach me the dance."

He laughed, turned to take a swig of his beer, then crossed to her left side and said, "OK. I stand here. And you put your hand on this shoulder. And I do this—" He touched her right hip and took her hand, felt his breath hit her neck. "It's an eight count. We'll wait for the right song, but I'll show you now. Rock, step." He rocked back on his left foot, let his right foot join the left. "Kick. Together. Kick." He kicked one foot then the other. "Hup!" He bent a knee and hopped. The floor felt sticky below him, and a urine smell wafted over from an open bathroom door.

"Looks like aerobics," Ellen said.

"Oh, no, I hope not," he said and went on. "Low! And you get down like this." He crouched on the floor, as if avoiding an overhead missile—or maybe just a flying beer bottle. "Then, as loud as you can, STOMP!" He stomped the floor, as if breaking the wine glass at a Jewish wedding. "So," he summarized. "Rock, Step, Kick, Together, Kick, Hup!, Low, Stomp." They tried it a few times, but then Ellen wanted to practice alone. Alex sat with his beer and watched her: the bounce of her breasts with the hop and stomp, his instructions a mantra that he could read on her face. When he looked at her face. Jesus, she was sexy, with the shirt plastered to her front and the sweat at her throat.

"There's more to it, actually," he said, a twinge in his groin. "You're supposed to do a mirror Charleston and crosskicks, but I may just be too old to keep this up."

"Old!" she cried, as if aging were an impossibility, but she sat down, too.

His chest was still rising and falling from his earlier effort. Embarrassing to realize how winded he was, even with all the exercise of the last few months. But then the band started into "Rockin' Robin." "Gotta go," he said, grabbing Ellen's hand. "This is *the* song for the Shag."

They called it quits around one, having taken breaks only for beer. She'd said she wasn't a drinker, but dancing made her thirsty, and she'd downed almost as many as he had.

"So," she said and looked toward the exit on the far side of the room. "I guess we should go."

"Right," he said, though neither of them moved.

"*Right* right," she laughed and jostled her side against him, a move that seemed decidedly intimate, now that they weren't dancing.

"So should we—" he began.

"Should we what?"

"Oh, I don't know," he said, as if the thought had just occurred to him. "Go home together?" And then when she didn't say anything. "Or not. There's the 'or not' option."

She turned and kissed him squarely on the mouth, as if to save herself from having to answer. But then she pulled back from his face and said, as if it were a painfully embarrassing thing to admit, "I'm not all that experienced."

"Not to worry," he said and leaned down to kiss her neck. "I am."

When did his life go this smoothly? Never. No slips, no awkward moments, no sense that he wanted her more than she wanted him. Even the field, when they passed it, not long after, cooperated. The fire was out, but the land was still smoldering.

At home, Alex turned on the light. In the car, his hand on her thigh, he'd thought about how he'd do this: the lamp on the hall table and not the overhead. Even so, he caught sight of his face in the hallway mirror. Pink brow, small chin, dark pooling in the folds of his face. A possum. That's what he looked like. A stricken possum. No young man. He wanted to tell her so, felt she needed to know that, despite the evening's acrobatics, he knew what he was. (Judge before you are judged and you circumvent judgment. A misconception, Alex knew. Years of listening to Valerie call herself fat, and eventually, he thought, "Well, yeah, you could lose a few." A thought that wouldn't have occurred to him without her assistance.)

Alex turned the light back off, then led Ellen through the dark to the couch. A complete dark. No streetlights out here. No furniture to stumble over either, as they made their way. Ellen sat, then lifted her face to kiss him. He kneeled, more clumsily then he would have liked, then folded her into his arms. They'd touched while dancing, but this touching was slower, sweeter, tenser. He didn't know what she expected, but he let her take his hand, touch the tip of each finger, as if considering its worth. Finally, he pulled her fully toward him. Later, he'd talk about how much he appreciated her small awkwardnesses in the moment, her hesitance about touching, and later still, she'd admit it was the first time she'd ever had sex. But at the time, they were both completely quiet. He rolled her over then under him on the couch. She leaned forward and their heads knocked together, a dramatic cracking of skulls, which Alex registered as a distinct white crackle of lightning but located deep within the sky of his brain, a bolt that separated the world into before and after. He was now in "after," whatever that would prove to be, and Ellen was saying—her earnestness the evening's only mood killer—"Sorry, sorry. Oh, I'm so sorry about that."

Chapter Six

JUNE 2005

❦

$\mathcal{C}$lara Massengill left town in April. Two months later, a note in Mose's mailbox asked him to stop by the principal's office during his free period. This was a surprise, but not an unwelcome one. Perhaps the new principal hadn't meant to ignore Mose's earlier invitation for coffee. Perhaps he'd only needed to settle in before he could attend to the business of getting to know his faculty.

"Hello." Mose entered the main office and waved to Betty, Hyman's secretary. Betty had long, once-blond hair, and a prominent blue vein at her pale temple that made her seem vulnerable to Mose, closer to death than the rest of the population. "Clark wants to see me?"

"Oh, yes." Betty turned to look through the open door to Hyman's office. Part of their shared wall was glass, so Mose could see three boys, all slumped in chairs, legs extravagantly spread, a posture that suggested their boredom with whatever reproach they were receiving. Or perhaps the stance was meant as a general announcement for passersby: "I've got balls, right here, between my legs. Check it out."

"Have a seat," Betty said. "I don't guess he'll be too long."

In general, Mose liked his students. Karly with the blue ankle bracelet over her black stockings, Jenafer—she insisted on the odd spelling—who drew elaborate ballpoint vines up and down the underside of her fingers, "Sam" of the unclear gender preference, Thomas who couldn't help but smile when he gave the right answer in class. All their endearing efforts to distinguish themselves. And their tics, too: one constantly swallowing, as if puzzled by the surplus saliva in his mouth, another sucking on her lip, another pulling her sweatshirt sleeves down over her hands, making of her arms two giant worms, another flattening and folding then reflattening a cough drop wrapper, a girl using a paper clip to twist her lips, a boy freckled with red acne scars, running his fingers over an as yet unexamined lesion. And the hair! The shaving of it, the twisting of it, the pulling of it, the pushing of it (in and out of a headband, a rubber band, a clip) or the spearing of it (with a chop stick, a Bic pen), the reorganizing of it (into a pony tail at the back of the head, or at the base of the neck, or at the top of the scalp, a joke, a fountain of hair spurting from above).

What wasn't to like? They'd won Mose over with all these signs of battles within. And even when Mose didn't like the students, he tended to sympathize with them, especially those kids who chose Sudbury over dropping out. These kids had predictably sad stories—crack addict fathers or prostitute mothers. They were hungry, some teachers said. Hungry, right here in America. But they were also invariably fat. The fat seemed like just another bad thing that had happened to them. No one had ever given them good food. No one had ever suggested that they stop eating when they were full or that the world offered something more interesting than TV.

Still, some students were hard to sympathize with, no matter how miserable their childhoods. Like Matt Snyder, Devon Cryer and HoHo Coombs, the three who happened to be in the principal's office. No doubt Hyman was offering the boys firm but respectful words, such chastisement being part of the "school contract" that all members of Sudbury signed. At Sudbury, you could tell someone you didn't like something they were doing, but you couldn't say anything that would make another student or teacher feel emotionally, physically, academically or socially unsafe. The contract—printed on a large wooden plaque—was the first thing you saw when you entered the school.

"Grab Mr. Sheinbaum a chair," Hyman ordered loudly, when he noticed Mose. Devon, dressed like the others in baggy black, jumped up to get a chair from Betty's office. Meanwhile Hyman waved Mose through his door.

57

"You know these kids?" Hyman asked Mose.

"I do, indeed," Mose said. He nodded a hello to each boy. "HoHo, Devon, Matt."

Mose knew more than their names, of course. A science teacher had found a crack pipe on Matt. HoHo—from whence his name? an over-consumption of third-rate bakery products?—lived in a transitional home out by the highway. Devon once claimed that the Dramamine in his pocket was for the bus. "I've got a sensitive system. Those busses really give you the motion sickness." Taken in enough quantities, Dramamine—it turned out—could get you high.

"Well," Hyman coughed, "we're about to finish up here." Hyman focused on the boys. "You won't forget what we've talked about?"

"No, sir," Devon said, and the other two chimed in.

"Then we're through here. You can go." The boys stood and filed out. Mose could remember Clara Massengill describing three boys—not these three boys, but three boys who were in all their essential aspects the same as these three—as "arrogant, angry and fairly stupid." She'd added, "And I mean that lovingly."

When they were gone, Hyman propped his head on the knuckles of his folded hands and said, "You'll have to excuse it in here. I haven't quite figured out how to decorate."

The room was absurdly blank. Not a picture on the wall, not a book (save a dictionary) on the shelves. One wing of Hyman's desk held a computer. A spider plant, its brown leaves crispy as old paper, sat on the floor.

When Clara Massengill had occupied the office, colorful rugs covered the linoleum floor, and the shelves were filled with books and videos. On one wall, she'd assembled a photomontage of students past and present. There had been a large dry erase board on which students were encouraged to leave messages. "Ms. M. Does Rock." "Ms. M—I need to talk with you. Very soon if possible."

For all this, Mose never absorbed how bleak the room was: no window save the glass that faced Betty's office, fluorescent lighting, drop ceilings stained brown from some long-ago plumbing problem.

"Glad you came," Hyman said.

Mose flashed on his own high school principal's bland office, its only spot of color the aqua bottle of liquid antacid that he kept on his desk, like a trophy. But then all official adults looked dyspeptic in Mose's youth. They smelled of onions and had brown teeth and made you associate learning with decay.

"You settling in OK?" Mose inquired.

"Well, as you can see . . ."

"Oh, no, I meant into town. Finding what you need? The hardware store? The *shul?*"

"The what?"

"The . . . are you . . . I was thinking you were Jewish." Not that the new principal looked Jewish, but Hyman was a Jewish name.

"Nope, Episcopalian. So, listen, I was going through some things, and I'm concerned about the reading for your class."

"I'm sorry?"

"The reading. For your class. You don't seem to do much of it. You use . . ." He lifted a sheet of paper from his desk and read, "*A Concise History of the American People in Documents.* That volume is only 191 pages. Insufficient for a semester-length class."

"Yes, right." Mose cleared his throat. "What you might not know is that I don't work with books. My students listen to lectures. I taped them years ago. They've gone over well. Then they come to class for debates. I . . ." He let out a half-laugh. "I do the debates straight sometimes, or I come in character. You know, I'm Joe McCarthy or I'm Alexander Hamilton, and they have to discuss what they've learned with me."

"But no reading?"

"Well, a little. If there's an important document. They'll read 'The Gettysburg Address' and 'The Declaration of Independence,' but I don't use a textbook. What they need to learn is in the lectures."

"And tests?"

"No, we don't have tests. The kids do presentations. Two a term— that's what they get graded on. Quite a bit of work, since they have to run class for the day. And then in election years, they do their service-learning project. You know, they all have to spend an hour a week on a campaign."

"They're teaching each other?"

"Well, yes," Mose said. Surely this approach to learning couldn't be new to Hyman. "The kids here . . . a lot of them, their primary intelligence isn't verbal. To act out what they know by doing a skit or making a movie on the computer . . . they learn far more that way than by reading some textbook chapter on Populists."

"Well," Hyman said, "I'm afraid we need a little standardization around here. The other history classes don't work this way."

"Yes, we all choose our own approach."

"These kids . . . their high school diploma has to mean something."

"No one's arguing *that*."

"Right," Hyman said. "Well, I've ordered you some more appropriate books. They'll be in the supply room, before the month is out. " His forefinger double-tapped a piece of paper on which he'd scribbled two titles. "That's what I expect you to be using in the future."

"In this school . . ." Mose began. He'd been at Sudbury for twelve years, drawn to the school and Alex Decker, its founder, for knowing that certain kids—distracted by the tragedy of their lives—needed something different in order to learn. "In this school, we're pretty committed to academic freedom."

"Oh, I'm not questioning your academic freedom. I'd never do that. This is just about rigor. And standards. Getting everyone on board."

"On board?" Mose echoed.

"That's right." Hyman smiled, delighted, it seemed, to have been understood.

"I'll think about it." Mose stood. He couldn't remember anyone, ever, in all his years at Sudbury, telling another teacher how to run a class.

"Well, good luck with this place." Mose pointed at the office walls. "Some psychedelic posters and a lava lamp, I'd say."

"Oh ho," Hyman said. "Lava lamp. That's a good one."

"*Rigor*," Mose spat some days later to Smitty, who'd been told by Hyman that he really needed to have his students paint a color wheel and a gray scale, before the year was out. Smitty had stopped by Mose's apartment to fetch his raincoat. He'd left it in Mose's car when Mose had last given him a lift. Though Mose had been enjoying his morning alone with the *Times*, he had buzzed Smitty into his apartment building, then offered him coffee. He was embarrassed by the state of his rooms, a pile of unexamined mail on the counter, unwashed dishes in the sink, the wall-to-wall carpet studded with crumbs and small bits of tissue. Ellen came by on Sunday afternoons to clean for him, but this was Sunday morning, his apartment at its messiest.

"Rigor. Rigor mortis," Smitty said, brushing the fringe of his hair out of his t-shirt collar.

"That haircut makes you look like a rock star," Mose said disapprovingly.

"So you've said," Smitty said.

But it was the look of a rock star without the sex appeal, Smitty being aggressively neutral when it came to personal passions. For years, Mose had the idea that Smitty had a girlfriend back east, someone who was just about to join him in Madison. Finally, Mose realized that this wasn't the case, and that all that Smitty had back east was a woman whom he'd once had a crush on, someone on whom he could focus, when people inquired about his love life.

"What'll we do?" Mose said, bending to sip his coffee.

"We'll ignore him," Smitty said. "It's what the kids do."

"And," Mose asked, "when he notices all the American history books still piled up in the stock room?"

"You just hand them out. Say the kids can use them for reference, if they want."

Smitty's Buddhist practice left him uninclined for confrontation. As for the students: already they referred to Hyman as Cunt Clark, or Mr. C., which Hyman seemed to find endearing, not realizing what "c" the students were abbreviating. How the students must miss Clara, who always hugged the students, asked, "How *are* you?" She could come into a classroom and disrupt a lesson for the mere purpose of embrace. Hyman didn't hug. Instead, he told students he respected them, that he knew they would make good choices. Despite his respect, students now needed hall passes to go to the bathroom. And Hyman had cut the funding for the annual trip north to study Native American fishing habitats.

"I wonder why the kids don't *react* more," Mose said.

Smitty shrugged. "*They* can't do anything about it."

"Not so! They *can* do something about it."

But for all the projects they collaborated on in class, Sudbury students weren't the type for group action. They'd have to be *assigned* protest to resist. For now, they sullenly adapted, if skipping school could be considered adapting.

"You know," Smitty put in, "there are a few who seem to like him."

It was true. Some warmed to Hyman's strict discipline. And these kids weren't the talented students, the ones with progressive parents who thought Sudbury offered an opportunity, or the artsy kids who thought Sudbury would give them more latitude to be creative. Instead it was the kids who'd been actively recruited; kids with brutal upbringings or the tendency to pull urinals off walls. It was as if the tradition of sending "bad" boys into the army had merit after all. Though what could be more counterintuitive? Slim Hyman Clark—with his largely balding head, stiff posture and ugly blue suits—appreciated by a gang of boys dressed in black. Oh, the Midwestern punk! Bland face plumped with cheese curds, metal adorning an eyebrow, tongue stud tap-tap-tapping a tooth. A smear of purple eye shadow on one boy, a tattoo on another.

"Mr. C.," a few students would say and salute him, click their heels. A joke, Mose knew, a thumbing of the nose at Hyman's authority by overdoing the obedience. Hyman Clark would offer a tight smile and pass by, either ignoring the offense or (perhaps? could it be?) believing the greeting appropriate.

"And the rest of us?" Mose said, aware that Smitty was not the one to ask for faculty gossip. "What are the others saying? I heard Gloria grumbled when he cut the field trip budget. And Harrison over in science said, 'That's not what we're about,' when Hyman first suggested the bathroom passes. But no one's *doing* anything."

"Well," said Smitty philosophically, ready to take his leave. "They have their own concerns."

"So do I. But it still bothers me."

Mose's eye caught on a yellow envelope under a supermarket circular. How long had *that* piece of mail been sitting there?

"Well, I should head out," Smitty said.

"Take all your clothes with you!" Mose insisted, mock-aggrieved, and Smitty patted himself down, as if he stored his wardrobe under his current outfit. "I'm finally set. See you in the A.M.," he announced and departed, leaving, as it turned out, the raincoat for which he'd come.

Mose sat with his coffee a bit longer. Others at Sudbury might not like Hyman's manner, but no one said they sensed the man's disdain, his lack of respect for what they were doing. Oh, why had Mose said that dumb thing at the dinner party? "My wife, too. She came down with a little something. What she came down with was Death." Well, we did all come down with that someday. What, in fact, was so awful about what he had said? That it was a dumb non sequitur? That it made light of whatever had kept Hyman's better half at home? But Mose hadn't meant that. Surely Hyman Clark knew that. Why couldn't Mose get away with what others did with aplomb? My God, he could remember the first time he met Clara Massengill. "Sorry, Mass-a-what?" Mose said, pushing his earlobe forward, and Clara smiled warmly and said, "Massengill. Like the douche."

Mose laughed as he thought of this—Clara's pleasing outrageousness; he wondered how she was doing in her new job—then he turned for the yellow envelope. How many days had it gone unopened? Inside, the envelope contained a single sheet of typing paper and bore—as he saw later, when he went back to reexamine it—a Madison postmark and no return address. It was quite clearly addressed to Mose, down to the correct apartment number, which wouldn't have been obtainable from the phone book. On the paper and in the crabbed hand of a lunatic with a ballpoint pen, someone had written, "We know who you are, Zionist oppressor. We don't forget."

JUNE–SEPTEMBER 2005

Three other people—the gallery curator, the director of special programs and the theater manager—sat in a small circle in Valerie's office, ready to plan next year's season. It was June, so "next year's season" didn't mean the upcoming season (which would start in the fall) but the subsequent year's offerings. Valerie had already e-mailed her idea to the gathered.

"So . . . hate," Leo began uncertainly, the pads of his fingers pressed together for push-ups. The gesture was so un-Leo, even though he made it all the time, that Valerie half-expected him to add a Groucho face and waggle an invisible cigar.

"Yes," Valerie said. "Hate. You got something against hate?"

"Me?" Leo said, pretend-defensive. He was the director of special programs and had been at the center longer than anyone else. "Certainly not. I love hate. Hate's the best. But . . ."

"But what?" Though Valerie was the center's director, Leo was, to Valerie's mind at least, its heart. He was the smartest of the bunch of them, though sufficiently disorganized (or so everyone claimed) that he wouldn't have made a good director. Valerie, prompt and thorough, knew how to sweet-talk donors, but she had nothing of Leo's vision.

Kaavya—the gallery curator—answered Valerie's question. "Well, with hate . . . what would we _do_?"

"What would we do?" Valerie echoed, confused. The words sounded inelegant in her mouth. Kaavya spoke English with a strong Nepalese accent, which made her seem, for all her youth, remarkably aristocratic.

"What *is* an art exhibit about hate? I just don't get it. And what about films? A lot of films about skinheads? It will be a pretty dismal year around here."

"It just seems to me," Valerie began, though she was already unsure about her suggestion, "that hate is *the* topic of our times. Remember how after 9/11 all these people were saying, 'Oh, why do they hate us so much?' as if the answer weren't perfectly obvious?"

"I can see a play about hate, but a gallery exhibit?"

"Are you talking about hate?" Leo put in. "Maybe you mean religious fanaticism. Maybe *that* is the topic of our times."

"No, not really," Valerie said. "I mean think of all the people *we* hate. Don't you hate George W. and Donald Rumsfeld? Don't you hate all the apologists for their government? It's been how long, and I can't get that Abu Ghraib image out of my head. You know, with all the naked men piled on top of each other. Or the man on a leash. How can you not hate the person responsible for that? And just all the bloodshed in Iraq. Sometimes I wonder that there is anyone left over there to get killed. And what can we do? Add our name to an e-mail list? I used to trust my vote . . . that was the way I'd effect change, but this isn't a democracy. It's a stupidocracy. It makes me long for Plato's Republic. You know, we'd agree that we're all equal, but to vote, we'd insist on an intelligence test . . ."

"Maybe a morality quiz," Leo put in.

"Right!" Valerie said, though she suspected Leo was calling her on her self-righteousness. How impossible. When you were the most earnest and upset, you came off as a jerk. "I mean," she said, but with less passion, "we can't even get the good guys elected in this country."

Bonnie, the theater director, said, "What good guys?"

Leo nodded, though not in agreement. He was processing everyone's words.

The large windows of Valerie's office overlooked State Street. On the sidewalk below, a man palmed a single slice of watermelon, rind and all, into his mouth in one smooth gesture. Christ.

But no, Valerie saw, it wasn't watermelon; the man was slipping in his teeth

"People care about all that," Kaavya commented, hooking her finger around the spike of one of her high heels and pulling it up under her, as if for a yoga move that required the prop of expensive shoes. Kaavya was engaged to a man back home, though everything about her—today she was wearing a short camel skirt and a tight red shirt over her ample breasts—suggested a woman on the prowl. "But it doesn't feel immediate."

"Excuse me?" Valerie said, slightly incredulous. With her accent and polished ways, Kaavya had seemed quite smart at her interview. In the six months since she'd been with the Center, though, she'd revealed herself to be cheerful but almost willfully vacuous, as if she knew she *could* be more intelligent, if she tried, but intelligence would require her to think about painful matters, so she might as well avoid it altogether.

"I just mean those dangers aren't *immediate* in the way they would be if we were Iraqi citizens or even if we lived in New York, where someone might blow up the subway we were riding on."

"Yeah," said Bonnie, in her signature wry way. "It's the Midwest. No one would bomb us. They'd have to come here first."

Valerie flashed on the grainy TV pictures of the bombers on September 10, 2001, their activities in Portland, Maine, the night before they boarded planes to their death. All those stops at fast food joints, the avatar of American commercialism. Why hadn't they found some roadside stand and purchased lobster rolls? Or was that, too, one of the promises of the afterlife: shellfish to go with the virgins?

"Maybe," Leo said, "we're really talking about powerlessness. What we feel when we can't stop something that sickens us. Or maybe we're talking about our failure to understand evil. Or even dread. That the world we live in can hold these things."

"What do you mean?" Kaavya said to Bonnie. "Don't you remember that . . . that thing?" She pointed out the window and down State Street, in the direction of the University of Wisconsin campus.

"Oh, the bomb." Bonnie pursed her lips dismissively. "That wasn't meant to hurt anyone. And that was in the sixties."

"Actually, 1970," Leo said. Everyone in Madison knew this story. One night, during the Vietnam War, protesters blew up the university's

Army Math Research Center. They didn't mean to kill anyone; they just wanted to dismantle the lab. Still, a physicist, working late, died.

"It was different then," Kaavya said.

"No kidding," Bonnie snapped. She had the least patience of the group for Kaavya, though she focused her dislike on the girl's makeup—the eyeliner that rimmed her almond lids and the bright red lipstick on her mouth. "Come on, girl," Bonnie once hissed in Valerie's ear. "We're not in a porn video; we're in life."

"Because of the draft. If there was a draft, you can be sure you'd see the sort of protests you saw back then," Leo said.

"It's all self-interest now," Bonnie remarked. She was gay and slightly holier-than-thou about her sexual orientation, as if it gave her special rights when it came to political pronouncements. It didn't matter that she'd been raised in Greenwich, Connecticut, the only one of the gathered who worked because it interested her, not because she needed the income. "If I'm safe, you can go ahead and let the poor kids in this country go to the Persian Gulf and get blown up."

"It *is* the poor kids who are getting blown up, but I'm not sure that means it's all self-interest. I don't think we know *what* to do," Valerie began, but then interrupted herself. Her mind was too curlicue. She thought of Doug, when he was five, lying in his bed and saying earnestly, and apropos of nothing, "Mom, I want to die by getting old. I don't want to die by getting shot." Where had that come from? They never watched TV in their house, save for PBS. Doug hadn't seen movies. Valerie and Alex read their newspapers at work. "That said, let's try to keep to the topic at hand. With hate . . . I feel like you have to look at it to understand it."

"Actually," Leo said, "you look at it, and you don't understand it. That's the point."

"I don't know," Kaavya said.

"Well, have you had *other* thoughts about next year's theme? If we didn't do this, what might we do?" Valerie asked.

"Why don't we do something like addiction?" Kaavya said, almost cheerfully. "You know, food addiction, sex addiction, that sort of thing."

Bonnie, whose seat was slightly behind Kaavya's, rolled her eyes, then said wearily, "Oh, addicts! I hate addicts."

In the end, they decided in favor of hate. The season would be called "Surviving Hate," because, Bonnie said, that's what they all were—Americans, Iraqis, Israelis, Palestinians, gays, Hispanics, even the Christian right wing: survivors of someone else's hate.

Center staff took July and August off. It was how the board compensated for low salaries: long vacations, pretty offices and fancy snacks at receptions.

In the past, Valerie spent summer vacation in the garden or with the books she had been meaning to read. In the summer of her divorce, though, she made plans to see friends—endless lunches—as if she could eat her way to an understanding of who she was, now that she didn't have a husband.

When people asked—and they did, almost as soon as they sat down with her—how Valerie was doing, they meant how was she doing since the breakup. How were *things*? Invariably, their voices grew portentous and secretive, as if she might not know she'd split from her husband. Not that they were being nosy. They were hoping to be supportive; their intentions were good. That was the problem: no ill-wishers and still she felt wounded. And how could Valerie possibly answer the question, when she didn't know herself? She was crying, on a nightly basis— the breakup made her feel like such a failure—and talking with friends on the phone. By way of answer, it seemed easiest to offer the one thing that *was* true: it would have all been a lot harder if she and Alex had split when Douglas was younger. But Doug was pretty independent now, and though they agreed on joint custody, Valerie and Alex didn't shuttle him back and forth needlessly. Doug kept his bedroom at Valerie's, the same bedroom he'd slept in all his life. Alex could call any time, take Doug out for evenings or weekend outings. In July—when Doug left for his summer job at Camp Timberview—Alex and Valerie would get down to the business of filing papers. By mid-October, they'd officially be divorced. After the papers were filed, Valerie and Alex would have no reason to see each other. Even so, Valerie imagined they'd bump into each other.

But in the end, Valerie saw Alex only once before the divorce was official. This was in early September. Alex picked Doug up for a day of boating out on Lake Mendota. (Alex's boat—an expense at which Valerie bristled. For the rare times when they actually went out on the lake, why not just rent something?) While they were gone, Valerie busied herself with work, but then the hour of Doug's return came and went. Valerie indulged the usual fears: a drowning, a car crash on the way home, a mad gunman where they stopped for lunch, a vending machine toppling over, her son killed by snack packages.

It was a Saturday, impossibly still, one of those Indian summer days that made the opening of school so hard: kids fainting in the hallways, everyone too uncomfortable to concentrate. Lightning might crack suddenly through the sky's oppressive clouds and hit Doug, the beginning of the storm that would offer relief, everyone sighing with pleasure, not knowing that Doug Decker had been fried where he stood, witlessly touching a metal pole. People survived the deaths of their children; Valerie knew people who had. Her friend Pammy's girl had gone into septic shock after breaking her wrist; Darla's child had died— in her arms—after a car accident. Valerie admired them, and even so, in their circumstances, she'd definitely opt for the going-mad thing. She read the news—this many blown up in Iraq, this many drowned by the tsunami wave, this many crushed in a mudslide—and she couldn't quite understand why the wailing, far away as it was, didn't reach her here, halfway across the globe. "He's just a child," Leo had once wept in Alex's arms. Leo's twenty-nine-year-old son Devon, fresh out of rehab, had fallen off a balcony. He was drunk, of course. Only he didn't die on impact. Why Leo was told this, Valerie never knew. Instead, Devon froze to death. Winter in Wisconsin, a season when a boy, loved but confused, could do such a thing.

"Oh, Lord," Valerie gasped when she heard Doug and Alex at the door. "You're OK." She was nearly in tears.

"Why wouldn't we be OK?" Alex said, irritated. She catastrophized. That was his word for it. As if worry, in these dark times, wasn't a perfectly rational thing.

Doug—barefoot, the edges of his short legs damp—darted through the front door. "Hey, Valerie," Alex began more amiably, this time. She shouldn't have let everything fall apart so thoroughly. If Alex were still her husband, she could let him know what had been going through her head. Though had she? Back when they were married? Mostly she *didn't* tell him what she felt—the urge to do so had been conditioned right out of her. He always tried to jolly her out of her emotions. Or he

69

simply misunderstood her concerns and offered an earnest but irrelevant bit of comfort.

"Hey," Valerie said now. "Want some tea?" They'd be friends eventually, she guessed, if only because the thought of *his* dying made her panic. And guilty: she hadn't made him happy, any more than he had made her happy.

"Nah. That's all right. I just feel like you should know something."

Valerie's stomach sank. Did good news ever follow these words?

"The thing is, I'm seeing Ellen Hirschorn."

"Oh." She nodded her head, taking in this news as if entirely nonplussed. She scratched a nonexistent itch above her left ear. She kept her tone even, actually flat. "Me? I'm seeing an asshole. And I wish he'd get out of my house."

"Yeah, I thought you'd take it well," Alex said.

"Oh, fuck off," she said automatically.

And why was she so mad? Because she might never again have sex and here he was doing it with someone half his age? What did she care? *She* didn't want to be married to Alex anymore. Ellen was only getting everything that had driven her crazy for years.

Valerie would say, "Good God—all these people are dead; they held hands and jumped out of the World Trade Center. People just like you and me, and their heads are in one place, and their elbows in another."

And Alex would say, "Life's tragic. What do you expect?"

And Valerie would want to wail like a teenager: "But it's not OK. It's. Not. OK."

If she never had another one of those idiotic exchanges in her life, she could live in relative peace.

And yet how this new detail rankled: Ellen Hirschorn, the sweet-faced blond who worked at the Center's daycare; Ellen Hirschorn, the perfectly lovely twenty-five-year-old who was such a babe. Valerie couldn't quite keep her own eyes off the girl, on the rare occasions when Valerie visited the daycare. "You should have seen me!" Valerie enthused at some long-ago dinner party, then let her face fall into a slack gape, ogling an invisible Ellen. "Stop looking, I'm telling myself!" She put her hand on her jaw and pushed, making a show of her head's resistance to her hand's effort. A joke, of course. Had Alex somehow absorbed Valerie's admiration for Ellen's beauty, tucked the compliment away, so he could nab her as soon as he dumped Valerie? Now, when people asked what had happened to her marriage, Valerie said, "You didn't hear? I pimped out one of my employees to my husband." Not that she had any idea how Ellen and Alex had met. Or that she was fond of self-revelation. Still, she tried to be entertaining when with friends.

Chapter Eight

NOVEMBER 2005

❧

"*D*on't tell him you're Jewish." That was the first thing Mose said when Ellen told him she'd met someone.

"What? That's crazy. What year do you think it is?"

"It's 1939. It's always 1939."

"Mose."

"OK. So it's not. But it can't hurt to be careful."

Ellen and Mose were walking around the park by Ellen's apartment. They'd agreed on two laps, then a stop at an art opening. Ellen had lured Mose into exercise with the prospect of snacks. There would probably be something good to eat at the art show, and though her cousin could make a dinner of breakfast cereal, he warmed to others' efforts, liked nothing better than a tray of buttery hors d'oeuvres.

Mose broke a sweat, despite their easy pace. Even the red and yellow leaves at his feet seemed to slow him down. "Look," Ellen said, pointing to an oak tree, its bark covered with fist-sized lumps. "The warty tree." She'd been half-consciously waiting to share this observation with him.

"My," Mose said, taking it in. "Looks like a bunch of dwarves are trying to push their way out of that thing." The warts disappeared. Ellen saw tree creatures, standing on one another's shoulders, each trying to force himself (nose first) out of the prison of the oak.

"*Oy gut,*" Mose allowed as they turned the final corner. Did his difficulty portend an early end? Or just a painful old age? (Mose on an earlier occasion: "When the *oy vey* rate exceeds the pulse rate, admit the patient!") Mose was thin though not small; even bent, he had a substantial air, the shadow of his former frame present if not visible. In everything but fact, he was six-foot-two, sturdy and commanding.

"This is it," Ellen said with what must have seemed to Mose like too grand a flourish. The art gallery to which they were headed occupied the ground floor of one of the many Queen Anne Victorians near Ellen's apartment. Though it wasn't fully dark, small white lights were strewn along the gallery's porch roof and woven through a trellis covered in purple morning glories, tight-mouthed, withholding the kiss of their color, now that the day (and their season) was ending. Mose climbed the home's few stairs, then sat heavily on a bench by the gallery's door.

"I'm an old man."

"Not at all," Ellen said automatically. What was this? The impulse to deny the obvious? The fat man said he was fat, and you crooned, "You're not fat," as if a man's shortcomings were all the worse if the man *knew* about them.

"So what's your new beau's name?"

"See that's the problem," Ellen began. She had no "old" beau, but perhaps Mose didn't know this. Perhaps he imagined that she'd always kept this part of her life secret.

"Wait," Mose interrupted. "Did you see that article in last week's paper? The one about the *shul?*"

"I know. Terrible." Someone had spraypainted swastikas on the front door of the synagogue. But why was he bringing this up now?

"See. Hate crimes. Right here in Wisconsin."

"Maybe. Or maybe some dumb kids." The newspaper articles about the graffiti reminded Ellen of college, the uproar after someone wrote "nigger" and "fag" on a dorm room memo board. Of course, it was a terrible thing to do, but did that mean the whole lot of them, four years' worth of university students, were unrepentant racists? How stupid *was* her optimism? (Anne Frank: "I still believe people are really good at heart." Oh, dear.)

Mose looked up at her, his neck an uncomfortable S. "This tendency of yours to minimize. It's not going to serve you, in the long run."

Why do you let him talk to you like that? Barbara would ask, if she was here. *He's so insulting around you.*

"Especially in this climate," Mose went on. "Anti-America. Anti-Israel. Israel as the demon nation of the universe."

"I know."

"You know what your problem is?" Mose began.

"Ohhhh," she mock-moaned, as she joined him on the bench, "do I *have* to have a problem? Can't I just be perfect?"

"You've never been beaten. You don't know what it is to defend yourself." The suggestion, of course, was that he *had* been beaten or that he'd fought in a war he'd neglected to mention.

"Mose—" she said, letting herself be irritated. "You don't know everything about my life. Maybe I have been beaten. Maybe something has happened to me that you don't know about."

"What're you telling me?" he said, suddenly concerned

"I'm just saying you shouldn't make assumptions. No one's an open book." She smiled. "Even me."

Once in Chicago, on her way to visit Barbara, then in college, some black teens had approached Ellen. It was night, a city street—she didn't know where she was exactly, was just making her way from subway stop to dorm room, all according to Barbara's directions. One of them put his face in hers and said, almost kindly, "Sweetheart, I was just wondering if you'd like to suck my dick." His friends hooted, and Ellen thought that that would be it; they'd dared each other to say something crude, but not into action. But as she walked on, one boy grabbed her umbrella and tripped her; another pushed his hand between her legs. The third caught her falling, only to swing her hard against the back of a building, her head clunking against the brick and something wet dripping on her neck, the sting of pain making it unclear if this was blood or some viscous matter from above. She had been too frightened to think. That's what she realized later: that nothing had happened, because she hadn't been there to absorb it. The third boy pressed against her and said, his tone both reasonable and threatening, "We just going to see how you like it best."

Just then, an angry female voice called out, "Hey, *you.* You leave her

74

alone." This must have been from an apartment above Ellen. "I'm calling the police," the voice cried. "You dumbass kids. And my old man is coming down to kick your butts." A flash of eyes all around, a silent consultation—just talk? or was someone really coming?—then the boys took off down the street. Ellen ran, too, in the opposite direction, afraid they'd come looking for her as soon as she was beyond the shouting woman's eyes.

"So this incident that you are not telling me about," Mose said, in his best professor's voice, though it was clear he thought there was no such incident, "what did you feel after? After it happened?"

"Relieved. Relieved it wasn't worse," Ellen said, her manner clipped.

"But not mad?" His tone was wise, smugly distrustful. "You *should* have been mad. Whatever it was that happened. If someone hurt you, they were evil, and you should fight evil. You shouldn't make excuses for it."

"Evil," Ellen puffed, as if she didn't believe in such a thing.

Ten or so people came down the walk and clamored onto the porch and into the gallery. "Don't you want to know about this man I'm seeing?"

"Oh, of course, honey. I'm sorry. How'd we get off the subject?"

"OK, so the man I'm seeing is a little bit older than me."

"Well, you know Rachel had ten years on me. An age difference isn't necessarily bad." Ellen didn't remember Rachel. Or did in only the vaguest of ways. She had a half-memory of an apartment and an elevator with a gold scissor-gate door, her terror when the door latched shut, and the wall behind began to move.

"Oh, I know." She felt tired, not ready—though she had just *been* ready—to divulge Alex's name. Mose might have admired Alex as an administrator, but as a beau? He'd only register that Alex was divorced and Ellen's senior by seventeen years. "Well . . ." She tilted her head toward the gallery. "Why don't we go in?"

An easel blocked the front hall staircase. On it sat a large photograph of a man in his forties. He was tall, almost awkwardly so in that way of men who heighten and thicken without ever losing the winsome gangliness of youth. Stooping, as he peered into the camera, he looked as if he were trying to fit himself into the rectangle of the photograph. If not for the deep red crevasses about his left eye, he would have been handsome. They were more than scars. It looked as if someone, years ago, had tried to gouge his eye right out of his head.

"Welcome." A heavy woman in a big batik dress and head scarf handed Mose and Ellen a price list.

"Good response?" Ellen asked the woman.

"Far better than we could have expected. We even have some interest from the Center for Artistic Exchange. They're thinking about scheduling the whole show next year. Everything that's up now and all the images we have out back."

Why, Ellen here works at the Center! Ellen could almost hear Mose forming the words and her subsequent explanation: *Not really. Just the daycare.* She turned, before Mose could begin, and peered into the gallery's front room—white walls, gleaming wood floor, track lighting— then focused on the images. When she did, she saw a smiling woman, chin resting in the V of her hands, only where her fingers should be, there were ten truncated stubs. A second picture was an aerial close-up of a sleeping woman, her limbs brown and raw as picked chicken bones. She lay in yellow dirt and dry grass, a once wet–now dry rag covering most of her crinkly white hair, and a pink cotton dress, streaked with mud, bunched up around her knees. Her feet were white with dried dirt, as if she'd shuffled through a field of flour, before dropping down, for sleep. Ellen stepped closer to read the typed card next to the photo. The woman was from Darfur, it said, and had just been raped.

A stack of postcards on a table in the room's center read, "Faces of Torture: Photos and Stories."

"This is what you take me to see?" Mose said.

"No, no," Ellen began. "I didn't know." The posters tacked to neighborhood telephone poles and the co-op's bulletin board just mentioned an art opening.

"I suppose," Mose said, loud enough for the others in the room to hear, "if you're in an Argentinian prison, having your genitals prodded by a hot iron, it doesn't really cheer you up to know that someday folks are going to be sipping wine and considering how damaged you look."

"Oh, Mose," Ellen whispered. Was this fair? You were supposed to bear witness, after all. "We can just check out the other room and make our exit."

She tried to look without looking—a man whose arm ended at a stub below his shoulder, a plain-faced woman with a single straight scar running cheek to jaw, others with no discernible damage but a story to tell: the burnings and slicings that might be revealed, if not for modesty, if not for the shirt over the breasts, the pants over the genitals. Mose was right, of course; Ellen might have suffered—who didn't?—but she had never been beaten. Already she couldn't quite remember why she'd wanted to claim that distinction earlier. She looped the exhibition space, made a forcible effort not to apologize for the show. Once they were outside, they could say what they needed to. Till then, Ellen felt the strain of Mose's disapprobation, how it included her—how it always included her—till she offered up an opinion that matched his own. She tried to focus on the house itself. She loved old Victorians with their shiny wood floors, high ceilings and stately staircases, their unfussy grandeur.

The gallery had a second room. In it, Ellen overheard two young women comparing the pictures to images from Abu Ghraib. One woman said, "Those were pictures of crimes; these are pictures of victims." In a novel, this woman would be insufferable, pronouncing on such matters from the safety of a well-appointed gallery. But this woman was genuinely trying to figure things out.

"It bugs me," her friend said, "that all these photographs *as photographs* are so beautiful. If you know what I mean."

"I do," her friend said. "I completely do. I saw this book in the art section at the bookstore. Called *The Holocaust*, and it was such a damn beautiful coffee table book and all that I thought, you know, 'Who is this for? Eichmann?'"

"OK," Ellen said, her eyes tearing—it was unbelievable what people had to suffer. And more unbelievable: that people were capable of doing such things to each other. And yet who *were* these people? It was always far away: the committers of crimes, the parched and unblessed, the have-nots who thought the way out of a nightmare was to become a nightmare. How could you ever understand when you couldn't *see* them? They disappeared into ordinariness moments after their crimes had been committed. Ellen turned to Mose. Her "OK" had meant,

"Let's go," and he understood it as such, stepping before her into the front hall. As he did, a door under the stairway opened, almost hitting Mose in the face. He tottered back from the possible blow, then rocked into his own misstep and stumbled further. Ellen grabbed for him, but her movement had the effect of another push, and he began to fall, arms rotating to steady himself, but only propelling him closer to the floor, where he landed with a crash. "Oh, God. *Oh, God*," Ellen said, flinging to her knees. "Are you all right?" But with his osteoporosis, how could he be all right? He would be shattered inside, shattered in a million unfixable pieces.

For a moment, nothing happened. Mose was still: eyes open, chest rising and falling, rising and falling. Then, his lips parted.

"Yes?" Ellen breathed.

"Let. Me. Think," Mose said puckishly, as if bemused by his situation. Something in his face made it clear that he was scanning his body, trying to ascertain damage, a break or crack or something far worse. Shadows fell over him, concerned art patrons. "Should I call an ambulance?" someone asked.

"Can you get up?" Ellen whispered.

"Of course I can get up." This impatiently. And then, as if the information might mitigate the shock of seeing him on the floor: "This happens all the time."

But Ellen had never seen him fall, though she'd noticed his bruises. *It's nothing. I walked into a chair. Closed a bathroom door on my schnozz. Got into a battle with a cafeteria tray, only the cafeteria tray won.*

Ellen held her tongue. Comfort irritated Mose. But there was nothing amicable about the silence, no sense of agreement that she'd acted *just right* by withholding nervous consolation. He rolled onto his side, pushed himself onto his hands and knees, then with the help of a chair and Ellen's forearm, onto his feet.

Ellen turned to see who had emerged from what must have been a bathroom under the staircase. It was Valerie Crowley-Decker, of all people, her fingers still pressed to her lips, in the classic gesture of alarm or woe.

"Oh," Ellen said softly, a twitchy band of tree dwarves now occupying her, their noses tickling the underside of her skin.

"He's OK?" Valerie mouthed at Ellen, and Ellen nodded her head, said, "I think so."

"Don't worry," Mose announced to those gathered around him. "I feel great." He jerked his thumb toward Ellen. "My associate and I are going to run a marathon, so if you'll excuse us." People sensed the request in his joke; please turn away.

Valerie obliged, pivoting to the gallery owner to say, "I'll give you my card. Call me in the morning?" She checked her watch. "And I don't know why I said I could stay for dinner. I've got to get my son at band practice." But Ellen knew this wasn't true. Alex was picking Doug up after practice. Tonight Alex was going to tell Doug about Ellen.

"I'm sorry," Ellen whispered, as Valerie made for the door. She wasn't sure Valerie heard her, but Valerie turned and smiled unevenly. Ellen couldn't imagine her in jeans or shorts. She didn't wear suits, but she was always *dressed*. Today, it was a black sweater and wine skirt with wine stockings. Expensive-looking shoes. Ellen had imagined . . . anger, that Valerie would be angry with her. Ever since her first evening with Alex, Ellen had been avoiding Valerie at the Center, an easy enough task in the summer, when the regular staff went on vacation, harder now that the new season had begun. It was all too easy to guess how things might look to Valerie: her long marriage over, her husband almost immediately taking up with a younger woman.

"Oh, I know you're sorry," Valerie said. But, of course, she didn't know that; she didn't know anything about how Ellen felt. "Still I'm glad you said something. And anyway, it's not *you*, you know." Her manner was almost sisterly.

Ellen felt she had to offer something in return. "He speaks very highly of you." She paused. "All the time," Ellen added. Too eagerly? Alex *did* speak highly of Valerie. She admired that about him. You had to wonder when someone badmouthed a partner of many years.

"Well, I can't say the same for him," Valerie said sourly, then paused and added, "No, no, I don't mean that. He is great; he's really great." But her voice had too much of an edge to believe she spoke in earnest. "Anyway, you know . . ." Valerie waved at the space between them. "It's just a little funny."

"Right," Ellen agreed, her lips twisting, a tightening that Alex said he loved for being both wry and innocent.

"You know I didn't do that on purpose." Valerie fluttered her fingers toward Mose.

"Oh, yeah," Ellen said emphatically. "Of course. I didn't think for a second . . ."

"Well," Valerie hooked her long brown hair behind her ears. Ellen didn't imagine she ever tied it into a girlish ponytail or experimented with braids or did anything other than cut it, dutifully, at a good salon, once every six weeks. She was such an undeniable . . . grown-up. "We'll have to get together and have a chat." Valerie smiled with what seemed like real warmth, though her tone didn't suggest that they'd meet to talk about their situation, but about Alex. They'd be girlfriends, dishing about their guy's foibles.

But Ellen couldn't do this. Not if she wanted things to work with Alex. And she did. She *wanted* things to work, though it took her desire *not* to chat with Valerie for her to recognize this. She didn't want Alex to be—as she had supposed he might be initially—just something that happened on the way to finding her one, true love.

Valerie shook her car keys out of her handbag and smiled a final goodbye to everyone in the hall.

"What was *that* about?" Mose said.

"Can I tell you outside?"

"I don't see why not. I have something to tell you myself."

They stepped back onto the porch. The sun had already set, and it was chilly.

"So what did you have to tell me?" Ellen began, as they set off.

"No, honey, you tell me first," Mose said.

"No, you."

"You!" Mose laughed, but then said, "OK. I'll go first. What I wanted you to know was that I got a disturbing piece of mail."

"Mail?" Ellen began. "Oh, I was thinking . . . What mail?"

"Let me show you. I have it in Stanley."

When they neared the car, Mose said, "We'll get in. I'll warm us up." He didn't like to visit Ellen's apartment. With its futon couch and two wicker-back kitchen chairs, he could never get comfortable. Into the initial puff of cold from the heater, Mose said, "So I look under the

Times one Sunday, and this is what I find." From the way he said this, Ellen knew Mose had told the story before. Probably several times. It was one of his bad habits, retelling stories till he wore them out, even if—especially if—the story put him in a bad light. Like that "came down with Death" remark he'd made to the new principal last winter; he pulled it out as evidence of his foolishness whenever there was someone new around, but he did it so compulsively that Ellen began to wonder if he was proud of the faux pas.

Mose handed Ellen a plastic bag. In it was a yellow envelope, and a white piece of paper on which someone had scrawled, "We know who you are, Zionist oppressor. We don't forget."

"Oh, Lord. What's this?"

"It's hate mail. That's what it is."

"Who sent it, I mean?" She pinched the edge of the plastic bag as if the material itself were toxic.

"The postal inspector thinks it's a copycat crime. There'd been a piece in the newspaper about someone sending hate mail in California. It was the postal inspector who told me to put the letter in the plastic bag. To protect the letter from any more fingerprints." He seemed proud to have this insider information.

"But what does it mean? Is there some crazy skinhead out there, who wants to come . . . I don't know . . . break into your apartment and"—*stomp your face*, she thought—"hurt you? I better sleep at your place tonight."

"Oh, no, don't be ridiculous. I got this months ago. I'm guessing this has to do with everything that happened the other summer."

"Right . . . ," Ellen said slowly. Madison had a number of "sister cities," and in the summer of 2004, the City Council voted down a request to link Madison with Rafah in Gaza. It had been a close vote. Nine in favor, eight against, three abstaining. Not the eleven votes necessary to pass. And the mayor promised to veto the proposal no matter what the vote. Still, there'd been serious debate and eloquent opposition, including a much-publicized letter written by Mose.

"Israel's existence is precarious. If we assent to this proposal, we say yes to a community that has said yes to suicide bombers, we say yes to anti-Semitism clothed as liberalism, which sees the failings of Israel—and no one would deny the state's failings—without seeing the failings of the Palestinians. In saying yes to this proposal, we say Palestinians are victims only, not victims and victimizers. We say yes to a culture that is not democratic, and no to a culture that is."

The pro-Palestinian cause had picked up on this. "We Say Yes to Peace" appeared on the bumpers of a few cars.

"Hardly seems like a note they would send, though," Ellen said now. ("If Arabs don't have equal rights in Israel, then it isn't quite a democratic culture, is it?" Ellen had said to Mose last summer, and he'd shouted at her, "Do you think there would even *be* an Israel, if the Arabs were allowed to vote? You can't give rights if you have to commit suicide first to do it.")

"The Yes to Peace people?" Mose said, his hands on the steering wheel, as if the car were going somewhere. "I agree. You couldn't call *this* a peaceful message. But in the end, how peaceful were the Yes to Peace people? And anyway, that was a student group, and once the students graduated . . . I haven't seen anything with their name on it, since school let out last May."

"Wait," Ellen said. "You said you got this message *months ago?*"

"That's right."

"But why are you only telling me now?"

"Oh, sweetheart," Mose said. "I didn't want to upset you. It just occurred to me that someone other than me and the postal inspector should know about this. And now I see I *shouldn't* have told you."

"Not told me? Who do you think I am, that I wouldn't want to know such a thing?"

Mose looked confused by this question. "We won't talk about it anymore. You said you had something to tell me."

"But wait, we're not done with this. So are you saying that in the end, this note is just a random thing?"

"No," Mose said sharply. "Not a random thing. Don't you remember those swastikas on the synagogue door? I just told you about that."

"Yes, I know. I forgot."

"Forgot? How could you forget?" Mose asked with such outrage that it might have been the Holocaust—not some stupid graffiti—that had slipped her mind.

She blinked and turned abruptly from Mose. He often flared up, sharp-tongued, like this, but it hurt her every time, his tone of disgust and dismissal.

"So," Ellen began. She was glad she'd have Alex, later in the evening, to curl into, the reliable comfort of his arms. "My beau is Alex Decker."

"Your . . . what? The superintendent?"

"Yeah, that would be him." Mose's car faced the homes that fronted the lake. Between a large Queen Anne Victorian and a place that looked like a cement gingerbread house, Ellen could see the water, a charcoal gray in the darkening day.

"Oh, honey," Mose said with clear regret, "he's a bit more than a 'little older' than you."

"There are some years there," Ellen allowed. She concentrated on the lake. She wished it were still warm enough to go swimming.

"And you like him because . . . ?"

Ellen held up her hand. She didn't want questions. "I can't . . . I can't . . . you know, *explain* it." Mose didn't respond, but he was looking straight at her, waiting. She didn't turn to him, only said, "Um . . . he's really generous . . . not thing-generous, I don't care about that . . . but you know on one of our dates, he made me this ginger soup with all these vegetables, and he cooks for color as well as taste. He brought all the ingredients to make . . ." She pointed out of the car, toward her upstairs apartment. "He brought them in a big paper bag and just made it for me."

"Right," Mose said, though he wasn't agreeing.

"Like you always say, 'Only the heart knows what the heart knows.'"

"Soup," Mose said incredulously. "You like him because of soup?"

"*Noooo*, you know," she said and made a nervous flip-flopping gesture with her hand. "I can't really talk about this anymore."

"OK," Mose said, challenge in his voice. "So what shall we talk about?"

"Whatever," Ellen said. "Whatever you want."

"I want to talk about all those nice boys who always say hello to you when we go for a walk."

"Well, we can talk about whatever you want, but not that."

"Right," Mose said. "Does Barbara know about this?"

"Yeah, I told her right away."

"So this has been going on some time?

"Since the summer—"

"The summer?" Mose seemed entirely taken aback.

"When we were kids, you always said, 'Private is private.' Remember? It was private for a while. But it isn't anymore, because it just isn't. I mean the fact of it isn't."

Mose sniffed and cleared his throat. "What other stupid things did I say? When you were a kid? I need to know, because I can see that my Hell is to be damned by my own words."

"You said you loved us," Ellen said, gathering her purse off the floor of the car. She wanted to go in. "And that you wanted us to be happy."

"Oh," Mose said, starting up the car, something in him seeming to soften with the word. He leaned over to kiss her goodbye, missing, as he always did, her cheek, and kissing the air. "Thank God, I did something right."

"*You*," Ellen called when Alex pushed through the door later that night. "I'm so glad you're here." They kissed in the doorway for several minutes, her hands holding his face and his arms around her back, the simple passion of it canceling everything till she heard someone open the downstairs door, and she said, half her mouth engaged, "Better shut the door."

"Let's go in there," Alex said, cocking his head toward Ellen's bedroom.

"Let's." She stepped back. "Doug all right?" She wondered exactly what words he'd used to tell his son about her.

Alex shrugged. "I asked him how he felt about my news, but he just said, 'I don't want to talk about it.' The joys of parenting an adolescent."

"I'm sorry."

"Nothing to be sorry about."

There was just the bed in her bedroom and a single white chair and six stout candles that she'd put on dinner plates on the floor. "You know, something weird happened with Mose." They began to unbutton each other's shirts. Alex sagged into the bed, pulling Ellen toward him. She told him about Mose's mail, pulled away from Alex's kisses to say, "Should I be worried?"

Alex stretched. "I doubt it. There was probably something up at the U when he got the letter. Maybe something like the Palestinian Solidarity Movement; if they have an event up there, there's always a chance of some spin-off activity. Divest in Israel, or something. But I don't think it means anything."

"Oh," she said, eager to trust his words. Alex undid her pants, slipped his hand into her underwear.

"You're so wet," he breathed, and she started to have the sleepy, half-fluid feeling she got whenever his hands were on her. She wanted to describe the interchange with Mose further—the effect his words had on her. But she couldn't. She eased Alex's elbow through his sleeve, and he wriggled the rest of his shirt off. An irrational thought, but there it was: Mose's imperfections weren't good for the Jews.

Chapter Nine

NOVEMBER–DECEMBER 2005

*M*ose used Monday's free period to complain, over his newly acquired cell phone, to Barbara in Maine. "Middle-aged! And ready to
run around with the first pretty thing he sees."

"Of course, you wouldn't like her choice."

"What do you mean, of course?" Something about the smallness of
the cell phone made him feel like he wasn't really on the phone. He had
to press the "loudspeaker" button to hear Barbara, and even so, he
needed to jam the phone right into his ear.

"You've always been hard on her."

"Oh, here we go again, spinning the hits." Barbara never tired of reminding Mose of his failings as a parent, and this was her favorite com-
plaint: that he was too hard on his young cousins. "I pushed you," he'd
agree. "That's not the same as being hard on you. I wanted you to have
what I didn't."

Usually Barbara would say, "And it worked. We're insecure and
you're a confident son-of-a-bitch." From whence this vitriol? He loved
both the girls, had loved them always. Not that he hadn't made mis-
takes along the way, lost his temper and behaved badly. Once, he'd
grabbed Barbara fiercely, trying to hold her in the kitchen, so he could
make a point. He yelled and yelled at her, all through the college application process. She wouldn't do anything—fill out the forms, write her

essay—in a timely manner. She'd run out of the apartment, screaming like a banshee. She wasn't going to do it; she didn't *have* to do it. And he'd grabbed for her, ended up ripping the pocket off the back of her jeans, since she wouldn't slow her run, and he wouldn't let go of the pocket. Later, she'd let that pocket flop, flop along. She wasn't going to sew it; he'd just have to look at it and remember he'd kicked her. *Kicked her!* He hadn't done any such thing, but this was her claim. She'd slipped out of his grip and fallen to the floor, arms over her head for self-protection, and he'd kicked and kicked her. Where she got these things, Mose didn't know. What he did know is that Barbara never forgot incidents, imagined or true. No matter all the good things he'd done. The bad canceled everything out.

"Never mind then," Mose said now. He was sitting at his classroom desk, and his eyes drifted to the stack of papers before him. A bit of cottage cheese and half a boiled egg sat in a plastic container just beyond the papers. "Let me know how you're doing."

"D in the D," Barbara allowed.

"Down in the dumps? How come?" He lifted the plastic fork, stuck it in the cottage cheese, then put it down, the effort of bringing the food to his mouth suddenly seeming like too much.

"I just hate this place. It's cold. It's even cold in the summer. I should never have agreed to come here."

Nothing Mose might say now—*Can you think about a move? A warmer winter coat?*—would assuage her. Barbara had two modes—her current mode, irrational and angry, and her other mode, in which she was warm-hearted and even funny, an efficient fundraiser for the Center for Grieving Children, where she worked half-time. The reasonable and the unreasonable Barbara bore no relation to one another, and Mose never knew which Barbara he was going to get, on a given day.

"I'll never find a job." Her manner was hostile, accusatory, as if daring Mose to suggest her failure was anything less than complete.

"You have a job."

"That's not a job. That's asking rich people for money."

"It's a good cause; it's something you care about."

"I don't care about anything."

In this mood, she wouldn't ask about him. Even on her up days, Barbara tended not to inquire about his activities. Sometimes he simply offered information, less because he felt a need to unburden himself, than because he hoped to distract her.

"Well, honey, we have a new diversity initiative in the district. Everyone is supposed to go to weekend workshops—six hours each. No pay, of course. Diversity in hiring, diversity in the classroom, sensitivity training. All that." Mose's classroom was a mess—books stacked on the floor, maps hung unevenly from the bulletin board, the usual disarray—but Mose had the uncustomary urge to pick something up. Since Barbara hadn't said anything, Mose soldiered on. "That's right, honey. Hyman Clark set up the initiative—not just for Sudbury, but for the entire school system." Oh, the irony. Inflexible Hyman instructing others in "human resource management" and fairness. Mose would be damned if he'd go. Since when did he need Hyman Clark telling him how to behave to blacks or anyone else for that matter?

"Yeah," Barbara said flatly. She had a prescription for anti-depressants but often forgot to take the pills. Said she didn't believe in them. "They can't even do something like diversity training here. It's so white. It's like a state full of marshmallows. There was a Klan rally in Lewiston. I'm in the Land of Morons."

"I thought you said you were in the Land of Minivans."

"I'm in the Land of Morons in Minivans."

"OK, honey," Mose said. "Have you been taking your medicine?"

"I *told* you I don't believe in all that."

"It's a pill. What's to believe?"

"You think . . ." Mose held the phone away from his ear. He did not want to hear what she thought he thought. When he pressed his ear back to the phone, he said quietly, "I should go."

Barbara was silent. Seething and silent. She had clearly not gotten what she wanted out of this conversation. She never did, when she was in this mood.

"So, goodbye, sweetheart." He pressed the button to end his call. He knew when he next talked to Ellen she'd say, "Barbara says you hung up on her."

He had projects to grade, but there was no point in trying to use the rest of his free period for that. He'd spend the whole hour staring at a single page of student work, wondering how serious this thing with

Alex Decker was. He knew the drill: the second family, the husband too tired to help with raising the children, the wife widowed by the time *she* reached middle age.

"Hello?" a voice called into the classroom. Hyman Clark.

"Hello yourself," Mose said, as Hyman stepped into his room. "How have you been?"

"I didn't see you at yesterday's meeting." There was something in Hyman's stiff posture that made Mose flash on a student he'd had years ago, a boy who wore a cage under his clothes to straighten his crooked spine.

"No," Mose said. He never went to faculty meetings, hadn't gone since his first days at Sudbury when teacher in-service days meant his girls would be home from school on Wednesdays, the days on which the faculty meetings were always held. At a different institution, his absences would not have been excused. Now they were so long established, Mose was surprised that anyone would note them. "I haven't been in the habit of going."

Hyman frowned. "Well, I'd like to see that habit changed."

"I'll see what I can do."

"That wasn't the answer I was hoping for." Hyman's top lip darted up, then settled into an inexpressive line.

"I didn't go when my girls were younger, since I needed to attend to them, but you're right. Things are different now."

In the classroom, Mose never had cause to question his talents, but around other teachers, he hadn't quite overcome his self-consciousness about his past. He wasn't ashamed of his life in the trades but knew he mispronounced words. He couldn't write a simple memo without a dictionary by his side. His spelling was atrocious. He could imagine a training session where he'd be asked to step to the blackboard and sketch out some principle or lesson plan, and he'd make a gross error. Once Barbara had corrected his shopping list.

Mellon   melon
Spagheti   spaghetti

To hurt him, Mose knew. And he *had* been hurt.

Now Hyman appraised Mose's classroom, arching his head, almost theatrically, as he scanned the room. On the side blackboard, Mose had scribbled, "It's YOUR Constitution. What are you going to do?"

"What's that?" Hyman gestured to the words with his virtually non-existent chin—the man's face was as flat as a pancake.

"Oh," Mose breathed out of his nose, a sigh/laugh. "We decided to draft a constitution today. For Iraq."

"For Iraq? Don't you teach *American* history?"

"Of course, but I wanted them to see what they could come up with, if they were writing the blueprint for a new government." Mose knew he should just stand up. His height, diminished as it was, would even something in the dialogue, but it was too late to rise without seeming to want to usher Hyman out the door.

"And you think you can compare an Islamic country in 2005 to our nation in 1787?"

"No, but I can get the students to imagine themselves as founding fathers, as people trying to enact ideals."

"I see. And how's that book working out?"

"The . . . *New and Revised American History?*"

"The kids like it?" Hyman asked.

"How could they not, with a sexy title like that?" Mose smiled.

"I don't think so much about titillating them, given all the MTV they watch. Plus from what I can tell, they do a fairly good job of titillating each other."

Mose cleared his throat. "They all have the book and are using it for reference."

"Meaning what?" Hyman said. "You're not actually assigning it?"

"No, like I told you. I use the tapes. They listen to lectures for class." He'd won prizes for this—not just from the school system, but from the state. His student evaluations couldn't be more glowing. Why pester him?

"They only listen to a lecture at night?"

"Well, they do have other classes. All of their teachers can't be assigning them two hours of homework. Not if we want them to do things like sleep on a nightly basis."

"I see. Well, I'd like you employing approved methods of teaching."

What could Mose say to this? He wasn't going to assign the textbook. It was dry as dust. Things needed to have meaning for his kids, or they simply wouldn't come to class. It was why they'd chosen Sudbury in the first place; they needed their education to have clear relevance.

The bell rang.

"Perhaps we could talk this over some more after school today?" Hyman said.

"Actually, you'll have to excuse me. After school, I have to meet my daughter. She's got me on this exercise program . . ." Mose didn't have an appointment with Ellen, but it might be nice to surprise her at work.

"Perhaps tomorrow?" Hyman said.

"Actually, it's an every-day thing. This exercise."

"Well, I don't want to get in the way of your plans," Hyman said, drawing his hands back as if he were the victim of a holdup. Was he being sarcastic, trying to suggest Mose was putting his private needs before his professional obligations?

"I can come talk to you during one of my free periods," Mose suggested.

"Oh," Hyman said, as if he now had all the evidence he needed for some private case he was conducting, "that won't be necessary." He turned for the door.

Perhaps Mose *would* go see Ellen today. Of course, Mose knew enough about young women not to offer up his disapproval of Ellen's choice of partner. He could check up on her, though. Surprise her at work and try to gauge her true feelings. But then he never liked visiting Ellen at the daycare, partially because he wanted to give Ellen her space, partially because when he came upon her introducing the letter *J* to a group of four-year-olds, he couldn't help thinking, "My girl. She has not a thought in her head." Her aggressive simplicity rankled, and yet she was good. And didn't he, of all people, know how hard it was for a kid to turn out good?

Things that are red.

Things too awful to name.

Things in the dark.

It was early December. Mose sat on one of the high stools in Smitty's art room and considered the strange list on Smitty's board.

"What *is* that?"

"My list?" said Smitty, smiling slightly, clearly pleased. So many people treated him like a joke that he took any sign of interest as a compliment. "It's an idea from a tenth-century Japanese courtesan."

"See, I *thought* you'd been keeping peculiar company."

Smitty stared absentmindedly out the large windows that formed the east wall of his classroom. Mose blinked. The light, at midday and given the blanket of snow outside, was harsh and white. "Tired," Smitty mused, then said, "So the thing is she documented court life in her *Pillow Book*. She made lists, too. So I stole that idea for class. The kids are going to have to make a visual list, using one thing from the board."

"Sounds interesting. It's hero week for us." Mose had assigned his students to interview a "real American hero." In class, they discussed what it meant to *be* an American hero. Then students were to go out with tape recorders to do the work. "You know who's an American hero?" Brandi Clark had told him after that first class, when they discussed the assignment. "*I* am. I've been through a lot, you know." Her friend Charlene Court stuck her head back into the classroom and said, in the grave and histrionic voice of a TV announcer, considering scenes of battle-devastated children, "Won't you please, please, please, help the acne-prone."

"Charlene!" Brandi cried. "I'm serious."

"I don't disagree," Mose said. "Still and all, I'd rather you didn't interview yourself." Brandi huffed at the decision and made for the hallway, where she swatted Charlene on the arm.

Things that are red. Once, not long after Mose and the girls moved to Madison, Barbara had found and read Ellen's diary. Mose had given Ellen the diary for her birthday—an orange item with a gold lock and key. He wondered if, at thirteen, she was really too old for such things. By high school, girls seemed to favor journals, not diaries. More than once, Mose had found a girl in the corner of Sudbury's library, scribbling furiously in a book of blank, unlined paper, the urgency of the words clear in the tight press of pen on page. If disturbed, the student would lift the book to her breast: this was how you held babies, this was how you kept secrets.

Barbara had jimmied Ellen's diary open with a bobby pin and found this confession inside: "Tamar wanted to know who my ideal man was, and I said Peter Jennings. I didn't know I was going to say it even. Until I said it. Tamar said that was right, that I was going to be some important man's wife."

"So, Mrs. Jennings," Barbara said when the girls sat down for dinner that night. "How are you today?"

Ellen blushed, and when Barbara told Ellen's secret, Mose scolded her. Private was private. How would Barbara like it if Ellen snooped through *her* things? (In fact, there was precious little privacy in their apartment. They all shared a bathroom; the girls had no problem calling out, "What a stink," after Mose used the toilet. They didn't close the bathroom door themselves when peeing.)

"I wouldn't care," Barbara said, "if you looked at my things." Mose supposed this was true; Barbara would have liked the attention. And then as if this were his name, Barbara added: "Cousin . . . Cousin Jennings." She tittered.

"Say Jennings one more time, and I'll slap you across the face," Mose said firmly.

"Mrs. Jennings, what did that guy just say?"

Mose stood up, reached across the table and slapped Barbara. Instantly a jet of red splurted from her nose, a stream that seemed unstoppable. "Head back," Mose had ordered. "Pinch your nose here." A terrible thought: her entire life pouring out the faucet of her nose. *Things that are red. Things that are dark. Things that are too awful to name.* That long-ago Peter Jennings confession . . . maybe it was a clue to Ellen's current attraction. In Ellen's circumscribed world, the city's superintendent of schools would certainly qualify as an "important man."

"*H*ey," Smitty coughed. "What's up with you these days?"

"Nothing," Mose said. "Well, actually. Ellen's got a new boyfriend."

"That's great."

"Well, you know who it is, right?"

"No. How would I know?"

You'd know, because everyone at school knows, because the whole city knows. But general knowledge wouldn't be a reason for Smitty.

"She's dating Alex Decker."

"Oh, right," Smitty said vaguely, as if he'd heard a rumor to this effect but hadn't believed it. "Isn't he, like, old enough to be her father?"

"Not quite. But there's a stretch of years there." Biologically, of course, it wasn't impossible. Had Alex knocked up his high school girlfriend, he would have a daughter Ellen's age.

"They're not marrying or anything. But it's pretty serious." Mose had been reconsidering his desire for a grandchild, a hope that made his mind dart briefly to the surely already accomplished fact: Alex's pale ass pumping into Ellen. He shook his head, as if to loosen the image. *Things you don't want in your brain:* an aneurysm, an arterial malformation, Alex Decker, unclothed and aroused.

"Mail call," shouted Brandi Carter from the hall and rolled a media trolley into the room. "Hey, Mr. Sheinbaum. Hey, Mr. Nelson."

Mose was always surprised to hear Smitty's last name, especially as he'd long assumed his nickname was a shortened version of his surname. Brandi handed the teachers their mail. They could easily pick the envelopes up in the staff room, but all Sudbury students were supposed to have a job, and after the necessary positions were assigned (van vacuuming, window cleaning, dishroom duty, Xeroxing), a few tasks needed to be invented.

"For you." Brandi handed Smitty a stack of mail and mock-curtseyed.

"And you." She bowed for Mose.

"Thanks, Brandi," they called, as she wheeled her cart out of the door.

Smitty said, "At least he did *her* a good turn."

"What?" Mose said, alarmed.

"Decker. He did her a good turn."

Mose sniffed in relief. He thought Smitty had said, "He did her for a good turn." "What're you talking about?"

"Don't you remember that whole story, about how Brandi was living across the street from the Deckers? A foster situation, I guess. But then the house got repossessed, and she slept in a car for a few nights."

"No, I don't. When was this?"

"What? Oh, I don't know." Smitty flipped through his mail absentmindedly, then turned to pin a few items to a wall that he'd already covered with announcements for art exhibits and oddball photos of a Mrs. Butterworth syrup container next to the major sights of Europe. Mrs. Butterworth and the Eiffel Tower. Mrs. Butterworth in the Pantheon. "A few years ago. Something like that. You *must* remember. Everyone was going on and on, because it was such a nice neighborhood, but it turned out, once their story hit the papers, the couple just cleared out, left Brandi behind." Smitty squinted out the window again, seemed to lose the thread of his thought.

"Their story?" Mose prompted. The classroom was overheated. Mose had visited, in part, to warm up—the heater was broken again in his classroom—but now he felt a little sick.

"Yes, yes, *you* know. Somehow Brandi got placed with those undertakers, the ones who were selling brains for research without the permission of the . . . you know, the dead people. Well, not the dead people, but their families. Just yanking those puppies out of there and sending them to . . . Frankenstein's Medical Market. Can't you just picture it? A big box store with all sorts of parts. Aisle one, you've got your unattached limbs, aisle two would be for transplantable organs, aisle . . ."

"Smitty . . ." A chastisement Smitty was used to by now. His name: a request to stick to the point.

"OK, so no one is even thinking about Brandi," Smitty said, as he dropped the remainder of his mail into the trash, "but Alex Decker tracked her down. Some UW guy was letting her stay in his dorm room, as long as she kept balling him. And Decker talked her into going to Sudbury, got her set up with a decent family. Definitely a white knight thing. On Decker's part."

So many of the students had these sad stories. Even when there were loving parents behind them, they'd be waylaid by something: a benign brain tumor that left them with no capacity for judgment, a blue puffy birthmark that grew over their face then killed them before they were out of their twenties, an arthritis that made it impossible to rise for morning classes. You had to marvel at the numbers who were just walking around, all limbs attached, no fast-growing cells being blitzed out of their bodies, no predator about to push them in a van for some grisly, riverside rape and murder.

Smitty went to the board and wrote "Things that a white knight might do" at the end of his list. "What do you think?"

"I never doubted Alex Decker's liberal credentials."

"No, I mean the addition to my list."

Mose squinched up his nose. "Might be interpreted the wrong way. Racist even."

Smitty erased the words. "And to think I went to the diversity training workshop."

"Learn anything?"

"People who have less money are pissed off at people who have more money."

That had been the word around the halls: that the diversity workshops—everyone in the school system was supposed to attend—regularly devolved into discussions of the teachers and their lack of respect for the secretarial and custodial staff, as if public school teachers with their lavish $35,000 a year salary were the enemy. If you made $25,000 a year, perhaps they were.

"Well, good for you," Mose said. "You'd never stumble on that truth on your own."

"I know." Smitty yawned grandly, a vaguely repulsive, wet-armpit-revealing, belly-exposing affair.

Mose stared into his pile of mail. Given the advent of e-mail, why so much tree murder? He stuffed one memo after another into the trash can at his feet. "*Oy vey.*" He stopped. "I've had . . . I've already done lunch room duty for all of November, and now Clark's giving me January parking lot duty."

Smitty looked at Mose, as if waiting for him to get to his point.

"It will be winter, Smitty." Mose couldn't go on, didn't want to say that he couldn't do parking lot duty in winter. He could barely make it over the ice and snow to get to his car as it was. One fall, and he could kiss teaching, driving and independent living goodbye.

"Complain to your daughter's beloved!"

"Can you imagine?" The idea was galling, more so, because Alex Decker had already promoted Hyman Clark. Next year, he would be assistant superintendent of schools. Mose *had* imagined calling his union representative to complain about Hyman. But what would he say? The principal doesn't like me? I think he's picking on me? If so, why hadn't Mose just tried to resolve the matter on his own? Once Mose overheard Haskell, the gym teacher, yelling at a student who'd reported some affront. "Did you tell him? Did you tell him you don't like what he's doing? Well, don't come to me, until you've told him what you think. Use your words." The kid being reprimanded had listened sheepishly to Haskell's reproach. Apparently, you had to tell people you didn't want them to throw a chair at your head. You couldn't just assume that this was a foregone conclusion.

"Hey," Smitty said. "Maybe he likes you better than you think."

"Who?"

"Hyman Clark. Look." Smitty reached back into the trash for a green piece of paper, which announced that the annual Christmas party would be cancelled, out of deference to the Jewish and Muslim staff.

"Oh, yeah, the Muslim staff. Like that imam over in the cafeteria." There might have been some Muslims in the school system, but there weren't any at Sudbury. As for Jews, Ben Goldstein—the new math teacher—and Mose Sheinbaum were the only ones. And because of them, the others would be denied their annual egg nog and rum balls. Mose loved those rum balls. And anyway, hadn't the party always just been for "the holidays," so candy canes aside, you understood that you were celebrating Kwanzaa and Chanukah, as well as Christmas?

"Now," cooed Smitty, "isn't that sensitive of our leader?"

"At least we'll be rid of him by year's end," Mose said and tapped his watch. Mose could bear the man for another semester.

The bell rang. "Time to serve our clients?" Smitty asked.

Mose nodded, but then something caught his eye. He leaned closer to Smitty's wall. "Mrs. Butterworth at Stonehenge!" he said. "And who says this world isn't full of miracles!"

*M*ose scheduled an appointment to talk with Hyman later in the week. There was no way he could do parking lot duty. He'd just have to explain why. When Mose arrived at the main office, Mark, HoHo and Devon—the three boys he'd seen on his previous visit—were there, still dressed (if memory served, which it didn't always) in the same thug-black, affecting the same chair slump, as if they were lowlifes leisurely contemplating their next crime. This time, Betty didn't suggest Mose wait but motioned him into Hyman's office, never mind that the principal was clearly occupied.

Seeing him at the door, Hyman turned to Mose and said, "We were just talking about the Bus of Peace."

"The what?"

"The Bus of Peace," Devon said, "and we're going to be the Band of Peace."

"These gentleman have offered to play at an event I've proposed to the superintendent."

"Bands not bombs." Mark held up his fingers in a peace sign and smirked. You wouldn't think you could make a peace sign look violent, but he managed it. "Some of these kids," as Clara Massengill once admitted, "just have criminal minds. They'll dance around the truth, even when there's no reason to." Lying could be a habit of mind. Not a choice, but something you did as reflexively as scratching an itch.

"I just came for our meeting," Mose said.

"Can't say these kids don't care about the world around them." Hyman smiled.

"Yeah. U.S. out of Iraq. Peace in the Mideast," said HoHo. "And all that crap."

"Eloquently put," Mose said.

"We're going to make people see that peace is the way." Mark said this so angrily that Mose supposed Mark would make people understand all this . . . by punching them.

Mose checked his watch. "You know," he said, "I had something to say, but I'll just send you an e-mail."

"Right," said Hyman. "Good to see you."

Back in his classroom, Mose typed out a quick note, explaining that physical considerations prevented him from being able to take on parking lot duty in any season, but particularly in winter. Could he please be excused?

Days passed, and there was no response. Mose sent another e-mail. "Re: parking lot," he typed in the message subject line. "Don't mean to bother you, but I'm still hoping to hear back from you."

E-mail! Oh, did not the kingdom of America have the speediest of couriers? Still, Mose had avoided it for the first five years of his job. Computers scared him. He'd finally broken down and asked Barbara to explain how to find a book in the library; the days of thumbing through softly worn index cards were clearly over. Hard to believe he once knew so little. Now Mose felt like an IV ran from his arm to his computer. Imagine what would happen if he ignored a student's importuning in the way Hyman was avoiding Mose's messages! Complaints, at the very least, complaints to which Mose would have to answer.

A week passed. Mose let more words click across his screen: "Don't mean to be a bother, as I know you are busy, but can you just drop me a quick line and let me know when I can expect to hear from you re: parking lot assignment?"

No answer.

"What am I? Invisible?" Mose complained to Smitty.

"Sure," Smitty said. "To him you are."

Mose grimaced. They were standing in the hall outside the art room.

"What is it with that kid Devon Cryer's face?" Mose asked.

"The spots?" Smitty said.

Mose nodded. Devon had tiny red spots all over his face. Given his hair—blond but dyed purple—he looked like a Doctor Seuss character.

"Gloria says it's gang colors. Red and purple."

"Oh, not seriously," Mose said, though Gloria, as one of the younger teachers, tended to be knowledgeable about these things.

"I don't know. Can't get away with it in the clothes anymore. She could be right. Gloria says she wants to Record, Report, Remove."

Mose laughed. When faculty saw gang behavior—hand signals, graffiti and the like—they were required to record it, report it and remove it.

"Listen," Smitty said. "I'll do the parking lot duty for you, if you don't hear from him."

Smitty didn't tend to be generous in this way. He guarded his time. Mose said, "I wish I didn't have to accept that offer." And then he felt angry. He shouldn't *have* to accept the offer; Hyman shouldn't put him in this position.

Smitty patted his back and said, "You've driven me a lot of places over the years."

"You're a good man," Mose said. Smitty shrugged. It was nice of him not to say the obvious, that asking Mose to do winter parking lot duty was the equivalent of asking him to play hopscotch in the middle of the freeway: as absurd as it was dangerous.

At home, that evening. Radio on, frozen dinner consumed, tomorrow's lesson plan reviewed. Mose rested in his La-Z-Boy, eyes closed, mouth ajar, his own snores periodically jangling him awake, before he settled back into sleep.

The phone rang.

"Sheinbaum?"

"Yes," Mose answered, confused. He'd been dreaming of a traditional Jewish wedding—a beautiful chuppah, a groom in classic Chasidic dress, and a bride who came from the grave, garnered with worms and decomposing flesh, ready for marriage. Oh, Lord. Why did the mind choose such torments for itself?

"Hyman Clark here. Just wondering what year you're due for your merit review."

"Excuse me?"

"I didn't get you at a bad time, did I?"

Mose rubbed his hand over his face. Mrs. Butterworth had been a guest at the wedding. "Not at all." Where was his watch? "My merit review? They're every three years now, but not when I started, so I guess it could be . . . this year? Next year? I can check my records."

"Yes," Hyman said crisply. "If you'd do that."

When Clara was principal, the merit reviews were a pro forma thing. Clara recommended the merit raise. The superintendent signed off on the recommendation, as did the governor. Raises could be anywhere from 0 to 5 percent, and Mose had never failed to get the full 5 percent in his time at Sudbury.

"So I'll need to make a classroom visit."

"Oh, yes." Mose had forgotten that. The principal usually sat in on a class, before writing the recommendation. "Come any time."

"Yes, I think I'll do that." Hyman hung up the phone.

Mose stood. He was in his boxers and undershirt, having undressed when he came home and not bothered to don anything else. You needed another person's eyes to worry about appearances. He searched for his watch. Almost ten. He shuffled to bed but didn't rest. "What was the purpose of that call?" Hyman would have asked Rachel, if she were still alive. As it was, though, he only had the succubus of his dreams and a vague, disquieting urge for pancakes.

Part Two

THE SEASON OF HATE

Among all phenomena, it is really the only one
to which there can be so definitely attributed
the opposing values of good and evil.

—Gaston Bachelard, *Psychoanalysis of Fire*

Chapter One

DECEMBER 2005

$\mathscr{D}$oug loved someone who didn't love him back. That was Valerie's take on things. Her clues? The usual: long showers, incessant checking of the computer for messages, heartbreak music. Valerie had her version of the same, though she opted for baths, a close monitoring of her phone's answering machine and a different brand of heartbreak music. Plus her crush was objectless. "You think you can do so much better than me?" Alex used to shout during their fights. "You're an angry, crazy bitch." Later, he'd say, "Of course I don't think that. Of course." It was just something he'd said in the heat of the moment. But then he'd say it, again and again, whenever they fought. She said, "Fuck off," and "Leave me alone," which were fairly contentless bits of anger. Or so she thought. She didn't tell Alex that he was such a loser that no one would ever have him. And she didn't think that. Nor did she think the world was full of wonderful men ready to sweep her off her feet. Alex helped out more at home than most men she knew; he'd always been a more or less equal partner when it came to Douglas and cooking and keeping up the house. But that didn't mean Valerie might not be better suited to someone else. Like Leo from work. Not that she was sexually attracted to him. She wasn't. Their friendship was meticulously non-sexual. But oh, how Valerie loved talking to him. Just sitting around in their offices, analyzing their families (not the ones they were in now, but the ones they came from) or talking about the Idiot-in-Chief, as they'd taken to calling the president, or their co-workers, or Leo's love of fishing. A form of Zen meditation, it seemed to Valerie, though it did involve hurting another living thing.

"You get along with him because he doesn't live with you," Alex once said to her. It was the sort of charge she had to consider. But Alex wasn't right. Valerie got along with Leo because she did. And, in the darker moments of her marriage, she had to admit that she never talked with Alex the way she did with Leo or other friends. That on some basic level, Valerie wasn't interested in Alex the way she was in others. He'd seemed, early on, so knowable, then so known. It wasn't that familiarity breeds contempt, but knowability. Valerie got along with Leo because she'd never work through him, like some grade school lesson book that is done when it is done. He was more like the Bible or Shakespeare. There was always another way to go back to him.

As for Doug. About whom was he pining? Of course, Valerie couldn't ask, though her parents had always known whom she had a crush on . . . back in the day. Perhaps because her parents lived on the Bradbury Prep campus and knew all the boys in Valerie's class as well as she did. Still, they wouldn't have asked *whom* she liked. Valerie would have offered. She probably *wanted* others to know. She didn't kiss a boy till college. Having a crush *was* her love life.

In her kitchen, Valerie cut vegetables with some urgency. The early dark made her feel tardy, as if the meal for which she was preparing had already been presented and consumed and now, despite her untimely efforts, she should be readying for bed. And still—*thwack! thwack! thwack!*—her knife beheaded a carrot. It was only 5:45, but dark as midnight, a typical December evening, streetlights on, Christmas lights on, a sparkly sense of celebration in the air, though otherwise Valerie associated the end of the year with mandatory visits back east or to Des Moines. This year, for the first time ever, Valerie would be on her own for the holiday, Doug and Alex heading for the Iowa farm, and Valerie unwilling to suffer her parents on her own. Some actors from last spring's production of Sam Shepard's *God of Hell* had asked her to join them for the holiday. A smattering of others, she knew, would try to fix her up. But she didn't know how to conduct herself around men anymore. Maybe she'd never known. She thought of all those boys on whom she'd once had crushes—from age fourteen on, she always had a serious obsession going. How she'd loved them in spite of their obvious shortcomings—one was arrogant, another gay, another a womanizer, another seventeen going on seventy-seven, his world-weariness complete. Not that she recognized these flaws in her youth. She was too busy tallying up the times a boy greeted her in the school hallway or said something romantic like "You gonna eat that?" in the cafeteria.

As a girl, Valerie had railed at the bathroom mirror. Oh, how she hated the face, the ridiculous hair she always found there! But, in the end, she must have had a crush on herself, imagining, as she did, her own startling sensitivity and how it transformed inexpressive, whiny adolescents into doting, confessional heroes. Marriage, of course, had stripped her of that notion. Alex hadn't improved in her presence. He'd become his worst self.

The early dark made her too melancholy! The doorbell rang—a sixteen-note chime that Alex thought was funny, though by note eight, some reluctantly rising member of the household always griped, "I know, I know, I get the point already."

One of the neighborhood kids—chunky Amy Haffer–stood in the cone of light outside Valerie's front door. She wore flip-flops and a mere sweatshirt and jeans, despite the weather.

"Hello, Amy. Haven't seen you in a while."

"Hey, Mrs. Decker. Just stopping by to see your offspring."

"Come on in." Valerie waved the girl into the warmth of the front hall.

"No, no, I'd rather wait here. For the fruit of your loins. If you don't mind."

Cold gusted through the doorway.

"Sure." Valerie turned to shout into the house, "Doug! Your friend's here."

Amy Haffer! A girl with a ring at the end of her nose. Truly, like the pig of the Owl and the Pussycat rhyme. With a ring at the end of her nose, her nose, her nose. With a ring at the end of her nose. Just yesterday, she was sitting in a stroller, gnawing on a wet croissant. Now she was a little piggy, a horrible girl who regularly crashed her parents' car and lived in her girlhood bedroom with her boyfriend. The Haffers' acquiescence in this matter surprised Valerie. Sure, high school kids were going to have sex, but to do the sheets for them!

And fruit of your loins! Like the nose ring, a gross little attempt to shock. In her dream of the previous night, Valerie—she just now remembered this—was single and on a date with some dark-haired man. (You *are* single, she reminded herself.) But in the dream, this wasn't quite true. Still, a friend had fixed her up, and Valerie had impulsively gone to bed with the dark-haired man, who spurted a garden hose worth of semen on her, a horrible white stream that dripped off her mattress and onto the floor. Plunk! Plunk! So loudly that the friend who had set them up—in the dream she was sleeping in a neighboring bed—woke up, repulsed.

"Doug!" Valerie called again, then gagged on the "g" of his name, the wine she'd been drinking as she prepared dinner coming up her throat. Why was her unconscious so disgusting?

Amy rolled some papers in her hand into a tube, held the tube up to her eye, and looked, as if through a telescope, at Valerie. She seemed to be hoping this would put Valerie off. When Valerie didn't react, Amy brought the tube down and bumped the papers against her thigh, a nervous metronome counting out the seconds till Doug arrived.

"Ame!" Doug said affably, when he finally came to the door.

Good Lord. Could Amy be the object of his affection? Valerie had pictured Doug falling for some wispy, arty girl. He'd been a beautiful boy and was now weathering his awkward phase—the gangly limbs, the breakouts aggravated by the attempt to shave his limited facial hair. Valerie and Alex had saddled him with braces and now his lips barely fit over his teeth. His hair was dark, long and curly. Poorly styled. Well, a mess, really, as if some animal had scaled the length of him, only to crawl onto his head and die. Valerie would have liked Doug to cut it. "No, no, Delilah," Doug cried, each time Valerie mentioned the barbershop. "I'll lose my strength." And then he'd collapse theatrically on the ground, moaning.

He *did* look a bit like Samson. Or Jesus Christ. Jesus Christ with dental work.

"Tag you're it," Amy Haffer said and hit Doug with her tube of papers. She then shoved the sheets into his hand before running down the handful of brick stairs that led to Valerie's front stoop.

At the bottom of the stairs, she turned, squinched up her face and stuck her tongue out before she hurried away.

"What was *that*?" Valerie said.

"Oh," Doug sighed. "We've got to write a round-robin story for English class." He stepped back into the light of the front hall and looked down at the pages, reading cursorily. "Mom, got any good ideas about how to finish a story that starts like *Grapes of Wrath* then morphs into a tale of blood-sucking lesbians?" Then, as if in answer to his own question, he rotated his neck drunkenly and said, "What a freak."

Oh, my boy, Valerie thought. He had a goofy sweetness that she admired—one of those kids who liked to talk to grown-ups, who really wanted to *be* a grown-up. If he could, he'd skip the mortifications of youth and get straight to the seriousness of employment and grown-up novels. He wanted to be a lawyer. Or a playwright. Or a city planner. Bless him. And he'd recently discovered the saxophone, having played piano for years. Who knew where the new interest would take him? He even had a band that played at the occasional school function or adult party. At first, Valerie worried that he'd come home from practices smelling of cigarette smoke and pot. But to his ordinary odor—old socks, soap and semen, a combination on which Valerie tried not to dwell—he'd added only cat urine. His jazz combo practiced in the basement of Shannon O'Neil's house, and he always came home saying, "All my organs have been liquidated, and they're coming out my nose." He was terribly allergic to cats.

In the old days—which were the pre-Doug-being-in-love days—Doug would have followed Valerie back into the kitchen and read Amy Haffer's story out loud. Valerie would have laughed, then they'd have brainstormed ways to continue the tale. If Alex were home, he'd pay no attention. For an educator, he was surprisingly uninterested when it came to Doug's daily lessons. Secretly Valerie was glad. She liked being the one watching from the sidelines, reeducating herself from a point of . . . hormonal stability. It was too bad that you couldn't go to school twice. Once as a kid, and then again at age forty, when you'd really appreciate it.

Ba-beep-beep came the loud ascending ring of Doug's upstairs computer. He had e-mail. Doug curled Amy Haffer's papers into a long tube, hit Valerie playfully on the arm and said, "Well, got to get to work." But thirty minutes later, when Valerie tapped on Doug's bedroom door to call him to dinner, he was lying on his floor, staring at the ceiling, doing absolutely nothing.

"You all right?" Valerie said.

"Yeah, well, you know," Doug said unhappily, hoisting himself up.

But she didn't know. She'd been a lot of things in her life, if she could trust the words of others—she'd been an angry, crazy bitch!—but she'd never been a teenage boy.

Chapter Two

DECEMBER 2005

❦

His meeting with Hyman wasn't until five, but Alex arrived early, warming his hands against his cheeks and offering the usual pleasantry to the hostess about the cold, before taking a stool at the new bar. Behind the wall of liquor bottles, there was a restaurant—*Four stars. You have to try it*, people said, if you could stand the preciousness and vague grotesquery of a five-course tasting menu. The tables (a flight up, the whole place in the former offices of a life insurance company) looked out on the Capitol Building, lit at this hour like a Disney Land castle of democracy. But Alex couldn't see the dome now. The bar was relegated to a windowless corner of the restaurant. As he sat, he looked out on precisely nothing.

He ordered and thought of a sign he'd once seen as a boy, below a Des Moines diner: "Senior Citizens Happy Hour, 7–9 A.M." Was it supposed to be funny? He didn't get it. One day, there had actually *been* two old drunks, passed out in front of the diner. At the time, Alex thought they were fake drunks, propped against the diner for a joke photograph, but he never asked, and here he was now far from Des Moines, sitting down to his own early-hour Manhattan. Too early, he fretted, though he enjoyed, as he always enjoyed, the first burning sweet sip, its suggestion that day was done. No matter that day was far from done. If chocolate milk suggested permission the way alcohol did

. . . But there Alex left the proposition, noting only that it would be good for Wisconsin's dairy industry.

Alex pulled a thick stack of papers from his briefcase. He had to approve a math curriculum, finish the long-range fiscal plan for the school board and hire three new teachers. It was too much to do. It was always too much to do. And that was in good times. These days, he felt in need of an extra set of hands and eyes to get through his days. As a leader, Alex's skill had always been his ability to delegate, but that had been impossible since the previous October when Greg Shardon, the new assistant superintendent, entered Alex's office, rubbed his finger below his thick brown moustache, and said he needed to schedule a meeting, that he had to leave in June. "Excuse me?" Alex had said, disbelief and maybe a bit of outrage in his voice. The man had only been working for Alex for three months. But then Greg explained: he'd been diagnosed with ALS, Lou Gehrig's disease.

"Oh, Christ, Greg," Alex blurted. It wasn't like cancer, where you might have a good prognosis or beat the odds of a bad prognosis. Or even heart disease, where you might hope to live well, then exit the world in a few quick moments of pain.

"The thing is I thought I'd be fine for awhile," Shardon said, "but you may have noticed, I've been tripping a lot."

Alex hadn't noticed. "Lord, I'm sorry. You do what you have to do."

"It's just my family, and I . . ."

Alex stood and embraced the man. "You don't need to explain anything to me."

Though he barely knew the guy, Alex already cared about him. Greg was a tall, rangy man who loved hiking and fishing. He and his brother were going to hike the Grand Canyon over Christmas break. Hurry up and do it, while they had the chance, despite a weakness in Greg's right leg, a constant sense that it was going to give out.

Sitting at the bar, wishing the bartender would put out some fancy snack mix, Alex thought of how he had to drag himself to the gym each day, how he forced himself to go running or swimming. Mostly because he didn't want to get fat again. Certainly not because he loved it. If he'd been given Greg's diagnosis, the last thing he'd do was hike. He'd embrace sloth. Or maybe that wasn't true. What with Ellen in his life, he might push himself. But he wouldn't be doing it *for* himself. He'd do it for her. His mind darted briefly from Greg's troubles to Ellen, the creaminess of her skin, the brush of her nipples against his chest when they made love, the curtain of her long, straight hair falling over his face, making a small room in which they kissed.

From behind, Alex heard Hyman Clark say, "Ah, you're already here."

"Thank goodness," Alex turned and patted the stool next to him. "Come save me from my thoughts."

"That bad?" Hyman folded his coat neatly, slid his briefcase under his bar stool, then sat, almost primly, both hands placed evenly on the gleaming granite of the bar's surface.

"Oh, you don't want to know." Alex ran his fingers through the curls at the top of his head. "I'm so glad you suggested meeting here. It's gloomy in the office, what with the dark and everyone gone for Christmas break."

"The early dark. It was like this in Nebraska, too."

"That's right. I keep forgetting you're from Nebraska. I keep imagining Kansas, though I don't know why."

"No, not Kansas."

"Land of the chicken-fried steak." Alex remembered this from some long-ago conference: men from Kansas (themselves composed of so many slabs of glistening red flesh) blithely eating deep-fried steak, as if coronary obstruction were just a fiction invented to hurt their economy. "What'll you have?" Alex said, tilting his head toward the bar.

"A Coke."

"Remember, I'm buying."

"Yeah, no, a . . . a red wine."

Alex raised his hand for the bartender.

"So you have to go to a dinner after this?" Hyman began.

"That's right. Having my son and Ellen's father out to Ridgeway."

"Well, I'll get right to the point."

"Oh, sure, but enjoy yourself. 'Tis the season and all." Alex looked up at the bartender. "A red wine for this gentleman. And"—he pointed toward his empty glass—"another for me."

The previous year, there had been an exhaustive search for the new assistant superintendent. Alex couldn't bear repeating the effort, so not long after Greg Shardon told him about the ALS, Alex simply appointed Hyman Clark to succeed him. Clark obviously thought big—he'd spearheaded a diversity initiative for the entire school system—and test scores were already up at Sudbury.

"Yes . . . well," Hyman began. "I wanted to talk to you about the diversity initiative and related matters. First, though, if you can give me formal approval, we're ready to move forward on the Bus of Peace presentation for next month."

"Yeah. I think what has held that up is . . ." Chin in hand, Alex tapped his cheek. Hyman had e-mailed him something about the Bus of Peace. What was it? "Just remind me. Who are these guys exactly?"

"Oh, surely. HoHo Coombs, one of my kids, found them. On the Internet. A group of Vietnam vets and peace workers. They go around in a big bus, painted crazy colors, and do talks on non-violent solutions to the Iraq War and the Mideast situation. Their program is geared to kids. Music, slide show. A forty-five-minute assembly is what I'm thinking. No cost. They're actually looking for venues. The bus people, I mean."

"Well, OK, that makes sense. I don't see why we can't put approval for that through, especially if there's no charge."

"Right. No charge. So good," Hyman said. "That's one item off the list. As for the diversity workshops, we've got plenty of people on board. Plenty willing to talk and consider what this means for the schools. I'd say that a full 90 or 95 percent of employees—I'm talking support staff and faculty—have attended the workshops."

"Mmm," Alex said, sipping. He'd have to stop after this drink. Tonight, at dinner, Ellen and he were going to tell Doug and Mose that Ellen was moving into the Ridgeway house. A few weekends before, Ellen and Alex had made a rush trip to Chicago to prepare for this, buying pots and pans, a pretty set of celadon plates, silverware and bathroom hand towels. Still the rooms looked empty, and the house itself was far from complete. Nothing was painted. The upstairs floors were plywood, and the downstairs walls still needed to be sheetrocked.

"A tree house," Ellen enthused. She liked it bare, the Swiss chalet feel of the wood exterior and the white down comforters he'd procured for the beds.

"But I think we need to address the problem of those 5 percent who haven't gotten on the bandwagon."

Alex pinched the skin above his bicep. He hadn't been paying attention. He pinched himself again: *Focus, buddy.*

"We don't want some parent suing us for racism, accusing us of ethnically insensitive language. You've got those Hmong, east of town. Commit suicide at an alarming rate, especially the women."

Hmong? Alex remembered hearing about Laotian refugees back when he was living in Iowa, the trouble they had adjusting to Midwestern life. Otherwise, the population hadn't been on his radar screen—or in the news—for years. Hyman went on: "You can see the sort of bind we might land in. Insensitive remark in class and a dead kid. You see what I'm saying. I think it all means we need to address this, you know."

Alex bobbed his head, ordered another drink. "When I was Sudbury's principal, we used to have the kids do projects on Madison's immigration patterns."

"Right, yeah. Well, that's a whole different kettle of fish. Mostly I'm thinking about hiring, curriculum and classroom sensitivity. That sort of thing."

"You don't think we've covered this?"

"Sure," Hyman said. "But mostly I'm wondering about the faculty who would choose *not* to attend a diversity workshop. If you see what I'm saying. That gives me pause."

"I guess that's a good point."

Anything that smacked of political correctness was going to be popular in Madison. In 1970, radicals blew up the University of Wisconsin building that contained the Army Math Research Center. The kids who did it thought that the lab was cooking up a new way to murder Southeast Asians. It didn't occur to them that they might become murderers themselves. Supposedly one of the brothers who detonated the bomb now operated a juice kiosk near the university's library. People said the only clue that he'd ever had radical leanings was the name of one of his fruit smoothies: the Angela Davis.

Once, out of curiosity, Alex had visited the juice stand. He wanted to see what the bomber looked like, though he wasn't exactly proud of the desire. But the man wasn't there. The place was staffed by a kid who looked up, surprised, when Alex asked for a Razzamatazz juice drink. "It's the principal!" the boy had said and reached under the counter for something. He raised his hand—there was a camera in it—and took a picture of Alex. "That's for my art class," he explained. "I'm doing a project called Juiceheads. How you doing?"

Later, someone told Alex the bomber actually ran a falafel stand and hadn't, in any case, been manning his business for over a decade.

Hyman was still talking, so Alex held up a hand. "Hold on a minute," he said. "I'm losing the thread here."

At just that moment, a young woman behind the bar interrupted the men. "So—" She put a bowl of nut mix between Alex and Hyman. Apparently, she had replaced the original bartender. "I guess you don't remember me?" It wasn't exactly a question. Her white t-shirt was tight enough that Alex could see not only her nipples but the dark skin at her aureole. Could she be unaware of this? Who would want to be *this* exposed?

"You're Karen Schaeffer," Alex said quickly. "I remember you from back when I was still at Sudbury." Alex had the gift of never forgetting a name, a talent that had once made him consider a career in politics. "You graduated in 2002."

"That's right," Karen said, grinning. She poured an amber-colored liquid from her cocktail shaker into Alex's glass.

"This is Hyman Clark." Alex placed his hand lightly on Hyman's shoulder. "He's the principal over at Sudbury. Come fall, though, he'll be my right-hand man." Hyman bobbed his head, trying to suppress a smile. "No need to be shy," Alex encouraged. "You deserve the promotion. You shouldn't be embarrassed to enjoy it."

Mose didn't like Hyman. Or so Ellen said, though she never said why. It was true he wasn't exactly a fun guy, his stiff manner all the more apparent in the bar, where formality was a liability rather than an asset. But otherwise, as far as Alex could tell, Hyman had done well. In meetings, he never offered opinions. The worst you could accuse him of was being a toady, reliably seconding Alex on all issues—not exactly a flaw that Alex *minded*. Plus, the man was diligent. He got things done.

Karen didn't respond to Alex's information about Hyman. Instead, she raised her eyebrows and said, as if she were a dessert that no one could refuse, "Karen Schaeffer, and all grown up."

Alex winced as she moved down the bar to take another customer's order. "What a world," he whispered to Hyman. Even if he didn't love Ellen, Karen's aggressive manner would put him off.

"Right," Hyman said.

"Wish you were already on board," Alex confided. "Shardon. Poor bastard."

"Sorry?"

"Shardon. Poor guy. And his wife . . ."

"Oh, yes, yes. You've got a point there," Hyman said, though something about his manner made Alex think Hyman had no idea what he was talking about. "So what I'm suggesting is that we address some of the kinks in the system. Use the merit raises a bit more to suggest what we're hoping for. It'll be a way to protect ourselves . . . and build a stronger community. If you see what I'm saying."

"You know me," Alex fingered the top of his glass. "I don't like to micromanage. If there are personnel issues to deal with, go ahead and deal with them."

"Well, since you say that, another option would be to consider measures against those who are seriously resistant to attending the workshops. We have to consider the underlying issue here: that there are people who are playing by rules that are not the school system's rules. They're playing according to an independent system. But it's not as if it is OK to create one's own laws and ignore the laws of . . ."

The land. Alex thought he might say. *The laws of the land,* as if the school were a kingdom and Alex its benevolent monarch.

Hyman pressed his fist to the center of his chest, as if to suppress a belch. "Now," he went on, "I did make a few calls." Hyman reached down for his briefcase. "Technically, under new state rules, you can fire even those tenured into the system, if they have three worrisome merit reviews—that'd be three years without a merit raise. If you sign this"— Hyman pulled out a sheet of paper—"it makes it all legal, and really rewards those who can honor what we're doing, while only punishing those who don't, if they prove recalcitrant for three years. In looking at the history of the merit raises . . ."

Earlier in the year, Alex's office had circulated a study of merit raises to all the principals. Hyman placed his paper on the bar, put his palm firmly over it: ". . . you're in no danger of unfairly firing someone. No one's had that kind of consistently bad record, since that pervert gym teacher Jason Beauvtos, and you can see that you might have even used this system I'm proposing to get him out of the schools before things blew up."

"OK," Alex said, checking his watch. What a relief to have Hyman already thinking like an assistant superintendent.

Hyman passed over the document, and Alex signed.

"*I* think that's Doug," Ellen said, touching her fingertips to her left earlobe.

Outside, trees cracked in the cold, and wind sifted snow into the once well-plowed driveway. Alex hadn't heard a thing, so he went to the window and looked toward the drive. "Sure enough," he said, seeing the lights of Valerie's Subaru. He stepped outside. "Good evening," he called gaily down the hill as Doug stepped out of the car and made for the flight of wooden stairs that led to the living room's porch. "Mose just got here. Careful on the steps." And then in a louder voice to Valerie, who was pulling out the drive, "Thank you, thank you *so* much!" Overwork made Alex ill-focused and friendly, as if his lapses, whatever they might prove to be, could be excused by broad good humor. But then Valerie *had* been nice to ferry Doug out, all this way. Normally, it was understood that Alex would do the driving back and forth to Ridgeway.

"Jesus, it's cold." Alex hugged himself. The stars were bright, almost painfully clear, so they seemed not to be objects but holes in the dark fabric of the sky.

"Yeah," Doug said as he climbed the stairs. "They've got these new things for that. All the kids are wearing them. They're called *coats*."

"Ah-ha, *coats*, sounds very interesting." Doug ducked around Alex's attempt at a hug hello. "I'll have to look into this matter."

Doug stomped his boots on the porch, then loped past his father, nodding at Ellen, who was washing greens in the kitchen. Usually, Alex asked Doug to take off his boots; there was the plywood—overlaid with flattened cardboard boxes and a large area rug—to keep clean. Alex was aiming to lay the pine floor tomorrow, but he held his tongue, not wanting to get off to a bad start. Doug collapsed in a living room chair—item #XOP3 from Crate and Barrel—and offered a grunt of a hello to Mose, who was also sitting in #XOP3, a comfy armchair with a relaxed pillow and hidden swivel base. It was hard not to think of everything he owned in terms of catalog copy.

Doug dropped his blue knapsack to the floor. He rummaged in its interior, pulled out a book and then, as if he were entirely alone, began to read.

"Nice fire," Mose said of the blaze in the fireplace.

"Yeah," Doug said, lifting his head only slightly. "I guess."

When Doug was small, he always rushed to Valerie's defense. "Leave Mommy alone," he'd cry from the playroom, when he heard Alex and Valerie talking heatedly. They needn't be arguing. They could be debating some point of news, and Doug would read the pitch of their voices ominously. When they *were* actually arguing, both Valerie and Alex flushed at Doug's reprimands. They *should* stop fighting, if only for their son's sake. Instead, Valerie would hiss, "Even *he* knows you're being a jackass." And Alex would say, "You're such a crazy, angry bitch." At which she usually threatened to throw a dictionary at him. Their marriage was more than the sum of the low points, and yet it was the low points Alex thought of now, Doug's demeanor being so clearly that of the injured party.

At least he didn't turn on the TV.

"Hello," Ellen called from the kitchen, holding up her damp hands, as if this explained why she wasn't coming closer. Doug had yet to spend any real time with her, largely because Alex wanted to keep the issue of the divorce and Ellen separate. They *were* separate.

"That's my dad," Ellen said, pointing with a carrot.

"Call me Mose."

"All right," Doug said but didn't put his book down.

"Doug!" Alex said, still standing by the door, disappointedly surveying the scene. "For Christ's sake." He pantomimed the closing of a book. Not a suggestion, but an order. One that Doug ignored.

"Your style with him is too *managerial*," Valerie once said. "You need to have a *relational* manner to make him behave." In other words: "You act too much like a man around him. You should act like a woman." Apparently, the first requirement for parenthood was self-castration.

Mose wasn't deterred by Doug's manner, though. He crossed the room to lower himself onto the edge of the fireplace's enormous stone base. He'd aged a lot since Alex hired him twelve years ago, his gait uneasy even though he had only the rug to traverse. Peering toward Doug, Mose said, "What you reading?"

Doug held up the cover of his comic book. Alex flushed in embarrassment. Doug normally read real books.

"*Contract with God,*" Mose said now, bobbing his head at Doug's title. "Serious reading."

"You know it?" Doug said.

Alex joined Ellen in the kitchen, whispered, "Sorry."

"Mose'll make it work out," Ellen said. "You'll see."

"I *do* know it. That's Will Eisner's famous book. *This,*" Mose called over to Ellen and Alex, "is considered the first graphic novel." He turned back to Doug to say, "I always thought those books had a lot to tell me about my parents. Eisner, I mean, but also Superman, Batman and Robin. The Joker."

Doug rested his book on his thigh, said, "Were your parents superheroes?"

Mose laughed. "*That* would have been something, but no. You know all those old cartoonists—not just Eisner with the graphic novels—were Jewish. As I am." Mose cleared his throat and sniffed. He seemed to have a constant low level of congestion, whether he had a cold or not. "But you wouldn't really have known that my folks were Jewish from the way they acted. I mean the name Sheinbaum was an obvious clue, but otherwise they were pretty focused on getting a toehold." There was something intimate in the way Mose leaned forward to relate this, as if he'd already decided Doug would understand and enjoy his words. "My dad made flags—he was quite the patriot—but he died young, and then it was just my mom and my brother. She was a singer."

"Really?"

"A jazz singer."

"You're kidding," Doug said, livening considerably. "*I've* got a jazz band."

"That's something I'd like to hear sometime."

Doug rearranged himself in his chair, letting his book fall into his seat cushion. "Yeah, you can come to one of our gigs." Alex tried to discern irony in his son's voice, but it wasn't there. Doug had never invited Alex or Valerie to hear him play.

"I'll do that." Mose reached around to feel his lower back. "That's toasty enough," he said and stood for his original seat, the dorsal fin of his spine painfully apparent through his thin dress shirt.

"But I still don't get what you mean about your parents and the comics."

"Well, all those early comics, you know. The nerdy Jewish boy—that would be Clark Kent—assimilates and becomes a blond and powerful WASP. Now it seems self-denying, but for first-generation Jews in fascist times, there was real power in choosing to be the muscleman and not the wimp on the beach. You know, Hitler banned Superman from Europe, because he thought he was Jewish. And maybe he was. Did you know that Superman's baby name was Kal-El? That's Hebrew for "All that is God.""

"Pretty interesting."

Alex didn't remember Doug ever having a fondness for superheroes. As a boy, Doug's thing had been firemen and construction workers. Later, he loved building. He had a bedroom poster of vehicles made of aluminum cans, another of cars made to look like something else, Doug's favorite being a car that looked like a giant hamburger. These days, Doug was more of a minimalist. His walls were bare, though above his computer, he'd taped a quote from a book he surely hadn't read, Iris Murdoch's *The Bell:* "When something's fantastic enough and marvelous enough, it can't be in bad taste."

"And you have to remember," Mose went on, "that when Superman is a baby, he is cast off the planet Krypton, just like Moses into the bulrushes. And then Superman is found and raised by others, just like Moses. For years, I never got why my parents were so determinedly un-Jewish, and the comics explained a lot. What their anxieties were. Their fantasies."

You could see why Mose was such a popular teacher. He didn't condescend. His interest in Doug's book seemed pure. He managed to relate *at* Doug's level without coming *down* to his level, without meeting Doug's initial sarcasm with the sort of humor that (when Alex attempted it) always fell flat.

"There's a quote from Jules Feiffer. I hope I can remember it. Something about how the comics were the Jewish boy's American dream. Oh, I know." Mose slapped his thigh then declared, "'It wasn't Krypton that Superman came from, it was the planet Minsk.'"

"That's great," Doug said, genuinely appreciative. He was quiet for a moment, then said, "I used to wish I was Jewish. Sometimes I still do."

"When did you wish you were Jewish?" Alex asked, as he cracked ice for water glasses, but there must have been too much challenge in his voice, for Doug ignored him entirely.

"Well, you're a student," Mose said, waving at Doug's book. "I can see that. You've got that love of learning. Maybe that's why the idea of being Jewish appealed."

Doug nodded his head, as if perfectly willing to admit he was a scholar. Or that all Jews loved to learn. But then he smiled slyly and said, "So . . . wait. How is the Joker Jewish?"

"I don't know that he's Jewish per se, but he is a Goliath, of sorts, an adequate foe for the skills of Batman, who is David. If you think about it, the Joker isn't a dumb villain. He's a smart one. That's what makes him special. Of course, the only superhero who actually 'came out' as a Jew was The Thing. He doesn't much like going to *shul* though, or so I hear."

Ellen brought Mose a scotch, Doug a Coke. Alex came in with glasses of wine, and the two of them settled into the living room.

"Nice place," Mose said to Alex.

"Still a lot of work to do," Alex admitted.

"Here we go," Doug said, rolling his eyes. He arranged an invisible smoking jacket, folded one hand over the other, and said, from one side of his mouth, as if the other were busy with a pipe, "The country manse is an ooonnn-going project."

"I am," Alex turned to Mose to explain, "the stupidest person in the world. And Doug feels I need to be reminded of this on a daily basis."

"Did you see?" Doug mock-enthused, mimicking the presumably windbag enthusiasm of his old man. "There's an unfinished basement that's going to be an apartment for Doug!"

"Well, there is," Alex said earnestly, "but that's down the line." Now, the basement was filled with a shop's worth of (rented) power tools.

"I can have the walls painted"—Doug paused to suggest he was quoting his father—"any color I want!"

"Doug," Alex turned to face his son directly. "Cut it out. Ellen and I have a serious announcement, and I want you to behave yourself when I tell." No one said anything, and though the moment clearly was not right, Alex stumbled on. "Mose and Doug, we want you to know that Ellen is moving in with me. But, Doug, that won't change anything between us. I'll still see you as often as I do now, and Ellen really wants you to know that she doesn't imagine stepping in as a mother or anything, she just wants to be your friend."

"Oh, man, you guys," Doug said, still in a falsely excited voice, so Alex couldn't guess what he really thought. "This is so cool! You'll be shacking up and all, which is just so, you know, hip and nineties, or sort of groovy and sixties, or sort of who-gives-a-shit and twenty-first-century."

"Douglas!" Alex cried.

Doug clapped his hands together, leaned forward to Mose to say, "I hope that doesn't upset you. Being of an older generation. I mean, how do you feel about these two living," he lowered his voice for a pretend-whisper, "in sin." His voice veered upward as he spoke. An unexpected squeak. Something true—sorrow? fear?—edging through. He cleared his throat and said, flatly, "No, really, best to you."

"Congratulations," Mose said and raised his glass. "That is what I am supposed to say, no?" He turned and smiled at Doug, almost conspiratorially. Alex had been preparing, all day, for Mose's polite dismay, had even rehearsed a little speech about his feelings for Ellen and how he planned to take care of her. "*L'chaim.* It may not be how people did things in my day, but still you have our blessings." Alex tried to meet Ellen's eyes. Something in the tilt of her chin made him realize she'd already told Mose. A small—her first—betrayal.

Doug raised his Coke. "Down the hatch," he said and guzzled the glass. "Woaah," he added, shaking his head, his hair with its ludicrous Nazarene locks dancing about his shoulders. "This is real strong stuff." He burped extravagantly. "Could I have another?" he turned to Ellen, extending his glass. "A double."

"Knock it off," Alex said, even as Ellen rose to fetch him more soda.

"Oh, it's OK," Ellen said brightly, happy enough to refill his glass. "It's gotta be disconcerting."

"Yeah," Doug breathed, his voice serious. "Though not as disconcerting as The Thing getting circumcised."

"One shudders to think," Mose agreed.

"Dinner," Ellen said, "is just about ready."

"*I* guess," Alex said, later in the evening, when both Doug and Mose were gone, and Ellen was leisurely drying dishes and handing them to Alex to put away, "that that went as well as could be expected. Mose was a help, talking to Doug and all."

"What else would he do, dribble him around the living room like a basketball?"

"Oh, if only he had! Doug isn't usually that obnoxious. But, no, really, all the stuff about the cartoons. That kind of helped lighten things."

During dinner, Doug had told Mose about an episode of *The Simpsons*, in which the Simpson children try to reunite Krusty the Clown (a.k.a. Herschel Krustofsky) with his rabbi-father. Mose had laughed appreciatively at the plot line, and Doug expressed amazement that Mose had never seen the cartoon series, though when Mose confessed to not owning a TV, Doug nodded his head sagely and said, "I admire that." Finally Mose had offered to drive Doug back to Valerie's, and the two departed Ridgeway as if they were longtime chums ready for a roadtrip.

"I don't think he cares for me," Ellen said now. "But he obviously likes his new . . . what is Mose to him? An unofficial step-grandfather?"

"What do you think they're talking about?" On the drive home, he meant.

"That's just what I've been wondering! I've heard Mose's Jews-and-Superheroes speech before. He has these set pieces, you know."

"Well, they sound pretty good the first time around."

"Less so the tenth time, trust me. It used to drive Barbara crazy." She yawned. "I didn't guess they'd stay so late."

"They don't approve of us," Alex said, though the fact was so obvious it hardly needed stating. "Does that matter?"

"I . . . " Ellen seemed alarmed that he'd even asked the question. "I thought it wasn't supposed to. I mean, that's the idea, right?"

It was only in the morning, as he was readying himself to work, that it occurred to him to wonder what she meant by "the idea." The idea of *what* exactly? Them? Inappropriate love? But there wasn't really time to dwell on this. Ellen had stayed the night but already left for her apartment, so Alex could focus on the house. He really needed to kick things into high gear. It was one thing to live alone in an unfinished house, quite another to have Ellen there with him. In this, Alex knew, he shared an Old World attribute with Mose: he wanted to take care of Ellen. He believed she was his responsibility. He could ask himself to rough it with the bachelor accoutrements of the Ridgeway house. But he couldn't ask her, though Ellen—as the younger party and with a back undamaged by a childhood fall from a horse—was better suited for camping, indoor and out.

So, to work! He was down to the final steps, having completed the rough plumbing and electric, the cabinets, lighting and bathroom fixtures. Now there was the floor to lay. Tile for the foyer and bathroom; pine everywhere else, even though he knew all the objections to using soft wood. Drop a can on the kitchen floor, and it'd get dinged. (In a country house, though, weren't dings part of the point?) After the floors, he'd be through—save for paint and trim work. As for finishing the basement, he could do that next summer, when he didn't have so many work worries. Already Alex could picture friends wandering through the Ridgeway rooms, saying, over and over, "Wow. You did this yourself?"

And he'd say—modestly, he hoped—"Oh, no. I had some help."

It was more than just some help, though. It was Howard Williams, an energetic young carpenter, who worked with Alex on weekends. For Christmas break, they'd committed to a work binge. Alex even begged off on the annual Iowa Christmas with his folks, claiming he was getting together with Ellen's family. A lie, but one that would serve, giving him extra days to work. It was just as well. He always found Christmas at the farm oppressive—the front room filling up with pies, a ham, the turkey; the men out working ("Those cows don't know it's Christmas") and the women waiting with increasing irritation for their return. Mom still went to church, but otherwise the day consisted of a cranky anticipation for something that when it came always disappointed. The presents were mindless and from Wal-Mart. Valerie and he didn't exchange gifts in his family's presence. Their choices for each other—a bird feeder, an antique toolbox, a high-end bottle of bourbon—or for Doug—books, jazz CDs, a ticket for a Jerry Seinfeld show in Chicago—wouldn't make sense to his family, any more than their choices did to him. At least, Valerie was pleased with how things had worked out. She'd have Douglas with her instead of (as they'd originally planned) with Alex for the holidays.

*H*oward and Alex put in two long days of work, then on Friday—two days before Christmas—Howard left early. "Got to get the missus," he joked. Or maybe it just sounded like a joke, because what guy in his twenties talked like that? Earlier in the day, Howard had surprised Alex with a six-pack.

"You shouldn't have," Alex said, accepting the gift. He said this friendly enough but really wished Howard hadn't. Alex had nothing for him and, Christ, he knew what sort of budget Howard lived on. If Alex had still been with Valerie, she'd have reminded him to get something for Howard. She might have even bought the present herself.

"See you later," Howard said at 3:30 P.M. and drove off. At 4:00, both Alex and Howard were attending a church fundraiser for Greg Shardon.

Alex turned on the radio. He could work a few minutes more, before he had to clean himself up, too. He wanted to see how far he could get by Sunday night. If he couldn't finish, he couldn't, but he so hoped to have the floor, at least, laid for Ellen. He opened a beer. Next Monday and Tuesday, he'd cut the upstairs walls. He could roll paint on Wednesday. He had every day of the Christmas break planned out like this, unsure if the schedule was a goad to action or a reprimand. He had been ludicrously optimistic about what he could accomplish in a day. Not that this awareness stopped him from trying to keep to schedule. Despite the cold outside, he worked up a sweat, stopping only to drink two bottles of beer as if they were water. No buzz, no urge to pee. Howard had sprung for fancy stuff—Sam Smith Pale Ale, more than he should be spending on Alex, that was for sure—and it seemed a shame to be enjoying it alone.

He checked his watch and saw he was already late for the fundraiser. Not that he actually had to *be* there to make a donation. Alex turned back to his work, opened another beer. If he went to the fundraiser for two hours, how much could he reasonably expect to do before bed? His circular saw cut through a plane of wood, and then another. He loved the smell of the freshly cut wood, the dusting of wood shavings on the floor . . . loved it even though he'd daydreamed all through junior high wood class. He had been the only boy who ended the school year without a lamp that looked like a water pump. Pull the wooden pump handle, the light chain went down, and the lamp clicked on. Well, no wonder he'd flunked shop. As Alex always said when he spoke to educators: You have to make work mean something. No one works when the end seems foolish. It was on this thought that Alex's circular saw stalled in a knot of wood.

"Shit," he said and put a knee to his bench, leaned over to put the weight of his body into his right arm. "All right," Alex murmured. The saw began to move through the knot, then it leapt up and to the left, where it met Alex's left thumb and kept going, through that digit and into his forefinger.

"Oh, Jesus, Jesus," Alex cried, releasing the saw to grab his fingers and press tight, the realization of what had happened coming to him a flash before the pain did. His thumb was somewhere on the floor, and oh, sweet Jesus, blood. So much blood. He could not pass out, he thought, vomit rising in his throat, and his pants awash in something— blood, urine, sweat? The air of the room, its gray and separate particles, welled up and formed a wave, a distinct foamy apostrophe, which pushed him—once, twice, once, twice. The wave seemed determined to ease him onto his back. Was there some movie, some Spanish surrealist movie, in which a wave did just this thing to her male lover? But why would the ocean be here? In the Midwest? And just as he asked himself this, the wave crashed over him, and his thoughts went under.

Chapter Three

DECEMBER 2005

❧

*H*oward came back for his wallet. It wasn't on the dash, where he normally left it, and it couldn't be at home, because he'd paid for the beer this morning—one six-pack for Decker and one to bring to the church fundraiser, only now he wondered if it was OK to have beer in a church. Candy, his girlfriend, would know; she was the one who belonged to the place. Howard was just going because of Candy and because he felt so shitty for Shardon, whom he knew from a camping trip he'd taken as a boy. Shardon had been one of the leaders. He'd taught the kids how to dig up sassafras root for tea; something which the other boys thought was dopey, but which Howard had loved. The drink even tasted good—like root beer and dirt. After that, Shardon kept pointing out other edible parts of the forest—but just to Howard, the other kids could have cared less. Last Howard had seen Shardon–he'd been out walking the dog with Candy, on some new trails she'd found—the guy looked the same as he always did: mushroom cap haircut, full reddish moustache and flannel shirt. A real Smokey the Bear type. Only everything inside had changed, of course.

It'd been a strange day. Bright then foggy, as if even the day was doing fine, but then it remembered about Shardon and got all misty. Candy said people at the church were trying to figure out how to help

Helen, Greg's wife. Some guys had asked Howard to build wheelchair ramps into the house. Pro bono. He wasn't about to say no, though how he was going to go two weeks with no income he didn't know. Candy said that Helen and Greg were going to renew their vows, just after Christmas. It broke Howard's heart to see a couple like that being so afflicted. A happy couple, after all, and there weren't many of those.

Howard turned into the road that led to the Deckers' place. Strange to see Decker's car still parked. Howard would have been at the church with Candy half an hour ago, if not for the wallet. From the far end of the drive, a cloud covered the house so completely that the structure might not have been there. But out back the late-afternoon sun cut low over the field. The dried grass there, poking through the snow, gleamed, as if some on-site troll hadn't bothered to gather his straw before spinning it into gold. There is no God, Howard thought, when he considered Greg and Helen's troubles, the never-ending punishment of the good. But then there was that light, saturating the field, hitting an old shed—the one structure standing on the property when Decker bought the place—and making the building radiant. Truly radiant. OK, Howard conceded. Maybe there was a God. This thought coincided with a loud popping noise. Had the pickup hit something? Howard cut the engine. He could hear Decker's radio blaring through the basement windows. Had he completely lost track of the time? Alex must have turned the thing up loud, so he could hear over the power tools. National Public Radio. Not exactly the sort of thing that got you in the mood for working: Good evening and here are the tragedies of the world. Presented to you by some very intelligent people.

A low hissing sound. But that couldn't be the radio.

"Oh, shit," Howard said, as he dropped down from the pick-up. His tire was flat.

Later, that was part of the story: the flat tire, and how Howard couldn't figure out where Alex's car keys were. Or find Alex's cell phone to call for help. The holder for Howard's spare had long since rotted out of the pick-up's underside, and Howard had pulled the extra tire from the bed of his truck for a load of plywood.

Now, though, Howard entered the house and clambered down the stairs to the ground floor. "Hey, Alex," he shouted before he even reached the basement. He noticed two bottles of Sam Smith lined neatly on the bottom stair, ready for recycling. "Hey, bud," Howard called. "I forgot something." He'd barely finished his sentence when he saw the bright red smear on the sheetrock.

Chapter Four

FEBRUARY 2006

🎕

The Sudbury auditorium was full. All junior and senior classes cancelled for the assembly. On the stage, three men stood below a "Bus of Peace" banner. One—a smiling, broad-chested kid in a sleeveless red t-shirt—looked little older than Doug. Dark-haired and dark-skinned, he seemed to be part Native American, or Mexican, or Filipino. *Something*, at any rate. Or so Doug figured. The kid might have been a football player, if not for the metal peg below his meaty left thigh: his reward (Brandi Carter said) for signing on for two tours in Iraq. Next to him, there was an old hippy type with a frazzly gray beard and a red bandana twisted into a headband and wrapped about his forehead. The third man was Sudbury's principal, Hyman Clark, who kept pressing a fist to his chest as if he had indigestion. The lights dimmed, and the three men stepped to the side of the stage. A screen came down, and two upside-down images flashed from slide projectors at the back of the auditorium. The lights came back up, someone fiddled with the slides, then the lights dimmed again.

"Welcome," the principal finally coughed into a microphone on the side of the stage. "Welcome to a presentation by Bus of Peace, which has been touring the country to talk about non-violent solutions to Mideast conflicts. They'll be presenting a brief slide show and then Sudbury's own Band of Peace will be playing for you."

"The Bus of Peace tour," said a slide on the left-hand screen. On the right was a picture of the colorful bus that Doug had passed on his way into the building.

"You are the only person I know who would skip school to *go* to school," Brandi leaned over to whisper in Doug's ear.

"Got to check out the guy you're seeing," Doug said and nodded toward the stage. Brandi was dating HoHo Coombs, a member of Band of Peace. Doug thought he knew what was out there, music-wise. In town, that is. But he'd never heard of Band of Peace till Brandi said HoHo played with them.

"I dumped HoHo," Brandi said.

"Since when?"

"Since he went around telling everyone I had nice tits."

"Well, let me see," Doug said, pulling back, as if he needed distance to get a really good view of her chest. "They're all right."

"Oh, shut up," Brandi said, slapping his forearm. "They're fabulous, and he's a dickwad."

HoHo *had* been talking about Brandi, but what he'd been saying was that her left breast had a mole with three dark hairs sticking out of it and that you couldn't have her breast in your mouth without one of those dark hairs poking at your face. Kind of like sucking on a witch's warty nose. Or so HoHo said. That was how gossip was in high school. You could learn something this intimate without ever having met the guy who said it.

Up on stage, the hippy guy said he wanted to talk about non-violent solutions to the war in Iraq and the Israeli occupation of Palestine. On the left-hand side of the screen was the word "Peace." On the right, "Truth-telling." The hippy guy was saying that he'd driven a truck with a napalm thrower in Vietnam. Apparently, you had to do something ugly like that to really know about non-violence.

"So HoHo the dickwad is history?"

"That's right," Brandi said.

"And now I have to sit through this stupid assembly?"

"But with such good company," Brandi said, smirking and batting her eyes theatrically.

"I'm in love," Doug declared, the same sense of play in his voice. The truth was he'd always had a thing for Brandi since she'd been, ever so briefly, a neighbor, living with a foster family who turned out to be brain farmers, illegally selling organs for medical research.

"If only I wasn't already spoken for," Brandi said, hands to her chest. Girls who had seen her naked in the gym locker room said Brandi's breasts were just fine, thank you. There was nothing on them, save an occasional red welt, courtesy of HoHo. He'd rather give a breast a hickey than a neck. This detail fascinated Doug: he hadn't known it was possible to do such a thing to a breast, though it struck him as a rather good idea.

On stage, the hippy guy said something about resistance and supporting the oppressed, about what the folks in the audience could do, some practical actions they might take. Like standing between an Israeli tank and a Palestinian child. *That* was non-violent resistance. The man seemed to think the kids in the audience were going to get an opportunity to do something like this in the near future.

"I thought you said the dickwad was history."

"He is."

They were quiet for a while, nominally paying attention to the slide show. Songs of peace were coming; maybe there'd be a question and answer session after. Three kids, each in black boots and a faux leather jacket, mounted the stage.

"The asshole on the right—the one with the broken tooth—is HoHo," Brandi said. Doug had been imagining someone very handsome, but HoHo had a distinctly Cro-Magnon look: deep-set eyes and a protruding jaw, the effect of which HoHo aggravated by shaving his head, so now his entire skull had a five o'clock shadow.

"He looks like a thug," Doug said. HoHo removed his jacket, and his muscles bulged out of his shirtsleeves. School, it seemed, was just an interruption from a weight room somewhere. His snaggletoothed smile—you could see the broken tooth, even from out here in the audience—made him look demented.

"He *is* a thug," Brandi said. "I don't know why I thought he'd be cool to hang out with. He hates everybody. Just because his parents checked out on him. My parents checked out on me, and I'm still a sweetheart." Again the batting eyes. Brandi *had* been through a lot, but, as she always reminded Doug, "Your dad fixed things all up for me." Now, she lived with a Catholic family, over on the east side of town.

"Soooo," Brandi continued, "*that's* why I dumped him for Sam Meyers."

"You're seeing Sam Meyers!"

"What's so strange about that? I'm coming up in the world."

Indeed. Sam went to West High with Doug. Actually, Sam was the reason that Doug had told Mose Sheinbaum, just the other night, that he'd always wanted to *be* Jewish. What he'd meant is that he'd always wanted to be Sam Meyers.

Doug had studied Meyers a lot, trying to figure out what, what exactly, made him so compelling. He wasn't your typical popular kid, what with his spaced-out air. He wandered around as if he'd just misplaced something but couldn't even remember what it was that he'd misplaced. And though he was handsome—wavy, dark brown hair; boyish bemused expression—his looks were similarly undefined: he always needed a shave, never brushed his hair. Comical cowlicks stuck out in every direction. His shirt was frequently misbuttoned. A disarray that Doug associated with money. For some reason, the richer you were, the more you could afford not to care about your appearance. Girls were always coming up to Meyers to pat down his hair or to coo, "Saam! Your shirt is inside out!" But for all this Sam was surprisingly disciplined. A star student, he ran track and was on the wrestling team. He was always willing to talk in class, when people were quiet. There was nothing goody-goody about Sam, so he often ended up embarrassing the rest of the class into conversation. "I was thinking . . ." he'd start to say, and Doug sensed he had not a clue *what* he was thinking, but then he'd rattle off something about pear trees and Zora Neale Hurston or Elizabeth the Virgin Queen and how failing to marry, but always having suitors, suited her political purpose, or . . . whatever. He was definitely on the side of women, whenever a debate split on gender lines. In ethics class, they got into everything: abortion, same-sex marriage, the war in Iraq, immigrant rights. In the end, Sam seemed thoughtful and ego-less, which drew people to him all the more. Doug would have liked to *be* him, but the very want disqualified him. Desire being an ego-thing.

"Hey," Brandi insisted again. "What's so strange about that? You think I can't have a smart boyfriend?"

"No," Doug said. "You know I don't think that." On stage, HoHo was strapping a guitar around his torso. "What *did* you see in him?" Doug gestured with his chin to the stage.

"Same thing I see in you," Brandi said, deadpan. "Nice ass."

"Can we have questions?" an aggrieved voice called from one of the rows in front of Doug and Brandi. Then Mose Sheinbaum pressed himself up from his chair.

"Uh-oh, I better get out of here," Doug whispered. "He knows I don't belong here."

"Mr. Sheinbaum?" Brandi said, confused. "He's my history teacher. I *love* Mr. Sheinbaum."

"Don't spread it around too much, girl."

"How would you know him?"

"Because of my dad. I don't really want Sheinbaum to see me here. He'll know I'm skipping."

"Your dad! Your dad's so great. He won't mind if you skip."

"Let's just agree that you have really weird ideas about my dad." This was territory they'd covered before. Brandi idol-worshipped Doug's father, and Doug was glad for it, in some ways, but couldn't stand it, in others. He'd have liked to be able to tell Brandi about the way his father had been acting since he'd lost his fingers. He didn't treat it like a terrible accident. He treated it like a goddamn fall from grace, as if shy all of one and part of two digits, he'd left the camp of the eternally blessed.

The boy with the metal peg leg stepped forward to the mike, one hip rotating up to compensate for the missing calf. "Sure," he said affably. "We can take questions."

"I'm concerned about some of the language you're using and your notions of truth-telling. You talk about the Israelis and"—here, Mose stopped to hook the air with quotation marks—"the 'ethnic cleansing' of the Palestinians. That entirely and dangerously misrepresents what is happening in Israel now and what happened in 1948. It ignores *why* the Israelis came to Zion in the first place. It ignores the Balfour Declaration and the U.N.'s role in the establishment of Israel, the reason that Israel was established—which indeed was to provide a homeland for Holocaust victims, for Jews everywhere who were oppressed. Most of all, it ignores the Palestinians' failure to show the Israelis that they are able or even willing to be coexist peacefully."

"The thing is," said the hippy-looking guy, "the Jews took the land from the Palestinians. The Balfour Declaration would be all well and good if the people who lived on the land signed it, but they didn't. If you want to talk about a holocaust, why don't you talk about what it meant to force all those people out of their homes?"

Mose started to sputter, "That is just about the most offensive—"

"Hey," said the boy with the peg leg, in a let's-be-nice voice, "we're all about peace. I think we can agree on that. We all want peace. You don't want your children to look like me"—he looked down at his damaged leg—"because of a government lie. And we don't want people dying for no reason. Every day you look at the papers, and it is just death, death and more death."

"He's right," a male voice called out, and the mood in the auditorium changed—from silence to an uneasy murmur of expectancy.

"And," said the hippy, "the papers don't even tell the whole story. That's why *we* are about truth-telling, because you can't solve a problem if you don't know what the real problem is. The Zionist media is hiding—"

"Excuse me," Mose tried to interrupt. "Excuse me." When the hippy wouldn't acknowledge him, Mose turned to the students in the auditorium. He seemed far more hunched than Doug remembered him from their dinner together. "That is a classic bit of anti-Semitic rhetoric, kids. Listen to what this man is *really* saying."

"Actually, I'm speaking the very truth that people try to repress by calling it anti-Semitism—"

"OK. I'll see you," Doug squeezed Brandi's forearm.

"You're going to miss the Band of Peace."

"Thank God," Doug said, looking briefly heavenward, "for small miracles. Not that I'm not curious to see what makes HoHo's ass so nice."

"Shut up," Brandi said lovingly as Doug scooted out the aisle.

As he pushed through the auditorium door, the hippy man said, "No one is guilty. But if no one is guilty, how do all these bad things keep on happening?"

Weren't you, Doug thought, as the auditorium doors clanged shut behind him, *the guy with the napalm? Someone* is *guilty. And it's you.*

134

Chapter Five

MARCH 2006

❦

*M*ose frowned at his menu. "What did you say this was again?"

A waitress with a nose stud stood over them.

"It's Nepali and Tibetan," Ellen said. "You'll like it. You like chicken tandoori."

"Where's that?" he said, still scanning the menu.

"Well, it's *like* that. Only they don't have that. Try this . . ." She pointed to a stew with potatoes and chickpeas.

"That's what'll I have then," Mose said, smiling up at the waitress.

"So," Ellen said when she was gone. "How's things?"

Mose seesawed his wrist. He wasn't the type to ever *say* things were bad or to admit that he had problems. Or he wasn't the type to say such things to her. He saved his confidences—what confidences he had—for other grown men. Over the years, Barbara and Ellen had bullied Mose out of many of his retrograde views—that homosexuality was a disease, that a stay-at-home dad was just some fellow who'd managed to give unemployment a positive spin—but they'd never convinced him to abandon his trust in male authority. Plato's Republic had philosopher *kings*, not philosopher queens, certainly no philosopher princes or princesses. In the end, when you needed help, you turned to a mature man for insight.

"Work's making me a little upset."

"Really?" This was unexpected. There were times, over the years, that Ellen had thought that work went *too* well for Mose, that his success *there*—he was so often voted teacher of the year by the graduating students or recognized formally by his colleagues—made him overly persuaded of the rightness of his opinions.

"Come on, Mose," Barbara had once said, in a playful mood, when she was trying to convince him of something. Perhaps that homosexuality didn't necessarily imply the end of the planet, the non-reproduction of the species. ("And I suppose you and Rachel only had sex when you felt like having a child!" Barbara might have said. They could say that sort of thing in front of each other. Mose liked a good argument, and he didn't pretend to be a Puritan. Asceticism was for the crazy goys.) But, no, it would have been something more minor, if Barbara was trying to persuade him merely by cajoling. It would have been like today, a new restaurant he didn't want to try because the cuisine (Afghan? Vietnamese?) was unfamiliar. "Come on, Mose," Barbara had repeated. "Be like Gumby! Flexible!"

Mose had stared at Barbara, his hard you-are-an-idiot stare, though if either girl called him on it, he'd deny there was anything dismissive in the set of his face.

"You know Gumby," Ellen had tried to explain. "The toy?" But there was no point in this. Mose was a lot of things, but he wasn't interested in contemporary pop culture. And he wasn't flexible.

Now Mose said, "I'm just very disturbed by the principal. At first, I thought it was just a bad feeling the man had about me. Now, I'm thinking . . . well, I'm thinking he's an anti-Semite."

"Oh, my God! *He* sent you that envelope?"

"No, no. I still don't know who did that."

The waitress arrived with their meals. They were eating lunch quite late—after school—and there was no one in the restaurant, save the waitress and a man folding napkins into little yellow fans for dinner.

"Mose, I hope that envelope isn't going to make you start imagining—"

Mose held up his hand to stop her.

Ellen *grrr*-ed as if angry but then smiled. She didn't want things to get tense. Still, the ongoing issue of her cousin's persecution complex. It was why it made her so crazy, long ago, when he accused her of thinking of herself as a victim. *He* was the one who thought of himself as a victim—a victim of history. Good for the Jews, bad for the Jews, please. In her entire life, no one had ever made an issue of Ellen's religion. Alex wasn't Jewish, and they had never broached the subject, even now that Ellen had officially moved in with him. "That envelope was weird, I know that, but I don't think people care whether you are Jewish or not. Not in this day and age. No one has ever—and I do mean ever—made an issue of *my* being a Jew."

"You don't look like a Jew," Mose said. "You're as Jewish as a cannoli, so you don't know what it is like for the Jews."

"That's not fair," Ellen said. She attended synagogue a few times a year and accompanied Mose to Barbara's Maine home where, for the last several years anyway, they had Passover. At Chanukah, Ellen dutifully bought gifts and rolled out a batch of sugar-less sugar cookies in the shape of dreidls. It wasn't much, but it wasn't nothing.

"Last week, Hyman Clark arranged an anti-Semitic diatribe, masked as a peace demonstration, at Sudbury. It was outlandish." Mose told her about the event, ending by describing the Band of Peace, three students banging on guitars and shouting, "Peace, now! Peace, now!"

"Actually," Mose said, sipping some water, before he concluded his story, "only two of the students had guitars. The third played a kazoo."

Ellen snort-laughed. "Well, that sounds idiotic. The anti-Semitism of the left. If you're going to see it anywhere, I guess it would be here in Madison. People fall into easy language about the Palestinians as if they are all little Davids to the Israeli Goliaths."

"Thank you," Mose said, "for that helpful explanation."

"I just mean it doesn't mean Hyman is an anti-Semite. He probably just wanted to present all sides of the issue."

"Excuse me. If you are an educator, and someone makes a blatantly anti-Semitic remark at a public assembly, and you don't step in to address or challenge that remark . . . and you are charged—*charged*, remember!—with the education of our youth, then what do you call your behavior?"

"I'm just saying it's not like he's a Henry Ford who—"

"Hell-lo," Mose crooned and leaned across the table to knock gently on Ellen's head. "Is there anybody in there? This man has been harassing me. He purposely gives me the worst prep periods. He complains about my class, about my attendance at faculty meetings, about . . . do you remember the Hanson money?"

"Well, sure, of course." Kate Hanson had been at Sudbury, years ago. She'd died young, *very* young, and her husband set up a fund in Kate's name. ("I didn't know," Kate had apparently once confessed to her husband, "that I was smart until I met Mose.") Mose could use the money however he wanted. He'd bought tape recorders for his students, then saved the rest for an annual class trip to Chicago.

"OK, so the Hanson fund. Let me tell you about that fund." Mose leaned back in his booth, his getting-ready-to-lecture posture. "I'm submitting my bills to the office like I do every year, assuming everything is OK. But I start getting calls—the bus company, the audio store. No bills have been paid. So I resubmit. A month or so later, more calls. I ring over to payroll, and they say the funds are gone.

"'No,' I explain, 'it's a non-revocable trust. Set up by the widower.'

"And they say that's not what they mean. What they mean is that Hyman Clark says it's quite clear—it's 'on the books'—that you can't give money to an individual teacher or project, a donation goes to the whole school. If I want, they say, I can apply for a grant to get my bills paid. In the meantime, I have to pay the bills myself!"

"That's crazy."

"That's the sort of man I'm working for! He'd steal from a dead girl. And what for? *Bubkes!* One thousand dollars doesn't mean anything to him. It does to me, though, and he knows that. He's determined to get me."

But not because you're Jewish. Ellen wanted to interrupt Mose to say. But then why did she care *what* motivated Hyman's behavior? "So what did you do?"

"I called Kate's husband, let him know what was going on. He said he'd pull all the money, put it in a fund outside of the school if it came down to it. Wire it into my own goddamn back account, if it came down to it. And when Hyman hears this, he sends off an e-mail. 'So sorry, but Mose Sheinbaum must have misunderstood. No one was planning to redirect those funds. Of course, the money is still intact for Mose's class.' A lie. An outright lie!

"And it's not just me. He wants to get Goldstein, too. The new math teacher. Cancelled the holiday party because of me and Gold-stein. And your . . . your *boyfriend* promoted this guy to assistant super-intendent."

"So that's good, isn't it? He'll be out of your hair."

"Oh, good Lord, you are missing the point." He stopped, then said, "Honey . . . you sure you want to be with this man?"

"Mose," Ellen said firmly, her voice a reprimand. She knew how he felt, but this was the first time he'd given full voice to his objection. "Yes, I'm sure."

"And live out there in the woods?"

The woods, as if the Ridgeway house was not just a place in the coun-try, but a tented outpost in the wilderness or a fairy tale cottage, hidden beneath predatory trees, their limbs grasping, their bark patterned in swirls that looked suspiciously like gaping mouths.

"I don't know. Next year with this Hyman Clark bending Alex's ear. And then . . . watch out. Hyman could go after all the Jews in the dis-trict. The whole school system will fall apart."

Ellen nodded, less in agreement than in acknowledgment that there *were* many Jews in the city's school system, though this was hardly un-usual. Jews often went into education. Mose's own mother, Sarah, used to visit Barbara and Ellen when they still lived in San Francisco. Sarah would pull Barbara and Ellen into her lap—as if they were so many daisies that she'd gathered from the field—and say, "You know the Jews are *so smart*. People of the book. School is *very* important to us." The sisters would smile indulgently. "You don't believe me?" Sarah would say. "It's the truth. Philip Roth? A Jew. Leonard Bernstein? A Jew. Ein-stein, Golda Meyer, Emma Lazarus. Even Woody Allen, who is a bit of a *schmuck*. Geniuses . . . and they're Jewish." She seemed to feel per-sonally responsible for their gifts.

"Listen," Ellen said now. "Even if Hyman Clark *is* an anti-Semite, you know as well as I that he couldn't go after all the Jews in the system. He'd be out of there in a second if he tried that."

"Are you even listening to me? You should ask your paramour what he is going to do to protect the Jews."

"You're talking crazy now, and you know it. Besides, I never mess in Alex's work affairs. It's sort of understood." There *was* a tacit agreement between Alex and Ellen: she was young, so she didn't get "it"—"it" being the vagaries of local politics, or the emotions of a divorced wife, or the sexual designs that other men might have on her.

"Ellen," Mose said. "I will tell you something. I am not happy about your relationship with Alex. Yes, yes, I know it is not my place to say so, and in the end, if you are happy with him, it doesn't matter what I think. I know that, too. Then I start to wonder. Maybe there is a reason for this bond between you. Maybe there's a purpose to it. And the purpose of it is for you to say what must be said. You keep silent now, and you may find yourself unable to talk when you need to."

"When I need to? Hyman might be a creep, but"—she swiveled her head, taking in the freshly painted walls and clean lines of the new restaurant—"unless I am mistaken, this isn't the Third Reich."

"On this earth or in the world-to-come, I don't know. You have already been too quiet in this life."

"What're you talking about?"

"Do you think maybe if you'd said something to Alex about his drinking, the man might have all his fingers today?"

Ellen pulled herself back in her chair, rage—that unfamiliar liquid—branching through her circulatory system. "I. . . . I . . . ." The word that came to mind next was "forbid," one of Mose's words. "How dare you?" she said instead, feeling the liquid in her system turn to gas, as if her blood were now carbonated. She never spoke harshly to Mose.

"You know what the Sages say," Mose went on, without any rancor in his voice. " 'He who is merciful towards cruelty will ultimately commit cruelty towards the merciful.' " Then, warmly but firmly: "You think you are a kind and understanding person, but you cannot simply be kind and understanding to everyone and still hope to do good. The world is too full of hatred for that."

"I. . . . I . . . ." She thought to protest, but how could she argue with this? "Listen," she began, "you didn't do anything to aggravate Hyman Clark, did you?"

"What? What aggravate? What would I do?"

"Well," Ellen hesitated. Alex had told her that Mose was one of the few people at Sudbury who hadn't attended the diversity seminars that Hyman Clark had planned for the entire district.

"Yes?" Mose said, waiting.

"Didn't you . . . weren't there these seminars you were supposed to attend? About diversity?"

"I'm a minority myself; I don't need people telling me about how to treat minorities."

"I don't think people think of Jews as a minority anymore. I mean: we're white."

She'd heard Alex say this, actually. Jews and Asians didn't count, when it came to affirmative action decisions, because Jews and Asians had no problem unlocking the door to higher education.

"Excuse me," Mose snapped. "Would you like a census report? Five Jews for every 270 Americans. Two percent of the population. *That's* not a minority?"

"I'm not saying what *I* think. And it's not about numbers, but opportunities, isn't it?"

"And what opportunities did I have?"

He was right. Despite his mother's admiration for the great minds of the Jews, she hadn't been able to put him through college.

"Honestly, Ellen," Mose said, in a more consoling voice. "If you look at who didn't go to those diversity seminars, you'll find that it was the blacks and Asians and I-don't-know-who-all in the system. What could a day's course teach them that life hadn't already made abundantly clear?"

"Yes, I know, you're right. But like this assembly: how could a man who is *for* diversity be against the Jews? And maybe he didn't know what those Bus of Peace people were going to say when they came to the school."

"Well, then he had an obligation to address it afterward, and all he did when I started to ask my questions is cut the whole thing off by introducing the band. As for the rest of the stuff: he is merely tipping his hat to diversity to protect himself. And he knows I know it. And that's just another reason he wants to get me."

"Why are you so sure this is about you?" Ellen knew that if Mose were his own interlocutor, *this* would be the question he'd put to himself. A lesson from adolescence: people don't care about you, because they're not paying any attention to you; they're paying attention to themselves. Or so Mose said, and said repeatedly, but always as if offering the girls a fresh profundity. He meant to be comforting, assuring

141

Ellen and Barbara about some word or action they regretted. Not to worry: narcissism precluded judgment, because it precluded perception. No one gave a shit.

"If it's not about me," Mose declared, "it's about my kind. Same difference. And, Ellen, you are my kind. So it's about you."

Ellen reached across the table to pat Mose's hand, pale and splattered with light age spots. The intimacy felt uncomfortable and not just because they hadn't come to agreement. Touching Mose always felt awkward. "Well, maybe I *will* say something to Alex."

Mose shrugged, as if it was all the same to him, but then he said—as if this were the very reason they'd been discussing Hyman Clark—"I knew you would. You're a good girl."

And she would have said something. She would! She would have dug her cell phone out of her bag and called before her bike ride back to her apartment, but how could she accuse Hyman Clark when she'd never even met him, knew him only as the person who was going to replace Greg Shardon?

Mose wouldn't lie, but that didn't mean his accusations were true. Being Jewish *meant* being under attack. Crack a history book, and there it was. Under attack from the Egyptians, from the Babylonians, from the Syrians, from the Romans, from the Spanish. Eventually the Germans. And the Arabs. The Palestinians. It wasn't made up, the sense of threat, but that didn't mean harm was imminent.

Ellen had heard people say rude things about Israel, their disgust with Israeli policies bordering on racism, their sympathies with Palestinian suffering unquestioning. There was a Manichean belief system at the heart of every American's soul. It was the fairy tales, Ellen thought, the very ones she told kids at the daycare. Raised on tales of good and evil, Americans never quite got past the truths of Walt Disney. If you tried to make things more complex for the children, if you said maybe the monster wasn't *all* bad, they panicked. "No," they'd correct. "He was really, *really* bad."

Even Mose, when pushed, reverted to simple dichotomies, when it came to Israel. Once, when Ellen said she'd always been behind partition, that she supported a Palestinian state, Mose had said, "The Palestinians have a state. It's called Syria." And: "You can't be a refugee for decades. Jews didn't stand at the border of Germany for years calling, 'Let us back into our homes!' They picked themselves up. They made lives for themselves elsewhere."

Still Ellen couldn't quite believe that a contemporary high school principal would do something blatantly anti-Semitic, not the very principal who'd been working for diversity in the school system. Of course, a neo-Nazi kid might spraypaint something offensive on a synagogue. You had to go no farther than the back of a city bus to see that Madison had its dark side—homeless kids, addicts and petty criminals, their skin sallow and blue in the bus light, a whole destination-less crowd, trading bursts of outraged feeling or cynical commentary, the bus's exhaust through the window a reverse halo behind them. As for a man of stature, as for unmediated, planned anti-Semitism, Ellen remained unconvinced.

But by the time she got home, she had yet another set of thoughts about the matter. It was Monday, her day off, and she'd planned to spend the afternoon packing belongings for the move to the Ridgeway house. Her problem would be no problem if she simply met Hyman. She could . . . she could ask Alex to invite him to dinner. Alex *needed* to start doing social things again. Only, of course, he'd say no, if she asked directly. He'd have to be convinced.

Ellen found Alex at his office computer, typing with one hand. The other hand was still in its bandage, and he wore his new woeful look: *Little boy lost.* The sad face was what he'd gained, when he'd lost his fingers in the accident.

Last December, Ellen had raced to the emergency room after the phone call from Howard saying Alex had been hurt. There, Alex, edgy with morphine, not really himself, told her that his thumb and part of his second and third fingers were gone, told her this first with irritation as if she had somehow facilitated the loss, later self-pitiably, as if she'd no longer want him, and later still with a grimace, apologies and damp eyes. He couldn't calm down, he'd confessed, that first night, in the emergency room. He should try to sleep, he knew, but he just couldn't . . . calm . . . down. He spat out the words. She told him to try to relax his jaw, to loosen his face. He was all *tight*. "Sometimes, when I feel that way, you know, I'll just try to consciously do this . . . make a space . . ."

She put her hand to her jaw, to indicate how she loosened herself up. He listened, jerked his head toward her, as if he were trying to toss the damn thing off his neck, there being additional parts of himself he'd like to lose before the night was over. But then, he put his finger between his upper and bottom teeth, as if he meant to follow her instructions, to just create a little space between his teeth so as to . . . He yelped. "Jesus." Suddenly there was blood in the corner of his mouth. He abruptly flung his forefinger toward her. He'd bitten straight through his own skin.

"My God, what are you doing?" Ellen cried.

What he was doing, it turned out, was having a massive reaction to the drug that they had injected into his IV, the very drug that was supposed to calm him down.

"Parkinsonian lock," said the doctor who came with instructions to administer Benadryl. This was why Alex couldn't pry his jaw open, even with his own finger. "And have you been jerking your head like this?" The doctor did an imitation of the movement Alex had made earlier.

"He has!" Ellen said.

Tears were still in Alex's eyes. "I thought I was just being a big baby. I've been telling myself to just calm the fuck down. You know, don't make things hard on everyone and then I just see it again. My own fingers flying off my hand and blood everywhere."

The doctor looked down at a clipboard. "Yes, that's right. You might have a little hallucinating, too. Classic," he said. "If you're going to react in the first place. Which most people don't."

"Nice to be special," Alex said, weak-voiced, but clearly trying to win the doctor over. Not that the doctor was going to take the time to be charmed or annoyed. He closed Alex's chart, patted his gurney absentmindedly and walked behind the curtain to Alex's left, saying to the patient there, "Now what's all this?"

"Where I come from," a female voice said with surprising good humor, given that she'd been vomiting or dry heaving since Ellen arrived, "we call it puke."

"That right?" the doctor said, far more engaged than he'd been with Alex, and Ellen thought, *My god. The jackass is flirting with her.*

But then a nurse came in with a needle, and she focused back in on

Alex. The nurse removed the IV from a port on the back of Alex's hand and injected. "You'll feel better in fifteen minutes."

That had been day one of the accident.

Day two, the morning after, as Ellen was running downstairs to grab a coat and some of Alex's things before she headed back to the hospital, she saw blood smeared on the basement wall and splattered in fat circles on the floor. Howard, being a man, hadn't thought to mention that Ellen had some cleaning up to do. Ellen had to put her head between her knees, so as not to be sick.

Now what was it? Day seventy. Something like that. The injury still felt like the main fact of their lives. It made Alex feel closer to Ellen, or so he said. He was less eager to play the part of the all-knowing protector, more willing to let her care for him.

"Honey," Alex said. He had finally looked up to see her at his office door. "What're you doing here?"

Ellen peeled off her coat. Under it, she wore a brown, sleeveless sheath with a hem of pink lace. It was March, far too early for such clothes, but Ellen had put the dress on with pumps and beige stockings—real stockings and garters, purchased (as the dress had been) when Alex had last gone to Chicago. He said she needed more dresses, now that they were officially together, something to wear when they were invited out.

"So to what do I owe this nice surprise?"

Ellen didn't quite know how to answer. "It's so strange to see you here at work," she confessed. She had never visited before. "I hope you don't mind my coming. I needed to ask you for something."

"How could I mind?" He got up to close the door.

"So," she said and lifted herself to sit on top of his desk. She kicked off her shoes. "I was thinking of taking advantage of you."

"Oh," Alex grinned, "I wish you would."

"I know you're busy."

"Not *that* busy," he said and sat down, patted his leg twice, so she'd slide into his lap.

"You look good in the dress," he said and started to pull at the zipper that ran down the back. Before he had the dress off, he popped her bra open. She felt a little thrill at being unbound in his office. (The bras

145

he'd bought, too; far sexier than her old Jockey staples, yellowed under the arms. These were all lacy and low cut, so she was as much out of the bra as in.) He reached under her skirt, and on feeling her garters—it was the first time she'd worn them—said, half-campy, half-sincere, "Oh, my, my. Now, remind me, why haven't I invited you here before?"

"Let's lock the door," she said, standing, feeling both embarrassed and pleased, the power of being able to excite him, of being (as Valerie apparently wasn't) receptive to his touch.

"Smart girl," he said, kissing her on the ear as she rose. There was the audible snap of the bolt. Alex smiled. "I bet they all know what we're doing in here." He cocked his head toward the door, then stepped over.

She flinched. He sounded so ridiculous.

"What's the matter?"

"Nothing." Sometimes it felt like years, rather than months, since she'd lost her virginity. Her unexplainable virginity which she now guessed had to do with that day in Chicago, with the black boys on the street, with that time when the act that was supposed to demonstrate love really demonstrated hate. And she'd run from it. And kept running and running. Or maybe this wasn't true. Maybe this was just the sort of neat explanation she'd seen in books or movies, so she was trying it out on herself.

Ellen pulled back from Alex's arms. She remembered those black boys and their faces clearly. They had just looked like *people*. She couldn't get over it. How could you resist cruelty, when you couldn't even recognize it? Of his grandfather's death in Germany, Mose once said, "He didn't get out, because he couldn't believe it." He'd been a mystic. He believed all people—and things—had a divine spark within them. He believed a famous rabbi could fly from one end of the earth to the other in a single night. He believed that the same rabbi could converse with animals, stones and trees. But that one man could turn another man's skin into a lampshade? That civilized men would come into a house and beat a mother and children and drag the father away? No, that he didn't believe.

"Something *is* wrong," Alex said, clearly concerned. "What is it?"

Ellen shook her head. "I don't think your co-workers are all that interested in what we do." She tugged Alex forward by his belt loop, dropped to her knees and unzipped his fly.

"Now what did you want to ask me?" Alex said, above her, fingers and the cotton of his graying bandage in her hair, purposeful parody of the man undone by desire. "Because you can have anything you want."

"I can?" she said, starting to lick him, trying to get more in the mood. A college friend on how to perform oral sex: "Well, you know, it's sort like an ice cream cone. You do the top; you lick around, and then he asks you to swallow the whole thing in one bite." The description scared Ellen at the time. How gross. She didn't think she'd ever be able to do it, or do it correctly, but then Tamar had popped a lot of popcorn and invited Ellen over for an afternoon of porn movies. "You'll see," she said. "There's nothing to it." And they'd watched a whole slew of things: a college grad on spring break, a teacher advising his dumb female student on how best to get an A, an airhead being serviced by her car mechanic, a businessman walking in on his secretary busily masturbating in the office and instead of chastising her joining the action. It went on and on, and eventually got boring—all the bizarre shaving, all those wet parts meeting wet parts, and everything (breasts, penises, lips) revoltingly engorged. And yet, Ellen always needed to have one of those films—not an image but a bit of narrative—in her head as she made love, as if one of the film's characters could entice Alex, but Ellen Hirschhorn, no. She never could. She never would have anything to do with the whole terrible business.

Before she left, Alex said, "What was it you wanted to ask me?"

"Oh," Ellen began. She'd lost her sense of purpose. The whole idea had been to ask about having Hyman over for dinner, but it would seem too obvious now. Sex as a trade for a dinner party. What had she been thinking? "It's nothing. I'll tell you later at . . ."

"At what?"

"Home. I'll tell you at home."

"I thought you were staying in town tonight." That had been the plan. She was in her final week of living both at Ridgeway and in her eastside apartment.

"Nah," she said. "I'd rather be with you."

But that evening, Ellen still felt shy about her request. Alex and she were lying on the living room floor, thinking about dinner, both too lazy to get up. Alex had stayed late at work, and it was now almost nine.

They'd managed to build a fire in the fireplace but that was all. "Hey," Alex said, reaching into his wine glass with the pinky finger of his good hand, then dotting the red liquid on her lower lip. "You never told me why you came to the office today."

"I think I came for sex."

"No," he said and leaned over, licked the wine off her lower lip. Not something she really liked. "You said you had to ask me for something."

"I did?"

"You know you did." He laughed. "You are the worst liar in the world."

"Oh, yes. No, not *for* something, but *about* something. I was wondering if we could have a dinner party? We could invite Greg's replacement and his wife. Maybe some others."

Ellen could tell he found this strange. Well, it *was* strange. Why would she have to interrupt him at work to ask about having people over for dinner?

"Hyman Clark, you mean?"

"That's the one. And his wife. If he's got a wife."

"Yeah, he does. Martha. I'm not in a party kind of place right now."

"Well, not a *party* party. More like dinner. Sort of a getting-to-know-you thing to make this place"—she looked around the room—"ours. You know, someone from your life, maybe two people who I know."

"Hyman's not exactly someone I'm dying to have over."

Alex didn't say this with much conviction. Ellen knew it was true, but it was also true that Alex would give in to her. "I'm only suggesting him, because there's the . . . I don't know . . . the professional obligation, and I just want it to be someone who is from your life, but not from your and Valerie's life. If that makes sense."

Alex's eyes were closed now, the light from the fire playing over his face. "OK, that's fine with me. If you want to do that."

"Can I invite Tamar?" This asking of permission had its own purpose. If he thought he was making the decisions, the dinner might start to seem more like his own project.

"Hard to imagine Tamar and Hyman Clark at a party."

"I guess." Against Mose's version of Hyman as a controlling, vengeful principal, Ellen had Alex's version of Hyman as a helpmeet and hard worker. He signed his messages, "Smiles, Hyman." Alex felt this demonstrated the man's innocent lovability. Or, perhaps, his malleability.

Ellen thought, but didn't say that the word made Hyman sound stupid—and dangerous. Everyone she knew who used that sign-off had an appalling well of anger behind the antiquated, sugarcoated veneer. So maybe Mose's suspicions were right? In junior high, girls who put smiley faces under their names (or dotted their "i"s with hearts) were invariably full of venom.

"Well, but I've never had Tamar over for a meal, and she *is* my best friend."

"Sure. Invite Tamar."

Ellen leaned over and kissed Alex. "You're good for me," he murmured. He wasn't going to ask any questions about why the matter of a dinner party suddenly felt so urgent. Alex, unlike Mose, let Ellen be.

"And I'll ask her to bring someone. It'll give her an excuse to ask out this guy she's interested in."

If Alex had any further thoughts on the matter, Ellen never found out. He started to snore. The quick way he dropped off always shocked Ellen. She generally took an hour to fall asleep, her thoughts roiling, none of them so interesting but all sufficiently demanding that her body wouldn't abandon them for the night.

In the fireplace, the logs shifted and resettled themselves, as if they, too, were bedding down. Ellen knew she shouldn't wake Alex, though he'd be stiff if he slept out here. She'd be stiff, too, but she couldn't bring herself to sleep in the bedroom alone. It was hard enough, even when she was in the bedroom with Alex.

What had happened to Alex's fingers, no one said. When Ellen changed his bandage, she saw the crusty bloody wounds that resolved, over the weeks, into short scabby thimbles. Two stubs, almost pornographic in their stiff fleshiness. Everyone focused on a different aspect of the accident. How would he type without two fingers, Alex's secretary wanted to know. Doug wondered how his father would handle the deformity. All those stares he might get from strangers. Not that people would *purposely* stare, but Doug often found himself looking at a scarred face or a withered arm, less to gawk than to correct his vision, as if it were his eyes, not the vagaries of the world, that had placed a red raspberry stain on the librarian's cheek or had edited an appendage off the cafeteria worker. Mose worried about pain. And Ellen focused on those phantom fingers, the two digits that someone (probably Howard, maybe an EMT?) had to pick up and . . . and throw in the trash? Bring to the hospital in case someone might find them of use? To Tamar—and Tamar alone—Ellen referred to the Ridgeway place as the House of Two Fingers, as if part of Alex's hand was still there, liable to show itself if Ellen did something foolish—like try to hammer a nail into the wall where the fingers now resided or like try to sleep (without Alex) in a dark room.

Tamar didn't want to invite Robert Porter, her long-time crush, to Ellen's dinner party. Too embarrassed, she said. "I'm old-fashioned that way. I need to know he likes me first. Can I just bring a friend?"

"Of course."

"Just a second," Tamar said. "Call waiting." She blipped off the phone.

Ellen hadn't told Tamar that she was hoping for assistance in determining Hyman Clark's character. Not that Ellen knew how she would do this or how she would gauge Hyman's opinion of Jews. She supposed she could play a little klezmer music, then poke her face into his and say, "What do you think of this?" Or fork some roasted vegetable pasta into her mouth and ask the gathered, "How *about* that Gaza Strip?"

When Tamar came back on the line, she said, "Can I invite Kristen?"

"Kristen! Isn't she the one who used to be a man?"

"That's her."

"You're not inter—"

"Good God, no, I couldn't imagine. But we've gotten to be friends, after all. She's really funny."

"She's the one who flunked client relations, right?"

"Oh, yeah, yeah, but I see now that it was really just her sense of humor. She's great with people. She really is. It just took me a while to get a read on her. She's sort of forthright, I guess you'd say. But she's like a different person since she had her surgery. Just happier all around."

"Well, sure," Ellen said. "Bring whoever you want."

"And let me help. What can I bring?"

"How about . . ." Ellen reviewed the menu she'd been planning. "Oh, I know. It'll be Friday. Bring a challah. We'll light candles."

"Will do," Tamar said. "Maybe I'll even get ambitious and make one."

And there Ellen had it. Her solution to the problem of Hyman Clark. She'd light the Sabbath candles, say the blessings and take, as best she could, her measure of the man.

Chapter Six

APRIL 2006

❦

Martha wouldn't come into the store. A bad sign. She always stopped doing things just before she went off. Alone, Hyman roamed the poorly organized aisles. Back in Nebraska, the used bookstore that Martha and he favored was on the first floor of a neighbor's house. Cats padded over stacks of books. A glass jar—with remnants of a Ragu label—sat on a wobbly table. The honor system. Sometimes a plate of banana bread joined the jar. Or, come Christmas, neatly decorated cookies. But here there was the standard cash register and no food, only a dimly lit space located in a strip mall, bordered by other low-rent businesses: a fabric store, a Laundromat, a cellular phone distributor. Nothing very interesting.

"Do you sell," Hyman finally asked the kid at the register, "puzzles?"

"Puzzles?" the kid looked up, as if stumped. He wore a diaper pin in the lobe of his right ear.

"Like crosswords," Hyman explained. "That kind of thing."

"Oh, yeah. Aisle 6. Left side."

Hyman wanted a book of double acrostics—a bribe, and a test of sorts. *If he got her the book, would she come to the dinner party?* She'd agreed—both to the deal and to the notion that he somehow controlled their money, that she couldn't simply buy herself a puzzle book, if she wanted to. Another bad sign, this idea that Hyman had the power to order her around.

Hyman passed by a musty military history section, then one on the occult. There was no logic to this place. Then he came to it: word games.

Earlier, he'd wanted her to come into the store, but now Hyman was glad Martha wasn't with him, if only for his fear about how the store clerk would read them, as they approached the cash register. They didn't look like each other the way some long-married couples did. He was tall and angular, an Ichabod Crane, he knew, if not for the face, a rough-skinned oval with an unobtrusive nose, weak chin and dark hair fleeing from the white expanse of his forehead. As for Martha: she was short, dumpy by her own account, hair the nondescript brown of overcooked lentils. *Siblings*, the boy at the counter would assume, if Martha were with him. Not man and wife. It didn't matter that in all the important ways—height, shape, color of hair and eyes—they were dissimilar. They shared the look of having never quite arrived in the present century. Or maybe the look of having been left out of the century, as if time were just another dance for which they hadn't been chosen.

*B*ack in the car, Martha scribbled something in her tiny yellow notebook—spiral bound, a dimestore thing, no journal with creamy paper for her. "What are you doing?" Hyman said, as he handed her a plastic bag.

"Puzzle I read about." She held up the small notebook. "See . . ."

There were two columns of words. On the left, she'd printed, in her tight, even hand, "Evil, eval, oval, oral." On the left, "Good, goad, gold, gild, geld."

"You try to make one word go to the other. You pick the same number of letters, of course. And then just go one letter at a time."

"You pick your own words?"

"Mmm-hnn. Opposites."

"But how do you know it will work then? There should be a book, where you only pair words that someone else has successfully switched. Otherwise, how do you know you can get from one to the other?"

Martha ripped the page from her notebook and crumpled it. "I guess you don't."

"Oh, for God's sake, Martha. I only meant . . ."

"Take me home."

"There's the party." He touched the gold buttons of his suit jacket, looked not at Martha, but at a small snag in her tan panty hose.

"I can't do it," she said decisively, though they'd already settled the matter and were on their way.

"But I got you the book." Hyman might have been talking to a recalcitrant teenager. Then: "What will they think if you're not there? You haven't been at any event you've been invited to."

"I really don't give a damn."

Hyman stared at the steering wheel. He fought the urge to hit her, just reach over and smack her face with the back of his hand. Instead, into the car's silence, he said, softly, "We're starting over, honey, remember? We're starting fresh."

"You are," she said in the spiteful voice that she used when most depressed. "Me? I just carry myself wherever I go."

$\mathcal{H}$e took her home, glad he'd started as early as he had. Even with this detour, he would not be late. Martha and he were renting out in the country, such isolation being a bad idea, he knew, but she said she loved the old farmhouse: its wraparound porch and quaint kitchen. It reminded her of home.

"You're sure about this?" Hyman asked, as he pulled into the patch of dirt before their home.

"'Fraid so."

"What will you do?"

"Do?"

"While I'm gone."

"Read, I think." She'd found a copy of Clifton Fadiman's *The Lifetime Reading Plan* in the Nebraska bookstore, and she was making her way through the book's recommendations. This classicism in her . . . if that's what it was . . . had always drawn Hyman to her; she knew the beauty of old things.

Hyman said—one finger held up, his signal that he was launching into their quotation game—"'You are saved, you are saved: what has cast such a shadow upon you?'"

Instead of answering, "Melville. *Benito Cereno*," she said, in the grim, flat voice she used when most unhappy. "Exactly."

"Eval," he said, as she got out of the car.

"What?"

"Does that count? In your game? It's only an abbreviation, after all."

"Oh, goodness Hyman, I don't know." She slammed the car door shut, then waved a conciliatory, apologetic goodbye. Well, that was something, Hyman thought, as he put the car into reverse. So what if Martha and he were habitual receivers of the last portion of cake? So what if no dealer would even toss them cards for the poker game of parenthood? This was a new state, a new life. He had an invitation for dinner at the superintendent's. He'd be the assistant superintendent come June.

Hyman backed his car into the road. Something made him look back toward the house. "Hey, hey," Martha called. She was running down the drive.

Hyman rolled down the car window. "What?"

"I changed my mind. I'll come after all."

He was as surprised by her quick trot toward him as if she were in flight, her arms flapping and her skirt a giant tail feather, pressed back in the breeze.

"I told you," Hyman said, as she sat back into the passenger seat, his voice as triumphant as it ever got. "Things are changing. You and me, we made them change."

APRIL 2006

$\mathcal{F}$rom the start, Ellen had been excited about cooking for Alex. She had a battered copy of *Recipes for a Small Planet*, and from this paperback volume came congealed bowls of adzuki beans and brown rice, salads of black seaweed, which proved entirely resistant to teeth, sweets with the heft and taste of an anvil. There'd been a disturbing vegetable terrine, an unidentifiable jellied substance curdling on its surface, and a peanut butter and tomato soup so vile that Alex had eventually admitted to flushing the leftovers down the toilet.

"Let me cook for *you*," he finally said. "I can cook vegetarian." He made a Japanese soup with udon noodles and vegetables.

"Wow," she said over her first steaming bowl, the smell of garlic and ginger in her nose. "I thought when men cooked it was . . . like . . . hotdogs boiled in beer."

He laughed. "Pretty surprising thought, my dear. Given the century."

"I know."

"Why don't you let me cook for the next stretch?"

She did. He made crab cakes, Greek fish in a packet, pasta with Swiss chard and pine nuts, a frittata with zucchini, mint and dill. The pleasure of pleasing her, he said. Somewhat of a relief that she was one of those vegetarians who ate fish. "You like? You like?" he'd say, as she tasted each dinner. Then add: "I'm becoming a Jewish *bubee*."

"Bub-ee," she said. "Not *boob*-ee."

"I like it, but you know," she eventually admitted. "It embarrasses me. All those things I made for you. I mean, I guess . . . I guess I'm a terrible cook."

"You're pretty bad," Alex said.

But by the time they were living together in the Ridgeway house, things had changed. At first, Alex and Ellen had cooked together. Alex poured them each a glass of wine, and they lazily cut ingredients and talked or listened to NPR. He showed her how to smash garlic with the side of a knife, prep Swiss chard, cook a perfect pot of rice. After the accident, though, Ellen simply replaced Alex in the kitchen. "Stop," she called, one night, as he was holding a yam with the three fingers of his left hand, and trying to cut the rolling tuber with the knife in his right. "Just let me do it. I know you can do it, but I get so scared watching you."

He wanted to yell at her, he told her later—the first time he ever had the urge to do so. Instead, he put the knife down on the counter and walked into the bedroom. She followed, wringing (actually wringing) her hands, and saying, "Sorry, sorry, it's not you, it's me. I know you can do it. You're fine. I know."

This hadn't helped.

Alex kept his hand in a bandage long past the time he needed to, a mummy's hand, a cartoonish mitten. He never looked when Ellen dressed and redressed the wound.

"You know," he said, on the night of their dinner for the Clarks, Tamar and Kristen. "I guess I've been depressed."

"I think I knew that," Ellen said, as she pulled items from a grocery bag. "A lot's been going on." She sensed he felt his luck had turned with the injury, that it wasn't the lost fingers he was grieving as much as the damage to come. Her job, as the younger member of the couple, was cheer: to insist that good things awaited them, no matter what the tenor of her thoughts.

For Alex, the dinner for the Clarks and Tamar was something of a test, a chance to see if he was ready for conviviality, right here, in his incomplete home, where he'd let himself mope for several weeks—over Greg Shardon, over his injury—and where Ellen had tried to gauge his sentiments, going for her long runs while he read or attached himself to the computer for an evening of e-mail.

Ellen began to cut peppers for the salad.

"*Let* me help," Alex said.

"Oh, yes, of course," Ellen said blithely, as if she didn't see how things had changed between them, now that he was asking for her permission to use his own knives.

It was an evening, she knew, not for talk, but for NPR, which they listened to quietly, till first one car and then a second pulled up the drive.

"It's just a dinner party," she said as she went to open the door.

He said, tragically, and she let herself dislike him for the briefest of moments, "I know."

"*H*ere you go." At the side porch doorway, Tamar put a large paper bag in Ellen's arms.

"What is it?"

"Two challahs. I tried to make pumpkin challah, but it didn't turn out very well."

"I remember you," Kristen said from behind Tamar. "I wasn't sure I would, but now that I see you, I remember. You're The Beautiful Girl."

"Thanks. I think."

Ellen didn't understand how she'd failed to notice Kristen's original gender the first time they'd met. She had broad shoulders and big hands. Also an undeniably great figure. Just under six feet tall, she was dressed—as before—in a slim skirt with a tight, pastel-colored blouse.

"The knockers," Kristen said, as if she'd divined Ellen's thoughts. "The surgeon did a little extra work there."

"Well, uh . . . they're nice," Ellen said.

"*Aren't* they?" Kristen said, a just-us-girls whisper to her voice, though Alex and the Clarks were well within the house. "Actually . . ." Kristen's hands moved to her chest. Ellen panicked, as if Kristen was going to unbutton her shirt, flash her breasts at Ellen and say, "Take a look at these," as if that's what women did, when they got together: purchased six-packs of wine coolers and simply opened the double doorway of their blouses and cried, "Hey! What do you think?" But Kristen just flattened her shirt over her chest, so Ellen might have a better sense of her body.

"Well, great," Ellen stuttered. "Come on in."

*Hy*man and his wife were already sitting chastely on the living room sofa. Ellen had imagined Hyman as a large man—with a dark moustache and full head of straight, dark hair, cut awkwardly around a square face. Her secret version of authority, she supposed. But though tall, Hyman was slim and balding, his face a battlefield of old acne scars. "Lovely home, lovely, lovely home," he'd said, when he entered, taking in the high-ceilinged living room with the row of windows overlooking the back meadow. "Dear? Isn't it lovely?" His wife nodded, never offered her name, so Ellen fell to calling her Mrs. Clark. She was much shorter than her husband and slightly pudgy in her tan skirt and thick-soled shoes. With her oak bark–colored hair, chopped roughly at the cheek line, and her blocky, oversized sweater, she might have been one of the unfashionable girls of Ellen's grandmother's youth. There were different ways of being unfashionable now. There were sweat pants. But Mrs. Clark didn't seem to know that. It was as if she'd been sitting in the Nebraska prairie for decades, on a wheat farm maybe, with no car and no TV, no access to the outside world. She seemed almost stunned by her presence at a dinner party.

"No, oh no," Mrs. Clark had said, as if scandalized, to Alex's initial offer of wine. Then she added how maybe she'd try "just a little."

"So," Ellen called, waving Tamar and Kristen into seats in the living room. "Here's my friend Tamar. We go way back. We were in Hebrew School together."

"Pleasure," Hyman said, standing to shake Tamar's hand.

Tamar gave Ellen a knowing bob of her head. Ellen should never have let her know about her agenda for the evening. Subtlety was never Tamar's problem.

"And this is Tamar's friend from work, Kristen."

"Delighted," Kristen said, shaking Hyman's hand, then turning to Mrs. Clark and saying, "And you, you're?"

"Martha," Mrs. Clark said.

"Martha," Kristen winked and sat down next to her, the couch sinking so they were thrown together into a V of cushions. "I would love a chance to cut your hair."

"Oh, it's terrible, I know," Martha said, dispiritedly, putting a hand to her head. "I can't do a thing with it."

"Exactly," said Kristen. "That's why I want to get my magic fingers on it. I could really liven you up." She wiggled her fingers fiendishly. "That's my specialty. The *complete* makeover." She winked at Ellen. Kristen's own hair was down tonight, falling in big S-curls down her back.

Ellen smiled, then made for the kitchen, Tamar following.

"Lord," Ellen said taking the challahs out of the bag. "These are huge."

"Takes a challah to feed a village."

"And two?"

"You're supposed to have two. *You* know that."

"You are?" Ellen so often felt like a stranger to her own religion. She was part of the club, but she didn't know the rules.

"Yeah, can't have only one on the table. Something about generosity."

There was a rule, too, about waste, about not wasting food, but Ellen couldn't remember it, just dreaded the mornings of fattening challah French toast she'd feel obliged to after tonight's dinner.

"I feel so *young*," Tamar whispered. The men were in suits, and she was in her trademark low-slung pants with two sleeveless tank tops—one worn over the other—and both showing off the birds and green vine tattoos curling up her arms.

*B*efore long, Ellen called everyone to the table to light candles. If Hyman Clark felt any discomfort about partaking in a Jewish ritual, he didn't show it. After Ellen struck the match and Tamar chanted the blessings, Martha said, "Oh, the candles are so beautiful," and Hyman chimed in, "Aren't they?" He turned to the gathered and said, "What a lovely, lovely table Ellen has set."

Ellen passed a salad and some bread around the table.

Once she'd finished serving herself, Kristen turned eagerly to Martha and said, "Let's learn a little something about you."

Martha flushed. "Oh, me? There's nothing to learn."

"Au contraire. I know what everyone here does for a living, but you."

Martha looked at the others, then made a high nervous sound, almost a giggle, before balling her hands firmly into her lap and saying with great precision, "Well, I'm *free*lance. I've got a . . . a *health* condition, so I can't be working full-time, you know. But I write crossword puzzles, actually. Though lately . . . well, that's what I do."

"Health condition?" Kristen said leadingly.

But Alex—who was sitting at the other end of the table from Kristen—interrupted to say, "Crossword puzzles. How interesting. How'd you get into *that*?"

"Oh, that goes way back, doesn't it dear?" Hyman's voice suggested it would be best not to explore the matter.

Martha nodded but didn't elaborate.

"And children?" Kristen said. "Do you have any kids? Tamar told me that Ellen has a stepson who is almost as old as she is."

"Hardly," Alex put in.

Tamar said, "No, what I said was—"

"Actually," Ellen interrupted them both, "Alex and I are a couple, but we're not married."

"No, no, I don't have children," Martha said, something complicated in her voice. She seemed simultaneously withholding and encouraging, as if she'd like Kristen to push on—if only so she could stop her with a devastating remark.

Ellen stood to take the fish from the oven. The asparagus was already arranged on a platter. She spooned rice out of the rice cooker and into a bowl, then poured tomato chutney over the fish. "Help me pass all this around?" Ellen looked over to Alex.

"Right," Alex said, almost starting. He was entirely off in his own thoughts, she realized. "Of course." He shook his head, loosing himself from some unhappy daydream. Ellen felt a surge of affection for him. *Poor* thing. Was it wrong to love a man most at his moments of weakness? She did, though she'd never say so to Alex, her first bit of evidence that communication—in love or marriage—wasn't always a virtue.

"Oh," Kristen breathed, "I wish I *could* have some kids. I wish I could have a whole bucket load. But not till I find the right guy, if you know what I mean. Then I'm going to adopt."

"It's expensive. Adopting, you know," Martha said, her voice thinning, the story she wouldn't tell vividly before the gathered as if a television monitor had just descended from the ceiling to broadcast her news.

"Let's not get into that," Hyman said sternly and turned to Alex. "Have you heard . . . Gray Simmons is saying he'll run for school board."

"That right?" Alex said absentmindedly.

For months now, Alex hadn't been focused, the way he normally was, at gatherings. Ellen assumed the vagueness was something he had to work through, that she shouldn't ask him about it, that questions would only make things worse.

"So why didn't you have kids?" Kristen asked Martha. "Didn't want them?"

"No," Martha said. "I *did* want them. I miscarried."

"Hell, everyone miscarries," Kristen said. "Practically everyone I know. One in every three pregnancies, you know."

"Yes," Martha said, "I do know that. I miscarried six times."

"Oh," Kristen said, then turned to Hyman. "No wonder you didn't want to get into it. I'm awfully sorry. That must have been bloody awful." She paused, for a moment, perhaps considering how the out-of-character Briticism might be received. "I guess I mean," she corrected, "that must have been awfully hard."

There was a pause, everyone examining his or her dinner plate with real interest, to give the news its necessary few seconds of silence.

"That's quite something you have on your arms, young lady," Hyman finally said to Tamar.

"Yeah," Tamar said wryly. "I call it my permanent display of a temporary feeling."

"You *do not*!" Kristen said, then addressed Hyman. "She calls that her Museum of Made-Up Birds. This pink bird here"—she touched Tamar's upper arm with her forefinger—"is the Bird of Serious Regret. It has an 'Oh, no! Oh, no!' song. And that green one . . ."

"Don't tell them!" Tamar cried.

"I just want everyone to know what a great imagination you have," Kristen said, giving Tamar what struck Ellen as a hail-fellow-well-met kind of punch.

"Well," Hyman pronounced, the one word conveying his sense that Tamar might have found a better way to use her imagination.

How would Ellen ever move this conversation to something Jewish?

Hyman said something about Gray Simmons, what would happen

if he was elected to the school board, and Alex nodded, saying that Lacy Jagolinzer had been the only candidate to date. There weren't any women on the board, and people wanted a woman. Only she had no experience, and Gray Simmons—a lawyer who'd worked for the Council for Improving Secondary Education—did.

Ellen drifted. The vagaries of local politics bored her. But Tamar, bless her, talked gamely with the men, politely inserting questions. This had always been her gift—to sense what others wanted in a social situation and offer it up. Sometimes to her detriment. (There was a bad experience in a back room at a sport's bar. Another worrisome incident with the better part of a soccer team visiting from England. She'd really gone over-the-top for a while with the fooling around.) As for Martha, she kept quiet during the conversation, though Ellen sensed something edgy in her silence, as if she wanted to return to the subject they'd left, not to dwell on her loss exactly, but so she'd be the very thing her manner and dress suggested she couldn't bear to be: the center of attention.

*S*ometime after the meal but before dessert, Kristen asked if she could look around the house. She was hoping to buy something herself soon. "At first, I thought I'd love house hunting," she said to everyone. "You know, you see a bunch of places and pick what you like, but it's really been about seeing a bunch of ugly places that I can't even afford. Each time I go out, I lower my expectations, but you need to have a sense of what your money can buy. That's what the Realtor says."

"There's just the two bedrooms and a bathroom down that hall," Ellen said, pointing. "The basement's kind of closed up till the summer."

"Even so," Kristen said and wandered off.

"Can I get anyone coffee? Tea?" Ellen stood to clear the dinner dishes.

When Kristen returned, she said, "Very nice. But not me. You know. You guys are very into that spare look. Me: I'm all about clutter. That's what you'd think if you saw my apartment. What about you two?" She turned on Martha and Hyman. "Where are you living? I just really want a lay of the land, before I make the *big* decision. I mean, I've lived here forever, but I've always rented. I don't really know about places to buy. It's like a whole new world."

Martha brightened some and said, "We have a house in New Glarus. Out in the country with a wraparound porch." She drew a shallow W in the air, perhaps to indicate the shape of the porch's overhang. "It was a mess when we got there. It had gone unoccupied for several years. But once we cleaned it up, we couldn't see why. It's . . ."

"Lovely," Hyman put in.

"Well," Martha said, reprimand in her voice, "I wouldn't go that far. But it has wood floors and what's called a double parlor, two small front rooms. Not a level floor in the house, but I'm not rolling too many marbles around."

Hyman looked at Martha warily. "Hun—" Even from her side of the table Ellen could sense him reach over, put a restraining hand on her thigh.

"Where is it exactly?" Kristen asked, and when Martha told her, Kristen said, "Why that's the old Doanes house!"

"Well, I don't know *who* had it before us," Martha said. She reached for the bottle in the middle of the table and poured herself another glass of wine.

Kristen continued. "The porch wraps around three sides, right? It's up on a small hill across from a vacant church, and you've got all that land out back. Big fields with three trees spaced evenly along the far end of the field."

"Yes," Martha smiled. "That's the place exactly. We're actually planning to buy it, now that we've got the place cleaned up. I don't want to tell you what kind of filth we found there."

"You want to buy it?" Kristen said, uncertainly, and because of the hesitation in her voice, Tamar and Ellen turned to each other.

"What's up?" Ellen mouthed but Tamar just shrugged.

Kristen looked at Alex. "Did *you* know about this?"

Alex shifted in his chair. "I did know about the rental, yes. These plans to buy . . . no."

Hyman cut in. "Well, of course, you knew about the rental. You were so helpful in making that connection with that real estate agent, when we first got here. We were doing everything so quickly when we made the move up here. Everything happened very quickly with the job. The former principal announced she was leaving mid-semester, which meant we had to arrive rather quickly."

"And you knew—" Kristen began, clearly addressing herself to Alex. "Because everyone around here knows . . ."

"Knows what?" Tamar said.

Alex held up his hand. "Ellen's made an apple crisp for dessert. I remembered that you can't do milk"—he bobbed his head at Martha—"so I've got some soy ice cream for you."

"How nice of you," Hyman said. "Very considerate."

"If they are thinking about buying the Doanes house," Kristen said importantly, "someone here has to tell them about the Doanes house."

"What's going on?" Martha said, a bit of fear creeping into her voice. "What are you talking about?"

Kristen pulled her hands back and said, "Oh, *no*. I'm not the one who didn't tell you in the first place."

Alex coughed. "The thing is . . . Well, this was a long time ago. But Greta Doanes was this woman with . . . I think it was . . . well, she had two babies. And you know how sometimes, after a pregnancy, a woman—especially if she's locked up in the house and can't go anywhere . . . a long winter or something . . . will . . ."

"Have a postpartum depression?" Tamar suggested. "My sister had a nasty one. Whenever I'd call her, she was lying in bed, crying and eating peanut butter cups. You know how when you eat a lot of garlic, and you sweat, you smell like garlic? Her sweat started to smell like peanut butter cups. I *swear* I'm not making this up."

Ellen pressed her palm to her breastbone.

"Yeah," Alex said. "But you know once in a blue moon, you'll have someone who actually becomes psychotic."

"Good Lord," Martha gasped, and in her face, Ellen saw what she hadn't seen before, a barely repressed hysteria, something that suggested her eagerness to be horrified and her inability to handle anything even remotely disconcerting.

"So Greta Doanes killed one of the babies. She . . . um . . . she drowned him in the bathtub."

Martha screamed. A short, wordless shriek that startled them all. The sound—high-pitched, vaguely mad, but oddly pleased with itself, as if Martha had been waiting, for years, to let this particular cry out. The silence after the scream was almost more disconcerting than the scream itself.

"It's OK," Hyman reached over to pat her leg. "It's OK."

"I'm so sorry," Alex said tensely now. "I'll just get it all out. I'll tell

you the rest. Greta Doanes murdered her child. For which, she went to
. . . I don't know for sure . . . prison or a place for the criminally insane,
and after she'd served her time, she came back, and she drowned the
other child in the bathtub."

Martha threw her face into her hands. The back of her arms shook,
and Ellen couldn't tell if she was containing her emotion or hiding
racking sobs.

"It was the fields behind the house. And those trees. She kind of
went snow mad. Or that's what the papers said," Kristen added, as if extra details might cheer Martha.

Hyman stood and rubbed Martha's back, but she remained rigid.
Ellen gestured with her head to the left to suggest that everyone move
to the living room and give Martha and Hyman some time alone. But
Alex shrugged and cocked the right side of his mouth, as if saying that
might not be a good idea. Eventually, Hyman cleared his throat. His
face betrayed no emotion, but he said, "Excuse me. I'm just going to
step outside."

"Great party!" Tamar mouthed at Ellen, and then she whispered in
her ear, "That guy definitely doesn't like Jews with bird tattoos. My
money's on *that*."

Below the lip of the table, Alex was doing something Ellen had
never seen him do before, circling the forefinger of his right hand over
and over the stub of his thumb, a gesture she recognized from their
lovemaking; it was what he did to her nipples.

"Christ," Alex whispered. "I never told him, because I couldn't
think of how to tell him."

"Well, dear," Tamar leaned over and put her hand on his left forearm. "*This* wasn't the way."

Chapter Eight

MAY 2006

❦

In May, before Hyman Clark officially moved to the superintendent's office, Mose received his contract renewal letter with its standard cost-of-living increase.

And no merit raise.

He asked around. Everyone who was up for review in 2005/2006 had received his or her usual 3 to 5 percent.

"Is this an oversight?" Mose e-mailed Hyman to ask. The school day was over, and Mose was sitting in his classroom, one flight up from Hyman's office. He knew he could just go downstairs and talk to Clark directly, but he could no longer bear seeing the man in person, especially as he now always traveled with the Band of Peace students. The boys—clustered around Hyman, in their signature black clothes—made Hyman think of sleeping bats. "We're his protection," the kids laughed, as if they were boys from the hood.

Mose was polite enough in his e-mail. He said that since coming to Sudbury, he had always received a 5 percent raise, the best the school system offered.

But Hyman didn't respond.

Mose e-mailed again. "Wondering if you got my e-mail?"

No answer.

"Hyman—Could you let me know when I can expect to hear from you?"

Finally, an e-mail note came. "Mr. Sheinbaum—No error in the contract letter. Cordially, Hyman Clark."

Mose had the uncustomary urge to shove something into the smug planes of Hyman Clark's face. *Stupid baboon.* Back when Mose worked plumbing, people did indeed say "The check's in the mail" and fail to pay, feeling somehow that the plumber had no right to charge since his services—and thus the bill—were unexpected. The infuriating logic of the phlegmatic customer: *Now, don't get angry at me! You asked where's my money, and I told you. What more do you want?*

Same logic for Hyman: a question had been asked and a question had been answered. No one could say Hyman hadn't answered the question. As if there was anyone in the world who wouldn't respond to such purposefully cruel terseness with rage! While staring at the computer screen in his classroom, Mose wrestled the cell phone out of the depths of his overcoat pocket—he'd been all but ready to leave when the e-mail arrived. He called the superintendent's office. "On what basis," he asked, "are merit reviews determined?"

The woman at the end of the line sighed. "You can look up procedural matters on-line."

"I'm sure I can," Mose said. "But I'd like a human being to tell me. I'm very fond of human beings."

He was transferred and transferred again. He was afraid Alex would sputter onto the line with some sheepish explanation or nattering about the new grill he was buying for Ellen. (New gas grill, season's tickets for college wrestling, a flat screen TV . . . all *for Ellen.* Oh, please.) But, no, when a person finally came onto the line, it was the assistant superintendent, Greg Shardon.

"Hey, Mose, how you doing?"

"I'm all right."

"I hear you have a question."

Mose repeated his query.

"Well, you know it's all written in the handbook. You can check it out on-line."

Mose was quiet.

"But basically, you know, the principal's letter determines things.

I'll . . . well, normally Decker makes the decision, but I'll be frank with you, I made the decision for you. This year. Given the family situation. What with Alex dating your daughter and all. But I have to let you know, I don't have a lot of flexibility with these things. I have to . . . I have to use this chart and just . . ."

"So it's your fault?"

"Oh, no, no," Greg laughed uncomfortably. "In the end, I'm just a conduit, you might say. I do as the principal's letter advises."

"And that letter advised you not to give me a raise?"

"No, no, it just describes your teaching and service, and I plug the comments into a formula."

"And what's wrong with my teaching?"

"You know, I can't remember the specifics of any given case, but you may not have hit the bull's eye on everything. That'll happen, and there are people in the system who do hit the bull's eye."

"The bull's eye?" Mose asked, incredulous. He was tired, he realized. Too tired to mention the three years when the students had voted him best teacher of the year, the Outstanding Educators award he'd twice received from the state, or his many years of favorable teaching evaluations.

"OK," he said, furious as much at himself as Greg, for not summoning the energy to argue his own case. "I see."

All over this country, Mose thought, men subject to injustices go home and rail at their wives who—themselves nervous about money—listen patiently, even indignantly at first, then give into their irritation at the complaints, the pompous sense (because men are invariably arrogant in self-defense) that the men had been cheated, their obvious talents denied. Mose would have welcomed such feminine rage. Who, in the end, didn't want to be important enough for anger? But, of course, there was no one with whom to share his feelings, and Mose—having composed devastating letters in his head on his short drive home—heated a can of soup, then drafted one of those angry diatribes that people tell you to never send to your boss. Mose e-mailed it to himself, just for the pleasure of knowing his words had traveled. Then he called Smitty.

"You know," Smitty said, "you can ask to see the principal's letter."

"I can?"

"Yeah, and maybe you should. You know that if you go two more cycles with no raise, the new rule is that they can get rid of you."

"Since when?"

"Since . . . oh, I don't know . . . it's on the Web site."

The infernal Web site. Mose had succumbed to the e-mail, but that was as far as he would travel into the land of new technology.

The next day, after classes, Mose visited Betty in Hyman's office to ask to see his letter.

"Not here," Betty said. "You've got to go to the superintendent's. Everything's filed there."

"Can I borrow your phone?"

"In person, actually. You have to ask for it in person."

Mose drove to the superintendent's office. There Alex's secretary told Mose that she'd mail him the letter. They were only allowed to send it by mail. Registered. She hoped he'd be home some day next week to sign for it.

"Actually," Mose said, slowly, taking this information in, "that won't be possible, you see. As I have a job, I actually work for this school system."

"Well, then, I can't help you," she shrugged.

"Jesus Christ!" Mose snapped. "What's the matter with you?"

She looked startled. "Greg," she called into a neighboring office, as if she needed help controlling her unruly visitor. Greg Shardon appeared in the doorway.

"Mr. Shardon," Mose said, extending his hand, but Shardon wouldn't even lift his arm to shake. Maybe Shardon believed whatever crazy things Hyman had written in his merit review letter.

"Sheinbaum," Greg said. "You can't talk to Candy like that. I need you to calm down."

"Don't tell me to calm down. How *dare* you tell me to calm down? You set up a ludicrous bureaucracy. I'm a mouse in a maze. You say push a lever. I push. I push, and I push. Push again, you say. I push and nothing happens, so I do what any mouse in my situation would do. I go a little crazy."

"Just come into my office," Greg said. "Alex's gone to California, for a conference, as you probably know."

Mose shrugged irritably. "Why would I know that?"

"Well, I just thought—" Greg began.

"All I want," Mose said, "is to see my merit review letter. That's my right."

"You want to see it, you can see it. No reason to get upset. I'll send it myself. There's that rule about doing it by mail, instead of just handing it to you, but when he gets back, I'll tell Alex that you were upset, if you want."

"No, no," Mose said, his tone more even. "You don't have to do that. In fact, I'd rather you didn't."

How humiliating, as if he needed the man who'd taken Ellen as a concubine—the sick bastard—to help him. As if he'd trade Ellen *ever* for such a thing.

*M*ose had an appointment with Hyman, though he wasn't sure why. His secretary, Betty, had called to set things up, and when Mose asked what the meeting was for, Betty said, "Oh, I don't know. I assumed *you* knew. You know me, just the lowly wage slave."

"Hello, lowly wage slave," Mose smiled when he entered her office. She held up her finger to indicate that he should wait. She was talking on the phone, but Mose didn't get this right away, as she wore her phone headset whether she was on the line or not.

"Sorry," he whispered, finger to lips, as if shushing himself.

Greg Shardon still hadn't sent Mose his merit review letter. When Mose called to ask about it—an envelope should only take a day to get from one Madison location to another—Greg said that he was sorry, that he meant to call to say Mose's file had been misplaced. They were hunting for the letter and would be in touch when they found it. By then, Mose had heard the sad news about Shardon's health, so he didn't protest. Instead, he said: "Well, OK, that's all right. You just take care of yourself."

Now he wondered if Shardon thought that bit of goodwill meant that Mose was no longer eager to see the letter. If Mose's concerns were being routed through Shardon, the assistant superintendent, soon they'd be routed through Hyman, the assistant superintendent. To avoid nepotism.

Still, as Mose waited for his meeting, he tried to keep an open mind. There was a chance Hyman wanted to meet so he could tell him directly about the merit review letter. He wrote it, after all. He knew what it said.

Betty rolled her eyes and pointed at her headset. Apparently, the caller wasn't going to shut up. She gestured toward Hyman's office and mouthed the words, "Go right on in."

Hyman registered Mose's arrival by standing formally and indicating the seat he wanted Mose to take. Then he closed his office door.

"Listen," Hyman began, not sitting himself. "I heard about that stunt you pulled in Shardon's office."

"Stunt?" Mose said. "What are you talking about?"

"I'm talking about the fact that you are insubordinate, that you ignore curriculum choices, that you march in here like you own the world."

"March? Wait. I just went to Shardon's office to get a copy of my review letter. I'm allowed to read it."

"That's not what I'm talking about. I'm talking about how you come in here with an attitude and expect me to drop everything to accommodate you." Hyman's voice rose, and he lifted his forefinger and started to shake it at Mose. "You don't seem to understand that you are probationary now. You can only go three years without a merit review raise, and your tenure is revoked. Well, you've just gone one year."

"Excuse me, are you threatening me?"

"I'm sick of your behavior, Sheinbaum. Don't try to challenge me."

"I . . ." Mose tried to form a question, but the reprimand rendered him temporarily mute. He was dumbfounded.

"I've never," Hyman said, "met anyone as unprofessional as you. Not in all my years in education."

If Mose wasn't already planning to have dinner with Ellen, he would have called and asked her to come see him. He didn't even want to drive, not till he calmed down. Instead he asked if she'd meet him at school. "Sure," she said in her usual chirpy voice, not seeing that this uncommon request meant something was amiss. "I'll bring a picnic."

Mose and Ellen installed themselves in one of the two low couches in the staff room. "I don't believe I'll ever be able to rise from this thing," Ellen joked as she sank into the cushions. The room with its vinyl floor and dirty coffee pots was dingy. Unexplainable large tufts of hair skirted the floor. Mose saw Ellen noticing a hairball, skittering across the ground as if alive. He said, in a confidential voice, "This room . . . It's shedding."

"Here," she said, bringing items out of her backpack.

"What's this?" He unwrapped a roll-sized sandwich.

"Maytag bleu cheese and caramelized onions. It's good. Honest. You'll like it."

Mose took a dainty bite, then pushed the whole thing away.

"There's a root beer, too. If you'd like." When he didn't take it, she said, "You have to eat more. Have you been drinking your Boosts?" The chocolate drink was supposed to pack on the calories.

"I'm too disturbed to eat. I don't know what just happened."

"What do you mean?"

"I've just had a run-in with the principal." Hand to brow, then up and through his thinning curls, Mose repeated himself. "I don't know what just happened."

"Oh . . . about . . . I've been meaning to tell you that I had the Clarks over for dinner."

"Why would you do that?"

"I wanted to get a sense of Hyman myself. You know I was thinking of telling Alex what you told me about the peace assembly, but before I did, I thought—"

"What sense do you need? He's an anti-Semite, and he's trying to get me fired."

"I . . ."

"I didn't raise you right," Mose snapped. "I raised you so that you don't believe evil exists."

"No, I . . ."

"Don't interrupt. You find justifications. *Oh, this isn't a bad act, this is just someone acting out, because he had a bad childhood. This is just because of poverty. That is just because of oppression.* Poverty, illiteracy, *whatever . . .* these things exist. But they are not explanations for evil. They don't make it OK to do evil."

"I didn't say they did."

"Hyman is evil."

Ellen let out a long breath. "He seemed . . . sort of . . . ineffectual, when I met him. Cowed by his wife maybe."

"Ineffectual," Mose snorted. "That's an act. He just threatened me with my job. He just said I was the most unprofessional person he's ever met."

"He *what*? Why would he say such a thing?"

Mose described the scene in Hyman's office, enjoying—perhaps too much?—her clear shift in allegiance as his story moved forward. ". . . the most unprofessional person I've ever met," Mose repeated, finishing his story.

"That's crazy! Why would he say such things?"

"Why? Why? You are still asking why? You are still trying to find reasons?" If *Ellen* didn't understand, what hope did he have of explaining to others? "I think . . . I need to quit. I don't think there's any other way."

"No." Ellen put out her hand to calm him.

"I think. I need to quit. I don't think there's any other way."

"Quit? No, that's crazy. You love your job. We just need to talk to Alex."

"But don't you see that I can't? Anything Alex says . . . it'll just be because he's seeing you."

"Well, then, we need . . . evidence. If he was yelling so loudly, his secretary must have heard him. And . . ." Ellen tapped her temple, as if trying to encourage a thought along. "You need to go to the union people. Don't ever meet with him alone again. You need to document how he treats you."

"Evidence. I *have* evidence. Didn't I tell you about the assembly and the holiday party?"

"You did, but . . ."

"All winter, I was assigned to parking lot duty. I told him I couldn't do it, that my health precluded it, that it was dangerous for me. But he didn't listen. Wouldn't change my assignment. Wouldn't even respond to my e-mails."

Ellen pressed her hand to her cheek. "Oh, Lord. You did parking lot duty last winter?"

"Smitty did it for me. Not officially. Officially, I did it. But Smitty did me a favor."

"What kind of person would suggest that? I mean. Your balance—

it's so clearly . . ." she seesawed her hand. "But really, what does he want?" Ellen's own voice rose in indignation. "To kill you?"

"One wonders," he said, secretly delighted, and ashamed of his delight, Ellen's indignation clicking with his own—mortise in tenon, snap in snap—making . . . not a force to contend with (Mose didn't let his thought run *that* far amok) . . . but a whosebut, a wingding, a thingamabob (there were no *real* words for it) that could prove (*did* prove, lucky Mose!) that he was not alone.

At Ellen's prodding, Greg Shardon, Hyman Clark, Mose and Gleason Smith, a union representative, met at the superintendent's office. Everyone said Alex should recuse himself—the family conflict and all. But Alex didn't need to make a decision, one way or another, as he was out of town on the day of the meeting. This time, at a Chicago conference.

Mose arrived with Gleason, feeling uneasy because he couldn't quite remember if the man's name was Smith Gleason or Gleason Smith, and he didn't want to seem confused to the man who was charged with representing him. Gleason was tall, thin, boyish and big-eared, perpetually smiling, but clearly bright. He'd put his hand on Mose's forearm, when he'd first seen him in the parking lot outside the superintendent's office, and said, "Don't worry. This isn't new to me. We'll get a handle on this."

Upstairs, in a windowless conference room, Mose found Shardon and Hyman already sitting at a table, paper cups of coffee before them.

"Hello, hello, hello." Everyone greeted each other, politely enough. "Want coffee? Can I get you anything?" Then there was a pause. The men gravitated toward opposite sides of the table.

"Shall we?" Greg asked, and the men nodded.

Mose had been up all night, several nights running, considering and reconsidering how best to present his case. He opened his mouth to speak when Hyman said, by way of introduction, "Mose, we're meeting today because some major red flags have arisen with your behavior."

"I . . . *what*?" Mose said. "I thought we were here to talk about what happened at our last meeting."

"Yes," Hyman replied gravely, "you were completely inappropriate."

"I . . ." Mose had speeches all prepared, but they abandoned him. "You threatened me! You were yelling at me. You were . . ." Mose's voice rose. He couldn't latch on to the word he wanted. "You were shaking your finger at me!"

Slowly, his tone kindly and avuncular, Hyman said, "I would *never* do that to *any*one." He addressed his words to Shardon and Gleason. Then, as if placating a suicidal teenager, he said, "Mose, Mose, you're *very* emotional. This is why we're having problems with you."

"But," Mose said, astounded, "you *did* do it!"

"No, I didn't," Hyman said evenly, facing the others. "I don't think Betty will say that she heard any yelling."

"She . . . she always has . . . what does she ever hear? She always has that damn headset in her ears."

"Try to calm down," Hyman said. "And let's leave Betty out of it. I heard you calling her a wage slave, of all things. Here we are holding diversity seminars to try and normalize relationships between faculty and staff and you—"

"That was a joke. You can ask her. *A joke.*"

"Excuse me," said Greg Shardon. "We're really not able to legislate a he said/he said sort of situation." He had seemed neutral, when the meeting started, but now his manner was defensive, suggesting there was nothing to be done about whatever had happened.

Hyman continued as if he hadn't been interrupted. "There have been documentable problems all along, of course. With attendance at faculty meetings, with arriving for meetings with me and then departing before we even begin, with curriculum planning."

"This is nuts. Clara Massengill never had any problems with me. You can look at my student evaluations—"

"We're not holding a popularity contest," Hyman said. "We're just trying to get things on an even keel."

"What about my merit review letter? I'm being judged, but no one will present the judgment. I have to defend myself against charges that no one will announce. You're familiar with Kafka, maybe?"

"Thank you, Mose," Hyman said. "We've *all* read the classics."

The meeting went on this way. In the end, Shardon said they should stop, that he felt he understood where both men were coming from.

"And that's it?" Mose asked.

Greg triangulated his fingers into a dunce cap then tapped the hat against his pursed lips. "Hunh?" he said absentmindedly.

"Is it too much to ask you to decide something?" Mose said. "Isn't that the point of this meeting?"

"No." Greg's voice rose in irritation. "The point is for me to hear what you and Mr. Clark have to say."

"Yes, *and . . .* ?"

"No *and,* Mr. Sheinbaum. I'll get back to you if I need more information."

*O*ut in the parking lot, Mose turned on Gleason, "Why didn't you say anything in there? I thought you were supposed to help me."

"Tactical maneuver," Gleason explained, smiley as ever. "I say something, and they'll try to hang me with it later. Mostly I was taking notes, trying to see if they'd give us anything that we can hang *them* with."

"And?" Mose said, feeling briefly hopeful.

"And you're screwed."

"How can that be? I'm not lying and he is."

"I didn't say it the right way. You're screwed, but only for the moment. There's nothing you can do, right now. You've got no evidence. That guy is smooth and smart. Also twisted."

"And where's his evidence? He's making all this stuff up about me."

"You need to sit tight. You need to just hold on with all this."

"But why don't we . . ."

Gleason shrugged. "Because he can't prove anything. That's why. My advice is to wait. He's not going to do anything just now. He's got to produce that letter, if he wants to make the zero merit raise stick. Or he'll have to write a new one. Your job isn't quite in danger. Not yet. He'll have to prove whatever he says in the letter."

"I was . . . I've been given an award. For being a good teacher. From the Department of Education. My students *love* me. This isn't hubris talking. I'm good at what I do."

"Listen, I've seen this sort of stuff before. We're documenting these conversations. You need to resist when it is time to resist. For now, just try not to let it eat you up. Put it out of your head."

But Mose could do no such thing. His guts roiled, ready to explode.

He'd shat himself, a few days earlier, not able to get off the phone quickly enough, while talking to Ellen, the pressure in his bowels mounting with his anger . . . and then there he was . . . a gross old man in his basement apartment, knotting up the plastic bag that held his underwear, throwing the whole appalling mess in the garbage, and immediately ferrying his kitchen garbage to the bins behind his apartment. Because you had to get that sort of thing away from yourself as fast as possible, because the evidence of your body was always too awful to be true.

"I gotta go," Gleason said. "But you try to take it easy."

Mose got into his car, pressed his hand to his lower intestines, as if to say, "Enough, enough already." He started up the car, then looked up to see Gleason, in his own car, motioning for Mose to roll down his window. Across his passenger seat, Gleason said, "And by the way. Your missing file? Ten-to-one Clark stole it. Ten-to-one there's your evidence, and both Shardon and Clark know it. That's what'll keep you safe."

"So why don't we . . ."

"We can't prove it, that's why."

"I could lose my job."

"Possibly. Not likely, though." He smiled and waved goodbye, a young man who'd sailed through college and law school as a star student: straight As, law review, girlfriend ready to marry after graduation and baby on the way. What did he know of what Mose was suffering?

Mose turned off his motor and fumbled for his cell phone. He called Ellen at the daycare to report what had happened.

"I'll call Alex in Chicago," Ellen mused, like Gleason, weighing this (or maybe not?) as just one of many matters in the day. "He said he'd get Shardon to talk to Hyman if you wanted. At least we can get his reading on things."

"Oh, my dear," Mose said miserably. "Alex is part of the problem."

Chapter Nine

MAY 2006

The Center for Artistic Exchange didn't have enough money for a full-time secretary, so when the phone rang—in the midst of yet another meeting to work out the details of next year's schedule—Kaayva picked up. "Center for Artistic Exchange. May I help you?" she said, in her beautiful voice.

In the brief interval during which Kaayva listened to the voice on the other end, Valerie glanced at her notes for next season. They'd secured a gallery show for "Surviving Hate." Today, they were combing through lists of possible films and plays.

"Ms. Decker," Kaayva said. Valerie looked up, a little startled. Everyone used first names at the Center. "I think you'd better take this." As she handed the receiver across the table to Valerie, Kaayva looked at Leo and Bonnie and said, with atypical force, "Outside," and pointed toward the hall behind Valerie's office door.

"Hello," Valerie said uncertainly.

"Mom, oh, Mom." It was Doug, and he was sobbing.

"My God, what is it? What is it? Are you all right?"

"It's Brandi Carter. Brandi Carter."

Valerie knew the name but had to think for a minute. Yes, Brandi. She'd once lived across the street.

"What about Brandi?"

"She's dead. Mom, she's dead!" In his incredulity, she heard his child's voice, a demand for Valerie to make the poor girl un-dead.

"Where are you, honey?"

"I'm . . . oh, God, mom. She's all burnt up."

"Honey. Slow down. Tell me what's going on."

"There was a fire, a fire, and she got trapped and—" Valerie remembered hearing sirens earlier. "Must be quite a blaze," Leo had said, and only then had Valerie noted how many sirens there were, how long the sirens had been going on.

"I'll come get you. Where are you?"

"The synagogue."

"You're at a synagogue?"

"No, no. *She* was. There was a fire there. And now she's . . . Oh, my God. I don't know what to do."

"Jesus." Early adolescence in the post-9/11 era. She knew he'd *hear* about violence. (A laughing mother at the supermarket: "And I said, '*Kids*, I can't *believe* you watched that beheading!" On the computer, she meant, and Valerie had been stupefied. Could the world be this sick?) Still Valerie hadn't really believed Doug would be *subjected* to violence. Worrying about harm was supposed to be a talisman—something to keep actual damage at bay.

"Mom—" Doug coughed into the phone.

"Where are you?"

He'd slept with Brandi, it occurred to Valerie. Maybe lost his virginity to her, though they hadn't dated. Or if they had, Doug had kept the relationship a secret.

Doug's sobbing grew choked. He was incoherent. He hadn't even lost his grandparents yet. What did he know of death?

"Are you at Shannon's?" Valerie said. She thought Doug said yes. "Band practice?"

He snuffled a reply. "Yeah," he said hopelessly. "Shannon's."

"I'm coming, honey," she said. "OK? I'm coming." And then the unavoidable thought—*at least it wasn't him*—as she put the phone down and ran, a true run, for the parking lot.

*S*mitty never knew what to say. He knew that. He smiled when he shouldn't smile or failed to get jokes. And even when he called Mose about Brandi Carter he got things wrong.

"It's me," Smitty said. "Did you hear?"

"Hey," Mose said jovially, "I thought you didn't like to talk on the phone."

"So you didn't hear," Smitty said grimly. "Brandi Carter. She came down with a little something. What she came down with was Death."

"What are you talking about?"

"The funeral," Smitty sputtered. "The funeral's next week."

Part Three

ENGAGEMENT

It can contradict itself; thus it is one of the
principles of universal explanation.

—Gaston Bachelard,
The Psychoanalysis of Fire

Chapter One

MAY 2006

HoHo Coombs showed up, the night of the fire. On Hyman's porch, of all places, and crying.

The unfamiliar sound of the doorbell startled Martha into action. She rose for the porch light but stopped when she saw the boy with the bald head, cavernous eyes and black leather jacket, zippers like so many wounds in the skin of his coat. Martha stood in the dark front hallway, other dark rooms opening like butterfly wings around her. Hyman was looking at her back—the blouse there puffed like a bellows—but he could almost *see* her register the kitchen clock, ticking like an explosive at the other end of the hall. "Holy Jesus," Martha whispered.

Hyman came up behind her. There was, as always, a trace of pleasure in her fear. You lived with a person long enough, you knew what they felt and what she felt was relief. It was here, whatever she'd worried about, finally *here*. Outside large moths with their terrible meaty torsos flapped frenetically about HoHo's scalp, as if they'd been borne into being with the porch light and had to do all their living now, before Martha refound the light switch and killed them. "What is *that*?" she said.

"Just a kid from school."

Martha turned and studied him, apparently unconvinced. A car passed by, its headlights illuminating the room. Something flashed blue then green on Martha's face, briefly danced there and disappeared. The colors came from the crystals Martha had hung from fishing line on one of their first days in the house.

"What *kind* of kid?" When he didn't answer, she looked back through the window that gave onto the porch. HoHo might have been some bog creature that had swum up from the silty bottom of the lake, a miscreant aquatic who'd taken to land and found himself here, among more evolved life forms. "I thought we were starting over."

Hyman put both hands on Martha's shoulders and moved her aside, as if she were a large, inconvenient doll blocking his path to the door. "Just leave us alone. Would you?"

"No, I will not. He's wearing those boots. You know the ones."

"I don't dress them before they come to visit me."

"Oh, yes you do," Martha said, keeping her voice low, ugly. "If this is what I think it is, I'll leave you."

How many times had she threatened *that*?

And how many times had he replied, "No, honey" and "Don't leave" and "You know I'd be lost without you"?

Well, not tonight. He had too much on his mind for a row with Martha.

"Go to your room," he hissed at Martha and turned for the door.

"HoHo! This is a surprise," Hyman said warmly, pretending not to notice the boy's tears. He stepped onto the front porch. Just an hour ago, Hyman had gotten a call that said a fire in Madison had destroyed the synagogue. "Have a seat." It was chilly, but Hyman didn't want HoHo inside his home. He gestured to one of the porch's two rocking chairs. They were meant to look like white wicker but were really plastic and foul-smelling. "Please," he began but then held up his hand, like a traffic cop. "HoHo, are you on something? Because I can't talk to you if you're on something. My home . . . It's just like at school. I've got a no-tolerance rule."

"Mr. C.—" the boy said, half-sob, half-plea, but sitting uneasily on the edge of the rocking chair, elbows balanced on knees, body thrust forward for confidences. "I just had a bad day, a really bad day."

His eyes were red-rimmed, something unfocused yet racing there. A drug, of course. Methamphetamine?

"Mr. C. My girlfriend left me."

"I'm sorry to hear that," Hyman offered flatly, "but even so . . ." The round of attachment and detachment that made up the lives of teens had eluded Hyman as a young man. There'd been no one, and then there'd been Martha, who had waited a full ten years before agreeing to marry. She had trouble making decisions, she said. But Hyman hadn't fallen for that. He knew she'd hoped to do better.

So had he.

"She left me for, for Sam Meyers. *Sam Meyers.*" This last pronounced with incredulity, the comparative virtues of Sam Meyers and HoHo Coombs apparently being a matter of general knowledge.

"Can't say I know him."

"A Jewish kid, Mr. Hot Shit at West." When Hyman didn't say anything, HoHo sputtered, his voice choked with self-pity, "I thought you'd understand. "

"Understand?"

"This kid. It's like he was made to be king or something. Just a little shit, with a doctor father and a mother and a . . ." He stopped, looked up, finally made an effort to meet Hyman's eyes. "Don't you know *anything*?" he began, spiteful now. "Don't you even know that Brandi Carter is dead?"

"I *do* know that. I just heard all about it an hour ago. It's a great tragedy."

"*That's* my girlfriend. Brandi Carter."

"Oh, son," Hyman said, finally sitting in the rocking chair by the boy. So that explained the tears. "Why didn't you say so? From the start?"

HoHo started to sob. Maybe he'd gone on some bender when he found out. Since he'd gotten the news, Hyman had felt cold. Not cold as unemotional but chilly, the news an ice cube in his chest that refused to melt. He couldn't quite pinpoint the girl—there were so many kids at Sudbury—but he'd have to respond to the community's grief. Moments ago, when Martha called into the kitchen to say, "There's some kid at the door," Hyman had been wondering what he should do about Brandi Carter. Schedule a special assembly? Request money for grief counselors?

"Brandi Carter is my girlfriend," HoHo said again, perhaps hoping for fresh comfort.

"*Was*, you mean."

"Huh?" HoHo blinked, suddenly alert, his face smeary with tears.

There was something of the Neanderthal chipmunk about him—the fat cheeks combined with the receding forehead. Hyman had corrected HoHo automatically, not aiming for cruelty, but HoHo's apparent outrage at the correction—adults were supposed to be nice when you were sad!—irked Hyman. "Was," he repeated. "You mean 'was.'"

"Is," HoHo said slowly, as if the mere word might not only resurrect his girlfriend but send her running back into his arms. And then, more forcefully, "Is, *is, is*." He slapped his thigh with each declaration. Then he stood—the empty chair yammering against the porch in protest—and turned abruptly around, as if to face an assailant behind him.

"What is it?" Hyman peered into the dark. Even in daylight, there were no neighbors in sight. The isolation was part of what had driven the long-ago occupant of the house so mad. Martha had found this out. She'd gone to the local paper to find all the old articles on the murder.

"There's no one there," Hyman pointed out softly.

"You think I don't know no one's there. What do you think I came here to tell you? Brandi Carter is fucking dead."

They all used the word "fucking" this way—as emphasis, as boldface. Meaning: she was *dead* dead, *really* dead. But "fucking" still held its original meaning for Hyman, who could remember the first time he used the word, the dirty sin of it, his nine-year-old boy's sense that something would happen to him once the verb came out of his mouth.

HoHo kicked at Hyman's porch railing, breaking a single slat, then catching his boot on the remaining piece of rotten wood. He pulled his foot out and started to kick more systematically. The fence slat fell to the ground below. "Hey," Hyman said, rising. "Hey, leave that alone." Martha was watching all this. Hyman could feel her eyes on the back of his neck, could sense the rising hysteria within the house. *What is going on? What is going on? What. Is. Going. On.*

HoHo swung around, fists still raised, body perfectly positioned to punch. Hyman jerked his head back, as if the blow had already grazed his cheek.

"You scared?" HoHo said, perhaps sensing he had an advantage here. He was young and strong. Hyman was just a weak grown-up.

"I'm a little scared," Hyman admitted evenly.

HoHo looked down at his fists, as if they weren't his, but two chunks of meat that had wandered onto his wrists. "You know what these are . . . ?" HoHo inquired. Then he turned his fists toward his own face and kissed his knuckles, the press of his lips causing his fingers to bloom into two dippy peace signs. "Band of Peace," HoHo grinned.

Hyman nodded; the words seemed to calm HoHo down.

"Band of Peace knows that you can't solve a problem till you know who the enemy is."

"That's right," Hyman agreed. "I taught you that."

"*You* know who the enemy is."

Hyman laughed. "I've got some ideas." Then: "Why did you come here?" When HoHo didn't answer, something occurred to Hyman. "Did you *hurt* Sam Meyers?"

"Now why do you ask that?" HoHo said. "When you know that wasn't what happened?"

"What are you telling me?"

"Hey." HoHo put his arms up in protest. "Is it a court of law? Is this a court of law? Are there tape recorders here? Because . . ." he backed up along the length of the porch, head turning to and fro as if his words *were* being recorded, "if there are, I can tell you where I got my ideas. I can tell you . . ."

Hyman saw his opportunity. He grabbed the front of HoHo's t-shirt and twisted, surprised by the heat of the boy's chest. "Listen, punk. You're nothing but a punk. Don't come here and threaten me."

HoHo pushed him away, and Hyman stumbled toward Martha's rocking chairs, their plastic stink.

"I don't need to threaten you," HoHo said. "You threaten yourself."

Chapter Two

MAY 2006

At the graveside, Rochelle Bernstein wept, the heart-rending sobs Ellen associated with newscasts from Iraq: a mother finding her child blown apart, life newly unbearable. "Jeez," Ellen whispered to Mose, a chilly gust twisting her black dress about her legs. "You'd think she'd get a grip."

Not that the irony was lost on any of the group clustered above the casket, late on a May afternoon. They were burying a Holocaust survivor, a Torah that had escaped Poland (thanks to a steamer trunk) only to burn in Madison, Wisconsin. Faulty wiring, everyone said. "Oh, please," Mose responded, sure of foul play from the start. But the synagogue *was* old and poorly kept, a former church meeting hall—which accounted for the arched windows and stained glass—that had been transformed into a *shul*. No pictures of Jesus, but squares of purple, red and yellow. As if to acknowledge the inappropriateness of stained glass in a synagogue, the windows, all of them, went unattended. Never cleaned, the squares, heavy with dust, looked black, save for when the sun shone at a favorable angle, purpling the already dark-hued velvet chairs. White chips flaked the sills; lead paint surely. The story was that the windows in the kitchen—where Brandi Carter had gone to drop off pastry for a Friday-evening service—were painted shut, impossible to open, even if they hadn't expanded with the heat. No one knew she was in there anyway. She was planning to surprise her boyfriend. "I baked this Jewish stuff," she had told a friend earlier in the day. "I'm going to go to the service with him, and when he sees a honey cake by me, it's going to rock his world." She danced around her friend as she said this, pleased by her own unlikely domesticity and the trick of sneaking the evidence of it into a house of worship.

A sudden wail from Rochelle Bernstein, as if someone had stabbed her. No one liked what had happened, but *really*. It wasn't as if they were attending yesterday's funeral for Brandi Carter, a citywide sobfest. Ellen had crowded with Mose, Alex and the others into the giant cathedral—no matter that she'd never met Brandi—then fallen apart along with all the high school kids. A clutch of them came to the service dressed as Brandi Carter had apparently dressed—shirt layered on shirt and tied at the midriff, wild colorful stockings and flared short skirts. "I'm going to have a lot of time," Sam Meyers, her boyfriend, said in a disintegrating voice before the mourners, "to think about her death. I've got my whole life to think about her death. Right now, I want to think about her life." After, a whole slew of people rose to tell stories about Brandi. Mostly it was kids, her classmates, but Alex stood to say something about how hard her early life had been, how she'd come into her own once she'd met her new family. Her foster father wrote something down, but two sentences into his speech, he dropped his head, pinched the bridge of his nose and started shaking with silent sobs. He couldn't do it. A student—the one who'd seen fit to share a story about Brandi, drunk at a party, wondering whatever happened to the noble tradition of the wet t-shirt contest—rubbed the man's back, and then his wife stepped forward to lead him to his seat.

You buried a Torah, because God's name, once written down, couldn't be destroyed. Still, save for Rochelle, the gathered were dry-eyed, waiting (it seemed) for the service to end, so they could return to the heat of their cars. It was unseasonably raw, the cold all the worse for the sharp wind, sending the pulverized remnants of last fall's leaves scuttering like mice about the cemetery. At the base of a tree, just beyond the coffin, a few crocus tips poked through the crusty soil. They looked unhopeful. Less like a sign of spring than three ghastly green fingers, clawing their way out of the earth.

Every year since he'd become superintendent, Alex had to face a student death—a car crash, a suicide, a fatal illness. Now this. If there was a reason, he'd told Ellen, to get out of his line of work, it was so he'd never again have to break bad news to a parent. But, in the end, Alex wasn't the one who told Brandi's foster parents. The police did that. Which left Alex to turn his concern to Doug, who became hysterical the day he learned of the death, and hadn't returned to himself since. He'd gone to Brandi's funeral, but wouldn't go to school, wouldn't meet with a grief counselor. He lay in bed, head pressed to his pillow, and when he rose—reported Alex, who was probably in his son's room now—he cried out, as if newly informed of the death and unable to believe it: Brandi Carter was *still* dead. When would she just *snap out of it?*

As for Mose, he didn't say how he felt about the tragedy, but then he'd always been stone-faced, when it came to death. Ellen and Barbara hadn't been encouraged to emote, after their early loss. *Just plug on.* Life was for the living. Now, the rabbi nodded at the cantor, who took a sparse shovelful of dirt and tossed it onto the coffin. The sound of dirt hitting wood—always the most chilling part of the service. At Ellen's parents' funeral, a distant aunt had stumbled when it was her turn with the shovel. One foot slid into the grave, and people grabbed for her, as if once she slid into the hole—dead or not—she'd be buried, too. Ellen wondered if Jews sat *shiva* for a Torah, but she didn't ask. It seemed too shameful not to know.

Mose's turn came for the shovel, but he faltered with its weight. "Let's do it together," Ellen whispered, and they did. When they turned away, Mose put a hand to his face and said, "Oh, Lord, she was only a child."

After, Ellen and Mose walked in silence to Mose's car. "Oh, Lord," Mose had said. Did he believe in God? Ellen had never asked, not outright. Once, back when they still lived in San Francisco, Mose had asked her sister if *she* believed in God, and Barbara had said she was "an agnostic." She'd just learned the word in *Thirty Days to a Better Vocabulary.*

"You can't be an agnostic," Mose said. "That's saying nothing."

"But it's the truth," Barbara protested. "I *don't* know." Still, she was clearly shaken; she'd thought she could rest on the word. She was old enough to comment on the *licentiousness* of—no, the *libidinous* nature of—contemporary advertising but young enough to believe that if Mose said she couldn't be something, then she couldn't be it.

Why didn't Barbara ask Mose if *he* believed in God? She must have supposed that he *did*. Or that Mose would pretend to believe to protect her from the obvious burdens of faithlessness.

Ellen joined Mose in his Buick. She owned a car—she'd bought one when she moved out to Ridgeway—but Alex had borrowed it for the day, so he could be with Doug. Alex's own car was in the shop.

"Mose," Ellen began.

"Hmm?"

"Do you believe God is good?"

Mose put the key in the ignition but didn't start his car. A stranger might have been put off by his manner, but Ellen knew this was his "thinking" silence. Finally, he said, "Did I ever tell you I once thought about going to law school?"

"No."

"Well, I did, but I knew the hours wouldn't allow me to be home enough for you girls." He fell silent again, then began in his teacher's voice. "Is God good? How would we make the case? Awesome, we know, yes. Powerful? Yes. Beautiful? Yes. Good? Well, the rabbis will say He is in hiding; He doesn't show his face, as He once did. No Red Sea parting for us. He works; we just don't see how He works. We have to trust His ways. What can we say? We can believe in this, but we can't agree or disagree. It's a proposition that never will have sufficient evidence to prove or disprove. Still, you ask, 'Is He good?'" He stopped to look at the cemetery. He might have been seeing the Torah, or Brandi Carter, or far beyond the city's graveyards to Israel, Iraq and Darfur or maybe beyond all that into history, the great scream of grief of a survivor, no matter what the political or religious affiliation. "I don't see how He can be."

Oh, Mose, Ellen would have liked to cry in sympathy or recognition, but in the economy of her peculiar family, such affirmation was verboten. Only one person was allowed despair at a time.

"So," Mose pressed his hands together, right and left shaking to seal some private agreement, and said, with surprising cheer, "next stop, Valerie's?"

"Uh . . . yeah." Ellen looked down at her lap, an imaginary "to do" list there. Item #1: Bury the dead. Item #2: Meet Alex at Valerie's. "That's right."

Ellen wasn't comfortable with cars. Her sister wasn't either. How could they be with *their* history? Barbara waited till she moved to Maine to learn to drive. Ellen learned in college. A boy in her dorm taught her. As for Mose: despite his meager teacher's salary, he bought a Buick Regal, a tank of a car, as soon as he settled in Wisconsin. A car was a necessity, he explained. Also a weapon, the girls understood, and the family interacted with the bloodletter in the driveway as best they could. Still, the car was the place for confidences, the place where Mose might be alone with Ellen while they waited for Barbara to come out of the library. Or it was where Barbara and Mose sat as they waited for Ellen to finish ballet class. All through their teen years, whenever Mose needed to make an off-hours trip to school, he contrived to make the journey a treat, picking one girl to drive to school with him. Neither Ellen nor Barbara ever construed the company as a favor. Instead, they'd gotten lucky, picked for special attention.

And it was special: Ellen in the passenger seat confided everything: what boy she fancied, what teachers she liked, how anxious math tests made her. Now, though, what could she say? That she was terrified of Valerie? That she thought it inconsiderate of Alex to ask her to pick him up at his ex-wife's home? After two days of funerals, such emotions seemed trivial, and still the chore loomed.

"Head over to the west side, and I can give you directions from there," Ellen said, studying her map.

"OK," Mose said and started to drive.

Earlier in the day, when making plans, Alex hadn't seen that it would be far better for him to pick Ellen up, rather than have her meet him at Valerie's. He'd argued that he didn't know when the funeral would end, that he couldn't be sure how much time he'd need with Doug, and finally Ellen assented.

"Plus you see Valerie at work all the time," Alex had said. "It won't be a big deal." But that wasn't true. Ellen and Valerie rarely saw each other. If they passed one another at the Center for Artistic Exchange, they merely nodded. The one time they'd run into each other in the women's room, they smiled—not awkwardly so much as with a sense of the oddness of the situation. Valerie and Alex talked, of course, to arrange things concerning Doug, but they did so on Alex's cell phone; Ellen never found herself having to make polite chitchat before she turned the home phone over to Alex. Ellen hadn't really *said* anything to Valerie since last fall, when they'd seen each other at that art exhibit about torture victims.

"What now?" Mose asked.

"OK, OK." Ellen squinted at a road sign. "You turn left at the next light and then left again." She'd driven by Alex's old house before, but only once, on a fact-finding mission to see what his life looked like before she was a part of it. "It's that brick house, the one up on the right. You can just pull to the curb."

Mose did as she said.

"Just wait a sec. I'll go get him."

Ellen darted out of the car and up the steps to Valerie's door. She pushed the doorbell. It rang for so long, Ellen guessed she'd somehow managed to jam the thing, just by pressing it. She took a key from her purse, tried to edge it along the rim of the doorbell to unpush the bell, but this only started the chime ringing anew. Her heart was racing. She knew Valerie saw her as an airhead, the midlife-crisis girlfriend, someone who wanted a sugar daddy, not someone who'd fallen in love with a man who was kind to her, with a man who offered the easy domesticity and attention to small creature comforts (that nice soup!) of which Mose had been oblivious. Alex danced with her, he cooked with her, and he didn't ever seem to want her to be something she was not.

Finally Valerie opened the door. She said, perfectly pleasantly, "You're going to have to come in. Alex is still trying to talk with Doug."

"Oh, my dad is with me." Ellen pointed down the short hill that comprised Valerie's front lawn.

"Well, go get him. I'll make you both tea."

"I . . ." But Valerie had already turned from the door.

Ellen ran down the steps, hugging herself against the cold of the day. Mose rolled his window down as he saw her coming.

"What's up?"

"Would you mind coming in with me?"

"Come in?" Mose said. "No, I'll just sit here."

"The thing is . . . it might be a long time. I think . . . Alex's still trying to talk to Doug."

Mose looked at his watch. "He's been talking to him for hours."

"I know." Mose had his own grief about Brandi, so Ellen hadn't gone into detail about Doug. "You see, no one can quite tell if Doug is going off the deep end or just having a normal reaction to the death. He's taking it so hard."

"There's no easy way to take it."

"I know. Valerie thinks maybe there was something between Brandi and Doug."

"No," Mose said authoritatively. "That's not right. She was seeing Sam Meyers. He was the one who talked yesterday at the service—the first one who talked."

"I know, I know, and Doug says that, too, but Valerie's got this idea. Anyway, I didn't tell you this before, but Doug's . . . except for the funeral, I don't think he's been out of bed since the night of the fire. Alex is really worried."

"Well, a smart boy. He's not going to be satisfied hearing that she's in a better place." Yesterday, that was where the priest had left the mourners: with an acknowledgment of the enormity of their loss and a sense of God's will being done, even if that will was beyond human understanding.

"Valerie wants to give us tea."

"Well, then we'll drink tea," Mose said and pulled himself from his car.

Valerie led them into an airy kitchen, its open white shelves laden with colorful plates in yellows, blues and greens, its substantial central table clearly made for a large gathering, the significant family event. *I didn't disrupt this*, Ellen reminded herself. *It was disrupted before I arrived.* Valerie brought over a blue teapot, mugs and a plate of chocolate-dipped biscuits. While Mose and Ellen had their first sips of tea, Valerie left the kitchen to call up the staircase. "Alex! Mose and Ellen are here."

Within a minute, Alex joined them at the kitchen table. "Quite a morning," Alex admitted to Ellen.

"For us, too."

"I still think there was something between them," Valerie began. Everyone knew she meant Brandi and Doug.

Alex sighed, as if irritated by Valerie's interpretation. "Everyone sexualized that poor girl. And now you, too."

"Yes," Valerie said evenly, "I'm the one who has a problem with sexualizing young women. Good point."

Ellen flushed. She reached out her hand to cup the warm teapot before her. "Pretty," she said of the pot. Its intense blue seemed to come from underneath its glaze, from deep within.

"More?" Valerie offered, and Ellen shook her head no.

Ellen was wearing her only black dress, a lacy thing that she'd found at a flea market a few years ago. It wasn't her style to dress sexy, but the dress *was* too short. You took what you could when you bought vintage. The hemline hadn't mattered when Ellen was standing at the gravesite, but sitting, the dress rode too high up her leg. She lifted herself slightly in the chair, to give the hem a firm tug down.

"So," Alex said, clearly for Ellen's benefit. "Doug has actually gotten out of bed."

"Well, that's good news," Ellen said, a shade too enthusiastically.

"Maybe not," Valerie put in. "He went out late yesterday, and I let him be. Didn't ask him where he was going. When he came home, he went straight upstairs to do the bed thing. I thought, 'Well, he left the house. That's something.' Then, this morning, I get a call from the police. Might I have been down at the synagogue, they want to know. Had I been down at the synagogue? Had I been to the site of the fire? I said no. So they came by and dropped this off." Valerie gestured to the marble topped kitchen island behind her on which sat piles of mail, a bunch of *New Yorkers*, a *Gardener's Eden* and a *Pottery Barn* catalog, as well as two books: Zadie Smith's *On Beauty* and Malcolm Gladwell's *Blink*.

Valerie twisted about in her seat to slip an eight-by-ten photograph off one of the piles. She slid it across the table toward Ellen and Mose.

"He made a shrine," Alex explained.

"He what?"

"Just look." Valerie's forefinger double-tapped the photo.

In the charred remains of the synagogue, there was a blue wooden cross. Stapled to its top was what must have been Brandi's class photo, slipped into a plastic sleeve for protection. The photograph itself was entirely unrevealing. A smiling girl. As for the plywood cross, someone had hung a plastic blue lei around it. In the ground below, fake yellow flowers stood next to a pinwheel with a ceramic angel in the center. A plaster of Paris teddy bear sat behind all this on an embankment, scrappy with brown grass, spent bittersweet and clumps of wet ash. The bear held a folded Ziploc bag. At his feet lay a flat stone painted with the words, "Love You Always."

"This is all his?" Mose said, eyebrows raised.

Valerie pursed her lips and nodded, one eyelid twitching slightly as if asking for a reaction that would make the photo less worrisome than she found it.

"I ask, because I could see other kids wanting to add things, *their* personal treasures."

"That's what I thought, at first," Valerie agreed. "A Princess Diana thing, but you have to see it for yourself. Something about it says, 'Don't come near. This grief is all mine.' I worried that the kids would tease him for that. You know how cruel kids can be."

"They're nicer now, I think," Mose said. "Nicer than how I remember them, when I was a boy."

Valerie stood to add more cookies to the plate, even though no one had eaten what was already there. "How you can look at that and not think there was something between them, I don't know."

"I don't mean he didn't love her," Alex said testily. "I just mean that there wasn't anything sexual between them. That's all I'm saying."

Ellen put her hand on Alex's forearm. "Maybe you and I should go see it."

Valerie looked at Ellen. "Why would you—" She stopped herself. "Oh, never mind."

"I'll tell you what . . ." Alex slid his chair back. "Let me go upstairs, just one more time. See what I can do. At least let him know I'm leaving."

"All right," Valerie said, and Alex left. In his absence no one spoke, the silence quickly growing uncomfortable. Ellen caught Valerie's eye but not knowing what to say instantly looked away. It was too awkward. The ex-wife, the girlfriend and her surrogate father. All in the ex-wife's home in a time of mourning.

"Poor girl," Mose finally murmured, meaning (Ellen knew) Brandi, but the words seemed to include Valerie, a mother weathering her son's grief.

Mose had been surrounded, all his life, by suffering females. Not that Ellen had ever put it to herself in exactly this way before, but his mother had lost her father and husband in the War, his wife died young, and then he had parented Ellen and Barbara, the orphans. Perhaps he knew what to say to women in trouble, though the evidence of her childhood was that he didn't, not quite. Oh, in the first flushes of grief, he knew what to say, all right, but when a sadness dragged on, he lost his patience, and withheld the very words (and they weren't all that complicated words, were they?) that might have brought comfort. Or maybe that wasn't it. Maybe it was just that "Life is for the living" philosophy. Maybe, as time progressed, it simply didn't occur to him that comfort was still needed, because he'd done what life required. He'd moved on.

Alex's cell phone rang, and Valerie picked it up from the tabletop.

"Maybe," Ellen reached out, as if to suggest she should take the call, but Valerie pressed a button on the phone.

"No, he's not available just now," Valerie said formally. "Can I take a message?" Then her voice softened. "Oh, yeah, hi, Jackson."

Mose mouthed a question: *Chief of police?*

Ellen shrugged. It could be. Jackson was the chief of police's first name.

Valerie was quiet, listening. "Yeah, of course, I'll tell him. OK. You, too." And then she hung up.

"What was that?" Ellen said.

"Oh, nothing. Nothing that concerns you."

Ellen looked at her lap, then up again. Heat filled her body. She turned to Mose and smiled nonsensically. He offered a quick return grin, vague and uneasy. He couldn't help. Or wouldn't. This was Ellen's affair.

Alex came downstairs, bending at the bottom stair to pick up a string or some other piece of crud, Ellen couldn't quite tell, only registered that this was not a bit of housekeeping one would do if one was a guest in someone's home. Back in the kitchen, Alex said, "He just wants to sleep."

Valerie pulled at a small piece of tissue on her lip, a habit Barbara used to have: of picking at her chapped lips, because she enjoyed the scrape of the tissue between her lips, but of not stopping till she'd drawn blood. "We'll give it time."

"I think we *should* go look," Ellen said to Alex. "At the shrine, I mean."

Valerie moved her hand from her mouth. "What's it to you?"

"Just concerned." Ellen's voice was small, though perhaps she *had* meant to aggravate. She could easily have waited till she was in the car to say this to Alex.

Valerie inclined her head toward Alex. "My husband. Take him. He's yours. Hands off my son, though."

"I don't . . ."

"Valerie, Jesus. You know she wouldn't—" Alex began.

Mose reached across the table and patted Valerie's hand. "All children," he said. "Have you noticed that all children, little ones I mean, at four or five, are beautiful? And smart, too. Who has met an ugly child? That's why I like meeting little ones. I like to see people at their best."

No one spoke. This seemed such a complete non sequitur. "Your son," Mose continued, "is safe with you. He'll get through this and be safe with you."

You gave mourners something when you gave them your optimism; you gave them something concrete to protest. *Oh, Lord, she was only a child.*

"Could *I* talk to him?" Mose asked.

Valerie stared, then looked around the table in disbelief. "Do you all think I am not capable of taking care of the son I love more than anything in the whole wide world?"

"No one's saying that, Val," Alex said. "Why would we? We're just trying to understand what Doug is going through."

"Only if you don't mind," Mose added. He was asking Valerie. Alex was irrelevant here.

She shrugged. A yes. Mose pulled on his dark coat, dotted with dandruff, as if he was about to step outside, not upstairs. "I'm not," he said, as if just taking note of his dark garb and general disarray, though both were standard with him, "a flashy dresser. That's for my next life." Something about the way he said this made Ellen picture Mose's next life, and see—as clearly as she saw anything, and even though she didn't believe in "next lives"—that Mose would be wearing his old coat there, too.

"Listen," Alex said edgily. "I can't sit here and just keep turning it over. Doug needs this. No, he needs that."

It was true that Alex liked to meet problems with action. He liked to get a job done, sometimes more than he liked to get a job done right, there being, he once told Ellen, no point in getting a job done right if that meant never actually getting it done. "So I *am* going to swing by the shrine with Ellen, then come back for Mose. Is that OK with you, Valerie?"

Assent, at this point, would be capitulation, but Valerie looked too tired for disagreement or maybe too tired for any scenario that would leave her alone in her kitchen with her ex-husband and his girlfriend. Suddenly all business, she stood and surveyed the kitchen table, saying, as if someone was trying to stop her, "I've really *got* to do these dishes."

The shrine seemed loonier, when you looked at it in person. The cross and photograph with its shiny, worthless detritus, the zany mishmash, had a certain Third World, Catholic look. Santeria. Voodoo. Some cross of mainstream and magical beliefs, as if the combination might allow Doug to speak to Brandi.

As if his thoughts were in accord with hers, Alex said, "Jesus, maybe he's having a complete psychotic break."

"No," Ellen said. "Not Doug."

"Oh, fuck," Alex said, an obscenity that wasn't usual with him. "I remember reading some article about schizophrenia in post-adolescent boys. No symptoms, then bang, off they go."

"It's just grief. It's just a manifestation of grief."

"*Crying* is a manifestation of grief. This is . . . Jesus, I don't know . . ." He rubbed his palm over his forehead.

Alex and Ellen stood on the ashy smudge of land where the synagogue had once been, as if poised upon the wet char of a giant's extinguished campfire, the smell like the back draft of a wood stove on a rainy day: acrid, burnt and sodden. The damp at their feet was all that was left of the firefighters' efforts. Ellen had gone to High Holy services here and practiced her Torah and Haftorah portion for her bat mitzvah, over and over in her faltering voice. There was a joke about a rabbi, priest and minister, each of whom had a problem with rats in their respective houses of worship. Someone had told Ellen this earlier in the year, when the center staged its terrifying production of *The Pied Piper of Hamelin*. In the joke, the priest and minister try unsuccessfully to get rid of their rats, and the rabbi says, "Rats! I can tell you how to get rid of rats. I rounded all of ours up, gave them bar mitzvahs, and they never returned." Ellen was like one of those rats. She'd hardly been back between her thirteenth birthday and today. How many times was it? Not many. Now cinder blocks lined the perimeter of where she'd once said her prayers. A large utility pole, blackened and worthless, lay where the bimah had been. Put fire and Jews together, and you couldn't help but feel guilty and sick, though within the week, she knew she'd be where she'd always been in relation to her heritage: interested in it as a culture, impatient with it as a religion.

Ellen leaned forward and touched the plastic sleeve that held Brandi's photograph. "What was the story? Of how you found her?"

"Oh," Alex rubbed his forehead. "Honestly, I don't remember exactly. She lived across the street but then those people left town. She was what the people at the homeless shelter called a couch surfer. She kept all her belongings in a cardboard box and went here and there. There were various college boys willing to let her bunk with them. One of the Sudbury students knew about it, and that's how I found her. It didn't take too much to convince her to come to Sudbury or go live with the McLellans. She was scared. Full of bravado, even then, but very scared."

"It wasn't Doug? Who told you?"

"I didn't even know they knew each other. I mean, she lived across the street for a time, but you know how it is, these days. You can live next door to someone and not even know their name. I didn't know the couple that skipped town. Don't think I'd recognize them if I passed them on the sidewalk."

Ellen bent to Brandi's photograph. Then she stepped back and said, "There's something weird about that photo, when you see it up close."

"I know," Alex breathed. And then he said what seemed obvious: "She looks so alive."

How strange that this spooked them, as if, when living, Brandi might have anticipated that this was the image that would represent her after death and comported herself accordingly.

"Can I help you folks?"

Alex and Ellen turned to see two policemen approaching, one with two dogs, the other an aging cop with the trademark low-slung belly. If he were a woman, midwives about town—and there were many— would knowingly exclaim, "Oh, you've already dropped."

"Hi," Ellen waved.

"What's with the dogs?" Alex asked.

"Nothing," the officer with the big belly said.

"My kid did this," Alex pointed to the shrine. "This girl's death has really cracked him up."

"Oh, boy," the other officer, the one with the dogs, said.

"Alex Decker," Alex leaned over Ellen to extend his hand to the men.

"Yeah," the officer with the dogs half-chuckled, shaking. "I know that. I'm Pete Stetson." He cocked his ear at the dogs. "They do the accelerant-sniffing."

Alex ran his fingers through the curls of his hair. "Not faulty wiring then?"

The fat cop grimaced, then said, "They found a gas cap in the rubble. The janitor told them there had been two red gas cans on the roof earlier in the week, but he hadn't thought anything of it. Although that in of itself is hard to believe."

"Old Arnie," Ellen put in.

"What?" Alex said.

"The janitor. Arnie Busar. He has Down's. He might not have realized what it was he was seeing." And then to the policemen, "You knew that? About the Down's, I mean."

The officer who hadn't offered his name said, "I didn't do the interview, but, hey, you think someone might have passed along that little tidbit. Fucking detectives."

"Arson, then?" Alex asked.

The officer shrugged but Pete Howards said, "I've been in this business twenty years. I still kind of got to wonder at the lengths people go to hurt one another."

"So—" Alex couldn't quite form his question. But then he said, "Was someone trying to hurt the Carter girl . . . or the Jews?"

"And which one do you think would be worse?" Pete said.

Alex looked at Ellen. "Hard to say." He was clearly trying for a philosophical tone. "Hard to say."

*B*ack at Valerie's, Alex suggested Ellen stay in her car. "I'll get Mose, then I'll have Valerie drive me to the garage."

"You don't want me to take you to get the car?"

"Val and I still haven't had a chance to talk things over," Alex said and leaned over to peck her on the cheek. "I don't know how long this will take."

"OK." Ellen slid into the driver's seat. She was glad not to go back inside, though she was disappointed that Alex was staying. She still didn't like being in the Ridgeway house alone, but she could hardly insist on her own needs now.

Not long after, Mose shuffled down the front steps and out to Ellen's car to say goodbye. He leaned into Ellen's window.

"What happened when you talked to Doug?" she asked.

"Oh, sweetheart. Nothing, really. I told him I'd lost people I'd loved, that time doesn't heal all wounds, that he'd always feel this loss. But that didn't mean he wouldn't feel other things, too."

"True enough." More true, Ellen guessed, for the *tone* in which Mose said it. If he wanted to, he could sound wise saying, "Hand me that corned beef."

"What did you think of the shrine?"

"I . . . I don't know . . . it sort of seems . . ."

"Unhinged?" Mose suggested.

"Exactly." It had gotten late. In the back and forth between the funeral, Valerie's house and the shrine, they'd missed lunch. "Should we get something to eat?"

Mose looked at his watch. "Ah . . . let's skip it. Soon enough it will be dinner, and I confess I'm tired."

"Yeah, me, too." She should tell him about the arson suspicion, but if the cops were so free with the information, it would probably be in all the papers tomorrow. And she didn't want to be with him the moment he learned; he always wanted to be alone when he was upset. Instead she said, "There's the summer, thank goodness. Doug can go as mad as he wants for the next few months, then dust himself off for classes in the fall."

"Or maybe the summer is a curse; work might be a distraction."

But clearly Doug didn't think so. On the drive home, Ellen thought of what Alex had already told her: that Doug had phoned the director of Camp Timberview, where he had worked the previous summer, to say he wouldn't be returning. "Ah, no," said Mrs. Mackee, she of the purple dresses and Marine Corps demeanor. "Why not? You're one of our best."

Doug said, "I just can't, because all those little kids are just going to die someday."

This observation didn't take Mrs. Mackee by surprise. "Well, last year they were going to die someday, too, but that didn't stop you."

Doug choked back a sob. "I know, but . . ."

"If I knew *I* was going to die someday," Mrs. Mackee announced, as if her mortality was genuinely in question, "you know what I'd want to do?"

"No," Doug said gently, "no," and he quietly placed the phone back on the receiver. Apparently he was afraid she'd tell him that she'd try to get a watermelon coated with Vaseline out of a lake, and he'd do the same, and he should come back to Camp Timberview and tell death not to be proud. Or something like that.

Ellen had gone to sleep-away camp once, when she was six. Mose had sent her and Barbara away for two weeks to an all-girls camp where they made macramé and hiked in the woods and learned how to do somersaults in a small blue pool, its floor slimy with algae. Ellen was the youngest girl in the whole camp, and the older girls treated her like their pretty little pet. Even so, half the time one of them was running away to fetch Barbara out of puppet making or drama class. "Your sister's crying," they'd call, flush with the importance of their errand. "Your sister's crying," and then a pack of concerned girls would run with Barbara back down the hill that led to Ellen's cabin. Barbara was only ten herself then. It became a camp project to cheer Ellen up, but the only thing she really liked was when her counselor sent her to the small cabin that served as the infirmary. Always freshly swept, with clean white sheets and itchy gray blankets on all the beds, the infirmary housed a nurse who dispensed Aspergum. When Ellen cried and said, "Mommy, Mommy, Mommy," the nurse came in with a cool washcloth, which she folded over Ellen's forehead. "It's OK," she'd say, stroking Ellen's hair. "It's OK." But even those moments—which veered into pleasure, released, as Ellen was, from the terrible daily strain of *not* crying—weren't enough to make up for the other moments, especially lying awake at night, head under the sheet in an effort to avoid the whine of mosquitoes, the tremendous expanse of night spreading away from her on all sides. Under the sheet, her head filled with the ghost stories the girls had shared around the campfire.

They came to her now, those stories, but in adulterated form, once she was back home. *I am the ghost with the bloody fingers*, she found herself reciting, remembering—but half-completely—a story from that long-ago camp. *You are the ghost with the bloody fingers. We are the ghost with the . . .* It was like she was trying to conjugate some foreign verb. Ridiculous. She rifled through old mail catalogs, turned the TV on, then off. Then on again. She flipped through the stations till she landed at a cooking show. She watched it, and the cooking show that came after. By the time it was over, she thought she should get dinner together. Or go for a run. But it was getting late for a run—even out here, a night run didn't appeal, the possibility of being waylaid by a sick stranger—and maybe Alex was going to stay for dinner with Valerie. She should do some sit-ups. Or something. It wasn't only the bloody fingers she was trying not to think about. Since the fire, she had to work not to imagine what it had been like for Brandi Carter, how it would feel to be in the synagogue kitchen, a room she knew all too well, and have a wall of fire come at you, how it would feel to have your shirt catch fire and then your arm . . .

Don't go there, as Tamar would say.

On the kitchen counter, there was a pad of lined paper with names on it. Before the fire, Alex and Ellen had been planning a house party for later in the month. Now the party seemed like a bad idea. Too soon after the tragedy. She should call Tamar and ask her opinion. Not that this was the question that truly occupied Ellen, but she needed an excuse to call Tamar. But when Ellen rang, her friend only said, "Well, what does Alex think?"

"I don't know."

"Well, ask him," Tamar said, in her signature bossy way. "Ask him right now."

"He's at Valerie's."

"Valerie? As in, the ex-wife?"

"The very one."

"Well, what's *that* about?"

"Oh, Doug, of course, and that girl who died. Doug's falling completely apart. I think he had a crush on her."

"Un-huh," Tamar said leadingly.

"What?"

"You don't think he'd fuck her, do you?"

"*What*?!" Ellen cried, thinking that Tamar was talking about Doug and Brandi.

"Valerie . . ." Tamar corrected.

"Oh, yeah. No, no. Alex and Valerie don't really get along."

"Though they were drawn together by the trauma of their mutual loss—" Tamar began theatrically.

"Tamar, this is serious."

"You know, Ellen. You're out of my league. Ex-wives. House parties. I'm still hoping to find a guy willing to neck with me."

"Right," Ellen said. She could hear Alex pulling into the drive. "Listen. I gotta go."

The first thing Ellen said when Alex stepped through the door was, "Let's reschedule."

"Huh?"

"I just don't see how we can have that barbecue now."

Alex looked confused. "It's not now. It's in two weeks."

"But . . ."

"Baby," he said and took her in his arms. "It's been the longest day of my life. I don't think I'm up for another argument."

"Right, of course, yeah," she said and kissed his wet, yeasty mouth. "Beers?"

"A few, and dinner. With Valerie. I'm about ready to collapse. Let's just go to bed."

"Oh, OK," she said, slightly disappointed, realizing that she'd been waiting all evening not just for his comfort but for his evaluation of the day—the time with Doug and Valerie, the police and the shrine—as if the whole point of the experience had been to come home and interpret it. But the point, she saw now, wasn't that at all. The point of the day—the point of any troubling day?—was to come home and finally just end it.

Chapter Three

MAY 2006

❦

"What's this?" Alex said, as he ducked into the front passenger seat of Valerie's Subaru.

A tremendous piñata in the shape of an elephant hunkered in the back seat. The inside of his ears were pink, his eyes blue, his trunk rising in a large S, ready to spray. Frills of gray tissue paper made up his festive skin.

"Dumbo," Valerie sniffed.

"Wow. You could . . . you could fill this thing with two turkeys . . . you know, skip the candy altogether." Years ago, at one of Doug's birthday parties, they'd hung a small piñata that the kids hadn't been able to break open. Nor had the parents, despite the two baseball bats they'd employed for the task and the many children chanting, "Break off its legs" and "Kill it." They'd used a saw in the end, been dismayed at the frenzy with which the kids grabbed the Tootsie Rolls inside: if you wondered why men started wars, here was your answer.

"Turkey . . . now that's an idea," Valerie said. "But we're raffling Dumbo off next weekend. At our fundraiser."

"Right," Alex said uncertainly. He hadn't followed her professional life—the public part of it—in the way that he suspected she followed his. The fundraiser was probably advertised in all the local papers.

By some silent agreement, they didn't talk about Doug until they'd arranged themselves at a booth in Shatterly's, a small pub out beyond the highway. Neither of them wanted to run into old friends, to hear someone inquire with evident pleasure, "Oh, you guys are back together?" When they were married, Valerie and Alex left the house so they wouldn't fight in front of Doug. Now they left to discuss Doug.

After a waitress handed them their menus and departed, Valerie began, her voice low and uneasy. "It's just . . . I mean . . ." But she couldn't get the words out.

"I know, I know."

Since his son's birth, Alex had worried over the possibility of Doug's ruin. Car accidents, drug addiction, a drunken stumble off a rooftop: the various male paths to needless destruction. But so far, Doug was a sensible, appealingly clean kid, cleaner indeed than his father, who'd spent his teenage years smoking pot, his college mornings drinking beers to mitigate the aftereffects of his nighttime high. There were ways to reject the path you were on, even as you committed yourself to it. That's what recreational drugs had seemed like to Alex: something his body could handle, like late nights at the school newspaper or binge writing of final papers, but something people didn't suspect him of. His manner, he knew, was always that of the get-ahead kid.

"How," Ellen had once asked him, "did you manage not to become an alcoholic?"

Was she asking because she thought he *was* an alcoholic?

He said, "Oh, I am an alcoholic. I really like to drink."

"I know that, but . . ." Ellen had continued. She'd excuse him anything, define him as he needed to be defined: someone who enjoyed drinking. Nothing darker than that. It was naïveté or else a form of generosity. By this point, Alex was what he was, and Ellen accepted that, no matter how it might look to a clinician or the author of a *Cosmo* multiple choice quiz. (How *many* nights of the week does he drink? How *many* drinks does he have?)

Valerie reached across the table and took Alex's hand. "He'll be all right, though?" A question and there was so much hope in it, so much need for Alex, whom Valerie had never admired, to have the right and acceptable answer, to reassure her that Doug would make it through whatever was happening to him. Alex felt his old affection for her.

"Of course, he will. He'll be fine."

"Right," Valerie said and started to cry, but soundlessly, letting tears drip down her cheeks, the very display—*Feel for me. I'm sad*—that used to enrage Alex. But it didn't bother him now. They'd both been trying to suppress their sorrow, so they could attend to Doug, but, Jesus Christ. Brandi Carter, that tough little girl. He still couldn't quite believe it.

"He's just overwhelmed," Alex said. "It's not just her death. It's *death* he has to make sense of. I remember that myself. The first young person I knew who died . . . it wasn't just about never seeing that person again. It was about mortality in general—my own, a squirrel's. You know, I'd see a bug squirming away from my tissued hand and think, 'There's the ugly truth of it. Nothing wants to end.'"

Valerie dried her face as a waitress approached. After ordering— beer for him, wine for her, a sandwich to split—they stiffened for some reason, talked a little about work, then drifted into the painful silence that characterized the end of their marriage. Sometimes he felt she had lots to say but thought it wasn't worth the energy to say it to him.

"When I was a kid," Alex started, thinking he could pull her back to him, if he told a story she hadn't heard about his past. Early in their relationship, she had been angered when he wouldn't divulge more about life on the farm, or his previous girlfriends, or his years in high school—all things he couldn't quite remember, but she never trusted *that* explanation. It was hardly as if it were a long time ago! But the truth was Alex had always been focused on who he would become, so he hadn't packaged the past the way she had. He'd weathered childhood, much as Doug used to suffer dinner . . . for the reward of dessert. "The first kid I ever knew to die was this kid—he lived maybe half a mile down the road—who fell down the stairs. In his house, you know, and died . . ." As he talked, Alex realized that his story was the story of a murder. Kids didn't die from tripping down the stairs. His parents, somebody, must have pushed him. *Holy shit*, that farm at the far end of the road, that family who always put out the most outrageous Christmas display—Santa and reindeer who raised and lowered their front legs, and elves running from the sleigh, each with a gift box in hand. And that poor kid—the one who'd died, with his sallow skin and dopey, unfocused eyes . . . No one talked about child abuse back then. People believed in spanking, not hitting, as if the two words implied different actions. But he didn't say all this to Valerie. He just told her how he remembered learning of the boy's death and how he processed the loss, coming to see that it just meant he had to live each day as if it were his last. "I guess," Alex finished his story, "I became a better person for it."

Valerie twisted her napkin. Perhaps Alex's conclusion—its simplicity and its bravado—irritated her. Or maybe she wasn't paying attention. At the end of their marriage, Valerie often drifted when his stories went on, as this one had, past a few sentences.

"Not hungry?" he said, looking at her half of the sandwich.

"No, I am," she said but didn't make a move toward her meal. She seemed almost nervous, as if they hadn't already negotiated a relationship and its demise, but were at the uneasy beginning of a new attachment. He reached out and pressed her hand with his own. "It'll be OK," he said. "Honest, it will."

"Right."

"We'll give him another week, then he has to go back to school. Class will distract him."

"Only summer's almost here."

"That's true."

"I just really want to go to bed with you," she said, as if this were a normal response to his words, and too, as if they'd never slept together, as if she'd been—in the past—forthcoming about sex. Which she hadn't. She'd been as uptight as they come.

"I . . ." Alex looked around the largely empty restaurant. This was . . . this wasn't just unexpected, this was . . . *what was it?*

And then he considered the possibility. What he missed about Valerie's lovemaking was desperation, a panic in the face of her own desire, related (Alex assumed) to how hard it was for her to let herself go. She sobbed on the rare times she came. Not sad, she explained. It's just too much. Too, too much.

Valerie looked down at her plate. Alex couldn't meet her eye either.

"We could go to the car?" Alex suggested. It was already dark, the parking lot all but empty. People wouldn't come till later. Folks ate early in Wisconsin, but Shatterly's was more of a place to drink than eat. Valerie nodded without looking up.

In the car, Alex quickly flicked his passenger seat back, and there was a ripping noise.

"Oh, Jesus. I'm so sorry," Alex said, turning to see what he'd done. The elephant was torn, a newspaper wound in its gray tissue paper skin. "I think I've emasculated your friend here." And then pretend-befuddled, because of course the elephant wasn't *that* anatomically correct. "No, no, that appears to be its tusk."

"Don't worry. I didn't know the seats could . . ." Valerie made a motion with her hand to mimic the seat's flip backward. There seemed to be an accusation in this, as if he had learned—by cheating on Valerie— how to turn a car seat into a lounger. If Valerie thought so, it didn't bother her, or not at the moment, for she was abruptly atop him—kissing his mouth though they rarely kissed during their marriage, always moved straight to the main event of sex, the lack of necking part of what Valerie claimed to hate about their partnership, no tenderness, no connection, just dumb biological need. Get it in, get it out. There you are. But now, as if tenderness—the very thing she always wanted—frustrated her, she moved for his pants, undid the zipper there.

"Ellen and I might get engaged," Alex blurted. What the hell was he doing? In fact, Ellen and he *were* engaged. They were planning an engagement party for later in the month.

"That's nice," Valerie said, taking his cock into her mouth, then slipping it out to add, "I'm giving you an early wedding present."

Infidelity had absorbed Alex during his marriage. A friend once confessed that he had said to *his* friends, "When do you find time to do it?" and Alex wondered if that meant that his friend's friends were all having affairs. Another friend said he thought people strayed a lot more than others realized. "I think a lot less," Alex countered. "I think people talk about sex in lieu of having it. Lots of fantasy, not much action." But then he'd flushed, thinking this gave too much away. And who knows, if Valerie had been giving him regular blowjobs in the car, maybe straying wouldn't have been so much on his mind. It wasn't that their sex life had been bad, exactly, but that they never seemed to be quite on the same page. Valerie would come kiss his neck in the middle of a ball game, clearly hoping for something on the rug, and he'd flinch—because it was a game he wanted to watch—and then she'd react to that flinch, as if he hadn't flinched but decked her one right there in the living room, and she'd get going about how he could never be spontaneous, how everything had to be 1-2-3 his way, and he'd tell her it was-n't that, and she'd say she knew he wouldn't do it on the rug, they al-ways had to march upstairs and then he'd say, "Good God, Val, do you want me to hurt my back?" and she'd say, "You know I don't want you to hurt your back. Just because I want you to lighten up doesn't mean I want you to . . ." And on and on they'd go, and she wouldn't have the little nooky on the rug that she'd daydreamed about, and he'd miss the ball game, both of them too busy fighting to get any pleasure out of the evening.

And even so, he'd never cheated on her. He'd feel like too much a jerk, if he did. (He felt like a jerk cheating on Ellen, the shame overtak-ing him as he wiped semen off his stomach with a tissue, tucked himself back into his pants and put the tissue into his pocket. He'd have to throw *that* away before he got home.) The cost of being caught—to his marriage, but also to his life—was simply too high.

Thinking about infidelity, though, that had become an activity in its own right, a way of stepping out of his life—the life not quite of a pub-lic figure but of a leader, the one in charge, bound to civic-mindedness, the education of the city's children. He felt born to it, really, to leader-ship and stature, felt born to it precisely because he hadn't been born to it. He'd been born to a dairy farm, to skinny men and fat wives, Re-publicans and Sunday supper, to a belief in the importance of work, a sense that education was a silly affectation. A defense, of course, this take on learning, a defense that became all the more entrenched when confronted with learning, which Alex's brothers, at least, could manage to portray as decidedly feminine, a sissy activity, the "liberal"—here a sashay to their hips—arts. Christ, how he hated all that.

On some level he'd married Valerie because the DNA that pro-duced her was decidedly not the DNA that produced him. Not born to privilege, she always insisted, but she was: the privilege of people who like to think, the privilege of people who used money, when they had it, to buy culture, not a bigger tractor. Privilege without the hard cash that would have made that privilege easy, but privilege all the same.

But still, fooling around with Valerie? What was he thinking?

He'd never even dreamed of cheating on Ellen. With whom? Do-ing what? Why would he want to?

So he might very well ask himself—well, he was asking himself, now that he'd picked up his car from the repair shop (shop long closed, key under the floor mat) and started driving home—what it was he had just done.

"Don't tell Ellen," Valerie had said, when she first started kissing him.

"No, of course not."

"I wouldn't want to hurt Ellen."

"That makes two of us."

Or all of us, he might have said. Everyone liked Ellen. *No one* wanted to hurt her. She was the sort of person you couldn't imagine hurting. ("Because she has no edge," he could imagine Valerie saying, "because there is no *there* there." But that wasn't true. People who didn't think she was bright just didn't see the subtlety of her intelligence.)

Alex thought he should feel more upset by his own behavior, but somehow it didn't feel like he was going home to Ellen after betraying her. It was just Valerie, after all, and he'd already chosen Ellen over Valerie. And what was he going to do? Say no to Valerie when she was upset? The idea of saying no hadn't crossed his mind. The closer he got to Ridgeway, the more it felt like he'd just done something he'd been doing off and on for much of the past decade. He hadn't cheated on Ellen; instead Valerie and he had had a farewell fuck, a final bit of business, like sorting out their mutual funds, a necessary part of the divorce.

The next morning, Alex found himself back at his son's rank bedside. The scene—even Doug's clothes—identical to the previous day.

"I'll never get over it," Doug told him.

"You will. You don't think you will, but you will."

"What you can't seem to understand," Doug said, furious, "is I don't want to get over it. I'd never forgive myself if I did."

Not knowing what to say, Alex decided his job was simply to listen. Doug was quiet for five, maybe ten minutes, and then he said, "It should have been me, not her."

More silence. Then: "I just want to call her up and talk to her about it, you know? Like I'll get on the phone and say, 'God, Brandi, you'll never guess what happened to you.'" And so on, through the morning.

215

Finally: "I wish I was dead."

"OK," Alex said, clapping his hands. "Get up, get up. You're taking a shower, and I'm driving you over to Mose Sheinbaum's."

"What are you talking about?"

"Your mother said that you liked talking to Mose Sheinbaum. Is that right?"

"I guess."

"OK. So shower. You stink. I'll be back up in fifteen minutes."

Downstairs, Alex dialed Mose and asked if he'd mind talking to Doug some more. Yesterday, his words had seemed to help, and help would be a help right now. He'd run out of ideas on what to do for Doug. They agreed Alex would bring Doug by Mose's apartment within the hour.

"So," Alex said to Valerie, who had come into the kitchen while he was on the phone. "I've got a plan."

"I heard. Sounds good. He was up last night, when I came home. He got up, and he ate a sandwich."

"That's progress."

"And"—she pointed over her shoulder, as if "last night" was located somewhere behind her neck—"we won't do that again." It wasn't a question or a mournful statement of fact. It was a decision.

"No, *no*," Alex said, in perfect agreement.

"I have some pretty strong beliefs about how people should act."

"I know that." He resented her for chastising him. *She* was the one who had started things.

"Only my longings don't go with my beliefs, I guess. I don't think you know *that*."

Alex recognized her heated tone. This was the way she talked when she believed herself to be most confessional, revealing her deepest secrets, though most of the time, Alex knew them already.

"If I read a novel about this"—her hand gestured between them—"I'd be a disgusting character. My behavior would be totally reprehensible. But I think of myself as a good person. I really do."

"You *are* good."

She twisted her lips in disagreement.

"Oh, Val . . ."

"One thing I'll say for you." She was no longer looking at him, but out the back window at the black-capped chickadees, the most reliable visitors to her bird feeder, no matter the season. "You don't judge people. It's a nice quality. It really is."

Doug came down the stairs. He looked haggard, from all the crying he had been doing, but he was dressed in clean clothes: jeans, a t-shirt, his high-top sneakers.

"Oh, Mom," he said and went to cry in her arms.

"Hey, baby," she said, stroking his hair. "Let *me* drive you over to Mose's. Alex should really get home to Ellen."

"No, I'll do it," Alex said, but Valerie held up her hand. The decision was made, and Alex might have welcomed it, only he wanted, during the car ride, to find out exactly what it was that Mose had said yesterday. In the end, what *were* the words that helped?

Chapter Four

JULY 2006

❦

*I*t was July, and there was only one subject: Israel and Lebanon. The TV news, Mose, the University of Wisconsin Divest from Israel Campaign—there wasn't an opinion put forward on the matter that didn't offend Ellen or make her squirm: the Divest From people who likened Israel to the whites of pre-apartheid South Africa, Mose who shrugged and said, "What can they do, with enemies always amassing at their borders?" Ellen bumped into a woman from *shul*, one of the older members who dutifully comprised the morning *minyan*, who said she hoped they "bombed the crap out of all those people," this being the complex thought to which daily prayer had brought her. And then there was the morning tragedy of the newspaper. "I look at it, and I'm like 'Arrrrgh,'" Ellen said to Tamar, who was the only one who seemed to understand. What could you say? There was nothing to say; there was only something to regret.

And then one day the MadCity Freedom Puppeteers and their giant grim reaper puppets staged a protest, a banner stretched from one end of the façade of the Center for Artistic Exchange to the other and reading, "Stop the Racist Israeli State Now!"

"What's that?" the kids at the center wanted to know. It was knights, dragons and castles week at the daycare.

"It's just something that grown-ups disagree about," Ellen said.

"What? Is that puppet bad? The one with the sword."

"He's definitely scary, isn't he?" Ellen said and handed each child a paper bag to color. Later, she'd cut holes for the kids' heads and arms. They were to wear the knights' armor for an end-of-the-week Medieval Faire.

Ellen couldn't believe Valerie had permitted the display. The banner was pinned to the Center, not just outside on the sidewalk, so it seemed to be a representation of the views of those inside. Technically the Center was closed in the summer, but the daycare kept running. There were no plays or public events. Instead, the Center rented out space. The Children's Theater of Madison was in occupancy, a thumping boom box playing music for *The Wiz*, and skinny girls occasionally walking by the daycare's windows dressed in costumes: Jackie O, a frowsy fifties housewife, a large green alligator. Ellen had spent too much time trying to imagine the story into which these three characters might fit. There had been a Red Cross blood drive earlier in the month, and for most of July, the MadCity puppet people constructed their enormous puppets—some twenty feet high—in the theater's fly space.

*I*nsofar as Alex and Ellen's life had fallen into a pattern in the few months they had lived together, that pattern reversed with the end of the academic year. Ellen was home by six, but Alex was always already there, working out of a makeshift basement office, instead of staying late in Madison for meetings or other business. Typically, Ellen went for a run, then settled into Alex's plans for the evening—for there was invariably something, even if that "something" was only "a night in, working."

Tonight, Alex wanted to talk about their engagement party. They'd originally planned a party for June, but after the fire and Doug's depression—which was still very much with the boy, though he no longer wished himself dead on an hourly basis—they'd rescheduled for August. If not for world events—the Israeli-Lebanon conflict on top of the Iraq War—July might have been a month of reprieve, the worst of the end-of-the-year events over (Greg Shardon's retirement party planned, thrown and endured, all its funereal sorrow cloaked as an appreciative tribute); Mose now reading and visiting with friends, instead of worrying over Hyman Clark; Alex taking breaks from work to garden, the house no longer smelling of toxic varnishes and fresh paint, but of dirt or the weedy wildflowers Alex put in small drinking glasses about the kitchen. Ellen imagined even *the ghost with the bloody fingers* had taken a rest, or just decomposed, like any wayward rodent, between the wallboards of her imagination.

Ellen joined Alex out on the porch, hair still damp from a post-run shower, feet bare and pulled up under her, eyes trained on the fields and woods beyond. Alex had mown a swath around the house, and the air smelled sweet and green. "Here," Alex said and deposited a large envelope in her lap. "Invitations." He went back into the house and returned to the porch, carrying a drink precariously in the remaining fingers of his left hand and a pad of paper in the right. "Shall we?"

"What?" Ellen cocked her head.

"Guest list. Round two." Alex held up the pad of paper with the names they'd come up with weeks ago.

"Oh, right," she said. "Do you know what was at work today? A big banner by those MadCity puppet people. It said Stop Israel's Racist War, or something like that. I couldn't believe Valerie would allow it."

"Why wouldn't she?" Alex said, slipping into the porch's other Adirondack chair and putting his scotch on the table between them.

"Because it's not true?"

"Val's always been one to let all sides have their opinion."

"But I'm not sure that's what it was."

"Well," he allowed, reaching into the neck of his t-shirt to scratch his back, a small spot of eczema that he refused to put cream on, an itch that had lasted the whole of their relationship. "Have a look." He indicated the envelope on her lap. "I hope you like them."

She pulled out a stack of color Xeroxes on cardstock.

"These are them? Wow—not quite what I expected." She'd imagined the standard: folded, off-white cards, noting day, time and a number to RSVP.

Instead, the invitations were titled "The Ridgeway Follies" and designed to look like mini–movie posters. A photograph of Alex's head sat atop the pen-and-ink torso of a woman dressed as a kitty cat and swinging on a trapeze swing. Ellen's head was perched on that of a dancer, gamely kicking her legs and fanning a top hat. About these figures, curlicue words promised "Dancing!" "Vaudeville! "Kiddie pool!"

Under the figures, the invitations read:

Come to the show, May 26th, running one day only, to celebrate the engagement of Ellen Hirschorn and Alex Decker.

And in even smaller print:

Act I.   Kids Can-Can. 12–2:30. Hiking and Ziegfeld berry picking. Kids (and water toys) welcome. Muffin baking optional.
Act II.   Afternoon Sports. 2:30–4:00. Soccer in the meadow. Kids still welcome.
Act III. Drinks and dinner. Six on, strictly NC-17.
Act IV.   Evening performance. All acts welcome. X-treme mime. Karaoke equipment provided. Eight till???

Gifts prohibited. (Don't even try, if you want to be fed.)

"You like it?"

"It's funny. It's just . . ."

"What?" And then before she had a chance to answer, "You've never seen me in party mode before. I can be quite the impresario."

"Oh, that's fine, I know. It's just not quite my style. Not that that makes such a big difference, but . . ." But maybe it should, she thought, if I'm hosting the party, and yet she'd more than willingly given into Alex's request that she let him handle the invitation, that she let him surprise her.

"But you said I could . . ."

"Oh, I know, I know. I'm glad we're doing it this way. The barbeque and all and everything low-key, but there's part of me that worries that Barbara will think this"—Ellen tapped the invitation—"is silly. And that Mose will think it isn't a serious enough way to announce a marriage."

"My dear, you worry too much about what that family of yours will think."

"That could be."

"Is that why the banner at work bothered you so much? You could imagine Mose reacting to it?"

Ellen laughed. "No, honey," she said. "I was bothered by that all on my very own. It was irresponsible of her."

"Free speech, though, isn't it?"

"For me, that's free speech the way a Klan rally is free speech. It's not true, and it's hate-mongering."

"Wait . . . I don't get that . . . they want to stop the war. I mean, they might be . . ."

"It's not stopping the war if you come up with some overly simplistic version of what is going on, of who is oppressing and who is oppressed, if you present something that just fans the flames, that . . ."

Alex stood up and kissed the top of her head. "Your father's daughter, after all."

"My cousin. You know Mose is really just my cousin."

"Right. Well, let's get down to the guest list. Let's just start from scratch," he said, crumpling their old list. "Rather than trying to resurrect what we did before."

Alex passed her a sheet of small white stickers. Ellen was to go through the invitations, crossing out the "May 26th" that Alex had had printed and replacing the date with stickers that read "August 19th."

Alex lifted his pen. "You go first on the names."

"OK, well, Barbara and her husband, Tamar and a date. Mose, of course. Tamar's parents." Ellen listed some more names—friends from her university days, several of her co-workers at the daycare.

"OK," Alex said, writing all this down, then adding some of his own friends to the list, but saying the names out loud, so Ellen would say, "Of course," or "I like them," before he wrote the names down.

"Hyman Clark," he said abruptly, looking up. "Geez—I don't see how I'm going to get around inviting him if I invite anyone from work."

"Oh, that would kind of be a drag."

"We could just keep Mose and him away from each other."

"Like anyone is going to sign up for that job," Ellen said. "It's not like he's the most fun person to talk to, and . . . oh, if you have him, you've got to have her, what's-her-face?"

"Martha . . ."

"Yikes." They both laughed a little. "She's kind of scary."

"No argument there–let's put them in the 'invite and pray they don't accept' category." He drew a line down his pad of paper, then looked up at her. "Done?"

"Yeah, OK," she said, not quite uneasily, but with a sense she'd have to revisit the subject when she was more in the mood for argument. At the moment, she was trying to make out a bird in the tree—a hawk, she thought, though sometimes she'd get all excited by a stately silhouette and realize that she was looking at nothing more than one of the property's ubiquitous ravens of which she was obscurely scared. Last week, one had gotten stuck in her compost pile. She'd looked out and noted it, looked out an hour later and saw the bird was still sitting there. This was on Saturday, Alex gone to visit Doug. She found her binoculars and saw that the bird was trying to take off, its horrible beak opening in a terrified caw, its large wings flapping anxiously. She panicked. She knew she should take a shovel and go out to the compost to free the bird, but she couldn't. It seemed like a little package of death out there. Was it just that famous Edgar Allan Poe poem that made her think this, or had Poe inscribed the obvious: the greasy ink of their too-big bodies was portentous, both too alive and too decidedly *not*, a carrion-loving, bird-shaped blackness.

In the end, she called the police. The man who answered laughed— "Well, this is one for the books"—and she apologized profusely, but they sent someone over anyway. She went out to meet the police car in the drive, but when she walked the officer behind the house to the compost pile, the bird was gone, a large pile of white droppings in its place. Ellen resumed the round of apologies that she'd started when she'd first called the police.

The cop held up his hand. "Hey, honey. I got a daughter myself. And she'd have called the police, too. Don't give it a never thought." He'd meant to say "another," of course, but he'd made that odd mistake—a "never" thought.

Now Alex followed Ellen's gaze. "Hawk?"

"That's what I'm thinking."

They were quiet, looking at the bird, and then Alex turned his attention to the meadow, said he would rent a tractor to mow it for soccer. "Listen," Alex said softly. "I know this is going to sound weird, but how would you feel if I asked Valerie to come?"

"I don't know." She put a few more stickers on invitations. August 19th, August 19th, August 19th. "You're serious?" She looked up, amused. "To our engagement party?"

"Not because I *want* her to come, just in the interest of . . . I don't know . . . future harmony. I just think of how strange it would be if everyone I knew were at a party with her, and I wasn't invited. I mean, she won't *come*. I can guarantee that, so it's more of a politeness. And you know that I already told her we were engaged."

"Yeah." Ellen took a sip from her water bottle. "When I first came out here, this place seemed so lonely. Now I feel this sense of . . . oh, I don't know . . . well-being. Like nothing, nothing of the ordinary world can reach us here. We might be on a camping trip. We're home, but we're also off somewhere." She looked down at the invitations. "I wonder how it will feel to bring so many people to this space."

"It's completely fine if you don't want her."

"No, no, I guess I don't mind. I mean, I like Valerie fine, you know. It's just strange."

"She won't come. This is definitely one for the 'invite and pray they don't attend' column."

"Oh, I know. But she could. And that might be all right. That might even be interesting." She laughed, a light, little laugh.

Alex wrote Valerie's name down on his list. "Of course, I might change my mind ten times before I put the invitations in the mail."

Ellen laughed, a more knowing sound than before. By now, she was onto this character flaw of his; without a lot of advice from others, he had trouble making decisions.

"And Doug, of course," Ellen said.

Doug had found summer work, teaching sailing on Lake Mendota and waiting tables on weekends. He was a long way from emotionally steady, but he met his obligations, even if the owner of Café Breton told Alex she'd found Doug, last Saturday, crying in the walk-in refrigerator, the one semi-private spot in the restaurant. "That's another reason to have Valerie here," Alex said. "Just in case the engagement party is hard on him."

"OK. I don't mind."

"Then it's settled." Alex leaned over to give Ellen a scotch-scented kiss, before standing for the kitchen. To get another drink, Ellen knew. The silence inside the house would be profound, save for a low, low hum that Ellen never tried to describe to anybody and that she couldn't attach to anything *in* the house. *Those fingers, those fingers.* Outside, even in the quiet, she could always make out something: a distant car, the wind stirring the treetops, a noisy crow. The inside sound, Ellen finally decided, was the hum of silence.

"Maybe you drink too much," Ellen said from the porch.

"What?" Alex called, though she had the distinct sense he had heard her.

Ellen put the stack of invitations on the porch table and stood to stretch. "Oh, nothing," she said to the hills before her. "It's nothing."

Chapter Five

AUGUST 2006

❦

*W*hat did Vitamin D deficiency look like? Maybe Martha had it. She went out of the house so rarely. When did she see the sun? Rickets. What were rickets anyway? Some disease of children, of Third World children from one of those countries that all blended together, as far as Hyman was concerned. But when he imagined the damage, he imagined white children with wasting bones, their eyes giant blind orbs in their heads.

Computers were making Martha's life worse. There was now a program for crossword puzzles. She used to do it all by hand. It took the fun out of it, she said. These days, she could only get work doing crossword puzzles for youngsters—big volumes printed on cheap paper and published by Dell or Scholastic. She wanted to do puzzles for the adult papers, but she'd gotten no encouragement there.

Hyman thought he'd cheer her up tonight. He had the news of a second invitation to the Deckers'—a party to celebrate Alex's engagement—and while Martha hadn't had a good time at that first party, he felt sure she'd join him at this second.

"Hey, there," he called into the dim room where she was reading a book. "How's your day been?"

"Oh, you know," she said flatly. "Yours?"

"Well, good, quite good. We've got another invitation to the Deckers'. A party for their engagement. I was hoping you'd want to go."

"That's all right. You go. You have fun."

"It's not till next week. You might like it? Not just a work obligation. So if we're being invited to this sort of thing, we've really arrived, you know."

Martha gave him a look that he couldn't read, then said, "Just noodles for dinner, though I made you a salad. My stomach's driving me nuts. I didn't think I could handle anything but noodles. I'm really sorry."

"Noodles are good." Pasta, he thought to say, everyone calls it "pasta" now.

"So . . ." he said leadingly, waiting for her to respond to his invitation.

"You know what your problem is," she said, and he realized that she was enraged, that she'd been furious ever since he'd stepped into the house. "Your problem is that you get ahead of yourself."

Hyman could not bear the idea of a fight just now, Martha puncturing his good mood. She'd been thirty and still living with her parents when he met her. Her father had hit her, even into her twenties. A situation from which he'd saved her, though it occurred to him now and then that what she wanted, more than anything, was for him to slug her, as if having grown used to such attention, she couldn't quite manage without it. She practically backed one into thinking about smacking her: everything about her manner said, "Hit me, come on hit me. I *dare* you. You know it's what you want to do." There were times when Hyman would very much have liked to oblige.

Chapter Six

August 2006

He wasn't going to come.

"But Mose—" Ellen began. She was at the kitchen table, arranging tulips in a vase, as she talked on the phone. How could he not be there?

"Honey, I'm far too sick." He snuffled once, then blew a wad of something into what Ellen knew was the cloth handkerchief he carried around in his pocket. They were talking on the phone. He said the only thing that would make him miss her party was the possibility of vomiting on the bride-to-be, and that, he had to confess, was a real possibility.

"Is this about Hyman Clark? We couldn't help but invite him, but you—"

"No, no. I wouldn't let him make me miss your engagement party. I'm really sick."

"What will Barbara think?"

"She'll think I'm sick. I'll see her later in the weekend, but really I'm coming down off this fever, and . . ."

"Right, oh, of course. I'm just sorry you won't be here." She shouldn't feel like he was denying a blessing by staying home, but that was exactly what she felt.

"But, listen, honey, that's not the only reason I called."

"It's not?"

228

"No, I got something in the mail today that I want you to see. I'm going to put it in the mail."

"What is it?"

"It's another piece of hate mail."

"You're kidding." Ellen put her hand to her check.

"I got it in May, just after graduation, I came back to my office and I found it on my desk."

"Why didn't you tell me?"

"I'm telling you now."

"I meant in May. Why didn't you tell me then?" When he didn't answer, Ellen said, "Well, what was it?"

"I'll tell you what it was. It came in a yellow envelope. On it, someone wrote, 'Thought this might interest you.' And inside I found . . . my merit review letter."

"Mose! I can't believe it! So what did it say, why didn't you . . ."

"Ah, she can't let me finish a sentence without interrupting."

Though she was on the phone, Ellen clapped a hand over her mouth and mumbled, "I'm sorry. I'll shut up. Finish."

And he did, saying that he had wanted to show her the letter right away, but he was aware that there might be "interpretive differences" and, too, that she'd want to show the letter to Alex, which might not be good for Mose, might prove politically difficult later on. So he'd sent it off for some independent confirmation.

"And that means?" Ellen asked.

"I sent into the ADL."

"You're kidding? The Anti-Defamation League? It's that bad?"

"Maybe you won't think so. That's why I sent it off."

"Well, read it to me. Will you? And . . ."

But Mose said no. He was going to mail a copy to her, along with the ADL letter. *That* had just come today. When she had read both, he said, they should talk.

"Don't make me crazy. I hate mystery," Ellen said.

"No, no . . . if I read it out loud, I'll inflect it the wrong way or something. I want you to read it, as you'd read it, then tell me what you think."

A loaded proposition made no easier by the astonishing swiftness of the United States Postal Service, which contrived to place the letter in

Ellen's rural mailbox at 11:03 A.M. the very next day, when Alex and Ellen were doing the last neatening for the party. "For you, for me, for me, for me, for you," Alex said as he sorted the mail, which largely consisted of catalogs.

"That was fast," Ellen said, picking up the envelope with Mose's handwriting. She'd told Alex last night that the letters were coming. "I guess we had better see what's in this."

"Now?" Alex said, his mouth gaping open. In flashes, there was something so decidedly dumb about Alex's manner that Ellen froze up, thinking she had made a mistake and wondering if it was a mistake that she would be able to weather over several decades, but then he'd close his mouth and seem perfectly intelligent once again.

"I'm sorry," Ellen said, her finger already breaking the seal of the envelope. "I couldn't stop myself from reading this if I tried. Sort of like you with cookies." Alex made Ellen hide sweets when she bought them. Presented with a quart of ice cream or a bag of cookies, Alex's instinct was to consume the whole lot, whether he was hungry or not. When he found her low-fat, oatmeal raisin cookies in the broom closet, he marched them out to her and—untasty as they were—asked her to re-hide.

But his appetites were entirely controlled when it came to the mail. He could leave a personal letter unopened for days, a restraint—or lack of curiosity—that puzzled Ellen, when it didn't madden her. How could he resist?

"OK, OK," Alex said, waving the papers that Ellen was unfolding toward himself. "Read to me."

So Ellen began.

Dear Sirs:

Mose Sheinbaum is one of those of whom it can be said are born teachers. He is a twelve-year veteran of Sudbury, having come to the school with no teaching experience, and parlayed his way into a full-time position in American History.

The child of New Yorkers—note: a jazz singer mother—who kept *Partisan Review* around the house, Sheinbaum engages with his students. On the day in which I saw him teach a class on the New Deal, Sheinbaum sat at the edge of his chair, feet and legs pushed back under his chair as if ready to spring. If you can summon up the curly-haired, bent-backed figure of a Chagall painting, head lifted to fix his gaze on the viewer, you'll have an analogue. Mose Sheinbaum fixes his hawk-like stare on his students, encouraging them with his signature New York accent. He is one of those teachers who is a performer, as much Woody Allen as Mr. Chips. (You can take the teacher out of New York but you can't take the New York out of the teacher.) And yet . . . his charm in the classroom (if it is charm, for some will find him aggressive, as he loudly exhorts his students to discuss matters entirely outside the bounds of his specific expertise) . . . this so-called charm is offset by a laxity outside of the classroom and a failure to participate in the larger school community. He does not assign his students a sufficient amount of homework—he seems to think books are out-of-date—nor does he make larger efforts by assisting in school-wide activities. He coaches no teams, nor does he attend faculty meetings. He has failed to attend the diversity workshops, required of all faculty and staff. Indeed, Sheinbaum is argumentative. He asked for a meeting with me, then failed to attend the meeting, arriving only to say he was leaving. Students are fond of Mr. Sheinbaum, but then they are fond of the easy way out. A more rigorous teacher would not please them. In the end, Sheinbaum is not, as we say, a team player. As a role model, Mose Sheinbaum certainly fails students, forgetting that resistance is a skill most students already have. In past years, Sheinbaum has received a full, and perhaps unjustified, merit raise, given these shortcomings. He was a personal friend of the previous principal, which may account for her fiscal irresponsibility. In keeping with your office's requests that I cut back my budget by 5 percent this year, I suggest no merit raise for Sheinbaum this year. At the very least, this should offset what certainly have been overly generous—if not entirely inappropriate—raises in the past.

Sincerely,
Hyman Clark

"OK," Alex said, too calmly for Ellen, "so now we know what he said."

Ellen felt a little queasy. She had expected something different from Alex. "You don't think that's borderline anti-Semitic. I mean . . . what difference does it make that Mose's mother was a jazz singer or that his hair is curly or—"

Alex said, "Why don't you just read the other letter?"

She did, trying to bite back her irritation with Alex. It was from Josh Greenstein, civil rights counsel for the Midwest ADL. In it, Greenstein explained that "New York," "hawk-like," "curly-haired," "Chagall" and "Woody Allen" were all code words for "Jewish." References to an African American teacher's curly hair, Greenstein observed, would hardly have been tolerated. The repeated references to "New York" struck Greenstein as particularly interesting, given that Mose had been born and raised in San Francisco. Greenstein said that he and his executive director were prepared to convey their concerns to the Madison School Board, should Mose wish.

"Oh, boy," Alex said, returning to the original letter, trying (Ellen imagined) to decide whether the letter was genuinely discriminatory or merely insensitive, the letter of someone too oafish to see how it might offend. "How come I am only seeing this letter now?"

He already knew the answer. Still, Ellen said, "I guess because the School Board approved the letter, so it never came to you. You weren't overseeing Mose's review, because of nepotism? Right? And then it got lost, so . . . here it is."

Alex put his fingers to his forehead, rubbed his left temple with his thumb.

"Back when you were doing the job search for Hyman, was there anything obviously questionable? I mean, did people have a problem with him?"

Alex squinted. He was trying to remember.

"Well—" she stopped. "You would have checked his references, of course."

"Yeah," Alex said. "I'd have made those calls myself."

"Well, what did they say? About Hyman?"

"I don't know. I mean, I can't remember specifically. Good stuff, I'm sure, or we wouldn't have hired him. I'm sure there are letters in his file."

"And when you called, you just called. Who did you call?" Mose had told Ellen something else last night, but it was so unbelievable, she still wasn't ready to tell Alex about it. Even though she had plenty of reason to believe Mose's words.

"His colleagues, I'm assuming. I don't remember. I'm sure it's all in the file. If he were an easier guy to read, I might just . . . You know how stiff Hyman is."

"We should try and ply him with some liquor tonight. See what he reveals," Ellen laughed. "Unless he comes to the blueberry picking part of the party. Then we're out of luck."

"Oh, God," Alex groaned. Then he reached over and swatted Ellen's bottom with the ADL letter. "It's our engagement party! We can deal with this all later. For the day, let's try to think of something else."

Chapter Seven

AUGUST 2006

❦

"*W*ild mint!" Alex exclaimed to Barbara. "I found it in the meadow." With his good hand, he grabbed a handful of unchopped leaves and shook the leaves in the air. "Smell! Wild mint!" There was something too delighted in his manner, as if he hadn't just picked the stuff but invented it.

"How nice," Barbara said mildly. A substantial pile of lime halves, their innards expended, lay by the chopping board.

"Have a drink. I'm making mojitos; there's wine in the fridge, beer out on the porch. Oh, and there's the lady of the hour."

"Ellen!" Barbara cried at the advancing figure of her sister in a brown, clingy sundress, looking, as she always did, gorgeous, though, save for the pretty dress and the band on her right finger, entirely unadorned. ("Don't you hate her?" some friend in Maine had asked when she'd described Ellen's great beauty. Barbara knew that was what she was supposed to feel: jealousy. But it was impossible. The legacy of their parents' deaths. You couldn't hate beauty in your children, and Barbara had always felt part-sister, part-mother to Ellen.) She embraced Ellen, imagining Alex behind her considering how lucky he was to land the pretty sister. "Hey, the fat one," Barbara knew people thought of her, as if she'd had the bad taste to eat her way out of her natural good looks.

"You look great," Ellen said.

"Oh, I do not. I never do."

"Jack." Ellen embraced her brother-in-law. "What do you do when she says such crazy things? Tell her to shut up, I hope."

Jack smiled but didn't say anything. There was no way to win this debate.

"Oh, things have just turned around here. For a while I thought it was going to be a Mary Tyler Moore party," Ellen said.

Barbara laughed. "I haven't heard *that* in a while." As younger women, they'd supposed themselves doomed to throw parties that mimicked the sitcom character's multiple flawed efforts to get people to enjoy—or attend—her fetes. Someone jostled Barbara from behind. "I'd say you're safe on that score. *Look* at all these people."

"I know. It's been like this all day."

Barbara was confused. "So not a Mary Tyler Moore party?"

Ellen waved her hand. "I know. I'm just babbling."

"You've got such a . . . such a house."

"I know. I'll show you around. And your bags? Well, we can get them later. Come on." She turned, Jack following. He always seemed perfectly willing to let Barbara boss him around. If anyone got annoyed about the situation, it was Barbara. "He's so nice. He doesn't get mad at me. He *should* get mad at me. I can be such a jerk."

"Barbara!" someone shouted, and there was Tamar, Ellen's oldest friend.

"Sweetheart," Barbara said and hugged her. "Come for a tour of the house?"

"You go. I've been."

"How did you two get so grown-up?"

Tamar raised her arms in protest. "Not me. I'm still a babe in the woods. It's that one." Tamar bobbed her head in the direction in which Jack and Ellen had gone. "You can't even recognize her anymore."

Barbara felt dirty from her travels. If their flight hadn't been so de-layed, she'd have been able to take a bath before the party.

"That's Alex's ex-," Tamar leaned forward to confide, her eyes dart-ing to a trim woman with dark hair, talking with a teenage boy.

"Not really," Barbara whispered.

"*In-deed*. He invited her. Didn't think she'd *come*."

"I better catch up with Jack and Ellen. Come find me later?"

"Yes, you go," Tamar said, motioning with her hand.

"Wild mint," Alex cried to a newcomer at Barbara's back. Later, when Ellen left them briefly alone in the guest room, Barbara whispered, mournfully, to Jack, "Oh, Jesus, he really *is* an asshole."

And Jack—who always withheld criticism, whose patience alternately amazed and infuriated Barbara—said, "He's marrying a woman eighteen years his junior. You were expecting maybe something else?"

"*God*," Barbara kept saying. "This house . . . it's such a . . . a house." Ellen didn't know what to say.

"I mean it's so grown-up." There was something undeniably insulting about her admiration. "It's like you've gone over to the other side."

"Well, it's definitely different from how I was living."

"Yeah, from dorm room disaster to walla-walla-bing-bang."

"You know," Jack said, silent all this while. "I'm going to go get myself a beer. Give you two time alone."

They were sitting in the guest bedroom, a room with a large white pouf on the bed, wood floors and a single white upholstered chair. No pictures yet on the white walls or above the Shaker-style dresser. As soon as Jack was gone, Barbara moved from the chair to the bed where Ellen was slouching. "So . . ." she began, a voice readying itself to hear confidences. "How *are* you? I mean, *really.*"

"I'm good."

"This is what you want?"

At first, Ellen didn't know what she meant, then she said, "Oh, Alex. Well, of course."

"You know," Barbara said, her older-sister-as-mother routine. "I had a friend whose mother knew on her honeymoon that she'd made a mistake, but it took her a decade to do anything about it. She was too embarrassed. Her folks had thrown her this big wedding, and, God, you've got to think they'd hate themselves if they knew she stayed in a ten-year marriage just because of the expense of a one-day party. You know?"

"We better just go for hot dogs and beans at the wedding, then."

"I'm serious," Barbara said.

Ellen readjusted the straps of her dress. "Listen, I know he's older, and I know that's going to have consequences later on, but I went and talked to a shrink at the University Hospital. With Alex. We went together, just to do . . . oh, what would you say? The Lolita test. How sick were we, and all that? He said, 'Look, you love each other. How many people can say that?' And I explained about Mom and Dad, because I know that Mose thinks this is a marrying-to-get-a-father-figure sort of thing, and, you know, I can see why he'd think that but . . ." She shook her head. She didn't want to go into everything in the midst of a party. "The shrink said we were lucky. To be in love. We didn't have to question that."

"What an asshole."

"Barbara!"

"A male shrink. I wonder what a woman would have said."

"Thanks. Thanks for the vote of confidence."

"No, no," Barbara said, taking Ellen's hands. "I just want you to be happy. I don't want you to get hurt."

Ellen let Barbara hold her hands for a moment, then said, "I am happy. I'm not going to get hurt. I'm a little more . . . I don't know . . . I have changed in this last year. In a good way, I think."

"If that's what you want. That's what I want." She clapped her hands together to suggest everything was all settled now. "And Mose, how do you think he is?"

"Oh, Mose," Ellen rolled her eyes. "Now, that's a long story. You know he's been dealing with all this stuff at work. The principal, who he hates. But, of course, he wants to see you tomorrow, even if he's still sick." Ellen pointed to the towels she'd put on the top of the dresser. "Bathroom's outside to the left. Wash up, and then come join us?"

"OK."

Ellen turned to go, but then she came back and said, "Don't go on your first impression of Alex. Who he is when you first meet him isn't who he is when you know him."

Or maybe he was. Maybe he seemed one way at first, another way after time, but then, after a much longer time, he went back to being the man he'd first seemed, as if he had a mask and a face under the mask that few people saw, but the face got so used to wearing the mask that it molded itself to it, became indistinguishable from it.

But wasn't everyone like this? Or like so many different people that the record at any one moment didn't mean anything? What did the gregarious man who'd hounded children into the woods and around blueberry bushes this morning owe to the man who'd bitten his own finger in the emergency room last winter? Or to the person she'd been in bed with last night, the one whispering, "I'm going to come," as if it wasn't quite a nice thing to do, as if he needed to give her fair warning.

In the kitchen, Alex was still holding up his eight fingers, stained a vibrant green, and exclaiming over his harvest. Hyman Clark stood in the middle of the living room, talking with someone Ellen didn't recognize. Hyman was holding the mojito that Ellen had given him earlier. As he'd drunk most of it, she brought him another, slipped one cup out of his hand and slipped another cup in, then said, "Hello. I hope you are enjoying yourself."

"Oh, certainly. Pleasure to be in your home again."

"And Martha?"

"Not here, I'm afraid. Came down with something."

"Funny. My cousin, too. I guess there really *is* a flu going around. Always strange to get sick in August."

"Isn't that so?" The man with whom Hyman had been talking— sensing perhaps more small talk than he could stomach—drifted away.

"You know," Ellen began conversationally, "Alex just told me that you were in Cartwright, Nebraska, before you came here."

"That's right."

"It's so beautiful there," Ellen said.

Hyman blinked, then gave Ellen an almost pie-eyed look. He dunked into his drink, then came up for air, blotted his wet lips on the back of his hand and said, "You know it, do you?"

"Yes, outside of Lincoln, right?"

"Well, not all that close," Hyman said.

"That's right. I didn't mean Lincoln. I meant Omaha."

"Not all that close to Omaha either."

"I see. And what was the school like there?"

"The school?"

"Where you worked? Before coming here?"

Hyman twirled his plastic cup, looked down at the green-flecked whirlpool of ice and clear liquid in his glass. "The mint in these makes you not realize how much you're drinking, I'm afraid." He looked back up at her then said, "They're good, I mean." He drank, head tilted back, narrow Adam's apple popping as he swallowed, a parody of a man throwing one back. When his cup came back down, it was empty.

"Want another?"

"That would be lovely," Hyman said, abruptly jerking his cup toward her.

Ellen took the cup but didn't move toward the kitchen. "The high school," she repeated, prodding. "What's it like?"

"Oh, what can you say about a place like that?"

"The thing is . . . that's what I'm wondering . . . what *you* can say. About a place like that." Her hand was at the back of her neck, as if she needed to brace herself for what she was doing.

"It was brick with . . . *halls*, of course. But then if you've . . . You say you've been to Cartwright?"

"I have." And then, when Hyman didn't say anything, she added, "Many times."

"Well," he smiled unevenly. "Then you know what it's like."

She nodded. She felt almost sad for him. "I'll get you that drink."

$\mathscr{S}$he poured him one and then another. In college, she remembered being at a State Street bar where the happy hour drinks—two-for-one—were served this way. Everyone sitting at a table with two rum-and-Cokes, two beers, two wines and so on. This was in the days when Ellen didn't drink at all, thought alcohol was like caffeine and sugar—something she should keep away from her body. "Mr. Clark," she said, handing him the two drinks. "I thought you might want *both* of these."

"You thought right, you little bitch."

"What?" Ellen said, stepping back, hand to her throat, the moisture from the cups dappling her breastbone. Had she heard him correctly?

"You thought right, you little witch," he repeated. His manner was suddenly jokey, the way it might be if he was any guest aiming for some witticism about alcohol. "It's *quite* the potion."

$\mathscr{A}$lex didn't find his way to Ellen till much later in the evening. He leaned in to kiss her, his breath hot yet minty in her ear. "Have you seen Doug?"

"I think Doug took off with a friend."

Alex led Ellen over to the fireplace. The room was crowded, but aside from the few people sitting, most people were crowded around the kitchen table laden with food, or over by the windows, where Alex had put a few small tables for people to rest their drinks. "I have to tell you something about Hyman," Ellen said.

"Oh, it's your engagement party. We'll deal with him on Monday."

"Promise you won't get mad at me?"

"Why would I get mad at you?"

"Well, yesterday, when Mose was going on about all this, he told me one other thing. And . . . You know he's had Hyman's resume, from back when you were doing the job search, and he wondered, you know, if there had been any problems with Hyman in the past, any evidence of bad behavior . . ."

"Honey—" Alex said, indicating the others in the room, though for the moment no one was paying any attention to Ellen or Alex. "It's hardly the time."

"I know, but just let me say. Mose called the Carter School of Cartwright, Nebraska. That's what was on the resume. You know, where Hyman used to work. And the phone was disconnected. No forwarding number. So yesterday, you know, before you came home? I told Mose I'd do a little sleuthing. I called information. Only I couldn't get the number, because . . . um . . . there is no Cartwright, Nebraska. I checked on the Internet, too. No such school. No such town."

"You're kidding!"

"Just now, I asked Hyman to tell me a little about Cartwright. I said I'd been there. Wondered how that'd strike him and all. He freaked out. I mean he obviously knew I was lying, and he just sort of panicked. Or at least that's how I read it. Like he knew I'd found him out."

"Oh, Jesus," Alex said.

"Hey, you two," Joe DeLouis, a vet whom Alex knew, a stocky guy who always wore striped dress shirts and gray trousers, came to clap the groom-to-be on the back.

"Hey, buddy," Alex said, turning. Then he leaned over to Ellen and said, "I'm going to slip outside. Think I need a little air."

"Want me to come?"

"No, no. I just need to think without"—he waved to the room—
"all this."

"Right," Ellen said.

Alex walked away. He'd put on some weight in the last months, his
torso heavy over his thin legs and flat rear end, his bottom striking her
as both poignant and ridiculous, jeans hanging loosely, despite the
growing flab above his belt. Ellen saw him stop, put a hand on Hyman's
shoulder and say something, before he left the room via the porch.

"You ever have a pet?" Joe DeLouis asked her.

"Um . . . no. Allergies."

"Too bad, I've got . . ."

Ellen couldn't concentrate—was it *witch* all along, or had he actually called her a bitch? And what had Alex said to Hyman? At length she
excused herself for the bathroom. Once there, she neatened hand towels, cleaned and dried the soap dish. For order, she had a talent, not that
it did her much good in the realm of human affairs. She didn't think
she'd return to the living room party, but hide temporarily in the chair
that Alex had placed in the hallway that led to the bedrooms. It was a
strange location for a comfy chair, but Alex considered the spot his
home's "reading nook," the hallway dead ending, as it did, at a large
window. How did the nonexistence of Cartwright fit—if it did—with
Mose's charges? What *was* Hyman's story? She couldn't gauge anything
about him. She fished and fished and still nothing quite broke the surface, save perhaps a general defensiveness and a weighty blankness, a
determined refusal to let another human being in.

No wonder Martha was half-mad.

*A*lex was drunk. He hadn't had more than usual, but his lower lip
was buzzing, and he felt dizzy. He couldn't remember the last time he'd
actually *been* drunk—the bar for giving himself a high having risen over
the years. But here he was, in something like hiding, standing, at any
rate, under the second-floor porch, wondering about what Ellen had
just told him.

"Can't find anyone good to talk to up there?"

"Jesus—" Alex jumped. "Valerie, Christ. I didn't know you were out
here. Where's Doug?"

"Going home soon, if he hasn't left already. The Simons were going to give him a ride back into town." The Simons were old friends; they ran a bookstore/coffee shop near the apartment that Valerie and Alex had rented fifteen years ago, when they'd first moved to Madison.

"And you?"

"Me? Are you wondering why I don't get out of here myself?"

"It's a reasonable question."

"It is, indeed. I was wondering that myself." She looked out into the dark, to where when it was light, one could see the land rising into a small hill, the starting point for this morning's blueberry hunt. "I guess . . ." Valerie began slowly, "I've been sticking around aiming for broadmindedness." She reached up and kissed him squarely on the mouth, her breasts sliding with the fabric of a new (he noted) dress against his chest, her arms wrapping around his back, noting (wouldn't she?) how easily he'd regained the weight he'd lost after the divorce. It had always bothered him that he had a fat back. He didn't know anyone else whose back got fat when they put on extra pounds.

He kissed her neck, then they were making out like teenagers. She had nothing on Ellen, but she was familiar—and yet unfamiliar in this new guise: the other woman. He reached a hand under her shirt. "I didn't cheat on you. When we were married. You know."

"I didn't know, for sure. One way or another." But there was nothing blaming in her voice.

"I wanted to," Alex said. "But I didn't."

"Congratulations," she said, kissing him with great tenderness, "on your self-restraint."

"I love Ellen, you know."

She pulled away from him and said, "I do. I do know that. Who wouldn't? She's a sweet girl." She waited a beat, then said, "And hot."

"She's that."

Valerie reached into her pocket, took out a hair band and tied up her hair up. "Let's not do this again. I mean, I know I started it, but let's not do this again."

"Yes," he said, kissing her. "We won't."

She cleared her throat into his mouth, a move that was sufficiently unappealing that he stopped. "You know, it's strange," Valerie said, folding her arms across her chest. "But I actually *like* Ellen. I really do.

I can't not like her. What happened in the car back—" She made an "over there" motion with her head, as if Shatterly's parking lot were just over the hill. "That had nothing to do with Ellen. If I ended up with her at some confessional—or the secular equivalent: maybe a book group where we'd all had too much white wine, and started talking about our men. Well, if Ellen said that the guy she was engaged to had cheated on her, just a few weeks before he gave her the ring. I'd say . . ." Valerie stopped, lowered her voice into that of a concerned schoolmarm. "'Oh, my dear. Have you thought about this man? And who was this woman he was with? What darkness motivated *her*?'"

Alex said, "Everyone loves her. That's part of her charm."

"And that's not my point," Valerie said in an irritable voice that was all too familiar to Alex.

"Let me change the topic," Alex said.

"I wish you would."

Alex pulled the letters Mose had sent out of his pocket.

"Will you read these two letters and tell me what you think about them? I just got them this morning. The first one is Mose Sheinbaum's merit review letter. It went missing for a time for some reason, but then Mose got it. The second's from the Anti-Defamation League."

"The Anti-Defamation League?" Valerie said with interest.

"Yeah. Mose didn't like the tone of the merit review letter, so he sent it there."

"Jeez," Valerie said and began to read. Alex looked out toward the trees and the star-sprinkled sky. It'd been a clear day and now he could see everything.

"Huh." Valerie grunted after she'd read the first letter, said, "I see" after the second. She looked up, an exaggerated "Well, well" expression on her face.

"So?" Alex said. "What do you make of all this?"

"What do I make of it? Let's see. This Hyman Clark might just be unaware of the implicit prejudice in his language. You could give him the benefit of the doubt."

"You think?" Alex said, hopeful.

"Then again, in this day and age, if you weren't too smart but wanted to say, 'Let's get rid of this loud-mouthed Jew,' isn't this how you'd say it?"

"So which is it?"

Valerie folded the letters, extended them back to Alex. She then clapped him on the back, as if he were a fallen sports hero, and said, "Hate to say it, buddy, but this requires an independent thought."

"Yes!" he said, relieved, "that's exactly what I'm asking for." It had been hard, he realized, not having her advice, these many long months. He never vetted his work affairs with Ellen. Why would he?

"Oh, Alex. *You. You* need to have an independent thought."

"Valerie, have I ever told you that you can be a real bitch?"

"Yeah," she said, walking out into the dark, presumably toward wherever she'd parked the car. "You mentioned that, once or twice. If memory serves."

Suddenly Hyman was at Ellen's side. When she didn't stand to talk, he surprised her by propping himself on her chair's armrest.

"I don't know what you told him." His voice was hushed but urgent. "I don't know what he thinks I've done." Hyman moved closer to her—the effect of the alcohol, Ellen supposed, his judgment off. A frothy bit of spit flew out of his mouth and landed on her cheek. "Your fiancé seems to think I don't like the Jews, but I have nothing but the utmost respect for the Jews . . ." He put his hand on her forearm, as if to assure her.

What if she *had* made a mistake? Read malice where there was only stupidity? She'd bumped into Smitty once, in the grocery store, and they'd discussed Mose's problems with Hyman. Smitty had bobbed his head at all Ellen had to say, then offered in a voice that managed to be simultaneously sympathetic, wry and uninflected, "Well, it's traditionally been very hard to live with the master race." But that had been a joke, of course. A comment on the man's personality, not his actual political affiliations.

"Really," Hyman said now, putting his other hand on Ellen's shoulder—a plea that might have been a dance move. "I'm a Christian myself, but that doesn't mean I don't respect the rights of others. Jesus was a Jew, after all." He laughed, a convivial chuckle, as if Ellen might appreciate having Jesus in her particular club. Ellen pushed herself back into her chair as his hand tightened on her forearm. Hyman leaned into her retreat, the corners of his mouth red and damp with spit. "You may know that I instigated a diversity . . . a diversity "—he couldn't quite grab on to the word he wanted—"a diversity *thing* at the schools and . . ."

Leaning even closer—practically on top of Ellen—Hyman interrupted his own words to say, "Please, please, you know I wouldn't—"

Hyman's head was so close, it was all Ellen could see, and she was on the edge of feeling that he presented a physical threat, when she heard Alex, just behind Hyman, saying, "Get your hands off her."

Hyman looked up, clearly shocked at the implication that he was making a pass at Ellen.

"Hands off her," Alex repeated, "and you're fired. I'll fax you a formal dismissal on Monday morning."

"What?" Hyman began. "You're kidding, right? Right?"

"If you would," Alex said, extending his arm cordially, as if he wasn't telling Hyman to leave, but nobly encouraging him to precede him into the ballroom of the outdoors.

Chapter Eight

AUGUST 2006

❦

*S*ome old friends of his parents gave Doug a lift to Mose's apartment. "Hello," Doug burbled into the apartment building's intercom, "it's me."

"Hello, me."

"Doug, I mean."

"A visitation in the night," Mose called back and buzzed him in.

"You don't mind?" Doug said, on entering.

"Mind? What's to mind? But you'll see I'm not at my best." Used Kleenex were scattered on the floor around Mose's La-Z-Boy. A book was cracked open in the seat of the chair.

"We'll sit," Mose said, indicating the small table and two chairs that sat by the "bar" separating his small kitchen from his living room. The apartment was a lot nicer than the stuff Mose put in it. Doug could always tell when something had been bought by Ellen, and when it was just the ratty old furniture that Mose had been schlepping around for years. It didn't take too much to guess that Ellen had been the one to pick the actual apartment—a slick redo of a former elementary school with fancy fixtures and a shiny kitchen counter, but otherwise the same sheetrock and flat gray carpeting that Doug saw in the apartments where his college friends lived. Mose's building had a view of the lake, but Mose's apartment wasn't on the lakeside. It was in the basement, which was actually the ground floor. His place opened on to a small patio that he never seemed to use.

Doug didn't even try to explain to his friends why he so liked the old man. What could he tell them anyway? Not one of them could distinguish between the world without Brandi and the world with Brandi. Even her foster parents said, "It's God's will." As if life didn't make one bit of difference, as if it was just a thing you bumbled around in for a designated amount of time, before God, souring on your efforts to make a mark or pay off your mortgage or make peace with your adult children, said, "Well, fuck, that's enough of *that*." Mose was different, though. He wife Rachel had been dead for decades, and he said there wasn't a day that went by that he didn't miss her.

"So that's why you never remarried, huh?" Doug said, not needing Mose to answer and so not fully hearing him say, "Well, not exactly."

There was another thing that Mose and Doug shared: a lack of fondness for the bond that had drawn them together. Doug was old enough not to have fantasies of his parents getting back together, but fantasize he did. And Mose clearly didn't want Ellen to marry Alex. "The best thing we can do to drive them apart," Mose had said that first night, when he drove Doug home from the dinner party at Ridgeway, "is to support them entirely."

"You're all lonely here," Doug said now as he settled himself into Mose's apartment, readying himself for one of their unlikely dives into Jewish mysticism or Philip Roth's sex obsession or Yiddish curses. Bar mitzvah training for the Unitarian in despair! Not that it was always Jewish. One night Doug said, "What is existentialism? I mean, I sort of know what it is . . . but not exactly."

And instead of saying something like "What do you know?" and Doug saying something dumb like "It's gotta involve black clothes, cigarettes and acting like a general shit," Mose said, "Well, let's find out." Then he'd shuffled over to one of his bookshelves, pulled out Sartre's *What Is Existentialism?* and read out loud, only stopping (when his voice got hoarse) to summarize the major points.

Now Mose said, "Lonely, what lonely? I have my friends." He pointed to the brown volume lying on the seat of his La-Z-Boy. "My friends and my tissues. A summer cold, which I may have represented as something more to Ellen, but I'm counting on you not to tell the truth. Did you enjoy the party?"

"Not at all," Doug said. "I heard there was some sort of bitch-slap between my dad and Hyman Clark, though."

"Is that so? Now that interests me."

"It does? Why?"

"I'll tell you why. Because that Hyman Clark is not who he says he is."

"I'm not who I say I am. Nobody is." After a moment, Doug added, "Not that I have any idea who I am."

"Yes, yes, the great existential questions, but that's not what I mean. I'm not being profound. I think he literally isn't who he says he is."

"Like, what isn't he telling the truth about?"

"Maybe his past. He might have lied about his past."

"Have you ever googled him? Just to find out?"

"Computers and I are like oil and water. We don't mix." And in case the reference confused Doug, Mose drew a large circle in the air, and put a line through it, the symbol for philosophy, also prohibition. Doug could take his pick. "Though I do do the e-mail."

"You never googled anything?" Doug couldn't believe it. He got up from the kitchen table where he'd been sitting and went over to Mose's computer. "Hey, aren't you a Jew, with the Jewish love of learning? You got to get hip to this." Doug fiddled with Mose's computer, then said, "You've got the Internet connection."

"No, I don't. I just have e-mail."

"Same difference. You're doing it on your phone, though. You gotta get off that. Takes too long. But here, we'll look him up."

Doug explained the whole concept of search engines to Mose, then pulled up Internet Explorer and explained how to get to Google. The machine was ridiculously slow. He didn't know how Mose could stand it.

"So you're telling me," Mose said, finally catching on, "I could type 'ham sandwich' into that thing, and anything ever written about a ham sandwich will just appear?"

"Yep. Here we go." Doug typed "ham sandwich." The first listing that came up was for a band named Ham Sandwich.

Mose laughed appreciatively, as if he'd just been shown a really good magic trick.

"So *now*," Doug said, as he typed. "We'll do Hyman Clark." Hits came up on the computer, but they were all related to the school district's Web site or the local newspapers. "Weird. You'd think there would be something that goes back a little further."

"Well, my friend. Interesting observation. Just yesterday Ellen and I were phoning around to see if we could find out anything about the man. But unless our research methods, as they say, were very much misguided, Hyman Clark's previous employer—according to his resume—doesn't even exist. Nor does the town in which he once taught American history."

"Oh, man," Doug said. "How cool is that?"

"Cool?"

"Like a mystery. You and I can figure it out. It'll be like CSI."

"CSI?"

"Oh, never mind. It'll be like Doug and Mose: the dynamic duo."

Mose looked at Doug, then down at his own body, and did a double-take at what he found below his neck. "More Laurel and Hardy, I think. Natasha Fatale and Boris Badenov. Rocky and Bullwinkle. Dudley DoRight and . . . ."

"Whatever," Doug said, his mood abruptly turning. His interest in Mose's affairs had briefly distracted him from the matter at hand: his depression. He was depressed, Brandi was dead. He wasn't supposed to act like he gave a shit about anything.

"Let me show you something." Mose went into the kitchen, where he rustled through a stack of papers on a shelf before taking down a large Ziploc bag with a yellow envelope in it. "Nope, wrong one." He put that bag back and took down another. "The postal inspector told me about keeping correspondence in a bag. To preserve fingerprints."

"And you need that because . . . ?"

Mose didn't answer but went into a long explanation about what a merit review was—though Doug more or less knew about this through his dad—and how this year his own merit review letter had gone missing, and how he'd had some dealings with Hyman Clark, who seemed to be angling to get him fired. Doug didn't quite get what the letter had to do with getting fired, but one day the missing letter showed up on

Mose's desk. It was in a yellow envelope, and someone had written "Thought this might interest you" across the front.

Mose passed the bag to Doug. On one side was the yellow envelope with the words; on the other the merit review letter.

"You can skim that, if you like," Mose said, as he more or less ushered Doug's eyes to the letter. "Or skip it altogether. I can paraphrase. It says, 'Mose is a loud-mouthed Jew.'"

"No way."

"Yes way! That's the sub-text. You know what sub-text means?"

"No, I haven't a clue," Doug said flatly. "I'm a moron."

"Just asking, my touchy friend. Just asking."

"And that other envelope?" Doug said, pointing to the shelf.

"That? No that is something else. From last fall. Even more unappealing, I regret." He lowered his voice, dramatically, and whispered, "Hate mail," his eyes shiny and pleased, not—Doug guessed—at the good luck of being loathed, but at having something that might interest the under-eighteen set.

"Let me see."

Mose went over to the shelf and retrieved the other bag. "This time the outside of the envelope is normal." Mose showed Doug one side of the plastic bag. The envelope had Mose's address but no return address. "But, inside . . ." He flipped it over. There, on an unlined piece of paper, someone had written, "We know who you are, Zionist oppressor. We don't forget."

"But Mose," Doug said, pushing the plastic bags across the table to the old man, "it's the same handwriting."

"No," Mose said, and drew his face close to the two plastic bags. He lifted his head.

Doug waggled his eyebrows.

"Good Lord, you're right!"

"Didn't Ellen notice?"

Mose put his fingers to his lips and tapped. "I suppose . . . I suppose she never saw the handwriting on this." He pointed to the plastic bag that contained Hyman's letter. "I gave her a copy of the letter, but not . . ." And then: "But it doesn't make any sense."

"Well, at least Hyman Clark can't have sent you that Zionist message, because whoever ratted him out on this merit review letter sent that message, right? That's what you're thinking, isn't it? That whoever sent you the merit review letter was doing it behind Hyman's back. Like maybe Hyman had figured out it wasn't going to fly once you questioned it, so he was trying to permanently lose the letter."

"That *was* what I was thinking. Now I don't know."

"Well, who knew his business?"

"Your father."

"No. I mean seriously. Was there a sketchy secretary or vice principal or even a kid who was pissed?"

"Vice principal, no. We don't have one at Sudbury. Budget cuts and all. Secretary, no, I don't think so. Kids? That could be anybody."

"If someone had access to the letter and then gave it to you, it'd have to be someone close to him, who then wasn't close to him. Right?"

"Your mind, it just . . ." Moses rolled a finger, suggesting a rapidly advancing machine.

"I watch a lot of crime shows."

"I suppose the TV has to be good for something."

"So, can you think of anyone?"

"Anyone who was close to him and then wasn't?"

Mose looked at the floor for such a long time that Doug started to get nervous, but then Mose began to rock slightly, a trembling that Doug would have taken for an incipient seizure if Mose hadn't looked up and said, "Well, there were three kids who seemed to spend an awful lot of time with him. Devon Cryer, HoHo Coombs and—"

"Brandi Carter used to be involved with HoHo, you know."

"No, I didn't."

"Yeah, but he spread some shit about her, so she ended that."

"Well, I can't tell you much about HoHo, but he dropped out of school last May, just before graduation. The truant officer was around asking after him. I guess he's hard to locate."

"Meaning?"

"Meaning I guess he doesn't live at the address the school has on file for him."

"So . . . that's a possibility. I mean that's a connection at least."

"Not one that makes any sense though," Mose said. "Does it to you?"

"No, but . . . I don't know. It's something, so we could just go talk to him. See what his handwriting looks like, you know. That'd be the obvious thing to rule him out or in."

$\mathcal{M}$ose had a special relationship with Harvey Mein, the truant officer. Last year, when he asked his students to write about an American hero, Laura Gleason had asked if she could write about anti-heroes instead. She wanted to write about people who had jobs that made other people hate them. A collection agent, a meter maid, a probation officer. She wondered how people dealt with people yelling at them all day, an interest she claimed she came by naturally, having lived with her mother for the last sixteen years. The idea was promising enough that Mose let Laura do it. Harvey never quite understood the premises under which he was being interviewed. "People don't hate me," he'd told Laura. (This as quoted in her "A" paper.) "I do a service for the city. Education is a good thing. Wish I'd had more of it myself." Laura had pressed him on the matter of his actual encounters with recalcitrant students, but here Harvey's hearing aids regularly shorted out, and he said, "I just bring them in. Try to get as many as I can a day."

He sounded, Laura Gleason told Mose, like a dogcatcher. But a dogcatcher who was honored by Laura's attention. At the assembly where Mose's students read bits of their papers to the American heroes whom they'd interviewed, Harvey Mien, eyes damp with emotion (or an allergic reaction to the mold growing in Sudbury's heating ducts), embraced Mose, then said, "It didn't occur to me how much of a hero I was till I met your Laura Gleason. Your kids have done something important for all of us."

Since that time, whenever Harvey ran into Mose, he hugged him again and said, "*My* hero."

It was probably illegal for Harvey Mien to share personal information about students, but share he did. He had no idea where HoHo was staying now—though the boy had once lived with his mother in a transitional home behind the Eastgate Mall—but he did know where he was hanging out. A tattoo shop named Blueleg.

"$\mathcal{C}$heck. This. Car. Out," Doug said as he slid into the passenger seat of Mose's Buick.

"Glove compartment sleeps six," Mose said.

"Truth," Doug demanded, looking directly into Mose's eyes. "How many times have you told that sorry joke?"

"Too many times to even count." It was the evening after the engagement party, and Doug and Mose were off to find HoHo. The signature music and news from National Public Radio—so many dead in Iraq, the unlikelihood of a ceasefire between Israel and Hezbollah—filled the car.

"Do you mind?" Doug said, turning off the radio and rolling up his window, so Mose and he could hear each other. "Can I ask you a question?"

"Please do."

"How come you knew the synagogue fire was arson? Even before they said so in the papers?"

"Synagogues don't just burn down."

"They could. Couldn't they?"

"There's another reason, but I'm sworn to secrecy on that . . ."

Doug smiled. "What are the chances I'm not going to make you tell me, now that you've said that?"

Mose was quiet, absorbed with changing lanes, and then he said, "Just because I like you doesn't mean I don't find you a degree too smartass at times."

"I hear you, sir." And then, when Mose didn't go on, Doug said, less sarcastically, "But really, won't you tell me?"

"I haven't even told Ellen this. But since we've left our lives and are now crime fighters from your TV show. . . ."

Doug snorted.

"I'll tell you, but the police don't want me to tell anyone, so I don't want *you* to tell anyone."

"The lips they are sealed."

"Do you know what a panzer boot is?"

"No, I keep telling you, I'm a moron."

"Young man, how do I know what you do and do not know? Have you ever seen one?"

"I don't know. They're supposed to look like Doc Martens, right? A lot of kids wear boots."

"I don't know about the Doc Marten, but the way the panzer boot is constructed." Mose stopped then said, "Forgive me if you already know this, but the way they are constructed is with swastikas, four swastikas on the soles. So when they walk, they make prints in the snow or rain, or in the case of the synagogue, the dirt. When the police saw some of these prints after the fire, they went back to last fall and any clues they had in the defacing of the synagogue. You may not remember but there was a swastika drawn on the synagogue last fall. And then I got that letter, so they . . ."

"Brandi's death is connected to your hate mail? HoHo might have killed Brandy?"

"I'm saying nothing of the kind. All we know about HoHo is that he was close to Mr. Clark, and he's dropped out of school. As for anything criminal, I'm sure the police have been talking to HoHo. An ex-boyfriend is always an obvious suspect, when a young woman is killed."

They found Blueleg, a corner shop in a part of Madison that Doug had never seen before. The storefront itself was empty, but its side door was ajar and outside sat three adults—HoHo, a young man with a baby, and an older woman. When Mose walked up and asked if he might have a word, HoHo looked up, suspicious. He and his friends were drinking beers, not bothering to hide the green bottles from general view. "You're not the police," HoHo said.

"No. I'm Mose Sheinbaum, I teach history at Sudbury."

"I know who you are. What do you want with me?"

"I just have a few questions. It shouldn't take long."

"And who's that?" HoHo looked past Mose at Doug.

"Just a friend, who has some questions, too."

HoHo looked over at the man with whom he'd been drinking. The man wore a black biker's vest, blue jean shorts that stopped at his knees and Birkenstocks. "I'm not inclined for a chat just now—"

The man snorted. His facial hair—a few days' growth—made him look scruffy and unwashed. The white-haired woman next to him (in a lawn chair, the other two were sitting on overturned buckets) said, "Be nice." She was enormous, having fattened into a large sack with two smaller sacks for breasts, both of which strained against her faded pink shirt with its flower appliqué. The baby, in a purple skirt and white tights snugged over plump diapers, was the cleanest thing in sight.

"Please," Mose said, "we won't take much of your time."

"Hey," the man said, putting the baby down on the sidewalk and standing. He had nothing on underneath his black vest, the effect meant to be more scary than sexy, for who would want to show off skin so pale that it looked blue or to reveal a few dark hairs snaking from chest to stomach? "I don't think you heard my friend."

"Hearing's fine," Mose said. "It's my back that's a problem. We only want—"

The man stepped forward, and Doug put a cautionary hand on Mose's forearm. "Maybe this isn't such a good—"

The baby released a loud wet fart, and the man said, "Jesus. You change her, Mom?"

The old woman put her hands up and said, "I did it last time."

"Crap," said the man and swooped the baby up and carried her into the back of the tattoo shop.

"Ahh," said HoHo, groaning as he stood. "It's all right. We can talk in there. We'll go around the front."

Doug and Mose followed HoHo around the corner and into Blueleg. The front room of the shop had a few white plastic chairs, a teetering coffee table with an empty ashtray and white walls covered with tattoo designs, orderly squares of paper featuring twisting snakes, blue maidens with weeping eyes and cartoon characters with testicle-shaped noses. There was none of the intricate scrollwork that West High girls tattooed on the small of their backs, none of the Indian designs that cuffed boys' biceps.

"You have one of these? " Mose said, clearly meaning a tattoo.

"Nah," HoHo said, taking a seat, "I'm too scared of needles. Aren't you?"

"Not really. You get to a certain age and you're more scared of what's not in the world than what is."

Doug groaned inwardly. This was just Mose being Mose, trying to sound wise, but HoHo would read the words as a challenge: try to scare me if you can.

"Well," Mose began.

"Oh, wait," Doug interrupted, as if something had just occurred to him. "We gotta get your advice about how to get out of here. We got pretty lost coming, as it was."

"Don't come down to this part of town much?"

Doug shrugged, embarrassed, his pampered life in the pseudo-sub-urbs next to whatever existed on this scrappy nowhere street. "Just if you could get us back to the Capitol area, then we'd know what to do."

HoHo started giving directions, but Doug said, "I'll never keep this straight." He reached into his backpack for a pen and piece of paper. "Can you write it down?"

HoHo rolled his eyes, but he scribbled the directions down.

"Great," Doug said, when HoHo handed the piece of paper back. Then he turned to Mose and said, "Yep."

Mose had parked at the curb, so he said, "Excuse me." He stepped out of the tattoo parlor.

"Wait!" Doug said, standing. "I don't think we should . . ." But Mose continued out of the shop. "*Really,*" Doug hissed at the door but then turned back to HoHo.

"What the fuck is going on?" HoHo said.

"What do you mean?" Doug said, trying to sound nonchalant.

HoHo snorted. "You really know who to hang with for fun."

Mose came back into the store with the yellow envelope sealed in its plastic bag.

"Why'd you give this to me, HoHo?"

"What the fuck are you talking about?"

"That's your handwriting. You just gave us the evidence. I'm guess-ing the police could find your fingerprints on this envelope, if they were so inclined."

Doug couldn't believe Mose. HoHo could just grab the envelope, if he wanted to. He could just beat the shit out of the both of them, if he wanted to. What was the point of confronting him?

HoHo tilted his chair onto its two back legs, then rocked forward with the heels of his two, hefty black boots. His jaw jutted abruptly to the right and back. Doug felt light-headed, like he needed to sit down, though he was already sitting down. There were swastikas on the soles of HoHo's boots. Doug saw them when he tilted his chair. He wouldn't have even thought to look for them, if not for the conversation Mose and he had just had in the car. He was looking *right at* Brandi's mur-derer.

But wouldn't the police have seen the boots? If they interviewed him? Or maybe Mose was wrong? Maybe the police hadn't interviewed the ex-boyfriend? Maybe they had no idea who the ex-boyfriend *was*, though how could that be? Wouldn't someone have just told them?

"Hey," HoHo said, pissed, "didn't you want that letter? Weren't you whining to everyone about your missing letter?"

"I did," Mose said, perfectly calm, no sense that he read anger in HoHo's voice. "I did want it."

"So, why not just thank me?"

"Thank you," Mose said simply. In the quiet that followed, noises came from the tattoo parlor's back room, the man from the sidewalk, gently singing, *"Johnny, we're sorry. Won't you come on home? We worry, won't you come on—. What is wrong in my life that I must get drunk every night? Johnny, we're sorry."*

"I still wonder why. Why you gave it to me, I mean."

"I'm a nice guy," HoHo said. "Not many people appreciate that about me."

"I'm just wondering about motive."

"No motive," HoHo said. Mose let the silence linger. Eventually, HoHo said, "This is what I'm noticing about this world. Everyone thinks the only way to be connected to something is through a bad motive. The police came here to ask me where I was when that Jewish place burnt down. They said, 'You were Brandi Carter's boyfriend,' and I said to them, 'Now, wouldn't that be my alibi? Why would I burn my own girlfriend up?'"

Mose said, "Well, you can't be a stranger to the notion of a crime of passion?"

HoHo stared at him blankly.

"Domestic violence, surely you've heard of that."

"Oh," HoHo said dismissively, and Doug realized HoHo's eyes were wet. "That's for people who don't love each other."

"Well, maybe they did once," Mose said. And then slowly, "My friend, Doug here, knew Brandi Carter, and he says you weren't her boyfriend. That a guy named Sam Meyers was her boyfriend. You were the ex-"

HoHo dropped the front legs of his chair abruptly to the floor and stood up. "I am so fucking sick of people talking about things they don't know the fuck about."

"My mistake," Mose said. "Please," he gestured to the chair, but

HoHo didn't sit down. "Why'd you drop out of school? In a few more weeks you'd have had the diploma."

HoHo started to leave, huffing as if he couldn't be bothered to listen to this anymore, but at the door, he turned and said, "So I'll tell you what . . . I sent that letter, because I thought you'd like to know what kind of man the principal is."

"And what kind of man is he?"

"Same as you, same as every other adult I ever met. He's someone who tries to get someone else to do his dirty work."

Chapter Nine

SEPTEMBER–DECEMBER 2006

❦

$\mathcal{V}$alerie felt a little sorry for Hyman Clark. He'd struck her as scared, the one time she met him: the measured way he talked, how tightly he gripped his coffee cup, as if it were a ballast in the storm-tossed ship of the high school's hallway. She wondered how conscious his errors had been, if he *knew* he'd gone after minorities in the school system. For there had, indeed, been a pattern to the faculty members who were denied merit raises: the two Jews at Sudbury, the Cuban Spanish teacher, the African American woman in guidance. Hyman said it was just a coincidence.

Hyman's life seemed dry and unhappy. He had no children. His wife—who wrote crossword puzzles for a living—never came out with him. She had some social phobia and a bowel disorder. How odd to know these two things about her. The one time Valerie had met her was at a New Year's party at the university's art museum. Hyman's wife had been drinking too much—and she clearly wasn't a drinker, was just trying to loosen herself up. She'd latched onto Valerie, then started to confess ridiculous things: that she had a recurrent dream about throwing up shit, that she'd wanted children but had been traumatized by miscarrying on an Omaha bus, blood running down her legs and everyone stepping away from her, as if she spontaneously bled just to shock others.

Valerie had worried about Mrs. Clark as she told these stories. Mrs. Clark! Valerie didn't even know the woman's first name. She'd been wearing an A-line skirt, thick brown shoes and a white blouse with a Peter Pan collar and a ribbon at the neck, a girlish outfit.

Not that Valerie was on Hyman's side. But she saw how he lived for his job and, too, how readily people took to the idea of an evildoer, how nicely another's guilt absolved one. The newspaper headlines were accurate and damning, without necessarily resolving the matter: "Hyman Clark Denies Wrongdoing," "ADL Cites 'Code Words' for Jewish," "Minorities at Sudbury Denied Raises," "Hyman Clark Calls History Teacher 'A Woody Allen.'"

And then the trial started.

On the stand, HoHo Coombs admitted to setting the fire. There was no point in denying it, given all the evidence against him. But he said he hadn't wanted to hurt Brandi Carter. He thought the synagogue was empty. He was sick of how the Jews got everything. And who told him that the Jews got everything? Why that, he said, would be Hyman Clark. Hyman Clark had taught him a lot of things about America and the rights of white people. He showed him how certain people talked about their rights, but what they were really doing was getting special treatment, finding a way to keep the white man down. And those swastikas on the synagogue last fall? Yeah, HoHo had done that. At Hyman's instruction. Hyman had even told him where to buy the boots he was wearing.

There was a "For Sale" sign outside of the Clarks' home. Valerie supposed there'd be a moving van soon enough and a quiet departure. Any future employer could type Hyman's name into a computer and find all he needed to reject Clark.

But the Clarks couldn't leave for good till HoHo's trial was over. The trial started in September. By October, the newspapers were speculating that Hyman would be named a co-conspirator.

Of course, Valerie should stop referring to the fall as the Season of Hate. Of course, of course, of course. But when people rang to ask about the season's schedule, she actually had to dig her fingernails into her palms to stop herself from blurting out the words. Now they were well into the season. The photography show on torture would open next week. Later in the month, the Hate Plays, specifically geared to high school students, would open. The Center's book club would be reading David Grossman's *The Yellow Wind*. They'd had so many documentary films to choose from that they were starting a new series—a film and discussion, the first Thursday of each month, sometimes with the filmmakers on hand.

The theme for the season had been Valerie's idea, but the Center wasn't offering one play or show that she wanted to attend; she was glutted with it, the bad news. The planet was melting, people kept killing each other and she wanted a break from catastrophe. She needed to find a friend who'd go see *The Devil Wears Prada* with her. If she didn't hurry, it would be out of all the cinemas.

Valerie went down to the gallery to check on the progress there. While she was looking around, Leo came in with lunch and more spackle for the preparators. He said, "So did you hear?"

"No, hear what?"

"Hyman Clark hanged himself. His wife found him this morning, out in their barn."

"Oh, Christ," Valerie clapped her hand over her mouth.

*O*n the day of the synagogue fire, HoHo had received an important letter. Ellen sat through his whole trial, so she heard all the testimony. He received a letter from the Marines, who had decided he wasn't good enough to go over to Iraq and fight for this country. "Not even good enough to fucking die," HoHo said at the trial and added that he'd maybe swallowed some pills he shouldn't have and had something to drink, and gotten to thinking about all the things Hyman Clark had been telling him about the haves and the have-nots in this country, and who gets what, and how Hyman knew how HoHo felt about things, because he'd always been a victim, too.

Was he telling the truth? Who knew? Hyman was dead, and Martha wouldn't say anything useful. "Haven't you people," she said to reporters and lawyers alike, "already done enough to him? Don't you people ever, *ever* stop?"

And then the newspapers' coverage began to change: had the media unfairly convicted Hyman? Could you conclusively say that there was a pattern of misbehavior when there were only four minorities at Sudbury High, if you counted Jews as minorities? Which plenty of people didn't. In a letter to the editor, a prominent lawyer wondered why the Jewish community had gone after Hyman Clark. In this day and age, didn't Jews have bigger and better battles to fight? It was like Lebanon. If the Jews saw an enemy with a gun, they dropped an atom bomb.

At Angel Towers, where Mose still volunteered once a week, a tiny elderly woman came, as always, to her apartment door, distinguished from all the others only by a *mezuzah* made of tiny blue stones. She accepted a hot lunch from Mose, then said, "Why'd you make trouble for us?" It wasn't good to give the *goyim* a reason to be angry with the Jews.

One Friday afternoon, before the trial was all through, Mose came to pick Ellen up at the daycare. He wanted, he said, to take her for a walk.

"You do not," Ellen said.

"Well, then I want to cheer you up."

"I don't want to walk."

"That bad, huh?"

"Oh, no," she said. "I'm fine, I guess."

"Well, let me buy you a cup of coffee."

"Coffee," she said, putting her hand to her stomach, as if the beverage were already there, tormenting her. "What about a cookie? That's what I want."

"Sure," Mose said.

Instead of leaving the Center through the basement door, which led to the parking lot out back, they climbed the stairs to the Center's lobby, so they could exit onto State Street; find one of the candy-laden pastries that Ellen—in a happier mood—called "Instant Diabetes" cookies.

But the lobby was full—a closing reception for the very same torture show that Ellen and Mose had seen a year ago in the gallery by Ellen's old apartment.

"I spy a cookie," Mose said, heading for a table, laden with platters of cheese, fruit and cookies. "Which makes you just about the cheapest date in the world."

"Mose," Ellen said, her voice high, "what if HoHo is lying?"

Mose knew what she was thinking. "Sweetheart, you didn't put the noose around that man's neck. Neither did I. A grown man makes his own decisions."

Ellen didn't leave Alex then, in the fall, when the scandal broke and others were accusing him of sloppiness and poor judgment and sometimes worse, but later, in December, when the trial was over, and HoHo was sentenced to two years in prison. She couldn't explain why she was leaving him any more than she'd been able to explain her initial attachment. It had been right before and it was wrong now.

Ellen sat through the trial with Mose but Alex didn't attend, embarrassed as he was by his part in the affair. He wanted the whole thing to just go away, he said. Ellen moved in with Tamar and found a new job, at a daycare within walking distance of Tamar's apartment.

The subject of Hyman's past remained unresolved. It was as if he'd been imagined into life on the day he started working at Sudbury and dissolved on the day he hung himself. Maybe Martha knew the truth, but she wasn't saying anything. "Throw me in jail, if you like," she threatened the reporters who came to her house. "You people. You people, you murdered my husband. I don't know, I don't know how you live with yourselves."

Mose slapped his head when he read Martha's words in the paper. "Someone was murdered. And her name was Brandi Carter. How the perpetrator becomes the victim, I'll never know."

Synagogue burning was a federal crime. Ellen supposed that soon enough, what with social security numbers and falsified documents (if there were those), the truth of Hyman's past—which might have absolved Ellen of her guilt over his death—would come out. But if the authorities learned about it, the public never did. Absolution was there, Mose claimed, in the secrecy. If it wasn't shameful, why hide it?

.

Chapter Ten

OCTOBER 2006

❦

At the moment of death, your life flashes before your eyes. Or so Hyman Clark had always heard. But that wasn't exactly the case for him. His life came to him in the context of his troubles, an aborted version of the whole, so even in the end—*even then*—he was shortchanged, bilked, hornswaggled. . . . *I was cheated*, Hyman would have told Martha if he could have unknotted the rope at his neck, like any old tie, pulled his feet out of the air and placed them firmly on the barn floor. *Someone cheated me.*

And so:

Hyman had never been a teacher of American history. But no one in Madison knew that. No one save Martha. He'd been a CPA in Lincoln, Nebraska. He worked for Jenkins and Smith, until the incident.

After, he tried working out of his house, but no one—no one who needed a CPA—wanted to hire him. He had friends, but they weren't people with money; they weren't people in power. Which is what started the whole thing in the first place.

Even though Hyman wasn't a teacher, Hyman knew about history; he'd had a strict education, learned Latin, read the Great Books, studied calculus. But no college of course. That was for rich kids, though he did manage two years at the community college. No one ever gave him a chance for anything else. His dad fixed clocks for a living. What a joke! All those timepieces in a one-car garage that had been made over as a workspace. As if people fixed clocks anymore, as if they didn't just buy new ones. His family had a giant horizontal freezer in the corner of the shop. For venison. Hyman got teased about it, on the bus. What? Did his family eat squirrel? Did his family eat chipmunk? Fox? "Hey," a voice piped up once, "squirrel ain't bad." All the kids on the bus were the same. They lived on failing farms or in tiny, one-street towns with a grain silo at one end and a church at the other. In between, maybe a diner or a failing lawyer's office. None of the towns was big enough for its own school. The school bus rounded up kids from six separate municipalities, stopping for a kid or two, then tunneling through the plains, the white of the fields—when you could see them behind the gray banks of snow, indistinguishable from the gray white sky. Or that's how Hyman always thought of it, though there had been seasons other than winter in Elvin, Nebraska.

In his final years at Jenkins and Smith, every time Hyman bid out a contract—to the state, to the university, to a church, you name it—he lost it. To a refugee. Martha laughed the first time, he told her that. "Don't you read the papers?" he asked her, but Martha didn't. He brought her home a library book: *The Middle of Everywhere: The World's Refugees Come to Our Town.* A percentage of all government business had to go to a Bosnian or Tajikistan or Afghan refugee. That's just the way it was in Nebraska, in those days.

When Tom Bell at church asked him about doing something for the Populist Party, he was all for it. It was time he argued for his own rights, for the rights of plain Americans. After hours, he let Tom's group use the photocopier at Jenkins and Smith, and then they agreed they'd have a meeting to honor some of the group's stellar members. People who'd gone to marches back east or simply helped get the word out: distributed flyers after work, giving time to the movement. What they wanted to say was that people—OK, white people—were getting screwed from both sides, giving their taxes to a government that wouldn't hire them, that had rules to make sure that they couldn't get work, even if they were the most qualified for that work. So Hyman set it all up: a meeting for the People Against Tax Tyranny (PATT), which he called—and why not?—a financial planning session.

The date. July 19th, 2004. Tom Bell and he met for a dinner beforehand—just burgers and Cokes, the relief of air conditioning at McDonald's—then over to the AmVets. It was the third PATT meeting that summer. A hot summer. But weren't they all? Normally twenty or so people showed for the meeting. That July 19th, there was a news van and a police car by the AmVets. At first, neither Hyman nor Bell thought anything of it. Some event must have preceded them in the building. People clustered on the steps. Not PATT members; they didn't mill around. They usually headed right into the building, though then Hyman noticed Dave Cartwright and Steven Ansach, sitting in their cars, windows up, motor running. Well, of course, the AC. But Hyman saw that he was wrong about that, too; there *were* a few PATT members on the AmVets steps, and it looked like they were arguing with the strangers.

Hyman heard someone say, "You can't tell us that. This is a free country."

It was early evening, but still hopelessly hot, that heavy, enervating Midwest heat. A policeman stopped Tom as he went to open the glass doors that fronted the building. "No meeting, sirs. The meeting is canceled."

"No, it's not," Hyman said, confused. He would have been the one to cancel the meeting.

A sweaty-browed man with a big gut stepped forward and said, "Bell, your privileges are revoked. We will return your rental fee, but from now on you are no longer a member here." Bell had been in Vietnam, which was why they'd been able to rent the space out in the first place.

"Nazi!" a woman on the stairs said.

"We don't approve of your views," the man continued to say to Bell. "We can't let this meeting take place."

"It's a financial planning meeting," Hyman said. "I'm an accountant."

"Good try, Mr. Clark," the man continued. How did he even know his name?

"Hey, we got a right," Tom Bell began.

"Yep, you do, and I got a right, too," said the big-gutted man. "And my right is to tell you that you can't use this space to spread your ideas."

A man on the steps said, "My great-grandparents died in the Holocaust."

"What do you want," Hyman said, "a prize for suffering? You think you're the only one who has suffered?" That was the thing with the Jews—they were so articulate, they could argue for a cakewalk for themselves, no matter that if you went far back enough in anyone's history, you'd find an unfairly murdered relative. They'd even set up the camps in Europe like amusement parks, so people could have a beer and go scare themselves. As if it had all ever happened the way they said it happened.

Someone cried, "Go home." Hyman felt unaccountably faint.

The man with the big gut said, "We know what this meeting is. We know it is a meeting of the Nationalist Party and . . ."

"Hey," Hyman said, a sudden thickening—the burger?—in his chest. "We're Populists."

"You're bigots," a woman in the crowd said.

"It's legal to be anti–affirmative action," Hyman said. And pro-white. Blacks had their own clubs and groups. They had their own colleges even, but white people couldn't without being called racist.

"Anti–special privileges," Tom Bell echoed.

"And anti-Jew and pro-Hitler," another person in the crowd said.

"I'm a patriot," Hyman began. "I'm not—" He heaved once and leaned toward Bell. "Jesus, Tom. I've got to sit down."

"You all right?" his friend asked.

"Actually—" Hyman's breathing sped up. He sensed something . . . what was it? . . . a pressing fullness nudge his chest, then explode like a slow-motion firecracker, light raining down into his arms and legs. "My heart," Hyman said, his voice rising, almost as if asking Tom if that was what it could be.

"Let him in," Tom said. "He's ill. Let him in so he can lie down."

"Sorry," the big-gutted man said. "I'll do a lot of things. But letting the Klan meet in this building . . ."

"The Klan?" Tom said.

"Listen," the man said. "I don't care what you want to call yourself. You know what you are, and I know what you are. We know you want to have an awards ceremony in there."

"Sit down, Hyman. If he won't let you in, just sit down on the steps." Hyman sat, feeling somehow apart from the scene around him. "Since when is it illegal to have an awards ceremony?" The heat formed in squiggles above the parking lot, and behind him, Hyman heard someone saying something about an ambulance. Tom and the big-gutted man argued on, and words—"nationalist," "anti–affirmative action," "lecture"—came to Hyman but not much else. His hands were unaccountably cold, given the heat, and when he found himself in an ambulance, a young man's warm hands pressed over his own, he didn't think to object. There was a tight feeling on his arms, as if he'd grown suddenly too large for his clothes.

It was Martha who had to tell him the rest: that everyone thought he'd faked the heart attack, that his boss had called to let him go, saying he couldn't condone Hyman's views . . . or what an association with him would mean for the business. "Is that legal?" Hyman asked Martha, and Martha had stared at him, dumbfounded.

When he was stabilized, but still in the hospital, Martha found paper and pen. "I'll take what you need to say down."

"Huh?" Hyman said.

"I think," Martha said, "if we're going to stay living in this city, we need to clear things up."

So they'd written a letter, together, going back and forth on the words to make everything clear. "I am not," said the letter to the editor that appeared in the *Journal Star,* "a white supremacist. Nor am I a member of the Nationalist Party." Now wasn't a time, Martha insisted, to make his feelings about affirmative action known, to clarify what he meant to be working for with PATT.

Tom Bell kept on with PATT. Hyman dropped out. Not that anyone seemed to care. He could feel eyes on him—in the post office, the supermarket—in a way he never had before. He could feel that and the draining bank account.

It was Martha's idea that they leave town. What a shock that had been. Not the idea, but that Martha would have it. It was her idea, too, that they hide their past, that they erase the experience that had thrown their lives so off kilter. They'd do it, she said, by making the road from where they came untraceable. And when that proved too difficult—

they could change their names, but not find new social security numbers—she said, with the sort of composure that was rare for her, "Well,
never mind. We won't erase the past. We'll just obscure it. You'll do
something so no one will ever suspect you of being involved with that
PATT business."

"Like what?" Hyman laughed. "Apply to be the affirmative action
officer at a state university?"

Martha had rolled over in bed to look at him, her hands in prayer
position below her right cheek. "Yes!" she said. He could almost take it
for the cry of pleasure she never released in bed. "Oh, yes!"

And after that, it was all just an elaborate puzzle to Martha: how to
create a believable resume, how to draft glowing but distinct letters of
recommendation from the principal, guidance counselor and English
teacher of the non-existent Carter High School of Cartwright, Nebraska; how to design the very letterhead stationery on which Carter
colleagues expressed their sincere regret that Hyman Clark was looking
for work outside their town.

"And if I actually get a job, and someone tries to check my references?"

They acquired a second phone line. Martha chirped, "Carter
High," whenever she answered, hooked up an answering machine for
the rare hours when she was away from home. Finally, an Alex Decker
from Wisconsin called to ask for James Arden, the principal. "He's not
here right now. Can I take a message?" Martha said.

The man at the other end of the line hesitated. "Well, actually, is
. . . um . . . Jennifer Fitch available?"

"The English teacher?" Martha said. "No, can I have her call you
back?"

The man laughed. "How about Sharon Felter?"

Martha giggled and said, "That's zero for three." Then, as if en-
deavoring to be helpful, "They happen to be in a meeting together. Bad
luck. Can I have them try you back?"

And then they did try him back: Tom Bell (who was ready to play
the principal) and Martha herself (changing her voice as much as possible) as both English teacher and guidance counselor.

Martha had never broken a law in her life. Never lied, never stolen penny candy, never . . . never anything. But she saw how people could act against their own natures. It was family feeling. You could do a lot for family feeling.

Did she love him? That's what he thought, after she'd engineered the whole thing, and it had worked, Jesus H. Christ, it had worked. Maybe she loved him, after all.

EPILOGUE

*Y*ears later, when Ellen was married and living with her husband and children far from Wisconsin, she'd think of herself at twenty-five and twenty-six. She might be folding baby clothes in the nursery while her husband, Toby, and Dana, their eldest, tried to entertain the twins. Toby would have, say, a stuffed pig in his hand, and be responding to something silly that Dana had just made up. Maybe Dana said she wanted to visit the Island of the Lost Dolls, which was a place Toby and she re-imagined every night. "Oh, well, that'll never happen," Toby would say. "That'll happen when pigs fly." And then he'd look at the stuffed animal pig in his hand and cry, as if astonished, "Wait! They *do* fly," and he'd toss the pig high in the air, across the room to Dana. She'd laugh and laugh, and the twins would look—as much as babies can look—amused, and then in the midst of Ellen's pleasure at the group of them, there in the nursery, playing, there'd be regret. Had she done the right thing, back in Wisconsin? She had never found a comfortable spot to put the events of those years after college. And now that Mose was dead, there wasn't anyone, really, with whom she could consider the matter. Even Tamar said, "You have to let it go already."

Once, before she'd left Madison, Ellen saw Martha in the supermarket, looking blankly at the meat counter.

"Can I help you?" the butcher had said.

Martha had started and said, "No. Oh, no!" before turning back to her cart.

Ellen glanced at Martha's purchases as though at clues to a mystery she still hoped to solve. White wine, saltines, a package of chicken breasts, frozen cookie dough ice cream, Swedish meatballs, pickles, two bags of radishes and a Hungry Man frozen dinner. Even the food didn't make particular sense.

So, what of it? What of it all? Mose, Alex, Valerie and Hyman. Ellen didn't know, though at moments she imagined herself and the others as hapless actors, unwittingly cast in some biblical story, where being right meant being rewarded and being rewarded meant demolishing your enemy. She wondered about those biblical stories. She hadn't yet started to tell them to Dana. Still, she wondered. How good were they, in the end? Not good as stories—they were good stories, all right—but how good were they, you know, for the Jews?